Twilight Moods

AFRICAN AMERICAN EROTICA

EDITED BY

JOSSEL FLOWERS GREEN

Twilight Moods

This is a work of fiction. The authors have invented the characters. Any resemblance to actual persons, living or dead, is purely coincidental.

Cover art by Lydell Jackson - www.siennastudios.com

Interior Design by Nancey Flowers
Edited by Chandra Sparks Taylor
First Flowers in Bloom trade paperback printing August 2002

For more information, or to contact the contributors, address correspondence to:

Flowers in Bloom Publishing
P.O. Box 473106
Brooklyn, New York 11247

Or visit: www.nanceyflowers.com

ISBN: 0-9708191-2-9

10 9 8 7 6 5 4 3 2 1

First Paperback Edition
Printed in Canada

CONTENTS

Twilight Moods

ACKNOWLEDGEMENTS

Twilight Moods started out with a simple telephone conversation and a suggestion between three spirited individuals filled with zeal, a passion for the art of writing and entrepreneurial hearts. Knowing that they had a great idea, they decided to seek assistance in pulling this project together. Three multiplied by six helped increase their numbers to eighteen wonderful contributors whose stories are amazing to say the least along with a great introduction.

A few calls were made and the results are in your hands today. After receiving the first submission the editors knew that *Twilight Moods* was gold. These wonderful stories are for your sexual pleasure and will arouse you to the fullest.

A personal thanks goes out to our contributors. We also appreciate all of those that assisted us with this project behind the scenes.

Now, sit back, relax and prepare to open wide and say ahh.

Jossel Flowers Green

Introduction
by
ZANE

*P*eople often ask me to define erotic fiction. Erotica is the perfect combination of realism and sex. *Twilight Moods* fits the bill well. All of the stories in the anthology flow with style and draw the reader into the characters from the beginning.

In "Watering Cherry's Garden," William Fredrick Cooper weaves the delightful tale of Vaughn Rivers, a young man frustrated after catching his girlfriend with another man. His friends take him to the Hideaway, a strip club, where he immediately falls in lust with Cherry. After watching her onstage and thinking of her constantly, Vaughn finds himself back in the club two nights later. Cherry appreciates the attention and invites him back yet again for a "private performance." One thing leads to another and Cooper entices readers with one of the greatest sensual poems of all times, which leads to an escapade with Cherry that is guaranteed to arouse.

Sandra Ottey takes a different approach with "Blue-Collar Lover." Gina Blackwood was raised to believe that blue-collar workers were beneath her, but things change after she runs into her friendly air-conditioning man in the parking lot of Home Depot. Dante is the kind of man Gina's mother has always warned her about, however, Gina finally realizes that life is all about making her own decisions and her life takes an interesting turn in the back of Dante's van. Women who have thrown caution to the wind in the name of "hellified sex" will definitely appreciate Ottey's sensuality.

Harvey Barron is the subject of Tracy Grant's story "Twist." Harvey runs into his ex-girlfriend Devin James at a conference for the National Society of Black Engineers in San Diego. Harvey has always regretted his mistreatment of Devin and is disappointed to discover that she is engaged to a schoolteacher. After a day of sightseeing together, they realize the flame is still burning and they take advantage of the moment. The romantic setting of a pier is a unique twist—no pun intended—to the storyline and for those who have lost loves and regretted it, this story will surely hit home.

Courtney Parker creates a delightful, complicated character in "Holdin' it Down." Twenty-three-year-old Portia is a spoiled rich girl who has always been attracted to roughnecks from Compton, South Central, and Watts. Portia is rebellious and even though her parents grant her every luxury she desires, she is head over heels in love with Jamal who is serving a two-year prison sentence. Portia is determined to save herself for him. She sends him explicit letters accompanied by nude photos of herself and allows him to run up her phone bill with collect calls. Portia faces a dilemma when she becomes close to Chris, an attorney with whom she shares a lot in common. Parker surprises readers with an unpredictable ending. Surely, this tale will be the subject of many conversations held by avid readers.

Marlon Green continues his mastery of erotic writing with "Shar-baby." Sharlene is sick and tired of her boyfriend, Jerry's emotional abuse. He intentionally insults everything from her clothing to her appearance in general. After giving her a hard time and insinuating that she looks clownish, she escapes by driving to a local lake that she frequents. She is approached by Daren, who readily admits that he has checked her out on several occasions but had never taken the opportunity to speak. Sharlene explains her situation to him as he listens intently. Daren assures Sharlene that Jerry is just trying to keep her down to prevent her from possibly creeping. Later, Sharlene hears Daren on a radio show answering relationship questions from callers. She is so intrigued that she heads back out to the lake to seek him out. What evolves is a powerful lesson as Sharlene learns to appreciate herself again and demand what she deserves.

These are merely a few of the sensual tales within the pages of *Twilight Moods*. As an erotica writer, I was overjoyed to read a book that actually touches upon the elements that shed a positive light upon the craft. Erotica is an art form and not everyone can write it but the editors have done a marvelous job of compiling vibrant, engrossing, and definitely sexy stories.

The fact that the majority of the writers either started out self-published or continue to be self-published was even more appealing to me. This just proves that when people take risks, they can achieve their dreams and their passions.

Sit back, relax, pour a glass of wine, and immerse yourself into the passion held within these pages. You are definitely in for a treat.

Peace and Blessings,

Zane
National Bestselling Author of
Addicted, The Sex Chronicles: Shattering the Myth, Shame on it All, The Heat Seekers, BlackGentlemen.com, and *The Sex Chronicles II: Gettin' Buck Wild*
www.eroticanoir.com
www.streborbooks.com

Bobby Q's Sauce
by
Lolita Files

*T*hanks for the meat."
He said it without even turning around.

She laid the package on the table and watched him, his back to her, standing at the stove stirring a pot of something with an odor so pungent and rich, it made the small room a sauna.

As if it weren't hot enough. South Beach in the thick of summer already had all the steam it could stand.

Veline dragged her hand across the back of her damp neck, then wiped it along the top of her thigh. She could feel the faint tautness of muscle. Compliments of Krav Maga, Pilates, squats. And fucking. She never knew how good fucking could be for the thighs.

"What's that sharp smell, mustard?"

He didn't respond. She didn't expect him to. Roberto Cristof Quiamas III guarded his recipes with the fierceness of a crackhead. A desperation that, without much provocation or threat, would send him into frenzies of stashing papers scribbled with esoteric codes in places around the house where no one ever bothered to venture. Veline always laughed. It wasn't that hectic. No one cared. Besides Balzac, their sunbathing lazy dog, it was just the two of them, and Veline didn't even like to cook.

He didn't like anybody in his lab. That's what he called it, this space where he honed what he considered his art. In it, he concocted astonishing delicacies that went beyond excitement. They aggravated the senses. Bobby's talents were a form of military attack. He loved watching his culinary prisoners of war swoon at the presentation of his work: spinoffs of Argentinean meat pies stuffed with ground pheasant and sage, plates fat with fried flying fish surrounded by jasmine rice and sweet, succulent plantains drizzled with rum honey.

It wasn't rare for Veline to hear him in the kitchen with his mortar and pestle, mashing sugar into limes without mercy, splashing it all together with *cachaça* and pouring it over crushed ice as he made *caipirinhas*. Bobby was a kitchen god. It was where he did his best work. Almost…

She loved the mystery of his imagination. Five years into their togetherness, he still found ways to exceed her needs. He did things with spices and food that made all her p's sing: her plate, her palate, her pussy. Bobby knew how to add just enough scotch bonnets to a dish to preheat her sex so that it would be nice and wet, ready to cook once his meat was to par. A fiery Caribbean man with the perfect blend of Afro-Latin traits, he was sensitive when it came to his passions—food and lovemaking—reacting with far too much gravity about them both.

He never gave Veline the chance to be dissatisfied, in the belly or below. He fed her in the morning, in the evening, in the afternoon. *Media noches*—those tasty Cuban sandwiches—deep in the night. He ate her in the morning, in the shower, in the car, at the movies, in the store, at the beach, on the causeways, on Ocean Drive, at Aventura, Bayside, on the Metro Mover, at The Gap, in thunderstorms, during hurricane warnings.

"My grandfather taught my father to eat *chocha*," he said, as he kneaded Veline's breasts the same way he had kneaded the risen brioche dough just two hours before. "My father taught my brother and me. My uncle taught my cousins. My grandfather's father taught him. All the men in my family are trained to eat pussy. Well. Not that tongue tiptoe shit, either. My great-great-great-great-great-great-grandfather was a Conquistador, and he said that a real man would never leave his woman to chance. Real men relish pussy. They eat it like it's a meal."

"A Conquistador?" she had moaned as his tongue traced a ring around the fullness of her left nipple. "Are you sure? Didn't seem like you listed enough greats to go all the way back to Conquistador days."

He bit down in protest. Veline cried out. With instant repentance, his tongue followed the road map of her body down her belly, into the tiny pit of her navel. He toyed with it, awakening the nerves just inside the perimeter.

"We are proud of our Conquistador heritage," he said. "And my mother's Ashanti lineage. You should be too. Look at what it's given you."

He raised his head and body, leaning back, on display. She drank him in, with all his exotic beauty. His enormous gorgeous sword jutted out with the subtlety of a Tyson hook, golden and noble, rampant and wild, its head raging in her direction—sort of—because it was bent a bit. To the left. Bent to fit. It hit all her corners just the way she'd prayed a dick would do.

"You're not supposed to pray for dick," her self-righteous sister once said.

"That's why you don't have any," had been Veline's reply.

She looked at Bobby above her, his dick from heaven, hot, curved, and hard, *prêt-a-porter*. Ready to wear.

"Oh yes," she cried. "Look at it. Give it to me. I want you to put it inside me now. I wanna feel it now."

"Not now," he whispered. "I'm not done. You're not ready yet."

That comment always angered Veline, if just for a moment. Who better than she could say what ready meant? Her cat was cooked. On high. Burned up. For Bobby, that wasn't enough. He wasn't content until the flames ebbed into a slow, deep simmer.

He bent down anew, his tongue razing a path across her hairless mound. He made a lateral move over the flat plains of her pelvis, the expanse of skin that covered her hipbones.

"This is my favorite part of a woman," he said, groaning.

"Whuh?" she murmured. Her eyes were closed, her words slight, as she lay soaking in the heat of his breath against her skin.

"This," he said, running his fingers across the area with a touch that was both light and worshipful.

He rose again, studying her, weak before him. He parted her thighs with commanding force, hovered above and between them for a moment—like a gull over the sea—then plunged in.

"Aaaaaaaaah…"

"Mmmmmmmm…" he breathed, slurping around the wetness, "…ambrosia."

"You mean nectar." Veline couldn't help herself. A too-smart woman, a trashcan of intellectual waste, it was her nature to correct.

"Ambrosia was the food of the gods. Nectar was their drink."

"I know what I mean," Bobby answered, his tongue still on its hot feathery beat. "I eat you. I'll let you know when it is I drink."

He pushed his face so deep between Veline's legs, she imagined that he might climb in. Punch drunk, she squirmed against his cum-streaked nose, wet forehead, and damp cheeks, thrashing about the bed while he attempted to pin her still.

"Just be. Let your body be."

She couldn't. She flapped and fluttered, screamed and scratched, as he lapped at both sets of her labia. She came and came, her body wracked with hiccups of delight. Bobby rose again, triumphant.

"Needs some banana," he declared with a throaty patois.

Veline fought to retain consciousness, her head swimming as Bobby sank his dick without mercy and measure deep into the bottom of her drenched canal.

She hollered at once, erupted, and fainted.

Bobby bust an immediate nut at the sight of her, limp and lifeless below him.

"I am Lord of Pussies," he whispered with a grin.

"You are King of One," she managed to reply.

Bobby ate every day, just as his Conquistador forefather had instructed his future clan of scion to do. Veline came to believe that it was, in fact, eating and not drinking, that he was doing.

After the strength of his first declaration of the difference between the two, it made her go to the bathroom, get a hand mirror, and check out her stuff. Had he been nibbling away at it, piece by piece? She studied for signs of lost pussy. If anything, it looked bigger, fleshier, fat with a sense of satisfied peace. New York pigeon fat. The kind of fat that came from being fed something others might consider filthy on a regular schedule.

It wasn't like Veline didn't return the favor. Because Bobby was so intense a man, in the beginning, she had tried to take off the edge in myriad ways. Her obvious choice was failsafe—the blow job. The early days of their relationship found her dropping to her knees under tables in restaurants, annoyed as Bobby speculated far too long on the ingredients of some exotic Haitian or Scandinavian dish. Proud of her fellatial skills, she would wrap her tongue around the fat, engorged copper tip, clamping her lips tight, sucking the arrow until it spewed its juice. Head was her forte. She knew how to give it with just the right amount of pressure and depth to induce the desired results.

Despite the amazing girth of Bobby's dick and her initial struggles to get her mouth to adjust, she'd been able to bring him to orgasm with the same degree of skill and timing she'd used on others less endowed. But it never reduced his intensity. Not even once. If anything, it stoked him more. The first time she blew him this way, in a corner of Thai Toni on Washington Avenue, at a table that faced the window and the folks on the street, she raised her head in victory— cum still coating her tongue and coursing down the back of her throat— to find him sated but frowning, swirling sticky rice around in his mouth, trying to gauge if peanut or sesame oil had been used in the chef's wok.

Busting a nut was nothing to Bobby. The release was elysia. He expected heaven every day. As heady as constructing a fabulous meal. But it never took the edge off. And it never took away his desire to know more, to get better, to be the best.

At cooking. At sex.

This quirk, when it came to cooking, was both a boon and a bane to Veline. While it frustrated her on occasion, she chose in most instances to have fun with Bobby's high-strung nature and culinary need-to-know. It was a visible jugular with which she would take regular stabs, just for her amusement.

She once raced into the bedroom as he jotted down the ingredients of a hybrid pastry. A tasty creation that was part *pasteles*, part *empanada,* part guava turnover. It sounded like a gastronomic disaster, but it had been an exquisite thing, a recipe he knew he'd want to replicate again and again. Precision was a must. A little too much of the wrong component would mean certain ruin for a dish this tricky. The measures had to be exact.

He had disappeared to the room in an instant of them devouring the thing to note the contents, lest they escape him. Feeling evil and horny, Veline had advanced toward the bed with alacrity, just to see how he'd react. She knew how hair-trigger he could be. As expected, Bobby reacted like a trapped deer, his eyes wide with what

he must have felt to be genuine fear. He went into covert mode, ripping the scribbled page from his tablet and cramming it into his mouth. That was different, Veline had thought. His typical move would be to tear it to shreds. She neared the bed and watched as he struggled to get the dry clump of paper down his throat. Veline's undiluted laughter
· burst free. Bobby was insane.

Bobby also had Attention Deficit Disorder, which was why it was necessary for him to record recipes with such immediacy. Not while cooking, but the second the meal was done and consumed. Veline had fucked him up. It would take him months to craft the exact same guava empasteles again.

Her presence in the kitchen now was a miracle.

She watched the Miami summer-cum-oven heat distill into a fine mist across the breadth of his deep caramel back, the muscles undulating in waves as his arms alternated stirring the contents of the pot. He wore a wifebeater, what Veline considered the official garb of all Panamanian men. His tribe, anyway. Every male from his family wore one, from the bambinos to the baldheads. Old and young, the Quiamas men always flashed some torso skin. She understood why. They all had strong, wide shoulders; thick, muscular arms; and chests as wide as the Atlantic. You could even see vestiges of it in the ones with potbellies.

Bobby had told her they all had big dicks too. That had proved too much information for Veline, as she found her eye gravitating beyond her control from crotch to crotch every time the family gathered.

She had brought back goat ribs from the butcher. Today's dinner would be something experimental. Bobby wanted to try a new kind of sauce on the ribs, which he would be preparing soon to go on the grill. The two of them sweltered in the kitchen now, him adding a pinch of this and touch of that to the pot.

"You want me to marinate the meat?" she asked.

Nothing from Bobby. Not even a turnaround. He reached up and opened the cabinet above him, pulling down a bottle of apple-cider vinegar.

Veline was too hot to be ignored. Her skin was clammy. Her

pussy was drenched. The sight of Bobby in the wifebeater, his back muscles taunting her, was proving a bit much.

She unzipped her jean skort and stepped out of it, setting her loins free. Veline seldom wore panties. It was something Bobby didn't allow.

With one hand, she pulled the bows of the halter at the nape of her neck and the center of her spine. The top fell to the floor. She stood quiet in the kitchen, naked from the ankles up.

With silent footsteps, she came up behind him, touching his neck. Bobby continued to stir. She pressed her lips light against his neck, licking the film of sweat. Salt. A slight bitter taste. She lapped harder, dragging her taste buds against his skin. Bobby reached for black pepper with his right hand, his left hand not missing a stroke at the pot.

Determined, Veline slid lower, maneuvering between his legs so that she was facing his crotch. There was only about six inches of space between Bobby's body and the hot stove. She managed to fit, nary an inch of space between her and the heat of the oven door. Had she not been so ready, the temperature would have been overbearing. Instead, it served to rile her more.

She unzipped his pants, pulling the burnished lion from its cage. His dick was hot, as hot as the stove, as hard as the terrazzo floor beneath her. She pulled him into her wet mouth and sucked. She ran her tongue around the rim, then closed her lips over the shaft, her cheeks caving in with the pressure of the wind within them and the movements of her tongue. She gazed up at Bobby.

His brow was knitted as he concentrated on the contents of the pot. The sole giveaway was the almost-imperceptible heave of his chest beneath the unstained wifebeater. Veline's suck was cruel as she grabbed his hardness with her left hand, pulling him into her mouth, playing with her pussy with her right. She sucked and sucked and sucked, her eyes burning a hole into the underside of Bobby's chin. After a time, he moaned. Moaned. And moaned again. She could feel things spurting from his epididymis up through his urethra as she held him, pleased at her perfect record for delivering the goods. She had long trained herself to know what those epididymal/urethral spurts meant. It was the sign of the imminent cum. Bobby was due to pop any moment now.

This time, she wouldn't let him get away with cumming without breaking his position at the pot, leaving her to gulp him in and exit his lab, banished to business elsewhere.

She waited until the nut felt inevitable. She stopped playing with herself and grabbed the backs of his thighs, sucking him hands free. She could feel his hamstrings quiver. It would be any moment now. The tadpoles would be free.

Without warning, Veline tackled Bobby to the ground. Weak from the balls up, Bobby fell backward, his arms barely breaking his fall. The wooden spoon he had been stirring with dropped along with him, splashing scalding, sticky sauce on both of them as it ricocheted across the room.

Veline pounced, mounting him like a puma, riding him vicious, Paula Revere spreading the necessary word. It was Bobby's turn now to scream and thrash beneath her, panicking as the measures of ingredients in the pot fled his head, destined to be lost in the wake of the nut. He freaked over which mattered more—release or the recipe—unable to decide on either. Veline's face closed in on him, his eyes once again wide with the panic of the loss of perfection.

He popped, grabbing her waist, ramming her ass down, down, down on him, as he thrust up, up, up, crazed, deep inside of her. She stilled her body so she could feel his dick jerking inside the walls, waiting for him to release his grip upon her hips. It was all too much for Bobby. He lay back against the hot terrazzo and closed his eyes.

Veline, unfinished, rose and stood above him, turned around, and backed her bottom onto his face. Bobby opened his eyes just in time to see her brown fleshy cheeks nearing his mouth.

"No," he attempted to cry, but Veline was on him, positioned in place.

"Taste it," she said.

Bobby's head attempted to move to the side.

"Taste it," Veline demanded, tightening her thighs around his head, forcing him still. She felt his lips part a little, then felt the hot appearance of the tip of his tentative tongue, delicate at first—almost frightened—then bold and probing, curious. Bobby grabbed onto her thighs, taking her from a squatting position to a sitting one, and pulled her in, lapping at her lips, pleased at the discovery of a new, pleasant addition to this already-familiar but delicious dish.

He was still lapping when Balzac stuck his head through the doggie door, watching them.

Veline pushed herself up from Bobby, gazing down at his cum-smeared face.

"I drink you," he said.

"Yes," she smiled, "you did, didn't you? You drank us."

"Nectar. That was nectar."

"That was nectar."

Bobby looked up at his wife, shaking his head.

"I've lost a recipe because of you."

Veline walked off, stopping to gather her clothes from the floor.

"I'm sure you'll find it again," she said.

Bobby made a smirking sound as he stood. He watched Veline leaving, her supple brown back curving into the perfect orbs of her ass, down into well-toned thighs and confident calves. Veline felt his eyes upon her, smiling with accomplishment as she put her palm against the swinging door that led out of the kitchen, into the rest of the house. She needed to see his face, to revel in his defeat.

When she looked back, she saw his bronze dick, hooked, blazing, bold, and ready, beckoning her again. She lingered a moment, studying his rod's landscape, then pushed the door open. Her honeyed words made their way in on the last swing of the hinge.

"Thanks for the meat."

Crooked Letter I
by
Phill Duck

*W*as it at Pigeon Point beach in Trinidad where the sun kissed her soft skin? Where it left a splendid etching of her thong bikini because she'd been too coy to reveal the dark black wisps of pubic hair that streamed between her thighs. Was she lying on a silk sheet but propped on her elbows licking roti crumbs off her slender fingers? Did she dip her toes in the warm, teal-colored water? Did the water caress each toe with the skill of a lover?

Or was she on the Beaches Varadero of Cuba staring seductively at the red sky through expensive shades? Sipping *mojito*—a faint hint of lime and rum on her breath. Was she there when the sweat dripped from her pointed chin and pooled between her breasts? Was it the soft winds in Cuba that tickled her nipples and made them embarrassingly erect? When she undid her hair from a bun and shook it back down to the nape of her neck, did flakes of sand fall on her shoulders?

Where was she when the *oooohhh* rose from her throat? When that tingling heat like Vicks VapoRub settled around her abdomen. When that ecstatic breath gripped her chest and she struggled to push it out like a fetus. When she reached for support and finally found flesh to rake with her manicured nails. When she closed her eyes and turned her head to the side. When she let that final releasing *aaahhh* slide from her lips. Where was she?

She was in her lover's bed. Her lover was in both Cuba and Trinidad.

The beauty of this woman is in her balance. The Trinidad of her father. The Cuba of her mother. Trinidad gave her the coffee. Cuba gave her the cream. Combined they made her skin the complexion of untreated maplewood.

She'd been created by a sculptor. Thighs muscled through the upper portion that contoured like the small end of a wedge as they approached the knees. Calves—dancer's calves—that jiggled with her hips when she walked. Her stomach, flat and rippled. No crease or stapler mark through her middle, yet she was still as perfect as the airbrushed beauties in a girlie magazine. Smallish, golden breasts with dark coins centered perfectly. Dark, brooding eyes. Subtle eyebrows but inquisitive lashes. Straight, angled nose. Full lips. Long hair, the strands like silk fingers. The coffee. The cream. Trinidad. Cuba. The beauty of this woman in her balance.

"I think you killed me," she cooed as her lover rose from the valley of her love.

"Remember that," he said as he wiped her juice from his lips. "Remember that later and kill me back."

She leaned forward and gripped him by his muscular shoulders. "You know what you are?" she asked him.

"About four inches thick and eight inches long," he joked.

She smiled. "Like whoa…" Bit into her lip and looked down at him from eyes shaded by lavender-tinted lids. "No seriously. You're *mi cielo*. That's Spanish. My mother used to call me that when I was younger. It means 'my sky, my everything.' "

Instead of offering him happiness, the words discomforted him. He rose from the bed and headed toward the bathroom. His upper torso funneled to a trim waist. His legs, though thin, were defined like the jagged rocks of a cliff. Whenever he went out in public, someone usually stopped him and asked if he was Tyson—Tyson Beckford, the black model with the Asian eyes and blatant negro lips, not the boxer. No, he'd say and they would be outwardly disappointed until he informed them that he was Cumberland Recorder.

"You're not gonna say anything," she called after him. "I pour out my heart and you get up and walk off."

He stopped for a brief moment. "That's sweet, Simona. I'm really touched."

Before he reached the bathroom he shook his head and stood with his back to her. Lingered by the doorway and so she rose and came to him. "What's the matter with you all of a sudden? You're blowing hot and cold on me again."

Words clung to his insides, threatening to rise up through his windpipe like bile. Stinging, painful, ugly words. He fought them like an ancient gladiator, thwarted their attempt. "I'm cool."

"The truth?"

"I said I was cool."

"Yeah, you said." She moved from him violently and gathered her shirt and pants. She was halfway done buttoning her top before he'd worked through his stubbornness and was ready to talk.

"I'm worried," he called out to her, raising his voice as if they weren't in the same room.

She stopped dressing and sat on the side of the bed waiting for him to continue. He came over and leaned against the dresser in front of her. His boxers clung to the muscles of his thighs. She noticed the ready bulge and little else.

"You gon' stop staring at my shit and maybe ask me what I'm worried about?"

"I wasn't staring—" she ran her tongue over her lips to torture him—"just thinking."

"You need to be thinking about the album," he blurted. As soon as he had said it, he winced like he'd been punched in the kidneys. No matter what the laws of physics dictated he knew going forward could also mean going backward.

She looked up with a sharp suddenness. "The CD? I thought we agreed once we left the studio we didn't discuss the music. 'No mixing business and pleasure' is how you put it, if I recall correctly."

He cupped his face with his hands and let out a deep breath. His hope was that when he opened his eyes she'd be resting peacefully, or she'd be smiling pleasantly, that this frame of his dream life with her had been subtly edited away. When he opened his eyes she was watching him intently. Avoidance wasn't an option.

"I was wrong, Simona. We desperately need to discuss the music."

"So you're worried about the album, then?"

He furrowed his brows, thought carefully about his words.

Thelonius Monk's "Straight, No Chaser" or Ralph Tresvant's "Sensitivity?"

He chose the latter. "The sessions haven't been as good as they could be. The album's been pushed back twice already. The label wants to know what the deal is."

Simona threw up her hands. "I don't believe this crap. We're making progress—tell them it'll be ready soon." She rose from the bed and moved closer to him. "But really, babe. I don't know why we have to pretend we're not together. It's hard working like that. Cumberland, I swear to you, that's it. That's why I'm struggling."

Cumberland shook his head. "That's the way it stays. I've never gotten involved with an artist while I worked on her album. It messes up the creative flow. While I'm in that studio I have to be objective. I have to push and pull every ounce of talent out of the artist." He looked in the direction of his living room. "That's how I got those platinum plaques. Pulling every ounce of talent out of the artist. Can't do that if I'm thinking about what color panties she has on or she loves me, she loves me not." He took her by the shoulders he'd once said were her most impressive attribute. "I care for you more than any woman I've ever known, Simona. You have to realize Cumberland Recorder doesn't fall in love."

"But you have," she said.

Just as quickly as he'd taken her in his hands he released her. "Not in the studio, I haven't. The label pays me to deliver. The higher-ups want all twelve songs on *Crooked Letter I* done by June 10. Do the math, Simona. That's ten songs in two weeks. That ain't no joke."

"We can do it, baby." She tried to wrap him in the love of her arms but he brushed her aside.

"*We* ain't the issue," he said as the melody of Thelonius Monk danced in his head. "I've done all the beats. You're the one who has to sing over 'em."

Silence filled the studio as Cumberland cut the music. "Simona, do the hook again. And, please…try to really emphasize that last part." He cleared his throat and crooned in his burdened-by-tobacco voice, "*Giving you my looove.* Let it ride out. Let all your strength flow on that last part. Feel me?"

"Felt."

Cumberland prepared to count down to the moment the music would blast through the speakers and shake the walls. The moment Simona's ears would be filled with the beat, like sand at the bottom of an overturned hourglass. Whereas other producers counted down with

Twilight Moods

a simple *one...two...three,* Cumberland preferred to use the three syllables of his own name as markers. He felt it eased his artists. Usually it worked. Usually.

Cumberland rewound the reel and set the music to cue. Tightness had settled in his pectoral muscles. "Alright, Simona, get ready." He raised his hand and an extended finger and chopped through the air. "Cum...ber...land...Go!"

As the music softly built in her headphones Simona attempted to make amends for what had been a poor studio session thus far. She had her eyes shut tight, her hands covering her ears as she swayed like a ferryboat treading the deep blue. She concentrated on the significance of the words more so than the tempo and pace.

> *Fate brought us here*
> *Joy kept us strong*
> *Always want you near*
> *So I'm giving you my loooove*

The music cut abruptly.

"Better," Cumberland said. "I'll play it back a few times so you can get the vibe. Close your eyes and just feel it. Don't sing, just feel it. I'm gonna want you to hit even harder on the next go round. And really listen to the last part. Get yourself focused. You gotta make love to the record. Caress the drum part with your voice. Ride it on the drums."

Cumberland cranked the music again and turned to his stable of engineers and songwriters. Two marketing gurus from the record label stood close to the glass eyeing Simona like she was the main attraction in a peep show, gyrating her hips and swinging around a pole while rubbing herself in unmentionable places. Cumberland sat back in his chair, his hands forming a bridge under his chin.

"Not much you can do with her, Cumberland," Staley, his main engineer, remarked. He winked at Cumberland and called out to the record label honchos, "You guys better make sure you keep the camera on that fat ass of hers when you shoot the video because her voice is thin. *Thin as hell.* Shit, if this is how it is I need to stop punching the buttons and get myself a deal. Damn a Latin invasion. Ms. Iglesias in there is just a pretty Puerto Rican chick with no talent."

"Actually," one of the label execs corrected, "she's Cuban and Trini."

Staley laughed, looked to Cumberland for backup that never arrived. "Sheesh, that's worse. So which country do I blame for her not being able to carry a tune?"

Simona listened to the revolving tape of her voice playing over and over. "Make love to the record," Cumberland had said. She closed her eyes and imagined his hands on her waist. She pushed him back with a single finger to the chest. Climbed on him, his dagger poking into the meaty V-shaped box of treats just inches below her belly button. She worked her hips, grinding against his rock-hard penis. She licked her lips, cupped her breasts. Gave them her attention for the time being. She knew shortly that he'd remove her hands and replace them with his. Rolling her nipples over his tongue like butterscotch candy drops. Extolling their sweetness with a grunt. Suckling for that Cuban cream. Then he'd take a finger, one finger, and plunge it into her wetness. Stirring that Trini coffee.

The music stopped again.

"You hear that part?" Cumberland's voice cut through her headset as Staley and the record label execs bickered in the background, "How you let down at the end? You keep fading right before the *giving you my love* part. We've got to get you over that hump. I don't want to punch that in—that's cheating. I want you to sing all four lines together. If you can flow it as strong at the end as you did in the beginning…"

"I'm trying, Cumberland," Simona shot back.

"I know. I know. Keep going with this. The magazines are gonna need someone else to talk about besides Alicia Keys and India Arie. You can have them eating out of the palm of your hand. Simona Iglesias…*the Crooked Letter I. Chica Caliente.*"

Simona nodded and blinked, daring the unwanted moisture to trickle to the corner folds. Tears just wouldn't cut it at this point. She had to be strong. Still, her stomach twirled uncontrollably as she thought about Cumberland's more than fair request—"get over the hump." It had taken everything she had to get to the foot of the hill, getting over the hump was an unlikely proposition, yet, she wanted so badly to do it, for him. She could hear disappointment in his voice. Could see the questions in his eyes. How did she get this record deal? Who had she satisfied to get it? What had been the nature of that satisfaction? Her struggles with this song soiled the most important thing in her life. Dirtied the relationship she had with Cumberland.

"Give me one more moment to figure this out, Cumberland."

He pursed his lips, nodded, and reclined in his chair again. He tapped his fingers like a drumstick on the armrest as Simona searched her diaphragm for some semblance of talent.

"Sheesh, yo," Staley said. "She is murdering the label's dime. You guys got to feel raped up in here. I know I feel it for you. Clock is tick, tick, ticking. No record. Bunch of shit takes. I hope to God one of you is fuc—"

Cumberland raised his hand and voice. "Yo, dawg, chill. Aiight? She's gonna get it. I have faith in her."

Staley threw darts his way. "Get it. Get what? What's she gonna get, Cumberland? You hear her in there, man. You've been through this plenty of times. You know she doesn't have much ability. A little, granted, but not much. You…"

Simona thought about the girl group she'd started with. A multicultural En Vogue is how they'd positioned themselves. Kiya had the voice of an angel and sung the majority of the songs. She was beautiful as well, but stood just a shade over five feet, even with heels. Pamela was the group's Faith Evans—a gifted songwriter and singer. But *Pamela* was just the Americanized version of a Kenyan name that Simona and the others couldn't pronounce. The name change, however, couldn't hide her eggplant-colored skin. Simona was the only one of the three to never sing solos. Simona was the only one of the three with a record deal. Who could blame Cumberland for wondering how she came to get this deal?

Simona closed her eyes and placed her hands over her earphones. She swayed from side to side. Under her breath she ran the lines again. Cumberland's scent was on her nostrils. His hands massaging her skin. Even with her eyes closed she could see him clearly. She didn't want this to end. "Okay, I'm ready."

Cumberland swallowed. "Aiight, focus. Cum…ber…land. Go!"

Wee hours of the morning after their first studio session

The dictionary paints music as a collage of rhythm, harmony, and melody. To Cumberland it was about vibrations. Taking those vibrations and making them bend and twist to his command. Placing the *boom bap* of drums in the right place, at the right time, with the right tempo. That was the role of a producer.

He made love to her like he made his music. With a passion that threatened the flow of warm blood through his arteries. With a life-or-death sense of urgency.

He basked in her kittenish fur. Touched and teased it. Sucked and licked it. Left his saliva clinging to her black leaves like morning dew.

Her spine was his keyboard. His tongue—fingers. Along the small of her back he played Steveland Morris' "Golden Lady."

Her small golden breasts were maracas. He shook her inner core with his touch. Caressed them softly. Caressed them with force. Licked the underside. Licked around the nipple. Licked the nipple itself. Bit the meaty flesh.

He entered her tenderly. Theirs was a perfect fit. Two instruments meant to be played together. She moaned with joy on his in stroke. Took a breather on the stroke out. Moaned again on the in stroke.

They made intense love in the near darkness, unaware that the smile of the moon was watching them through the Venetian blinds. Vanilla incense mixed with their body musk. Created a humid funk that only lovers could appreciate. Shadows moved along the walls.

They made love standing. Her fingers interlocked behind his head and her legs wrapped around his waist gave them the appearance of saxophone and saxophonist. He blew the horn first against the canopy rail of his bed, then against his dresser, then along his wall.

The near-dark room with just a tad of moonlight.

The body musk and vanilla.

The alto or bass sax.

It was the twenties all over again.

Cotton Club in old Harlem.

Duke Ellington's orchestra.

They continued their dance of love as sweat fell from them like rain from a sunless sky. She moaned her approval. He grunted his from deep in his chest. A baritone grunt. Then, after they'd both had their

moment of great release, they slumped against the wall and slid to the
ground like sap on a maple tree. The sync of their rhythm, harmony, and
melody had been perfect. Their vibrations wonderful. The music they
created together, pleasing.

He could hear her singing in the shower afterward.

Fate brought us here
Joy kept us strong
Always want you near
So I'm giving you my loooove

Wee hours of the morning after their latest studio session

Cumberland sat on a stack of newspapers in his loft thumbing
through a crate of dusty records, searching for a horn loop to sample on
a hip-hop record he'd been contracted to produce. He reached for his
third cup of coffee and accidentally knocked it over. "Shit!" He took off
his T-shirt and used it to soak up the spilled coffee.

"You're tired. Why don't you come on to bed?"

He looked back and saw Simona. She wasn't wearing any-
thing except for one of his shirts. Strangely enough he thought about the
symbolism of their dress. She had on a shirt and no pants. He had on
pants and no shirt. Did this mean they balanced each other? Or did this
mean they were doomed as opposites? His Freudian observation didn't
last for long. The sight of her bronze legs brought forth an urge just
below his navel. The psychology of their relationship at the present
could be summed up in one word: desire. She was sexy as hell and
headed his way. He turned back to his records and fondled the spine of
an album jacket. He couldn't allow this desire to distract him from the
bigger picture. He wanted to love her. Wanted to hold her for a lifetime.
Yet he couldn't chase away these certain doubts.

She took a seat next to him. Sat in the worse way possible.
Indian style. He noticed that she'd shaved her pubic area. A second
look revealed the firm roundness of her ass. He shifted his position then
reached down and pushed aside the urge below his navel. Simona
watched him, a smile on her face.

"So you're not talking *and* not coming to bed?" she asked.

"Who said I wasn't talking?"

"Okay, you're talking...now about bed—"

"I've got work to do. You come in here for something specific?"

"I did—" she uncrossed her legs and sat down on the floor with them arranged in a V—"but bunk that. Now, I want to find out why you're treating me like this."

"Like what?"

"Cumberland, cut it out. It's too late to be playing this game. You're upset so tell me about it."

He turned his full attention to her. "Same ol', same ol'. Another raggedy studio session. I'm beginning to wonder."

She reached down and slid the shirt from under her hip. The lips of her vagina smiled his way. "Was choking me," she said as she rearranged the shirt. "So, you were saying. Wonder what?"

"Who you slept with to get this deal." The surprise and hurt in her eyes squelched the urge that had risen in him. He could see the playful sexiness ooze from her. Her shoulders slouched. He didn't regret his words though. They were his feelings and he needed to get them out before they consumed him to the point of madness.

"I knew you thought things. Knew you probably wondered. But I never imagined when you questioned me it would hurt so badly."

"It hurts me to wonder. No sense in me lying to myself…"

She looked down at the floor. "They felt I was the most marketable of the girls in the group and so they signed me to a solo deal. I didn't sleep with anyone."

Cumberland shook his head. "But Pamela and Kiya could really sing."

"Yeah, they could." It shamed him to see Simona's eyes filling with tears. Shamed him that he'd been the cause. She rose and stood contemplating for a moment and then left the room. He let her go without following.

Staley was working on a mix when Cumberland entered the studio. Cumberland placed his backpack on the couch and came up to the mixing board next to Staley.

"I put some effects on her voice just like you asked," Staley said. "With the backing vocals it really comes together. I don't know how you did it but you pulled another one out of old girl."

"We've still got six to do."

"One at a time. Ain't that what you said the other night when she started to cry and threatened to leave?"

"Yeah."

"I would've told her to take her no-talent ass out the door. Shit's crazy. Even the non-talents come up in here thinking they're divas."

"She's got talent," Cumberland defended.

Staley laughed. "I meant singing talent."

Cumberland let the comment dissipate. He went to his backpack and retrieved a reel and loaded it.

Staley worked the buttons. The music came through the speakers. Cumberland was nodding when the room suddenly went silent.

Staley's eyebrows met at the center of his head. "Yo, Cumberland, what's up with this?"

"What do you mean?"

"That's the ballad, man. We agreed not to try this song with her. You know she can't pull this one off. This song takes range—which she ain't got."

"I want to do the song."

"I want to find the money Bill Gates *lost* last year—six billion, by the way—but that ain't happening. Simona can't do it man, face the fact."

"Can't do what?"

They both turned.

Cumberland smiled. "You have a habit of sneaking up on people, you know that?"

Simona nodded. "Can't do what?"

Staley said, "He wants to do the ballad. I'm not about limiting anyone, but, Simona, honestly, you don't have the range to do this ballad. You think the other sessions were brutal. This one'll make you give up on the album for sure."

Simona looked at Cumberland. "This true?"

"Which part?"

"You wanting to do the ballad? Me not being capable, not having the range?"

"Depends who you ask."

"I'm asking you."

"I think it's a major stretch for you."

Simona shook her head. "So why try. Staley's right, I probably can't do it."

"Only one way to find out," Cumberland said.

Again, Simona shook her head. "I've already fizzed out enough with a roomful of people. I can't subject myself to any more humiliation, Cumberland."

Cumberland turned to Staley. "Bro, do me a favor. Turn down the lights in here and go out in the lobby. Don't let anyone come in. This is a closed session."

Staley's voice hardened. "Closed session? What are you doing, Cumberland?"

Cumberland reached forward and took Simona's hand. Her eyes widened.

"Me and my lady here are gonna try and make some music."

Fade out softly

Daydreaming at Night
by
Joylynn M. Jossel

*N*ot even ashamed to inform you of the erotic day dreams that ease the wait.

Hell, I'm not even ashamed to inform you of my intimate doings once the night gets late.

If I were dreaming I had asked not to be awakened. Now I know it was the hand of mine.

My hand, not yours, was responsible for the silent shouts and the muted whines.

So it was my index finger after all pushing the buttons for D'Angelo's "Untitled" to play.

It was I who poured the melted candle wax down my belly…damn, what can I say?

Do I think of you? Do I think of you often? What the fuck kind of question is that?

Hell yeah I think of you. I think of you licking me, rubbing me and hittin' it from the back.

I'm dying inside with no care for reality knowing this scenario exists only in my dreams.

I know what I experience in thought is a mere tease as real as the encounters may seem.

I guess what I don't know won't hurt me. Now you got me reciting lame-ass clichés.

Scared to miss it at night, but even more fearful of the aftermath that brim over my days.

Almond Joy

The eleven vacationers jointly decided not to port the vessel that day as originally planned. For what Blue Pacific Yacht Club was charging per hour for the rental, it only made sense to utilize every waking moment on *The Opal*. Besides, the occupants consisting of six men and five women, including myself, had deserved this long-overdue splurge of finances and time. A pact had been made during the first semester of law school that this outing was exactly how we would celebrate three aggravating years of learning the law and how to manipulate it.

With the exception of Sherry, who got pregnant second semester and had to put law school on hold, we all kept our word. Mar-Mar was married so his wife, Earth, joined the celebration along with her cousin, Koya.

Jawan and Daria went summer semesters and graduated before the rest of us. They held out on the celebration until we walked the stage. They were able to do most of the planning beforehand. It was Daria's dude, Flem, whose dad actually had the membership to the yacht club and was able to hook us up.

Tico flew in from Colorado, where he relocated from Florida the day after graduation. Tico graduated top notch. Can you believe that son of a bitch got a damn near perfect score on the bar? Firm and corporate representatives chased him down like chickenheads to an NBA star.

When the largest African-American publishing house, Green Rainbow in Bloom, waved those ridiculously obscene salary figures in Tico's face to solely represent them, he bought a one-way ticket to paradise. His paradise was my hell.

From the day I met him at law school orientation I knew he was the one.

His skin was as black as a bowling ball and yet I wished for it to be even a shade darker. You know the saying, the blacker the berry the sweeter the juice. Damn did I thirst for a sip of that smooth-ass cognac.

I'm all talk though, or should I say all thought. I studied with that man countless times until the wee hours of the morning. We performed mock trials together. We had dinner, went to lunch constantly, and even interned together. Not once did my bitch ass ever just tell him how bad I wanted him.

He always seemed so serious. I assumed that a woman would be the last challenge he needed in addition to law school. I soon learned that closed mouths don't get fed.

Unlike myself, Daria wasn't one to bite her tongue. Just as soon as she could worm her yellow ass into our study group she let Tico know just how bad she wanted him to fuck her and so he fucked her. She fucked him. They fucked until they got tired of fucking and decided to study with me again.

I could have kicked myself for all those times I had Tico right in the palm of my hand. If only I had been the modern woman and spoke up to him about how bad I wanted him. Daria showed me that Tico was the kind of chocolate morsel you let melt in your mouth and not in your hands.

Although Daria and Tico had sex, it didn't stop me from feeling the way I felt about him. It was just more reason for me not to speak on it. I used to sit in our study group pretending to be listening to their debates. All the while I would be trying to picture the two of them fucking—wondering if she sucked his dick and if he ate her pussy. I could just see her slamming his smooth bald head into her stuff. Of course the daydream always started out with them two, but Daria was always soon replaced with the vision of myself.

I probably fucked Tico more than a thousand times in my day-dreams and replayed each one of them to masturbate to every night. I had one of those standard six-inch vibrating massagers. I bought this little black jacket for it that had little bubbly censors on it. Those little bumps use to make me tingle something awful. I'm one of those women who stick to the clit when masturbating. I don't stick shit inside of me. My main button really gets my juices flowing. It swells up like a min-iature penis before it erupts like a volcano.

Once, Jawan had a sex toy party and I bought this thing called a butterfly. It's the cutest little pink butterfly with purple stripes. It has multiple straps to secure around my waist and it takes six AA batteries. This thing is the ultimate female masturbation assistant. It has a re-mote control with several speeds that operate a little sucking and grinding device that molds the clit. I'd always start off with it on low speed, but by the time visions of Tico brought me to my climax that sucker was on full speed.

Imagining Tico being inside of me occupied a colossal quantity of my thoughts. I'm surprised I even made it through law school. Knowing that school was my passport to keep company with Tico was a subliminal motivation in itself.

When Tico accepted the position in Colorado, I cried for twenty-four hours straight.

I fantasized about me confiding in him all of my hidden lust at his going-away party. He would take me in his arms and made love to me so passionately. He would pledge his true feelings for me, insisting I move with him to Colorado.

His going-away party came and went without my scuffling up the balls to confront him. I had even dreamed of giving it one last shot at the airport. I would chase him down as final boarding for his flight was called over the terminal intercom. I would show up wearing nothing but a black trench and three-inch strappy pumps. He would choose to abandon his commitment in Colorado after learning of my emotions. We would catch a taxi back to my loft but not before having mad sweaty sex that fogged up the taxicab windows and funked up the air.

I was too weak to even wish Tico farewell the day his flight to paradise departed. He went from being *the one* to *the one who got away*.

When Onion told me that Tico was going to fly in from Colorado and join us on the yacht, my clit quivered. I just knew that big Kool-Aid grin I was holding back would win the battle and burst through my face. Of course the only response Onion received was "Oh, how nice."

Onion and Tico had been best friends since undergrad. They were totally opposites in personality. Onion was anything but serious and loved the ladies. That's actually how he earned his nickname in law school. He went from woman to woman (or let him tell it, study partner to study partner) breaking plenty of hearts along the way. We called him Onion because in the end he always seemed to make the girls cry.

Onion's brother, Darik, and Onion's roommate, Nigal, would be joining us as well. The more the merrier (not to mention it cut down the cost per head). Anyway, I would be so focused on trying to get with Tico that the existence of anyone else would be irrelevant.

I knew that since Daria would be up under Flem, Tico wouldn't even think about trying to strike up that old flame, which otherwise would have been quite convenient for him. So nothing was going to keep me from getting Tico this time. I had secretly loved the hell out of this man for almost five years. This could be my last chance to stop dreaming and wake the fuck up!

The Opal is a sixty-foot shiny black boat with three inside levels and an outside top deck with a Jacuzzi. *Opal* stretched across the waters like an Egyptian queen, to the male passengers anyway. To the women, including myself, it was the most beautiful dick in the world that we couldn't wait to ride.

Opal came stocked with everything we needed for our three-day, two-night escapade. A crew was included with the voyage—from the captain right down to the cooks—and any ingredient they would need to satisfy our appetites. I craved nothing but Tico.

Our first night on *Opal* was spent claiming cabins and beds then reminiscing to day one of law school. I had hardly spoken two words directly to Tico. He was like Kryptonite—he zapped every nerve in my body. Here I was a grown-ass woman acting like I was in grade school. This was more than a grade-school crush though. This was inevitable destiny.

The second night we were supposed to port in the Bahamas and party, but decided that with eleven of us, we already had a party going on. *Opal* had more than enough fun to offer from the lower deck bar to the upper deck billiard-type lounge. The night fell quickly and I could hear the clock ticking. It was to be our last night on *Opal*.

Five passengers occupied the lower deck busting spades to some R & B grooves while the rest of us were in the lounge busting corks and pool balls. Everybody was eating, drinking, and just cooling out. The ambience was mellow.

In the middle of booming laughter and general conversation my met eyes connected with Tico's. No words were spoken but we both knew what was being said. I shrugged in agreement and we proceeded up to the outside deck. It was as if we were invisible because no one seemed to notice our departure. The talking and laughing continued as we exited the lounge.

The slight breeze thrown at us by the night didn't know if it wanted to harden my nipples or flare my chiffon sundress. With six in one hand and half dozen in the other it decided to do both.

This game of peekaboo the evening breeze played lasted the duration of our seven-step flight up to the outside deck. Tico hungrily licked his lips at the brief view of my pantiless ass as he played referee. Sometimes the game became so intense that my dress would slap down on Tico's face (like a bad boy being punished).

The abuse from my dress must have gotten to him. Before I could even turn to face him after leading the way to the destination of our tryst, I found his hands gripping the fabric of my sundress, the portion that was hugging my hips. It took only a moment for me to realize that a sudden strong wind wasn't the cause of the dress rising above my waist.

Even through the layered fabric his nails left a violent trail down my thighs that told a passionate story itself. My eyes closed and there was nothing but darkness. The abundance of stars piercing the night sky quickly vanished. Only sounds remained to describe the climax of this encounter. I couldn't distinguish whether the sounds came from the ocean's water smacking against *Opal* or our bodies briskly connecting.

I guess you could say feelings as well as sounds could describe the climax because Tico was inside of me. The feeling was one of completion. It was as if this was why I had been born. I wasn't supposed to leave this Earth before feeling such complacency.

He slowly penetrated me with just a couple of inches. His hands still gripped my sundress and mine clutched the edge of the yacht to keep from falling forward. There was a sigh of relief from me and a moan of fulfilled anticipation from him. I knew right then that he had longed to feel this way also, that he, too, had been born only for this very moment.

As he began to push himself deeper inside of me I didn't want to hold on any longer. I wanted to fall. I wanted to be swept away by the waves with him still inside of me, with him still gripping my hips at the expense of my sundress.

I felt as though I had to let go of the yacht, as though there was, in fact, a need for the cries of "man overboard." I felt as though I was already drowning in my own waters, in my very own private pleasure of waves. Wet, creamy, and steamy with body heat, my pussy lips began to suck in more of his ten-inch vessel.

At first I thought that I couldn't breathe because of the depth of Tico inside of me. Never had anything so long and so round been between my legs. I felt completely filled. I realized that I didn't want to breathe. If another breath meant that this feeling would go away, that this very moment would end, then I didn't want to breathe again.

Tico just stood there with seven inches of his fat dick inside of me. At the same time he was burning my neck with heated kisses. I cocked my ass in the air and pressed it against him allowing his hairs to just barely tickle my ass. I allowed my throbbing pussy muscles to lock down on his dick. After so long I couldn't just stand there anymore. I had to take the moment for everything it was worth.

Pushing him from inside of me I turned around and placed my perfectly round almond ass on the edge of *Opal*. Tico assisted me by slightly lifting me up. I was ready to cum. I was ready to cum hard and I wanted him to cum with me. While the others were inside busting spades, corks, and pool balls, I was only interested in busting nuts.

What took only seconds seemed like hours as Tico stood with his erect penis dripping with my natural juices. I went to pull him back inside of me but he was already there.

I pumped my pussy back and forth on his dick. I was working my hips like a porn star. I couldn't help but watch my thick clit grind on his dick as it went in and out of my walls. Each time his dick was covered more and more with my cream. I had taken in eight inches and it felt so good, so good that I wanted to cry. I closed my eyes again, but somehow a single bead of moisture fought its way through my tightly closed eyelids.

I buried my fingers into his back and took in all ten inches with one hard, deep plunge from him. He burst through my tight little pussy like football players bursting through banners during the Super Bowl. I was forced to grip the edge of *Opal* as Tico began pounding my pussy constant and hard.

Right as I was cumming I went to grip my hands into his ass to see if he could thrust any deeper. I wanted to be certain that I hadn't overlooked not one inch. My pussy was calling me all kind of bitches for letting this foreign vessel beat on it so. It hurt sooooo good though.

As I released my hands from the edge of *Opal* to pull Tico as deep into me as possible I found only empty space before me. I was alone on the deck.

I open my eyes only to find that the scene has not altered throughout this interval. Everybody was still eating, drinking, and cooling out. The ambience was mellow.

Ain't that about some shit? I thought. *Another fucking day-dream.*

I embarrassingly look down to find my hands gripping my inner thighs. I had managed to toggle my ass halfway off the chair to allow the corner of it to molest my clit as my hips had been slowly winding.

I looked over at Tico as he smiled mischievously at me. My eyes accidentally traveled down south to briefly graze over his hard penis. Our eyes met again and I smiled back. I listened to his eyes and they confirmed that I hadn't been alone on that deck after all. Together we had integrated our trance, and without a word we excused ourselves and proceeded to the outside deck to make our daydream a reality.

Shar-baby
by
Marlon Green

I am sick of this! Whatever I put on my man has something negative to say about it. I'll put on my chiffon sundress with the faded clouds. Where are my sandals? Here they are. This mirror can't be lying. He better not say anything bad about this outfit. As I walk back into the living room, my man's eyes stay focused on the TV.

"How do I look?" I ask while striking a pose, trying to lighten the mood.

"Huh?" he replies, his eyes remaining glued to the TV.

"You know them hoochies don't have anything on me. Are you looking?" I ask still posing. As he glances over he smirks at me and once again focuses on the TV. "Oh, you have this attractive woman in your face you would rather look at them than me?"

"Hell yeah. If you ain't talk so much maybe you would be more attractive."

"So now I'm not attractive?" I was trying to be nice, but I was getting mad.

"You look alright, but you just talk too much. Then when a brotha doesn't feel like talking you want to get upset. And why did you put that on? It's nighttime and you put on a bright-ass dress with clouds and shit. Go ahead and piss on yourself so that it will look like the clouds are raining." He then starts to laugh like that shit was funny.

"What kind of shit is that to say?" I turn and begin to storm back down the hallway. "Maybe I'll put on a skimpy bathing suit like those hoochies in that video you're watching. You'd like that." I'm fuming now. He gets on my last nerve. I can't believe I have a child by his dumb ass.

"I don't care what you put on because we ain't goin'. The movie started at 9:45."

I look at my watch, which reads ten o'clock. I want to cry. "Why didn't you tell me we were running late?" I yell from my closet all the way into the living room.

"You're the one who's late, not me, around here wanting to be Diana Ross and keep changing your clothes and shit. I ain't ask you for no fashion show."

That did it! I went through all this trouble to find a baby-sitter and he's going to try to spoil my night, but I refuse to cry. I quickly grab my orange shorts, throw them on with my white tank-top and my white tennis shoes, and storm back into the living room and grab my keys.

"Why you put that clown outfit back on? The orange in your pants don't match the swoosh on your shoes."

"Fuck you," I say as I turn the doorknob.

"Bye, Bozo."

I quickly slam the door and as I stomp down the stairs in the apartment building I feel free. Getting into the car I hear a voice from the balcony.

"You look like Homey the Clown!" my man yells.

I'm too embarrassed to speak so I simply ignore his statement. I fuckin' hate him!

I finally arrive at Laurel Lake. I am an Aquarius and I love the water. When I am feeling down or just need to get away from everything and everybody I come here. I know that it is in busy area, but it's lovely to be here at night.

I wish that I was taking advantage of this summer weather rather than simply sulking over that tired-ass man of mine. I'm sick of his shit. As I sit on the front of my car overlooking the lake I feel a sense of calm. I really need to come out here more before that man of mine drives me crazy. Going to tell me that I look like a clown. Please! I should tell him how silly he looks sometimes.

"Welcome to my lake," a masculine voice says.

Who in the hell is this? "It's late and I'm really not in the mood to meet anyone or to talk. Keep walking and mind your own business." I ain't got time for no shit.

"I'm not trying to meet anyone, but your coming out here tonight is strange. You normally come here on Tuesdays, Thursdays, and some Saturdays, but today is Friday."

Oh no! This is a crazy motherfucker. "Are you stalking me?"

"Stalking you? I drive that little white car that you always park next to. I would pull up, start jogging, and look up and see your car. I'd be like, 'Is someone following me?' Then I'd see this fine, caramel-mocha woman staring at the lake."

"Is that right?" I ask, going along with his little game. I'm beginning to get intrigued. I love how he looks through me. He is kind of handsome.

"Yes, that's right. I never spoke because the lake held you captive, however, I would fantasize about me one day holding your attention."

I can't help but to bust out laughing. "That was smooth. You're a player, right?"

"Far from it. I just speak my mind. You never have to worry about me misleading you," he says as he finally arrives next to me on my left. "You being here means that something has happened. You can talk to me about it if you'd like. Until then, I'm going to get you some Off! because mosquitoes also recognize pretty legs."

I laugh at his previous statement, but now I'm blushing like a young girl. This man is good for the ego. "Thank you. I normally wear sundresses out here."

"I know, but you still look good. I see you with your orange and white on. You got the Nike swoosh to match your pants. I see you coordinating."

"Yeah, but they don't really match. The oranges are two different colors."

"Sweetie, no one can tell. Only a jealous person or a hater would notice."

"You think so? Well, my man must be a hater. He said that I looked like a clown."

"And you fell for that? He made that statement to stop you from going out."

As he walked to his car, I began to think about all of the times my man called me names. There definitely was a pattern. After my admirer returns, I grab the bottle and begin asking questions. "Why does he put me down? Why does he mistreat me?"

He went on to tell me that my man wants to make me feel insecure and that it doesn't matter how good I look, if my man wants to control my emotions he'll put me down for no reason. My admirer said if I normally walk out when I get upset then my man does it to be able to leave without me questioning him or having to take me with him. That way he can spend time with someone other than me, be it his boys or another woman. That makes sense because he's never home when I return. I'm beginning to hate my man all over again.

"Do you need some help with that?" he asks.

"No, I have it. You just keep talking," I say as I continue spraying the Off! and rubbing it on my arms.

"Well," he starts as I catch his eyes shifting from my legs to my eyes, "your challenge is to find out if he is taking you for granted or has just plain lost interest in you. Being taken for granted can be fixed, but once he loses interest then chances are your relationship is over."

We talk a little while longer and, as interesting as he is, I can't get past what he is saying about my challenge. His name is Daren and he tells me how nice it is to finally talk to me and wishes me luck in my relationship. He tells me to keep the Off! to protect my pretty legs on future visits to our lake. I sit alone for a little while then jump in my car to go home.

In my four-minute drive I formulate a plan of attack, which will lead to my man and me making love. All of the arguing and fighting block the fact that I haven't had quality sex in more than two months. All he does is get his rocks off and go to sleep. And I'm not going to talk about how dead the romance is.

Just as I figured, my man is nowhere to be found when I returned. I quickly hit him on his cellular so he can get back here. "Where are you?" I ask. "Baby, I need you here tonight to hold me and to love me. My pussy is so wet for you. Where are you?"

"Go ahead with that, girl," he says in a playful voice. "I'm at the movies."

"You can't be serious. Why didn't you call me?"

"You had an attitude. I wasn't going to take you anywhere acting like that. Plus, I ain't even in the movie, I'm just hangin' out."

I get off the phone with another attitude. He would rather hang out at the movies than be with me. He'd rather be with his boys than in this hot, wet pussy. Men ain't shit. I can't believe I said that, but I'm lonely. I grab the radio and head to the bathroom to take a hot bath to calm my nerves. As I get in and begin to relax and unwind I lose myself in India Arie's song "Brown Skin." That song activates my fantasy and I begin to touch myself while the hot, oily water continues to soothe. As the song comes to an end, I discover that I am straddling the side of the bathtub with my hips gyrating. With one knee in the water and the other on the bathroom floor, I try to bring on an orgasm. It's just my luck that the radio personalities break my concentration by talking instead of playing another song. I can't cum with them running their mouths and I'm not getting up to change the channel. I gently roll back into the water and try to think of the last time I had an orgasm. "It's him! Oh shit! That's Daren on the radio!" I scream and sit up in the tub.

"…and that's the problem. Many girls create fantasies about their prince and the romance that they'll share. As they get older the sexual fantasies become more detailed and elaborate, and if they aren't fulfilled then part of them is dead.

"Girls fantasize about love. Boys fantasize about being sports stars and singers."

"Wait a minute, caller. We women dream of being sports stars and singers too."

"But you place emphasis on love. Boys don't. As we both mature, women are in touch with romance and love. Men are far behind in each. That's why a man's idea of romance is having a ménage à trois. He's out of touch with love and romance. And many sisters end up with these men and expect romance. When the man doesn't comprehend either she bottles up her emotions, acts them out on herself, or she has an affair…"

I can't help but to feel funny after he says, "acts them out on herself." That forces me to look at the part of the tub that I was just loving and wipe my juices from it.

"…The key is to find a man with fertile soil for your fantasies to grow. You can't hide from your fantasies because you can't hide from yourself."

"You hear that, ladies? It sounds like this brother has his thing together. So, caller, let all of the romantics know what you have planned tonight. Any romance?"

"I'm on my way to my lake to watch the stars' reflections in the water's ripples."

"Caller, stay on the line. The next song is 'U Got It Bad' by Usher and…"

I know that was Daren. I have to hurry up and get to that lake. Let me slow down before I slip and break my neck trying to get out of this tub. What am I going to wear?

I park next to Daren's car and look to see if I can see him. There he is. "Daren."

"Hey, lady. I'm so glad you could make it." He stands and helps me down the tiny hill leading to the bench. "That's a lovely sundress. It brings more beauty to your legs."

"Thank you for the compliment," I say as my blushing side-tracks my original thought. What was I about to say? Oh yeah! "I heard you on the radio tonight."

"You did?" he says without expression.

"Don't even act like it's not a big deal because it is. You were the bomb. How do you have such a deep understanding about love? I feel like I can just talk to you forever, just tell you my entire life and all my pain."

He straightens his expression and turns toward me. His eyes penetrate my soul. He seems to be looking at me with genuine care, not sexual intentions. I can see that I have his complete attention and I'm not used to getting that. My man prefers his PlayStation 2 and his boys over me. I bought that game for him, I ought to throw it out of the window.

"I want to know if my man cares about me and if I should be with him. He won't take me out, tell me he loves me, and all that he does is put me down. And to top it all off, I haven't had an orgasm in months. Like just now when I left you, I went home and he wasn't there. I called to tell him how hot and bothered I was and he brushed me off. What are you smiling about?"

"I apologize, sweetie. You caught me off guard with that 'hot and bothered' part. Look, it seems to me that you have all the answers. You know if he cares. You need to come to terms with yourself and realize why you're still there. Do you have kids?"

Bingo! That's it. I have a child by Dumb Ass. Instead of facing Daren I look to the lake for understanding. I am so confused that I don't know what to do.

"Hey," Daren says, gently placing his hand on my chin and turning my face to his. "A better day is coming." I try to look away, but he won't allow it. "Sweetie, just go home and give him all of your love. Do your best to forgive what he's done in the past. After your efforts you'll know if it's meant to be."

I can now feel the tears coming to my eyes. "What about my child?"

"Your child only benefits when there are loving parents in the home. Now go reconcile your differences and try to work things out. Don't attack him. Wait till it's time to talk and share how you feel. Be sure to listen attentively to how he feels."

I don't even wipe my tears. I just let them flow. "Ow! Why in the hell did you slap my leg?" I feel my Brooklyn attitude coming out.

"Where is the Off! that I gave you?" Daren asks as he turns his hand over to reveal a dead mosquito. I give him a soft kiss on his cheek for protecting me.

As I return home I see my man's keys on the kitchen counter. I then hear a voice coming from the bathroom. He obviously didn't hear me come in. I softly tiptoe down the hallway and try to eavesdrop.

"…yeah, I'll show you my place one day. Damn, you and I just had a good time and now you want to sweat me about where I live? Don't rush it, girl. Ay, ay, do I need to come back over there and put that thing on you again?"

That is all that I need to hear. I try to open the door, but it's locked. "Who are you talking to?" I demand as I try to break the door open with my hip.

"Ay, girl, I gotta go. My roommate is calling me," Dumb Ass says quickly.

"He has a girlfriend and a child, ho," I yell into the door so that bitch can hear me.

"What the fuck is your problem?" Dumb Ass yells as the door flies open.

"Who was that bitch?" I ask as I stare up at him.

"That ain't nobody. I was just joking around because I heard you come in."

"I'm your roommate now? Huh? You are so foul. You've been fooling around? Answer me!" I feel myself beginning to shake. My heart is beating so hard. "Let me see your phone." I know that her number is in there. I'm going to call that bitch.

"If you trust me you'd take my word. Fine, just take the fuckin' phone," he yells and shoves the phone in my direction.

I grab it only to discover that this motherfucker has taken the battery out. As I look to him he is busy laughing like everything's a joke. My feelings are crushed, but I'm not going to cry in front of him. I grab my keys and head for the door.

"Baby, don't leave. I'm sorry. I ain't going to hurt you no more."

As I turn around I see a pleasant look in my man's eyes. I love him so much. As I hug him I feel his dick not responding to my affection. Why isn't he getting hard and erect? When I reach for it he sways his hips to avoid my reach. "Let me smell your dick."

"I ain't gotta put up with this shit. I'll take my things to my mother's."

"Oh, is that where you fuck your bitches? Over your mother's?"

"Yup."

When I hear that come from his mouth I rush him. As he tries to push me with his right arm and turn his body away I finally get a hold of his dick as I force my right hand into his boxers. Just as I get a good grip on the base of it he pushes me in the face.

I feel myself going crazy as I begin to swing at him. His calling me a bitch several times only arouses my anger more. Before I can do what I intend his tall ass has grabbed me from the back, lifted me in the air, and brought me to the door. I kick and try to punch behind me, but I find myself in the hallway. He slams the door and reopens it to throw the bag I packed at me. As I look at the bag I begin to think about my daughter. She doesn't deserve this, and Dumb Ass doesn't deserve me.

"Jerry, give me my keys. Give me my fuckin' keys!"

"Step away from the door and I'll give them to you."

"As I step away I listen for the knob to turn. Upon hearing it I rush the door with my shoulder and try to barge in. "Open the door!"

"See, you want to be smart. I'll tell you what, walk your stupid ass out front. Your keys will be out there in the grass. All of the shit me and my mother have done for you."

I heard enough of this! "Fuck you, fuck your mother, and fuck that bitch you were talking to in the bathroom! See if you see your child again!" When I don't hear a response I rush outside to get my keys. It takes me five minutes to find them because his smart ass tossed them in the bushes. Ooow, I hate him!

After driving without a destination for thirty minutes I find myself back at the lake crying like my world has crumbled.

I feel as if I have been sleeping for days when I awaken. As I look out of my windshield trying to adjust my sleepy eyes I hear a tapping. As I turn to my driver side window I see Daren standing there.

"Step out of the car," he says with compassion in his eyes and in his voice. He then backs away one step as if he knows I'm going to obey. I unlock the door and before I move to open it I glance into my visor's mirror to get the sleep out of my eyes and to wipe my mouth. Looking at myself, I see dried tears on my cheeks. Before I can lick my finger and rub them away I feel my door swing open and I'm suddenly pulled from my car. I catch my balance in Daren's warm embrace.

"Come get this love, sweetie," Daren says as he holds me like a delicate flower.

I feel like shedding more tears, but I'm all cried out. Instead I witness the most beautiful sunrise I've ever seen. At this moment I could just fly away. I feel free of the stress…free of the pain that Dumb Ass has put me through. Daren has opened his heart to me and the break of dawn has given me further comfort. I now feel like living.

Today was incredible! I feel great. Around midnight I was at the lake, an hour or so later I was fighting with my ex-man, that bastard. Then returned to the lake sleeping and suddenly awakened by this knight in shining armor. Now I'm staring at my gorgeous nails with this telephone receiver between my head and shoulders.

"Hey, girl," I say in my cheerful voice. "I'm okay. You don't have to worry."

"Sharlene! Where are you? I've been so worried! You know your man was calling here all day asking questions like he was the FBI or some damn body. What happened?"

Tracey is talking a million miles a minute. I know she's happy to talk to me. I just let her speak till she runs out of breath.

"…because my son had his toys all over the floor. I told him that if I step on another one I'm going to throw them in the trash or give them away. So where are you?"

"It's about time you came up for air. Damn," I say and laugh. "Anyway, I have this friend named Daren and he took me to breakfast. But first he stopped in the dollar store and bought a towel, toothbrush, and toothpaste. Then we went to IHOP where I cleaned my face and we ate. Afterward he took me to a hotel and…"

"You gave him some ass?" Tracey asked.

"No, fool. He told me to shower. But, look, as we ate I told him everything that happened and he just listened. He didn't try to make suggestions. So after talking, I went to take a shower and after I finished washing my body he got in the shower behind me and put the shampoo in and massaged it with his fingers. Girl, it felt so good I could have died and went to heaven. Then he put the conditioner in and…"

"How does his body look?"

"I didn't see it naked. Anyway, he got out and then I got out and…"

"Then you gave him some ass?"

"No. Would you be quiet," I say while Tracey laughs in my ear. She is so silly. "As soon as I came out the bathroom I couldn't even dry my hair. He took me to this salon and got my hair, nails, and toes done at the same time. While the girl was doing my manicure Daren was massaging my feet. I felt like royalty."

"I'm jealous. What's Daren's phone number? Sike. How does your hair look?

"I got it like Nia Long's. You'll see it. Daren paid for everything, but I insisted on paying the tip. I then told Daren that I would tip him later."

"No you didn't!" Tracey screams. "Where is he now?"

"He went to get dinner, but after all of that this other woman gave me a facial."

"So you got the hookup. When y'all got back you gave him the ass?"

"No. Girl, you're pressed to hear some freaky shit," I say before I bust out laughing.

"That ain't it. Daren just talks too much for me. Are you sure he ain't gay?"

"Tracey, no more jokes, sweetie. Okay?"

"Go ahead with your story about your little gay friend. Does he have brothers?"

"Girl, you're married."

"Evidently I married the wrong motherfucker. I ain't had no foot massage, he ain't paid for my hair or nails, and I haven't gotten a facial, and he already got the pussy. When his ass comes home he better take me somewhere."

As Tracey goes on about her man I just laugh. She is so funny when she goes off.

"Ooops! Gotta run, Sharlene. My man is home so I have to hurry and wash my feet and get out the lotion. He doesn't know it yet, but he's going to massage my feet. Have fun with Daren, girl."

Minutes later I hear the door unlock and Daren walks in.

"What's up, Shar?" he says as he places a bag of food on the table.

I need some answers because no man in his right mind would do this for nothing. Daren's nice, but I know that he's up to something. "Daren, why are you doing this? Why the breakfast, spa treatment, ice cream, and Chinese food? Why?" As he pulls a bottle of Courvoisier out of another bag he turns his attention toward me.

"I'm doing this to celebrate."

"Celebrate what? I'm tired of you talking in parables like you're Jesus or somebody. Just tell me what's going on."

Daren begins to show a faint smile and as he sits on the bed with me his smile fades. Now he gently places my hands inside of his.

"This morning you felt like life wasn't worth living. Like love didn't love you, right? Well, you and I are celebrating a new you. A better you. How do you feel after all you've experience today?"

"I feel wonderful. I feel great."

"And that's how you should always feel. You only live once and your time is precious so if a man doesn't bring you even half of the joy I've brought you then he ain't worth your time. You were treated like a queen today and that's how you should see yourself. That's how I see you."

I can't take anymore. This man is so smooth with his words, and his caring for me has penetrated my heart. Tears begin to form as I concentrate on his words.

"Tears of joy?" he asks in a whisper.

"Yes," I softly whisper back while he leans toward me and delicately licks my left eye's stream of tears.

"It's been more than two months since you had sex?" he whispers in my right ear.

"Yes," I whisper once again as my hormones begin to react. Suddenly I begin to grow hot as my body starts to quiver.

"Well, how long has it been since you had someone make love to you?"

I knew that I would have to ponder that question for a long time to come up with an answer. Instead I feel Daren's warm, soft lips on my neck. I quickly throw my arms around him and close my eyes as my pussy begins to throb. It's been so long and my panties won't stand a chance against my juices. As he kisses me on the other side of my neck and my shoulders I feel myself being picked up. He's strong. Now he has placed me on his lap so I straddle him as he sucks and licks on my chin. His hands are rubbing my back. I'm about to explode. "Mmmmm…" Daren moans with delight.

I can't take this…I can't take this. "Kiss me, Daren. I need you to kiss my lips."

As we finally touch face to face I try my best to ram my tongue into his mouth. "Love me," I hear myself say as the passion gets hotter. Our tongues simply come together like old friends and he squeezes my ass. He then picks me up as my legs lock around his back and he puts me up against the wall.

I'm now reaching down to grab the bottom of my T-shirt so I can take it off. It's time to get the show on the road. As our lips briefly separate and my shirt passes by, he lifts me higher and buries his face in my breasts. My nipples are giving off sensations like I have two clitorises on the ends of my breasts! They haven't been touched or stimulated in so long. All that I can do is grab his bald head and feel his tongue go from one breast to the other.

"Baby, your breasts are so pretty. I love them, baby."

He's so expressive. I love his tongue action, but I wonder if he can fuck. "Oh…oh, honey," I shriek as he places my entire left breast in his mouth and tongues the nipple as his mouth remains attached. Every twirl of his tongue could be felt as my mind drifted away with thoughts of him being inside me. Please let him have a big dick. If it's small then let him know how to work it. Please. I need it. I feel myself being walked across the room as he continues to suck on my titties. I suddenly hear the radio come on as his right hand is once again placed on my ass. I need to take these panties off and get him undressed. I'm ready.

I'm working my hips now as we get to the bed. He places me down gently and seductively kisses my legs and then he turns me over on my stomach. Now I feel his tongue lick from the crack of my ass to my neck in one long, wet stroke. It feels good, but I don't want an overdose of romance. I want that dick inside of me now. "Honey, don't tease me any longer. I want you now." I then feel him reaching for my panties so I quickly turn over to help him take his shirt off. "Mmmm!" I say as I see his fine chest. He is built.

He squats and places his mouth between my legs. "Oh, oh, what the…ooow…!" I escape his tongue for the moment and sit back on the bed. He then lifts my legs as he gets on his knees. I can only moan with pleasure as he lifts my legs into the air and places his tongue inside my vagina.

"Concentrate on my tongue," Daren says as he begins to lick my right vaginal wall slowly. He then licks the left wall. His hot breath is making my pussy wetter.

"Suck my pussy, baby. Lick my pussy, baby." This feels so good. He's now making sucking sounds on my lips as his tongue kisses my pussy. My hips then thrust upward and my ass jumps off the bed as he seductively slides his tongue to my clitoris. He is eating this pussy like a professional. "No! Baby, no! You can't…you can't lick me like…oy…like…like…oh shit…I'm about to cum…I'm…I'm about to…aaaaah! Uaauaah! Oy…oy…." As I begin to make sounds I've never heard come out of my mouth I finally feel him come up for air. He then goes into the bathroom and runs the faucet.

I just lay across the bed with my feet on the floor. I discover that I can barely move as I try to stand. After I get myself together I decide to make my way to the bathroom and attack him. When I reach for the doorknob the water stops. When I open the door I see him placing a washcloth on the side of the sink and his pants to his ankles. I quickly drop to my knees and I'm eye to eye with his dick. Four or five inches! I'm going to swallow this little thing. May even pick my teeth with it. I place it into my mouth and I can feel his balls on my lower lip. I can feel his right hand stroking my hair and…damn, I'm choking as my eyes feel like they're going to jump out of my head. I continue to cough and gag. When I reopen my eyes I see an adult version of that baby dick that I was sucking a second ago.

"Boy, you hit my tonsils. Hold on," I say as I cough one more time. My throat is feeling funny. I compose myself and start sucking his dick again—this time with caution.

As Aaliyah's "Rock the Boat" comes on Daren slowly inches his way around toward the door. As he turns I walk on my knees and turn with him.

Daren tells me to get on the bed and that's when he quickly tells me the rules of the game we are about to play. Whatever Aaliyah says to do we have to do sexually. Then when she says to change position I have to take the lead and choose one. What can I say? Everything that he's done so far has made me feel like a real woman should. I lay on my back without hesitation and wait for Daren to roll on a condom.

As he slides inside the walls of my vagina, I explode with ecstasy. He works his ass by sensuously gliding from side to side and up and around. As Aaliyah sings I smile with erotic anticipation and sing along with her. When she says to take it overboard Daren and I jump up and I get on all fours. When she says to rock the boat we both sing along as Daren rocks my ass from side to side. He then follows her next instruction by going straight down the middle, in and out with a steady groove. Now Aaliyah says to change positions, which means it's my turn to take over. I turn around and get him to lay on the bed and I ride that dick until I drift off into the lyrics.

This is so exciting. I've never had this much fun while having sex. This little game of ours is off the heezy for sheezy! As the chorus comes on again I scramble to get on all fours again as he stands on the floor and pulls my hips toward him and starts rockin' by boat. Oooh, this dick feels so good as my hips and ass are rocked back and fourth, from side to side. Once again he goes along with the lyrics and sends that long dick right down the middle. My pussy is so wet. I know my walls are starting to feel funny.

Change positions…I have to think of something quick because it's my turn to take over again. I jump up and grab the bag of Chinese food and place it on the floor. I lay on the small, round table and open my legs wide. Daren follows and slides that dick back in there. Since the table is high Daren doesn't have to lean over. Oooh, I'm in love with this. I'm feelin' so good.

"Stroke it for me!" I scream as I begin to feel the passion go to another level. That's it! Oooh, that's it. "Baby, I'm cumming," I scream in a high-pitch tone. Daren then speeds up his rhythmic stroke and I feel that dick become even larger and harder as he climaxes along with me.

Daren lifts me off the table with a powerful thrust and lays on his back with his arms still around me. I push up off his chest, look him in his eyes, and as my energy drains from that orgasm, I fall back on top of him. I'm exhausted. It's been so long since I had some dick that I'm sure that I'll want some more soon. I want to sleep, but I'm hungry and I'm sure he is too. Nevertheless, I feel myself drifting off as I continue to contract around his dick.

I awaken about an hour later to Daren hugging me. Still on top of him, I simply squeeze his shoulders with my hands because there's no way that I can get them under his back because of the bed. As he releases his hug I push up off his chest and find the energy that I didn't have earlier.

"You are a real woman…a queen in my eyes. Is that how you feel?"

"Yes. I feel wonderful emotionally and physically." *Really I feel like marrying you, but I won't dare tell you that. Plus there's so much about you I don't know.*

"Alright, Shar-baby, it's time to eat. You have to get that sexy body up so we can see if that food is edible. You know Chinese food is nasty when it's cold," he says as he slips on his sweatpants.

As I look for my T-shirt and panties, Daren squeezes my ass. I just giggle and skip to the bathroom. After I freshen up I return to the bed to discover the food along with two glasses of Courvoisier. I sit down quickly because the broccoli and chicken smells so good. I dip my chicken in the rice and taste it. "Mmmm-mmm!" I moan as I wash it down with a sip of cognac. That's just what I needed. I grab my container and glass and walk to the side of the bed closer to the bathroom and lay next to Daren. Next I throw my legs across his waist and smile at the level of comfort I've reached. I feel so cozy.

"Daren," I say after I take another sip, "I've been giving a lot of thought to that stuff about fantasies you were talking about. You know something, I've been in a relationship for five years and have never come close to my fantasy. And you were right, I do feel incomplete. I've been a working mother and I'll continue to be. I love my child, but when can Mommy have some adult fun?"

After he asks me about my fantasy I eagerly explain it in detail.

"Sounds good to me. Come on and let's go get some ice cream," he says and he jumps up and places his shirt on.

I'm so turned on! I never used to go anywhere with Dumb Ass. Daren is spontaneous. Just jumping up on the drop of a dime and wanting to go out for ice cream.

"I'll be downstairs," Daren says. He kisses me on the cheek and leaves.

"Okay," I say. As soon as the door shuts I whip out my cellular phone and begin dialing. I hear a sleepy voice on the other end. "Tracey, I gave him the ass!"

While riding in his car I hold his hand and after he shifts the gear his hand returns to mine. He's holding my left hand so I use my right one to massage his thigh.

"Where are we?" I ask as I begin to observe our surroundings. All there is to my right is a neighborhood with woods to the right of it. On my left is an elementary school with woods to the left of it. "Where are we?" I ask again.

"We're at boot camp," Daren says as he gets out and closes his door.

I get out with him and he reaches for my right hand. As we walk into the darkness of this unfamiliar park I feel protected. We sit on a picnic table under a huge wooden canopy about fifty feet into the path. Daren then pulls out a bottle of Off! "You want some?" he asks as he sprays it on himself.

"Only if you'll put it on me," I say flirtatiously. As he massages it into my arms and legs with sheer seduction, I'm compelled to inquire. "Daren, would you have put the Off! on me like this the other night?"

"No, I would have done it nicely, like a gentleman."

"Yeah, right! No you wouldn't have," I say jokingly

"I'm serious. Back then I was trying to help you keep your love with your ex. I didn't really flirt with you at all. Did I?"

He had a point there, but he definitely had been all over me that evening. As I blush at him he leans over and kisses my lips and slides his tongue into my mouth. As I begin to enjoy the moment, the left strap of my sundress creeps down as Daren's lips escape mine and find a home with my left titty. There he goes working that tongue again. His mouth is on my titty, his right hand playing with the hair at the nape of my neck, and his left hand is going from my right hip, to my right breast, and back to my right hip. I'm getting wet again. "Daren, look," I say, pointing toward the bright light.

"The police. Come on, let's go." He leads me deeper into the woods. We turn several corners and come upon a small bench with no backrest. "Can you see the lake?"

I focus on a lake not nearly as nice as ours. I then sit down as Daren stands in front of me and strokes my head with his left hand. Next he leans over and kisses me and caresses my left titty with his right hand. My hands are free so I unbutton and unzip his pants and maneuver his underwear until his dick is free. This time I slowly insert it into my warm mouth as I hold the base of it with my right hand and grab his ass with my left. I'm careful not to underestimate the size of his dick so it won't have me gagging again.

"Oooh, damn, baby," Daren moans with delight.

I love when a man talks to me during sex. All that does is motivate me to suck Daren's dick even better. I lick and suck with even more passion as he continues to moan and groan. This long, black dick loves my mouth. I feel his veins protruding through his skin as I begin to slurp. I disregard my hands getting wet as I get deeper into my trade. As I slurp and suck his royal blackness I feel him massaging my scalp and squeezing my nipple. "Mmmm," I hum as he lightens the pressure. I want to tell him that I enjoy the piercing pain sent from my nipple through my titty, but I don't want to take the dick out of my mouth.

Suddenly my cellular phone rings and I have to answer it because of the noise it's creating. Shit! I forgot to cut it off after I called Tracey and I don't like the number that's on the caller ID. "What do you want?" I ask as I reluctantly take Daren's tasty dick out of my mouth, but continue jerking it with my right hand.

"Look," Dumb Ass says, "our child is asking for her mother."

"What? My mother's watching her this weekend. How did you get her?"

"I went and got her since you ain't want to come home. I'll bet you'll bring your ass home now. You ain't been over Tracey's, so where are you?

"Don't worry about it!" I say as I adjust my hand on Daren's dick, trying to at least make him cum since I have to leave. My daughter comes first. I hang up the phone on Dumb Ass. "Daren, I gotta go."

"It's alright. You don't have to explain anything to me."

We walk back to the beginning of the trail and discover that the police are still there, but the spotlight is off. Daren gets the car and returns to pick me up. As he comes to a stop and I get in the police begin flashing the spotlight.

"Fuck them!" I say. "I'm from Brooklyn and I ain't hardly scared of the police."

"You've been a little agitated since that phone call. Baby, just relax. You're a new woman and you have to be a better one than you used to be when reacting to your ex."

"Whatever, Daren," I say, letting my anger show. He had a point, though. My attitude was coming to a boil until his last statement. I'm calm now and I'm returning to my new self. I lean toward him in an apologetic way and place my right hand on his dick. He doesn't hesitate as he inches his shorts and underwear down.

"Aren't you going to finish what you started?" Daren asks, glancing at me.

"Uh-uh! Hell no! That's what happened to Teddy Pendergrass! I'm not putting my head down there while you drive!"

Daren begins to laugh at the top of his lungs at my remark, but I didn't say that to be funny. I just continue to play with his dick as he drives.

Everything was far from normal when I returned home. For one, Dumb Ass met me at the door. He hasn't done that since the first month that we moved in together—and that was five years ago. Actually, he was peeking at the parking lot from the balcony window—probably trying to see if I got dropped off or something. Whatever the reason, it was unusual. Since he normally doesn't greet me, it didn't seem strange when I walked past him, threw a nonchalant hello in his direction, and went to my daughter's room to check on her. Dumb Ass had already put her to bed and that's something else he rarely does. Then he had the nerve to smile at me. He wanted something, but I was sticking to my guns.

I didn't want to wash the scent of Daren's sweet lovemaking off my body, but I had to take a shower. While I'm in there I have to figure out a way not to sleep in bed with that fool. Ah-ha! It's a plan. I don't have to worry about Dumb Ass trying to make up with me by sexing me tonight. He'll be upset, I'm sure, but he'll get over it.

I suddenly feel Daren's hands softly stroke my hair trying to awaken me. I wonder how long I've been asleep. I open my eyes to admire his body and make love to him, but my eyes are tortured by the bright light. It's now that I realize that Daren isn't softly stroking my hair, but rather Dumb Ass is pushing my head.

"Hey! Wake up. Why are you sleeping so hard? Why is our daughter in the damn bed with you? She got her own bed. "You hear me talking to you. Why is our daughter in our bed?" he says as he pushes my head again.

I try to roll over and play sleep, but he continues the late-night harassment. "Jerry, this is a queen-size bed. There's space for you over there next to Shelly." I have to say something to stop him from touching me.

"Give her here so that I can put her back to bed," he says as he reaches for our daughter, but she's snug under my arm.

"Jerry, I miss her. If you put her in her room then I'm going in there to sleep."

"Whatever! You ain't slick. You just don't want to fuck."

"See! You have no class. How are you going to talk like that in front of her?" I say as I sit up and my eyes struggle against the light.

"She's sleep!"

"I don't care! You still don't curse with her around. Dag. Where's the love?"

"I'm trying to make love, but you have our daughter in here."

"Please. You haven't made love to me in four years. You better go in the bathroom and do the job with your hand. Better yet, call that woman you been fuckin' ." He leaves the room and I jump up to cut the light off, but it's worth it. I can sleep peacefully.

Two days have passed without me seeing Daren, and I'm losing my damn mind. I'm missing my mocha lover. My daughter is in day care and I've arranged for Tracey to pick her up. It's getting dark and I have to get to the lake.

As I pull up and get out of the car my cellular rings. "Hello."

"So glad you could make it."

"Where are you?" I ask as the reality of finally seeing Daren hits me.

"Just get on the path and walk toward your right. You'll find me eventually. Now, how have you been?"

He cares, he cares, he cares! It feels so wonderful when someone really asks about you with genuine concern. I talk with him while walking for three minutes. As I reach him on the opposite end of the lake he gets off the bench and gives me a big hug. I could just melt. Daren hugs me like no other. He leads me to the tiny docking area.

"Paddleboats? We're going on the paddleboats? Aren't they closed after dark?"

"Not if the price is right. Now mind your business."

I laugh as Daren helps me aboard. We paddle to the middle of the lake and begin to kiss. I'm the new me again. The two days in Dumb Ass's presence wore me down.

After getting off the paddleboats Daren leads me to a guy having a private picnic on a blanket. I've never seen anyone do that this time of night.

"Thanks, Brad," Daren says as the guy stands and leaves. "I appreciate it."

"Who was that? He looks familiar," I say.

"He runs the boat rentals. He guarded our picnic area while we set sail. Now stop asking questions and sit down. I'm going to make your fantasy come true."

"The picnic wasn't part of it," I say. I don't know where he got that.

"I know. It's the enhancement. We have peaches, strawberries, cantaloupes, and honeydew melons."

"What's in that bottle? Wine?"

"Apple cider. I ain't getting locked up out here."

I feel so special. I can't control my tears as I place my hand into Daren's and sit next to him. We begin to play, tickle, kiss, and tease as we feed each other fruit. Before we realize what's going on we begin to eat the fruit off each other's body.

"Wait a minute," Daren says as he slips a strawberry under my sundress. I feel that strawberry massaging my clit, but when it slightly enters my pussy, my eyes dart to Daren in astonishment. He then takes the strawberry and bites into it.

"Fruit has never tasted sweeter," he says as he slowly chews.

"You are so nasty. I can't believe you did that. Do it again." He goes through the same motion again with another strawberry, but I snatch it and eat it.

"Girl! Do you know how much I wanted another Shar-baby pussy-coated strawberry?" I laugh as he grabs another, dips it into me, and eats it. We then dip and share more fruit that is dipped inside of me. He eats one, then I eat one.

The next thing I know, Daren has dipped a piece of something into me and goes to get it face first. I've been waiting to make love by the lake, but this is an unexpected prelude to my fantasy. "Eat that pussy! Oy…oy…" I cry out in a voice altered by shrills. "Taste that fruit-flavored pussy, poppy. Lick it good." Once again he is working that tongue like a maniac. I've never had quality head before. "Daren, I'm cumming already. I'm…I'm…oy…oy…oy…oooh. I have to make sure that I have some energy left for the main event of my fantasy.

"Turn that caramel-mocha ass over, Shar. Here comes your fantasy."

I know the position. I've dreamed of it many nights. I'm just glad that I can finally put a face to the dark figure in my fantasy. I lay down on my stomach facing the lake and place my chin on the back of my stacked hands to keep my chin up. "Hurry so no one can stop us."

"I got this, Shar-baby."

Damn, I like that nickname, Shar-baby. That's a new one on me because… "ooh, that dick is good," I say as he slides into me. All of his weight is on my backside because I still lay flat. I now begin to make my ass jump up and down to give him more pleasure. At the same time I tighten and loosen my vaginal walls.

"How's that fantasy coming, baby?"

"Call me Shar-baby. Oooh, call me Shar-baby."

"Shar-baby, how's that fantasy coming?"

"It's perfect, baby. Better than I imagined. How does this pussy feel?"

"Your pussy feels as good as it tastes, Shar-baby."

"Say it again."

"Shar-baby."

"Say it again," I say as I pump harder.

"Shar-baby, Shar…baby…Shar…baby…"

Suddenly I get that feeling again and deep inside of my walls I begin to explode.

"Shar-baby, Shar-baby," Daren chants as he shoves his left hand into my mouth to smother my screaming orgasm. However, I still grunt in my bliss. Now I've cum already, but Daren is still pumping hard trying to get his. Whose fantasy was this anyway? His rhythm has broken and his dick is getting harder and larger. Here he cums at last. I muster up enough energy to throw the ass at him while he cums. He lies on top of me exhausted and I'm too worn out my damn self to even try to move. I just lay there and look at the lake while my pussy continues to contract. My fantasy is fulfilled. How sweet it is!

Just pulling up in front of my apartment building spoils my mood. I was in bliss a minute ago as Daren and I continued to feed each other fruit after making love. Now I'm back with a verbally abusive man. The only thing that I have to look forward to is my child. She and I need to move.

Walking up the stairs to my door is a sad moment. It feels like the closer I get, the slower I walk. I can feel Dumb Ass on the other side of the door. Before I put my key in the lock the door swings open.

"Took you long enough," Dumb Ass says while standing in the doorway.

"Hi," I reply as I maneuver between him and the doorsill.

"Oh, you're scared to touch me now? I can't get a hug? Give me a hug."

"You don't want a hug any other time. What makes today different?" I try to find something for dinner in the fridge, but I don't see a damn thing.

"I gave you twenty to pick up something for dinner this morning and you come home without nothing? Some mother you are!"

I do a good job of ignoring that question, but he's standing behind me. I decide to say hello to my daughter and take a nice, hot bath. She'll just have to eat some fish sticks, fries, and peas tonight. I approach her door surprised that I don't hear a sound. I open it and she isn't there.

"Oh, you forgot to pick up our child too? What kind of mother are you? That's neglect on your part."

That did it! "What kind of mother am I? What kind of father would have a child out of wedlock and not even consider marrying the mother for five years? That's neglect on your part!" I then storm into the bathroom. I quickly take off everything and jump into the shower. I wish Daren were with me to ease the pain.

The past week has been very strange. Ever since my fruit picnic and sweet fulfillment of my fantasy with Daren my world has turned upside down. It turns out that Brad, the guy who was in charge of the paddleboats and guarded our picnic area, knows my man. He told him that he saw me with some guy. Thank God he didn't tell him about the paddleboat ride and the picnic.

Nevertheless, what he told him was enough for my man to watch my every move and not let me out of his sight for seven whole days. He took off from his job for an entire week and spent time with me. Even bought me roses and played cards with me. I never liked playing Spades one on one, but since it was quality time with him I didn't mind.

And how could I forget my man taking me to the movies? He also cooked dinner for me three times. His spaghetti was nasty, but he tried. No doubt that the effort was there. Now I'm sitting, wondering how I can break away and get to the lake. I know that my man is going to break down soon to his urge to hang out with his friends. When he does I'll have my chance to go to the lake, and I'll hope Daren arrives. I have a lot of explaining to do.

"How have you been?" Daren asks as I approach the bench. I remain standing.

"Let's go somewhere private. I don't want that guy, Brad, to see me here with you. What's up with him telling my business? I knew he looked familiar."

"It's okay. He won't say anything else. He and I had a talk. Sit down and relax. Listen, he said that he knew who you were and he saw a little of what went down, but out of respect for me he'll act like he didn't see anything. Now, out of respect for his other friend, Jerry, he had to tell him something. I told him to only tell Jerry he saw you with a guy, that's it. Anyway, he told me that he gave Jerry some advice to tighten things up with you because you were too good to lose."

"Oh, he did, did he? That's why Jerry has been doing so much," I say as I begin to get upset that someone else put him up to the past week's good deeds.

"Charlene, you're missing the point. You should be happy that he acknowledges his mistakes and is now trying to do right by you."

"So what are you saying?" I ask as I look into his eyes and twiddle my thumbs. I know that I'm going to miss him, but I don't want to say good-bye.

"I see what's coming. I'll make this easy on you because I know that your family is important and you still may be able to salvage something good from your relationship."

"So what are you saying?"

"I'm saying that we can't meet anymore. There, I made it easy on you. Now you don't have to break up this affair of ours."

I begin to smile as Daren extends his arms to hug me. "You are so silly. Thank you for being there and thank you for the spa day and for helping fulfill my fantasy and…just thank you for everything." I then begin crying on his shoulder.

"It's going to be okay. Just be patient with Jerry, okay?"

"Yes," I respond as he releases me. He then kisses my forehead, tells me good-bye, and walks away while dialing his cell phone.

As I sit and stare at the lake I feel someone sit next to me. I look up to see my man. "What are you doing here?"

"I can't come here? I thought you'd be surprised to see me."

"Of course you can," I say as I think about Brad putting him up to treating me so well for the past week. "What's up?" I wonder why he's kneeling down all of a sudden.

"Sharlene, I've done a lot of dumb-ass stuff and…"

Dumb-ass stuff? You've been reading my mind!

"…I think that I should start treating you the way that you should be treated. I love you and I want to marry you. I'll do you right. I promise."

I've never seen my man cry, but his eyes are about to overflow. Wait a minute, did he just propose to me? "Jerry, are you proposing to me?" I can't believe this!

"Yes, I'm proposing if you," he says, smiling.

"Jerry, I once loved you more than anything. I didn't love you like that after the way you were treating me over the past couple of years. This past week opened my eyes that you could be the man you once were. I'll tell you what, let's keep loving each other and working on our love so that we can grow closer and appreciate each other. If we can do that then I'll be the happiest woman in the world and I'll say yes to you a million times. I want to be your wife, but I'm scared of being hurt."

"I can respect that," my man says. "I'm going to do all that I can to make this work. I'm sorry for everything bad I've done. I love you."

"I love you too," I say as we hug and I shed another tear.

"Now, can I stay and enjoy the lake with you?"

"Yes, on one condition," I say with a smirk.

"What is it? I'll do anything for you."

"Start calling me Shar-baby."

Anniversary
by
Rochelle Alers

rina removed her hands from her coat pockets and pulled the oversized collar up around her neck. The below-freezing temperatures had dipped into single digits with the setting sun, while the frigid mid-February wind lashed at her exposed flesh like hundreds of sharpened razors. Quickening her pace, she made her way to the entrance of a building taking up nearly half a block of prime Manhattan real estate. A slight smile lifted the corners of her mouth, softening her crimson-colored lips. At least her date had selected a hotel with old-world charm for their encounter.

Stepping into the revolving door, it moved automatically without her having to push it. Seconds later, she walked out onto a marble floor and into comforting warmth. Suddenly the full-length silver fox coat sweeping around her ankles seemed too warm and much too heavy.

Ignoring several well-dressed men who stole surreptitious glimpses at her professionally made-up face framed by a matching fur cloche, she strolled to the information desk and offered the clerk a friendly smile. He returned her smile, his bright blue eyes lingering on the curve of her full lips.

"May I help you, ma'am?"

"Can you please tell me if Mr. Emery Peterson has checked in?"

Trina saw in the clerk's eyes he was startled by the sultry sound of her low voice. If voices were compared to fabrics, then hers would be thick velvet. He reluctantly shifted his gaze to a computer monitor and typed the name Trina had given him. "Mr. Peterson checked in twenty minutes ago. He's in Room 1632."

Her smile was one of obvious relief. Emery had followed through on his promise to meet her at the hotel for dinner. "Thank you very much."

Trina felt good—as good as she looked. She'd taken the day off from her position as a buyer for Tiffany Jewelers and spent all morning and part of the afternoon at an Upper Eastside day spa. Her flawless brown face glowed from a European facial, and her body was relaxed and supple after a full-body massage. The brilliant red on her manicured nails matched the polish on the toes of her smooth and silken feet. She'd lingered at the spa long enough to enjoy a light snack, and purchase a dress as well as accessories and have her favorite cosmetologist make up her face.

She shifted when two middle-aged couples exited the elevator, laughing softly. They, as with most of the people getting on and off the elevators, were dressed in formal attire. It was Valentine's Day—a holiday that celebrated love and lovers. Entering the car, she pressed the button for the sixteenth floor. The brass doors closed silently and she closed her eyes briefly as the elevator rose quickly to her designated floor.

It stopped, the doors opened and her pulse quickened in anticipation of seeing Emery Peterson again. The golden glow from wall sconces created an atmosphere of subtle welcome as the heels of her silk-covered pumps sank into the deep pile of the carpet lining the hallway. She neared Room 1632, inhaled, and then let out her breath slowly. Raising her hand, she knocked softly, waiting for a response.

"Yes?" came a deep male voice from behind the door.

"It's Trina."

The door opened and she stared up at the face of the man who had managed to seduce her with only a glance. The instant their gazes met and locked she knew she wanted him—all of him.

He was as breathtakingly handsome now as when she first saw him. His smooth, mahogany skin; close-cropped mixed gray hair; neatly barbered mustache; and evenly balanced features reminded her of James Vander Zee's sophisticated photographic subjects. A tall, muscular, toned body complemented his exquisite face. The dark gray double-

breasted, single-buttoned suit jacket caressing his wide shoulders, veri-
fied the garment had been tailored expressly for him.

Emery Peterson stared at Trina—completely stunned by her
unabashed radiant beauty. Her velvety sable-brown skin; large, brilliant golden eyes; full, lush lips; and rounded face elicited a surge of
heat and heaviness in his groin that was totally unexpected. He'd always prided himself on his rigid self-control with most women; but
there was something about this woman standing in front of him that
was certain to prove him wrong. If he'd thought her beautiful at the
prior weekend's dinner party, then he was mistaken. Seeing her now
confirmed she was nothing short of perfection.

He extended his hand. "Please come in."

Trina placed her gloved hand on his larger one, feeling its raw
power as his fingers closed protectively over hers. Stepping into the
spacious suite, she glanced around his shoulder. Pale-colored drapes
were pulled back from a picture window, offering a view of the East
River, while lights from office and apartment windows and the ones
outlining bridges linking Manhattan with other boroughs created a back-
drop that resembled thousands of diamonds on navy-blue velvet. A
round table in a cozy alcove near the window was set with a gleaming
white tablecloth, china, silver, and delicate stemware.

Emery noticed the direction of her gaze. "I ordered dinner
from room service, but wanted to wait until you arrived to have them
deliver it. Now that you're here, I'll call them."

Trina flashed a grateful smile. She had barely eaten since
rising earlier that morning except for a light snack at the spa; a cup of
herbal tea, two slices of low-fat cheese, and three stone-wheat crackers
were hardly enough to give her the energy she needed to sustain her
throughout the evening.

Moving behind Trina, Emery's hands went to her shoulders.
"Let me hang up your coat first."

She felt his warmth, inhaled the clean, distinctive scent of his
aftershave, her knees trembling slightly. Her reaction to his closeness
never failed to elicit a craving that made her question her own sanity.
What, she wondered, was it about *this* man that made her react like a
cat in heat? Could she sleep with him tonight, and then leave the hotel
with only the memories of what they'd shared?

Yes, you can, a small voice reminded her. She knew she could because she'd done it once before. She'd met Emery at another hotel on Valentine's Day last year, drank champagne, shared her body with him, and awoke with him beside her in bed without experiencing any of the guilt the nuns had sternly lectured her about when she attended parochial school.

She removed her soft kidskin gloves and hat, pushing them into the pockets of her coat. The soft gasp of Emery sucking in his breath confirmed that she'd achieved the reaction she sought when she had selected her dress for their interlude. The clinging garment, with narrow crisscrossing straps, bared her back from nape to waist, while the revealing décolletage displayed a generous amount of full satiny breasts rising and falling with every breath she took.

Emery closed his eyes, gritted his teeth, and prayed silently. He was so close to exploding that the intense throbbing between his thighs was akin to a tortuous pain. He hadn't felt this horny since the onset of puberty. Once he discovered the gratification that came from ejaculating, it seemed as if he spent every free moment in the bathroom masturbating. His mother could not understand his penchant for showering several times a day. But that all changed once he had begun sleeping with women. He had discovered a natural outlet for his sexual frustration.

Even though he still claimed a very healthy libido, he was also very discriminating. Unlike many of his single college buddies and fraternity brothers, he'd always believed in relationships. For him quality was more important than quantity. Trina was quality—and more. When first introduced to her, he discovered her to be intelligent, unpretentious, and extremely sexy. She also projected a modicum of innocence that he found irresistible, a sensual innocence he had never encountered in any other woman.

He opened his eyes, removed her coat, and pressed the soft fur to his nose, inhaling the scent of the perfume clinging to the pelt before he hung it in a closet in the entryway.

He stood motionless, watching Trina as she walked over to the window. His gaze caressed the straightness of her spine, the soft curves of her full hips, length and perfection of her long legs in a pair of sheer black hose and heels. It reversed itself, moving up to her bared shoulders and the black shiny cropped curls hugging her well-shaped head.

"This view is spectacular." Her sensual voice floated back to him, snaring him in a seductive web from which there was no escape.

Unbuttoning his suit jacket, he closed the distance between them. "That it is." He stood less than a foot from her. "It is almost as spectacular as you are."

Shifting slightly, Trina glanced at Emery over her shoulder. Her eyelids lowered slowly. "You like the way I look?"

He went completely still. He even stopped breathing for several seconds. "I like your looks very much. In fact, I like everything about you, Trina." Reaching for her left hand, he stared at the wide platinum band with an inset of flawless princess-set diamonds on her third finger. "Your husband is a very lucky man," he whispered seconds before he kissed her fingers.

Closing her eyes, Trina leaned forward, her breasts grazing the front of Emery's stark-white shirt. "Don't," she pleaded softly, placing her fingertips over his lips.

Emery's arms circled her waist, pulling her closer. He felt the outline of her full breasts against the solid wall of his chest, press of her slim, toned thighs against his, and felt the moist sweetness of her breath sweep over his throat when she raised her chin to stare up at him. Trina was tall in bare feet, five-eight, but her heels gave her more of an advantage. After all, he was six-six.

"I won't talk about your husband if you promise not to mention my wife." His tongue darted out, moistening her fingertips.

She offered him a saucy smile. "You've got yourself a deal."

Dropping his arms, he returned her smile. "Let me call room service. If it's all right with you I ordered the same as last year."

"It's fine."

Trina waited while Emery picked up one of several telephones in the expansive suite and completed his call. The attractive lines around his large dark eyes seemed to devour her as he stared at her. A wave of heat rushed to her face, then moved lower to her breasts, and still lower to the place at the apex of her thighs. Moisture bathed the secret place concealing her femininity, and she doubted whether she'd be able to finish eating before she pulled her dress up around her waist to straddle her lover's thighs.

Her fingers curled into tight fists as Emery moved closer to her. He knew. He knew she wanted him. Wanted and needed him more than she wanted or needed food. He was her food—the sustenance to exist beyond the night. Emery Peterson's lovemaking was what she needed to sustain her until the next Valentine's Day.

He held out his hand to her. "Come, darling. Sit down." She took his hand and permitted him to seat her. He lingered behind her, bending down and placing tiny kisses on the nape of her neck. "I can't wait to taste you."

Lowering her head, Trina closed her eyes, and sucked in her breath. Emery had to know what he was doing to her. "Please put on some music." She didn't recognize her own voice. A rising passion had made it lower than her normal dulcet tones.

Emery hesitated. He could smell the essence of her femininity rising from her pores. There was no doubt that he'd aroused her as much as she had aroused him. He walked over to a massive armoire that concealed a large-screen television and stereo unit. He opened the doors, flicked on the stereo, and turned to a station that featured soft, relaxing music. The instrumental version of a popular song flowed from speakers concealed within the walls of the suite.

A sharp knock on the door garnered both their attention. Emery crossed the space and opened the door. They waited while a member of the hotel's room service staff placed several serving dishes on the table along with a vase of peach-colored roses and a bottle of chilled champagne. Reaching under the lower shelf of the serving cart, he withdrew a quartet of oil candles and lit them.

Emery reached into a pocket of his trousers and gave the man a bill. He palmed it at the same time a wide smile deepened the minute lines in his craggy face. "Thank you."

The slightly balding older man nodded his freckled pate. "Thank you, sir. I hope you and your lady have a happy Valentine's Day."

"We will," Trina and Emery said in unison.

Emery waited until the waiter left before he flipped a wall switch, turning off all the lights. The soft glow of flickering candle-light threw long and short shadows on wheat-colored walls. He sat down opposite Trina, his hungry gaze betraying his runaway lust.

"Champagne, darling?"

Picking up her flute, she extended it. "Yes, please."

He filled her glass and then his own. He held his flute aloft, she following suit. "Happy Valentine's Day."

Her lids lowered over her brilliant gold-colored eyes. "The same to you, Emery."

Both sipped champagne while sampling a platter of chilled shrimp, lobster, smoked oysters, and an exquisite crab salad. Trina drank more champagne than she would have normally, but tonight was special for her. It was the one night of the year when she let go all of her inhibitions.

Her eyes widened when she saw Emery stand up and remove his suit jacket. His right hand went to the knot in his tie. "Wait. Let me do that," she said in a breathless tone.

She dabbed the corners of her mouth with a damask napkin, pushed back her chair, rounded the table, and stood in front of Emery. His breathing deepened as she undid the length of silk around his neck. His chest rose and fell heavily as she unbuttoned his shirt. The sound of their quickened breathing shut out the soft strains of background music.

Hands at his sides, Emery stared down at Trina's head. She placed nibbling kisses along his breastbone before her tongue circled his nipples. He swallowed back a groan, his flesh swelling against the fabric of his briefs. He moaned aloud when her fingers moved between his thighs, cupping him possessively.

"What do you want?" she asked softly.

Closing his eyes, he threw back his head. "Everything."

She alternated sucking his breasts and biting gently on his nipples. "You have to tell me what you want, Emery."

"Lick me. Suck me. Fuck me, Trina."

"Where, my love?" she crooned.

"My ass."

"Where else?"

"My cock."

She laughed in her throat. Unbuckling his belt, she unzipped his trousers and pushed them down around his knees. "Aren't you forgetting someplace else?"

"My balls," he groaned in erotic torture.

Going to her knees, she pulled down his briefs, burying her face in the coarse hair around his long, thick throbbing flesh. She inhaled his scent, his maleness. Trina loved Emery's smell. It was masculine and potent. As potent as his hot seed whenever he ejaculated. He was the only man she'd slept with who could fill more than half a condom with his semen.

Her tongue traced the length of his penis, the velvety skin stretched over the swollen head, the vein-covered underside before she took him into her mouth. He tasted wonderful and smelled even better.

Emery felt the heat from her mouth, the roughness of her tongue, intermittent nip of her teeth on his sensitized cock, on his balls, and along the slight indentation of his ass. There wasn't a woman in the world who could suck him off likeTrina. The first time she'd gone down on him he'd cum in her mouth. She gagged from the sheer force of his exploding semen filling the back of her throat. He was just as surprised as she was, and he spent more than an hour apologizing to her.

They fell asleep in each other's arms, and when they awoke he made it up to her. He made sweet love to her, permitting her to take her pleasure before he took his—this time in the soft sweetness of her lush body.

Reaching down, he caught her under her armpits and lifted her effortlessly to her feet. He kicked off his shoes and trousers, then bent slightly and swept Trina into his arms. "Your mouth is driving me crazy."

She smiled up at him. "I thought that was what you wanted when you set up this date."

He returned her smile. "I don't want to go crazy by myself."

Curving her arms around his neck, Trina rested her cheek against his chest and listened to the rapidly pumping beats of his heart as he walked over to a king-size bed. He pulled back the bedspread, placed her gently in the middle of the bed, his body following. It was impossible to see his expression in the darkened space.

They took their time undressing each other. She gasped when his hand slid between her legs, pushing her thong aside to find her wet and pulsing.

"I'm glad you opted for the stockings and garter belt instead of the pantyhose," he whispered close to her ear.

"I remembered what you said last year."

Emery smiled in the darkness. Circling her waist with his large hands, he relieved her of the last scraps of fabric concealing her nakedness. He couldn't see Trina, but he knew exactly what she looked like even in the dark. She complained that her body wasn't in proportion, but he found nothing wrong with her full breasts with their large dark, prominent nipples. Her waist was small enough for him to span with both hands, and her ass, her ass was perfect. It was slightly rounded, tight, and flawless. In fact the skin covering her body reminded him of a smooth, whipped dark chocolate mousse.

Cradling her face between his palms, Emery covered her mouth with his, tasting himself and champagne on her tongue. He kissed her deeply, his tongue mating and dueling with hers. Moving down her body, he parted her legs and drank again—this time from the fragrant well of feminine libation.

Catching the tiny nodule of flesh between his teeth, he applied the slightest pressure. Her hips rose off the bed as she arched her back in ecstasy. His tongue lapped up juices flowing from her pussy before they dripped onto the sheet. He did not want to waste one drop.

Trina's head thrashed from side to side. She didn't want to climax before Emery penetrated her. Her fingernails bit into the firm flesh on his shoulders. "Stop!"

He recognized the desperation in the single word and slid up her body. Her hand closed around his cock as she guided him into the heat of her body.

She opened her mouth to scream, but he swallowed it with a kiss that siphoned the oxygen from her lungs. He'd entered her in one sure powerful thrust of his hips. The walls of her vagina closed around his large penis, holding him fast.

Emery moved slowly, deliberately. "Trina, you have the sweetest pussy in the world." She moaned close to his ear in response.

Her long legs circled his waist, pulling him closer. "Fuck me, Emery."

"How, baby?"

"Faster."

He increased his tempo. "Like this, baby?"

"Yes," she gasped. "Oh yes."

"What else do you want, baby?"

"Deeper."

Pulling back slightly, he plunged deeper, harder. Each time he withdrew, it was a little farther and a little deeper. He took long, measured strokes before quickening them. Their bodies were covered with moisture when he pulled out and, turned her over. Positioning her on her knees, he entered her from the rear, his hands covering her breasts. The sound of his thighs slapping against her ass created its own musical rhythm.

Holding on to the headboard, Trina tried not to concentrate on the hardened flesh sliding in and out of her body. She wanted to fuck Emery and have him fuck her until the sky brightened with the dawn of a new day. She did not want this Valentine's Day anniversary to end so soon after it had begun.

Reaching between their bodies, she held his slick, wet dick between her fingers, holding him firmly. "Sit up," she ordered. He complied and she hovered over him until she straddled his thighs. She took him into her body—all of his nine and a half inches.

She rode him, bucking wildly, while he sucked one breast before giving the other equal treatment. His hands held her waist, guiding her up and down the length of his rock-hard flesh.

Trina felt the slight tremors, the tingling sensation at the base of her spine. She knew it wouldn't be long before she climaxed. The soft sounds she usually made before she came escalated. The pulsing increased, growing stronger with each thrust of her hips.

She ground her buttocks into Emery's groin, trying to get close enough to him where they'd become one. Her fingers gripped the headboard as she tried forcing back the pleasure threatening to erupt and hurl her to another dimension.

Emery supported his head against the headboard, bit down on his lower lip, and rocked from side to side as Trina bucked up and down on his rigid, swollen flesh. His balls tightened, the head of his cock swelled, and he knew he had less than a minute before he exploded, leaving his seed in Trina's hot, scented body.

First came the heat, then the chills, and finally the dizzying rush of sexual fulfillment. The rush that always accompanied his climaxing stopped his heart for several seconds.

Trina screamed once, collapsed against his chest, waiting for the pulsing between her thighs to wane. She sat motionless, the rapid pounding of her heart echoing in her ears. Resting her head on Emery's shoulder, she waited to encounter sanity once again as his hands made soothing motions on her damp back.

"Did I hurt you, darling?"

She smiled, shaking her head. "No. You never hurt me when we fuck."

He chuckled softly. "I love it when you talk dirty in bed."

It was her turn to chuckle. "That's because I never talk dirty out of bed."

"I worry that I hurt you because you're so small."

"Not so small that I can't take all of your cock."

"There's an expression that says big woman, big pussy. Small woman, all pussy."

Trina laughed, slid off his body and onto the sheet. The sticky liquid on her thighs was a reminder that Emery hadn't protected her. It wasn't something she was concerned about.

Reaching down, Emery pulled a sheet and blanket over their naked bodies. The essence of their lovemaking was redolent in the room. They would get up later, shower, and make love again before they finally checked out of the hotel.

He pulled Trina close to his chest, dropping a kiss on the top of her head. "Do you think we made a baby, darling?"

"Maybe." Her voice was heavy with a lingering passion. "It would be nice if I did conceive on our second anniversary."

"It's only 7:45. We have at least another four hours before it's officially February fifteenth. We can try again before midnight."

She rubbed her nose against his smooth chest. "What if I don't get pregnant right away? What will happen if I get pregnant this summer?"

He kissed her again. "Don't stress yourself, Trina."

"But we promised each other that we would always celebrate our wedding anniversary by meeting at a hotel."

"And we will," Emery insisted. "Even if you're due to deliver the next day I still plan to meet you at a hotel to celebrate Valentine's Day and our anniversary."

"I love you, Emery Peterson," she whispered against his throat.

"And I love you, Mrs. Trina Peterson."

Music played softly, candles flickered, while Emery and Trina held each other until they drifted off to sleep. Just before midnight they woke in time to celebrate their second wedding anniversary in their own special way.

Moving Day
by
Nancey Flowers

A thin slice of light peeled through the window pane. The glare woke Sylvah long before the alarm, which was set to tear at a quarter to seven. Too lazy to disarm it, she allowed the non-syllabic sounds to spill into the air. Wearily she reached over to cease the clock and in another swift motion she flicked on the reading lamp. It was almost one year to the date that she and her husband Bläise parted ways. The yellow manila envelope containing the divorce papers sat on the bedside table. It had been there for more than two weeks, still awaiting her signature. She left it on the nightstand to serve as a blatant reminder that her marriage was really over. "I'll sign and mail you sometime this morning before the movers arrive," she voiced to herself.

Sylvah sat upright and propped her body on the cushioned headboard. She wasn't quite ready to leave the comfort of her California-style king-size bed or her beautiful four-bedroom home. This was the same bed that tore her marriage apart. It was the bed that she grew to love and despise almost simultaneously. It seemed almost impossible to hate a bed. After all, what could a bed do to you other than provide you with a fitful sleep or a little bit of discomfort? But this was Sylvah, and she was anal in that manner. She wanted badly to blame something other than herself for the disposal of her marriage, so she used the bed as a scapegoat. Sylvah felt that the purchase of the bed was the beginning of the end of her twenty-year marriage. Prior to the acquisition of the bed, the troubles between she and Bläise were practically non-existent. That was a little less than five years ago. They were better off cramped up on top of each other in their queen-size bed. At least then they still made physical contact with each other. Once they got the

king-size bed they stayed on their respective sides of the mattress—
Sylvah on the left and Bläise on the right.

Truthfully Sylvah knew the bed wasn't the reason her
marriage dissolved. Their problems began well over ten years ago. It
probably started when her sex drive disappeared. It vanished the day
she looked in the mirror and actually noticed her excess weight. She
had managed to gain twenty-five pounds in a matter of two years. That
was the beginning to the end of a wild and adventurous sex life. Her
desire fizzled. It felt as if the pounds crept up on her. There was no
warning. She couldn't run for shelter. No one else in the family had a
weight problem, so why was this happening to her?

Prior to the weight gain she and Bläise fucked like rabbits.
There wasn't a time or place that was inconvenient for them. They
enjoyed indulging in impulsive sex. They had done it in several places,
including a bathroom stall, the subway, the roof, a public library, the
stairwell in college, a swimming pool, and she even gave him head in
an elevator. The most memorable experience was when they made love
in the sauna during the black ski summit. Another couple walked in,
but exited once they saw what was going on. The act of getting caught
actually heightened the experience, causing spontaneous combustion
or eruption from both. Sylvah always wore clothes with easy access,
because with Bläise she just never knew. Bläise always told her that he
loved that little spark in her. On the exterior Sylvah appeared to be
reserved, but that was all a façade. Sylvah definitely had some freak in
her and Bläise knew how to whet her appetite. When he felt like being
adventurous he would arch his eyebrows and pucker his lips in that
sexy way that Sylvah adored and without a word he'd be driving her
like a nail into a wall. The kids didn't even slow them down. Sex
between Sylvah and Bläise was one of their favorite pastimes, however, all of that abruptly came to an end.

Those first two years of law school were the hardest and once
she managed to get through them she didn't do anything to lose the
weight. Bläise still complimented her and even voiced his satisfaction
by saying, "Baby, it's just more cushion for the pushing. You know I
like it from the back and you could never have too much ass for me."

She would laugh at his coy remarks and knew that he meant
well, but still she wasn't content with her appearance. Her body went
through some kind of metamorphism and she didn't come out looking

like a beautifully painted butterfly. She went from a size six to a size fourteen. The change actually required a brand-new wardrobe. Her bra size even increased. Sylvah who barely had a mouthful before the weight gain went from a 34B to a 36C. Her back got broader and her breasts grew fuller. That was the only thing that she didn't mind.

Their children even commented on her heaviness. Kenya and Zaire who were ten and twelve at the time said, "Mommy, you're fat." The weight gain and the words that poured from her children's mouths were a huge blow and Sylvah was too entrenched in her studies to recover physically. Whenever they went out to dinner as a family, Kenya and Zaire would caution their mother against after-dinner sweets. It was all out of love, but children merely spoke the truth, no matter how heartbreaking it was. Then when she finally started to accept her shapeliness it was simply too late. Bläise began finding other pastimes and they didn't include her. He'd go bowling with his coworkers and even began watching football games at bars. Bläise hated bars and complained about the smoke. He wasn't much of a social drinker either, but anything was better than being around a sulky Sylvah, and with time he adjusted. Adding insult to injury they owned a sixty-inch digital television with surround sound. Nevertheless, he got tired of her constant complaining about school, her job, money, the kids, and the weight gain. He told her that her mouth was like a fish swimming upstream—it never got tired.

Those were things that she needed to put in a chest and place in the attic of her mind. The fact that she and Bläise managed to share twenty good years was a blessing, however, she did have the good sense to finally walk away. It wasn't healthy to stay in a failing relationship. She witnessed the volatile situation that her grandparents had and it was horrible. It was painful and awful to be involved with someone whom you no longer loved. The kids were both in college and were old enough to understand, so it was time to move on with her life. A friend recommended that they seek counseling, but Bläise being headstrong and heart wrong refused. Deep down she was afraid of letting go. Afraid of starting over. Afraid that there wasn't anyone out there suitable or as compatible with what she and Bläise shared before things went awry. Afraid of another heartbreak. Afraid that no one would find her attractive, but that was the least of her worries.

The day before as she strutted down the street talking on her cell phone to her hairdresser, Kennedy, she caused a car accident. A three-car accident at that! It wasn't every day that a thirty-nine-year-old woman caused cars to come to a crashing halt.

"Woman, are you causing accidents again?" Kennedy asked, chuckling on the other end.

Sylvah merely laughed it off and kept her pace, however, the man in the third car jumped out and stated, "You know that you caused this accident, right?" He was looking directly at Sylvah. She blushed, smiled, and kept walking. Kennedy was still on the line eavesdropping.

"See I told you," he replied.

To make matters worse, the same man who accused her of causing the accident began calling for her attention again.

Oh great, Sylvah thought and said aloud. "I hope they don't need me to become a witness. I didn't see what happened anyway, and I'm not lying for these people."

"I hear you," Kennedy replied. "Tell them those exact words and keep rolling."

"Kennedy, I may have to call the police or find one out here real quick. This man is following me," Sylvah said as she spun her head around to find the man a step away from clipping her heels.

"Pardon me, miss. I'm sorry for bothering you. I just wanted to ask if you'd be interested in dinner and the theater."

Sylvah's bottom jaw hung open and her upper lip rolled, exposing the gap in the top row of her teeth. This was far from what she thought he had in mind. How could this be happening to her? Why was this man tripping? The fact that someone struck his car seemed to be the least of his worries and from the look of it, that little ding was going to cost someone a pretty penny. He appeared to be more interested in getting his mack on.

"Excuse me," Sylvah replied still in awe at the scene that was taking place before her.

Kennedy remained on the other end of the phone saying, "Mmph, mmph, mmph. Handle your business, Ms. Sex Goddess. What do you have on today anyway?"

"Kennedy, shut up," Sylvah said, laughing.

The man began to back away and a genuine look of embarrassment covered his face. The only words he heard come out of Sylvah's mouth were *shut up*. He was oblivious to her phone conversation. Unaware and unable to see the headpiece neatly camouflaged by her long hair he hung his head down in shame for taking up her time. Realizing that he thought she was talking to him, Sylvah pointed to the cord of the phone and he bared his teeth in a slight smile.

"Well, would you consider going out with me for a lovely evening of dinner and possibly a play?" he asked again. He bounced back like a rubber band and seemed to really be on a mission.

Sylvah looked over at the other two drivers who were exchanging information. One of the men beckoned the man who stood in front of Sylvah. "We need you over here," the man chided in an unpleasant tone.

"Give me a minute, will ya!" Sylvah's new friend replied.

This man was dead serious. Sylvah was in a good mood and Kennedy was urging her to give the man a response. A positive one. Sylvah didn't know what to do. He was a good-looking man, but she was still married—scratch that, soon to be divorced. What was a woman to do? Sylvah had never dated a white man before. For that matter, Sylvah never really dated. She had been with Bläise for more than half of her life. She had two lovers before Bläise and those encounters took place during her teenage years. She couldn't even remember the touch, feel, smell, or taste of another man. Yet, here this man was expecting to taste some of her deep dark chocolate. It appeared that he liked his women strong and black.

A white man. He wasn't your typical white man either. He was nicely dressed in an expensive navy blue pinstriped, double-breasted Italian suit. Probably Armani. A tie that resembled something that she could have easily picked for Bläise in the past in a heartbeat. He was driving a Lexus. It wasn't the current year, but it was definitely top of the line. There was no sign of a wedding band—not even the shadow of a ring. His shoes were either new or recently polished and his hands were beautifully manicured. Sylvah allowed the thought to run through her mind once more before answering. A white man. A Brad Pitt/Pierce Brosnan/Johnny Depp appeal. Damn what was the world coming to? It wasn't like he was asking her to marry him. He was polite and merely offered to take her out to dinner and the theater. She couldn't even remember the last time she visited the theater. Oh yeah, *The Lion King* in 1998.

Sylvah reflected that too much thought could damage the mind. She had a way of overanalyzing situations, but that was part of her being. That's what lawyers did. Sylvah dipped her hand into her handbag and retrieved a business card. Even before the tango-colored nails with the acrylic tips could reappear, he handed her his information. She quickly glanced at his business card and read his name aloud.

"Hunter Bolton. That's different," she said in a singsong voice.

"My parents are eccentrics. They loved the sixties. My middle name is Grey," Hunter said, smiling like he had just scored a goal.

"Really. Well here's my number." Sylvah placed the card into Hunter's open palm.

"Sylvah Lawrence, attorney at law. I may need to retain your services right now. Are you any good?"

"Well, Mr. Bolton, wouldn't you like to find out?" Sylvah said teasingly, knowing that Kennedy was taking all of this in.

"If you give me the time I have every intention of finding out," Hunter said as he backed away and headed toward the sight of the accident. "I have every intention of finding out," he said once more with a grin that gave Sylvah goose bumps.

"Woo!" Sylvah gasped. It was the only word that escaped her lips as she proceeded down the path and picked up where she left off with Kennedy.

Sylvah walked away from that accident with a confidence she hadn't felt in years. Her dress was simple but elegant—black pants that were fitted but not tight, a soft brown knit turtleneck, three-quarter length camel-colored suede jacket, matching handbag and brown python boots with pointy toes and sizable heels. Sylvah was a conservative dresser. Though she wasn't a prude, Sylvah strongly disliked it when women chose to bare all of their goods, leaving nothing for the imagination.

Forty-five minutes later when Sylvah entered the hair salon her arrival provoked standing ovations from the staff and patronizing customers. After all it wasn't every day that a beautiful lady like herself was able to cause a multiple car accident.

The events of the day before caused a smile to dawn on Sylvah's face. She was so ready to move on with her life. A year of sulking was definitely enough. Her friends complained because she was always in a funky mood. It was almost as if she had PMS (personal man shit) for an entire year, but she suddenly felt renewed. Refreshed. Rejuvenated. And in less than two weeks she would celebrate her fortieth birthday. Her best friend, Felice, was treating her to a five-day, four-night vacation in Jamaica. Their reservations were at the Hedonism II hotel located in Negril. It was a much-needed respite from her life of drudgery. Hopefully she'd be able to do away with her friend Barry McKnight for the week. He had been her lover for the past year. When they made love he swooned her like Barry White and he strongly resembled Brian McKnight. At least he did in her dreams, but she wanted and needed the physical, the real deal, and she was ripe and ready for some real fun and loving.

"Lord, let me sign these papers," Sylvah said, speaking into the air, allowing the words to ricochet off the walls and back into her ears. Rolling over to the untouched side of the bed she located a pen in the drawer of the hand-crafted beechwood nightstand. The document was long, but she knew exactly where to sign. She had her lawyer look it over with a fine-tooth comb. Obtaining a lawyer made practical sense. Doctors have doctors, so why shouldn't she have a lawyer? She reviewed the papers herself but didn't want to risk missing pertinent information. She knew the law, but divorce law was not her expertise.

Sylvah entered her marbled bathroom dressed in a gentle green terry-cloth robe monogrammed with her initials. Standing directly in front of the large sixty-by-seventy-two-inch silver-framed mirror she undressed and admired her new body. Her breasts didn't hold the same position they did twenty years ago, but they still looked fabulous. Large nipples encircled deep chocolate candy-apple size breasts. Love handles were still visible, but compared to last year they were almost absent. The cushion for the pushing refused to retreat, but it was fine by Sylvah. An ass was definitely an asset. Joining the gym was rewarding and before long all visible flaws would be gone. It was just a matter of time.

The steam from the shower made the mirror hazy, fogging up Sylvah's view. She extended her hand under the water to test the temperature before stepping in. Once inside the water pelted her skin like a dose of heavy rain in a tumultuous storm. The high output shower massager was set on level three. It was the most therapeutic of the six massage settings. The fact that the massager was also handheld made it an invaluable asset to Sylvah. She was in need of an invigorating shower session. There were knots in her back that needed kneading and a twinge between her legs that demanded the pulsating water's attention.

Sylvah squeezed the Satsuma body wash onto her loofah and worked up a gentle lather. Her hands traced her body in circular motions. Her body appeared to be covered in whipped cream and at that moment she wished that she had someone to lick it off her from head to toe. The thought stimulated her vagina and the desire for sexual release intensified. Sylvah reached for the showerhead and the sweltering water rinsed her clean, leaving suds around her toes. Her body glistened and she took delight in seeing her caramel-colored nipples rise to attention. Sylvah didn't deny herself, but instead used her left hand to massage her right breast. She took her nipple between her thumb and forefinger and began to toy with it. Her left breast was feeling neglected, so she turned her attention there. After a few moments she moved her hand down to bathe it in the moisture that was beginning to gather between her legs. She trembled from the touch.

Sylvah gently stroked her clitoris until it began to swell and became lubricated. A small gasp escaped, because she knew how to make herself feel good. She had spent time teaching Bläise how to please her when they first became lovers and would probably have to guide the next person as well. After all, no one knew her body the way she did, but it was always fun to explore. Sylvah's clit became thick and firm and sensitive to the touch, but she wasn't ready to cum. It was hard to stem the tide of the orgasm that was waving its way to shore, but she willed her body to hold off. Sylvah lifted her chin and held the shower nozzle above her head allowing the water to swab across her face and her neck. There was a small area between her neckline and shoulder that served as one of her weak spots and the sensation of the water further aroused her. Sylvah quickly removed the hand that was still rubbing her clitoris and replaced it with the showerhead. The heavy stream of water jetted from the shower nozzle causing Sylvah to cum upon contact. She managed to maintain the position of the nozzle as her body writhed from delight. The warm water seemed to prolong her orgasm, carrying her into a high that she imagined only a drug addict could comprehend. The sensation overwhelmed Sylvah, and her body slumped over from bliss.

Sylvah recently purchased another showerhead just like hers for her best friend Felice. All of her friends thought her to be crazy when she told them the pleasure that she received from the massager and just like skeptics, they laughed. But one weekend Felice came for a visit and her curiosity piqued after hearing Sylvah's incessant chatter about her shower massager, so she decided to give it a whirl. Sylvah was in the laundry room located next to the bathroom washing clothes when she heard a squeal. Tempted to yell if everything was all right she decided against asking, figuring that Felice must have forgotten to adjust the water before stepping into the shower. Sylvah proceeded to put another load of clothes into the wash and was adding fabric sheets into the dryer when she heard Felice bawl out, "Oh, my fucking goodness. Oh, shit…help me!" Sylvah slammed the dryer door shut and ran three paces to the bathroom door. She turned the knob and the warmth of the steam grazed her face and the fog hazed her vision.

"Sylvah, is that you?" Felice asked in short, steady breaths.

"Yeah. Is everything all right?" Sylvah asked, concerned although she remained standing in the doorway.

"Yes, I'm fine. I'm fine." Felice was still experiencing the aftershocks that accompanied her orgasm.

"Are you sure? Because I thought I heard you screaming for help."

"Girl, you're hearing things. I almost busted my ass bending down for the soap though. You know that if I had fallen I'd have to lay here on the floor and sue your ass for this faulty shower floor."

"Felice, you always finding something to sue somebody over, but you forget that I'm a lawyer and that shit won't fly over here."

"Whatever. Anyway get out of here so I can finish showering."

"Oh yeah. My bad."

Later that evening Felice confessed to having used the massager, but said that she was too embarrassed to admit it when Sylvah walked in on her. They ended up having a big laugh about it later, so Sylvah decided to buy Felice the massager as a thank-you for being such a great friend and for the trip. Now that they were both single they needed as much excitement as they could get.

As Sylvah exited the shower she heard her phone begin to ring. She quickly glanced at the small clock above the commode and saw that it was only eight. Who could be calling her this early in the morning and why? Sylvah grabbed her robe and sprinted into her bedroom. She had to get to the phone before the fourth ring, otherwise the machine would come on and a lot of people had a tendency to hanging up on answering machines.

"Hello," Sylvah said, kneeling forward and leaning on the bed to catch her breath.

"Is Mrs. Lawrence available?" the voice on the other end asked. It was way too early in the morning for telemarketers, Sylvah thought and was tempted to make her reply in the negative. But she decided not to be hasty.

"This is she. How may I help you?"

"This is Jason from Keep It Moving and Storage. I'm calling to confirm that our movers will be there at eleven this morning. Do you have any special needs that I should let my drivers know about?"

That was the wrong question to ask Sylvah after she just got out of that steamy and body-relaxing shower. She had lots of special needs, but was sure that that wasn't what the caller had in mind. Besides she didn't know if any of the men coming this morning would be able to help her out anyway.

"Jason, is it?" she asked not really waiting for a response. "Everything is packed and ready to go. I have a few small items that I need to put away, but those things will be done by the time your men get here."

"Okay, but just as a precaution we'll bring extra boxes. You just never know. You know?" Jason said and laughed.

"Yeah, whatever," Sylvah said, getting antsy. She was ready to cut him off.

"Okay. Well your final bill will be blah, blah, blah. If you should need any additional services, it will cost you extra. Blah, blah, blah. So we'll see you then. Thank you for using Keep It Moving and Storage."

"Thank you and good-bye," Sylvah replied, replacing the receiver on the base.

Why in the hell did he feel the need to call her so early in the damn morning? The movers weren't due to come for another three hours. Damn, she definitely could have missed that call. Less than a minute later the phone rang again. This time she let it ring until the machine came on. If it were important, whoever it was would leave a message. The extended greeting played while she applied the mango-scented lotion to her legs. She made a mental note to take Bläise off the recording when she moved into her new condominium. Now that she was going to be single she didn't want men thinking that she was still attached. Although that had its appeal, that wasn't the type of man that she was looking for.

"Pick up the damn phone!" It was Felice. "You know that your ass is home, so stop screening the calls."

Sylvah grabbed the receiver before Felice could mouth off any more crap, because she could and would take up the entire fifteen minutes of recording time if she wanted to.

"Woman, you really have issues. I could have had a man laying here with me and there you go cussing me out."

"Hello, may I please speak to Sylvah?"

"Anyway. I don't know why you're trying to play me. I could have a man in here if I wanted to."

"Sweetheart, no one said you couldn't, but I know you and it's been how long since that man left you. And when was the last time you got your groove on—and Barry McKnight don't count."

"You better stay tuned and don't touch that dial, because sister is hot. As a matter of fact I'm hot to death! Sister is causing car accidents and turning heads of white men these days. Girl, you betta recognize."

"What! You can give me the details when I get there. I'm on my cell and on the way now. Do you want anything from Junior's? I'm about to stop in for coffee and some breakfast to go."

"As a matter of fact, yeah. I don't have any food left. I cleaned the refrigerator two days ago and gave away all of the food and all of the canned and boxed goods are packed away. Get me coffee and a bagel with lox."

"Girl, this is Junior's not Lawrence's Delicatessen. I'll get you something good. See you in about thirty minutes."

"Okay. Hurry."

Felice arrived in record time. They were able to eat their French toast and corned beef hash before the movers arrived. Sylvah was sipping on the last of her fresh-squeezed orange juice when the doorbell rang. Felice popped up like a jack in the box upon hearing the chimes.

"Girl, you act like you expecting company," Sylvah teased.

"Let's see…you hired a moving company that is black owned, so you know these brothers are bound to be beautiful and buff. They lift heavy things, so they've got to be in shape, so to answer your question, yes, I'm expecting some company."

"I should have known that was why you volunteered to come over here and help. You always have some kind of ulterior motive."

"Don't act surprised," Felice said as she hightailed it to the foyer to answer the door.

Sylvah picked up the bags and the remains of their breakfast to empty the items into the garbage. She could hear Felice flirting with the movers as she took the bag out of the trash bin and tied the drawstring handles into a knot. Felice led three bronze-colored men to the kitchen. On sight none of them really appealed to Sylvah. The first brother was well built, but couldn't have been more than an inch or two taller than she was, and Sylvah never liked dating men that were close to her in height. The second brother had it going on and he was the perfect height for Sylvah, but he could use a serious tan. He seemed to be lacking in the melanin department and Sylvah liked her men to be at least golden-brown. The third brother had the height, the complexion, and the body, but the gaps between his teeth were so wide you could use his mouth as a dish drain to rest plates. To make matters worse his head was disproportioned. It simply appeared too small for his body.

Sylvah watched as Felice fawned over all three of the men and she knew that if her friend could have her way she'd be doing all three of them right there on her kitchen floor. Hell, and from the way the men were responding, Felice would get no rejections. All three of them were salivating.

Felice was a freak. There was no hiding it and for years Sylvah had lived vicariously through Felice to learn new tricks of the trade. Felice was a tall beauty with skin the color of raw sugar and a naturally cut hairdo. Her figure required a sign that read "sharp curves ahead."

Sylvah hadn't really noticed it before, but she realized that Felice's attire was a little on the skimpy side. Her friend was wearing a sky-blue baby tee that more than accentuated her ripe breasts and revealed her navel ring. Felice wore a 34D bra and for whatever reason her nipples were never at ease. They stood at attention 24/7 seven and since her breasts stood firm and upright she rarely wore a bra—and today was no exception. She had on tight black low-rider stretch pants and because her pants were low you could see the powder blue lace of her thong panties. If Felice were to make an attempt to bend over the movers would get a clear view of the crack of her ass.

Sylvah politely greeted the men, told them that they could get started in the kitchen, and walked past them to take the garbage outside. She trusted that her girl would be able to entertain them in her brief absence.

She took the large aluminum trashcans that displayed her house number on the side to the curb, then she walked back into her concrete yard and closed the gate behind her. Just as she was about to reenter her house she heard the gate creak and slam again. Sylvah quickly turned around to see her intruder.

"Hi. Are you Mrs. Lawrence?" the stranger asked.

This brother looked good and there were no complaints this time around. Sylvah was mad at herself for not looking her best. She had a scarf on her head, a sweatshirt from her alumni, Morgan State University, and tight torn jeans. Sylvah wasn't going for the sexy look, because she wasn't planning on meeting Mr. Umm Damn today. Mr. Umm Damn was about six feet one. His complexion was like a pancake when cooked properly and his body was banging. Mr. Umm Damn's hair was cut very low; he had beautiful teeth, which were showcased by an alluring smile; long eyelashes; and thick silky eyebrows. Where did men like this come from? Sylvah thought, trying not to froth at the mouth at this beautiful creature. Sylvah would've slammed herself into a wall if she were still walking.

"Miss, are you Mrs. Lawrence," he asked once again.

"Are you talking to me?" Sylvah asked, realizing shortly after that her question was extremely silly. After all, he was standing in her front yard and she was the only person besides him in it. Never in life did she think that anyone could look better than her now-estranged husband, Bläise.

"Yes, I am," he said, giving her an odd look.

"My mind is elsewhere today, so please pardon me. Yes, I am Mrs. Lawrence. Actually it's Ms. Lawrence. As of today I'm no longer married and since I don't believe that I'm old enough to be your mother, please call me Sylvah."

"Oh, I'm sorry. I wasn't trying to insult you or insinuate that you were old, because you don't look a day over twenty-five."

Sylvah knew that this bronze Adonis was bullshitting her and what he really meant to say was that he wasn't a day over twenty-five, which was fine by her. The late, great singing sensation Aaliyah sang it best, "age ain't 'nothin' but a number." She was flattered and didn't bother to suppress the burgeoning smile that tugged her lips due to his very forward compliment.

"If I had my paint, paintbrush, and canvas I would capture that celestial smile that you just laid on me. Your smile is past beautiful, it's divine."

Okay, Mr. Umm Damn was definitely interested in sampling the goods that stood before him, because he was stroking the oil on her canvas pretty thick. Sylvah became curious and wondered if he stroked up and down, round and round, slow and steady, or fast and hard. Inquiring minds wanted to know.

The usually reserved Sylvah decided to step out of character and play along with her new friend.

"Is my smile all that you like?" Sylvah inquired with a sly grin. "What's your name?"

Sylvah could tell that she put her new young friend on the spot, by the way his cheeks turned blush red.

"My name is Jason. I spoke to you on the phone earlier."

"Oh, so that was you. Well, please come on in," Sylvah said, leading him into the house. "So how long have you worked for Keep It Moving and Storage?" Sylvah asked, trying to get an idea of how old Jason was without coming out and asking the question directly.

"I've been working with this company since it was established five years ago."

"Really? So how does it feel to work for a black-owned organization? Is it all that it's cracked up to be?"

"Yeah, it's that and then some, especially since it's my company," Jason responded.

Sylvah stopped dead in her tracks, put her hands on her hips, and swung her head around one hundred and eighty degrees after his last comment. Now she was confused. Jason had to be in his early to mid-twenties and here he was professing to own one of the most successful African-American–owned moving and storage companies in the five boroughs of New York.

"Come again," Sylvah said.

"Keep It Moving and Storage is my company. I opened it up when I was twenty-two, which was shortly after I graduated from college."

"Really? I'm impressed. Who helps you run it? Your parents?"

"I keep it running," Jason answered smugly and rightfully so. Sylvah's line of questioning was unwarranted. "I'm an artist by trade, but I realized early on while in college that my art wouldn't support me until I made a name for myself so I was a double major. I studied business management and art history."

Sylvah made an attempt to retract her query. "I didn't mean to make it sound as if you couldn't run this company alone. It's just that you appear to be so young and I just assumed…well we all know what assuming leads to. Please accept my apology."

"Apology accepted," Jason said, extending his arm so that Sylvah could once again lead the way.

When they entered the kitchen Jason immediately surveyed the amount of work that needed to be done. He walked over to his employees and gave them directions on which rooms to begin clearing first. Within seconds the men divided into two teams and began doing their work.

Felice walked over to Sylvah with a huge smile on her face. Sylvah smirked back at Felice, because she knew that her girl had something up her sleeve and whatever it was she wanted no parts of it.

"I'm going to start organizing the boxes that are upstairs," Sylvah announced. "I still didn't put all of my clothes in the garment box yet."

"Well, wait for me. I'll come help you. After all, that is what I'm here for," Felice said.

"Oh, really? I thought you were just here as a showpiece today. Besides, I thought that you'd want to stay down here and keep these men satisfied—I mean occupied. What is wrong with me? I guess it's just a little slip of the tongue."

"Sylvah, you are not funny. Anyway, I still want to know what's going on with you and these white men. You still didn't tell me what happened."

"Oh yeah. Well bring your butt on upstairs and I'll tell you," Sylvah said. She then walked over to Jason to inform him of her whereabouts and told him if he needed anything to simply come upstairs.

Sylvah and Felice entered the master bedroom. They both went into the walk-in closet and began transferring the clothes from the wardrobe to the garment box. Within ten minutes they were finished and the only thing left to be done was to move the items into the truck. While they waited for the men to complete their work downstairs, Sylvah told Felice all about her episode from the day before. Felice told Sylvah that she should pursue a relationship with Hunter—at the very least a little rendezvous at which Sylvah scoffed. Although her curiosity piqued about the prospect of being with a white man, the thought of being with a sexy, strong, ambitious younger black man was even more appealing. Sylvah was lost in her thoughts when Jason appeared. Felice had to tell her to snap out of it and brought her attention to the sexy visitor that stood patiently in the doorway.

"Ms. Lawrence…I mean Sylvah, I wanted to take a look up here if you don't mind, so we could begin taking these items out to the truck."

Sylvah cleared her throat and pulled herself together. She didn't realize how much she desired this luscious young man. When she stood she could feel the moisture that began to form between her thighs, and now that he was standing only a few feet away her clitoris was experiencing a slight titillation of excitement. She was feeling a bit embarrassed, but she quickly realized that no one else would know that her panties were wet or that her pussy was throbbing. Sylvah felt like a bitch in heat and she knew that Jason could be the dog that she needed him to be.

"By all means. Please take your time and look around. I tried to organize things to make it easier for you guys. I put the larger boxes to the front and the smaller ones are back there." Sylvah pointed and Jason shifted in the direction of her finger. He moved closer to Sylvah and she could feel the warmth of his body. Unconsciously, Sylvah began fanning herself and Felice choked up a laugh.

"Girl, I'm going downstairs to let them know that they can begin clearing some of the upstairs rooms and to see if *I* can be of any assistance. It appears that there are too many black folks in this space and you know how we can draw heat."

Before Sylvah could object Felice was gone.

"Umm, are your guys almost done downstairs?" Sylvah asked as Jason circled the room.

"Yeah, just about. I have another worker who just showed up, so we have more than enough hands now."

"That's good. You'll be able to do your job a lot quicker and then you all can go home early."

"That's true, but I'm in no real rush."

"Oh, you don't have another job after this?"

"I have a job that I want to complete right here, right now," Jason said as he walked up behind Sylvah and put his hands on her waist. "Sylvah, if you don't mind me saying so, you are beautiful. I haven't been able to take my eyes off of you from the moment I arrived."

Sylvah was startled and quickly pulled away. She wanted him, but she had never been involved in a one-night or one-afternoon stand before. This was all happening too fast. She had to regain control of the situation.

"Jason, I don't know if I gave you the wrong impression, but I'm still a married woman."

"I thought you said earlier that you weren't married. It doesn't matter and I apologize if I've overstepped my boundaries. I don't usually behave this way. I was just so attracted to you," Jason said as he walked off sheepishly.

"Jason, wait," Sylvah called.

Jason stopped in the doorway and turned around to face Sylvah, who walked over and took him by the hand, closing the door behind them.

Sylvah craned her neck to invite Jason's mouth to meet hers. Jason's tongue moved with such precision that it felt like he was making love to Sylvah's mouth. His thick lips were pressed softly against Sylvah's and his mouth was warm and sweet. Jason looped his tongue around hers and did something that Sylvah had never experienced before. Then he kept her tongue in his mouth and slowly sucked on it the way Bläise used to suck on her clitoris. Sylvah could feel herself melting in Jason's massive arms. The kiss was intense and Sylvah felt another jolt of excitement in her vagina. When he was through he pulled back and gazed into her chestnut eyes causing Sylvah to swoon. She didn't know how and when things got so hot and heavy, but they had and she wanted more.

Kissing was usually considered personal, private, and very passionate. Sylvah couldn't remember the last time she shared a kiss like that with anyone—not even with Bläise. Yet here she was kissing Jason, this young brute of a man. She still couldn't get over his age. It really shouldn't have been an issue. Sylvah felt she deserved this young treat. Plenty of men dated younger women. As a matter of fact many men only dated younger women. What difference did it make if she decided to date a younger man? The important thing was that he treated her right. Hell, why was she getting so carried away? It was only a fuck!

Between breaths and on the way to the bed, Sylvah spoke.

"Jason, I'm almost old enough to be your mother." After further calculation she realized that she would have been a very, very young mother.

"Then teach me, Mommy. Teach me, because I'm willing to learn," Jason said as he bent to his knees and began unbuttoning Sylvah's jeans. Slowly he slid them off her full hips and sumptuous ass. His hands moved freely about her body and Sylvah laid back to enjoy the company and pleasure of Jason's hands, which seemed to be extraordinarily soft for someone who moved furniture for a living.

Sylvah's body yearned for the touch of a man, and she wanted this man inside of her. It had been almost two years since her body was caressed. Jason's fingertips grazed the damp crotch of Sylvah's panties, which he removed with his teeth. Sylvah wriggled as Jason darted his tongue in and around her vagina, using his tongue as a probe. Sylvah wondered how someone so young could be so good. Bläise didn't even please her like this. Jason moved his hands against her smooth bare legs and Sylvah's chest heaved up and down from elation. She chewed on her lower lip to keep from moaning aloud. After all, Felice or one of

Jason's employees could come knocking on the door at any second. Sylvah's breathing intensified when Jason's tongue hit her spot. She wanted to stop him, but it felt too good. Bläise was a good lover, but he never hit the spot that quickly. A simmering sound passed through her lips. Sylvah bucked her head forward. Jason used that as an indication and slowed his tongue down a few notches.

"Not yet," he said as he held up his head. "I want to taste some more of this sweet nectar."

He kissed her vulva and licked on her clit some more. From time to time he would stick his tongue in and out of her vagina to stop Sylvah from climaxing. When Sylvah could stand it no more she held his head on her spot, forcing him to bring her to orgasm. Sylvah's body flinched and her legs locked around Jason's head. As Sylvah continued to cum Jason stroked his tongue in strong circular motions and she imagined that he handled his paintbrush in the same manner.

A rush of cum gushed out of her vagina as her body continued to jolt. When her legs relaxed and her body became tranquil Jason moved up onto the bed to join Sylvah, but she wasn't quite ready for him to enter her. Sylvah wanted to taste Jason as well. Their lips touched briefly before her descent. She positioned her body upright and headed straight down south. She quickly unfastened his belt and pants and before long his large and very attractive penis filled her mouth. She utilized the strength in her jaws to suck his shaft and used her hand to jerk what couldn't fit into her mouth. She marveled over his beautiful piece of equipment, which was indeed a masterpiece. Sylvah could tell from Jason's expression that he was thoroughly enjoying her warm, soft lips and mouth wrapped around his penis. On occasion he would look at her and moan his pleasure and she kept her eyes on him the entire time. She placed her free hand on his balls and fondled them for further stimulation. This action seemed to turn him on even more, because he began pumping into her mouth faster and harder. The head of his penis was now touching her throat. Sylvah could feel the life throbbing and the veins pulsating in her mouth. His penis became thicker, so she slowly removed her lips in preparation for her ride on the downtown express. The next stop was Sylvah Street.

Jason reached for Sylvah's hand and pulled her to lie beside him. Gently he pried her legs apart and bent down to get one last taste.

He rubbed his fingers over her clit and sucked them. With tender thrusts he made his way past the gated region. Sylvah moaned and Jason covered her mouth with his lips. This kiss was even more passionate than their earlier one. Sylvah held on to Jason's neck and wrapped her legs inside of his to intensify the penetration. She found his rhythm and they waltzed to the same beat. Jason gazed into Sylvah's eyes as he put his arms around her waist to pick her up by the ass. Within seconds he was standing and lifting her up and down, plastering her slickness on his dick. Sylvah's ass was damp and he could feel her moisture trickling down his thigh, which heightened his arousal. Jason's breathing became faster as he inserted Sylvah's large ripe nipple into his mouth. He suckled her breast like a nursing infant, fast and feverishly.

Sylvah could feel another orgasm beginning to surface and she made no effort to hold it back. She pulled her body closer to his and clawed her fingers into his flesh. She bawled for the Creator as her body gave way to the bottled-up pleasure. Sylvah's seeping river caused Jason to lose total control. His body convulsed as he filled her with his hot liquid. His movements became languid. Sylvah closed her eyes, laid her head on his shoulder, and collapsed into his cozy embrace. Jason kept Sylvah in his arms as he walked them both back to the bed. He lay her down and faced her, planting soft kisses on her forehead, cheeks, chin, and lips.

A few moments lapsed before either one of them made a move and time seemed to stand still. Neither of them wanted to disembark their passionate excursion, but they each knew that they had to. After all, this was moving day and Sylvah's next stop was to Hedonism II.

Fuller, Deeper, Smoother
by
Timmothy B. McCann

*O*h shit."
    He didn't hear the words but felt them tumble from her lips. James saw the way her eyebrows pulled closer together as if connected by an invisible string. The way her mouth formed a soft O. The way she'd squeeze his triceps on the downstroke and released her hold on the pull back as if she had lost strength in her hands.

    She convulsed and he increased the pace. Her charcoal skin reflected the light of a single candle and James looked down on her—seemingly intent on driving himself through the pinkness of her body. Sweat dripped through the curls of his hair, tiptoed down his nose, and plopped on her breast. She became limp, yet her fingers pulled at the root of her locks. Her thick, brown lips formed the words, That's it, that's it, that's it, *yet no sound was heard.*

    He didn't need to hear her speak. He knew what she wanted by the way her body squeezed his, by the gooseflesh texture of her skin, by the aroma of sex that filled the suite.

    No matter how much he gave, she demanded more so he brought the bend of her knees over his shoulder and wrapped the other around his waist like a belt.

    She looked him in the eyes and inhaled.

    He moved his double-jointed pelvis and repeatedly thrust himself inside her.

    Deeper, fuller, quicker.
Her hands grabbed the headboard.
    Deeper, fuller, quicker.
Her toes curled, then spread apart like fingers.

Deeper, fuller, quicker.

James felt he'd given what she wanted but it was far from what he needed. She opened her eyes once again and as James looked down at his wife—he saw nothing. No love. No lust. No desire. Her jaw relaxed and before she screamed, she buried her face in a pillow to release all of her emotions. As she began to shiver from head to toe, he fell carelessly to the bed and wondered if their brief marriage would survive the working vacation. But the thing that worried him most was if he even cared.

12:00 A.M.

Ava Maria cried softly in their bed, in a land older than time. In a land where each breath seemed to be a personally wrapped gift from God.

He lay beside her, massaged his half-full penis, and looked through the oval window at snow-capped mountains in the distance. Behind them a pale blue moon had replaced the watery sun. The dark and erotic skies sparkled with heartless stones and palpitated like the eyes of a caged tiger watching its prey. Marrakesh had given birth to a brand-new day.

James tried to take his mind away from the obvious and concentrate on coming up with a new tagline for his audition. He whispered softly, "From the hills to the valley, the deejay that's taking you alllllllll the way." James shook his head. "In the midnight hour, the only deejay putting more pound in your souuuullll power." He shook his head again. None of the verbal calling cards worked and in less than forty-eight hours he'd have the most important audition of his life.

From their bed, James saw lush palms in the pitch blueness outside as well as the tops of trees, which looked like giant peacock feathers. He closed his eyes and felt a breeze that pushed the silk magenta curtains apart. The cool winds blew gently against the fine black hairs of his arm—a direct contrast to a day so hot he could still smell its vapors in his lungs.

James heard his wife fluff the previously used pillow. He heard her continue to cry but refused to respond because he knew she'd walked into a place within herself in which he could not retrieve her. She was in character.

Sheer opulence could best describe Suite 117. It was expected to be of the finest quality but the Les Cieux suite went beyond imagination. The designer's attention to detail was meticulous—from the stenciled religious verses on the borders of the floral-painted walls, to the beamed ceilings. From the tangerine and purple stained glass in each of the windows that cradled the afternoon sun, to the gold encrusted bowls filled with oranges each morning. James and his wife resided in a fairytale but knew eventually it would end.

She continued to cry.

A year earlier James lived in a cramped one-room cell without bars. He'd pace in the decaying unventilated apartment repeating the call letters to the radio station.

"This is WLCV, the voice of choice in Memphis and I am your pre dawwwwwn pilot on this ride through the land of love, so buckle your seat belt and enjoy the smooth soul."

He would stand in the corner to feel his baritone voice bounce off the dingy wallpaper. He'd say the words with more staccato and then soften them by rounding his vowels.

"Smooooooth sooooooul soooounnnds."

He'd left a position as a bank executive in L.A. for the promise of fulfilling his lifelong dream of being an announcer and eventually got his break. After two months, his radio show was number one in his market. But after ten months, WLCV was in receivership and was forced to liquidate.

As fate would have it, a college friend in Los Angeles listened to James's show while in Tennessee on business and arranged for him to have an audition in L.A., an audition James knew would change his life forever. KTWT was in one of L.A.'s tallest skyscrapers and while the thought of being in such a structure during an earthquake was unnerving, James would not allow his fear of heights to deter him from the possibility of achieving his goal.

James took another look through the window at the moon in the jealous skies, rolled on to his back and studied the contours of his wife's body. In his Mack truck voice he asked, "Ava, what's wrong now?"

Her damp and salacious locks flowed over the pillow as she said, "nut'n." But the word was said in the Ozark dialect of her character. Ava Maria eased her body to the corner of the bed, slid her feet into her mules and walked fully nude toward her Gucci suitcase. Her fingers ran over her lips as if she was feigning for a cigarette, although, to his knowledge she had not smoked in more than a year. Her character was a chain smoker.

"Nothing?"

She stretched and he stared at the curved shape of her ass, the rounded bottom that always got his dick hard, but for the moment it did nothing for him at all.

"Nothing? Ava Maria, why do you always do—"

"Do what?" Her normal speaking voice had returned.

"Why are you always in character when we make love? Why do you always get out of bed and go write? Am I fucking you or that white bitch? Sometimes I don't know."

"I'm not having this discussion with you again. Okay? Just go to sleep. We have to check out by—"

"You're not what? You're not having this discussion with me?"

Ava Maria neatly moved her clothes aside, put on one of her husband's T-shirts, and walked out of the room. He knew where she would be. The place she always ended up. In front of her laptop, wearing her headphones, listening to Miles Jaye and talking aloud to no one. "Bitch."

2:45 A.M.

She sat on a lavender marbled patio that was streaked by the dancing light of the moon. He was troubled. Despite the opulence of the room, it was unfortunately on the highest floor in the hotel. Although he protested, she booked it anyway because she needed the view to boost her creativity. Looking at the Moroccan horizon allowed her to envision her protagonist—Dr. Blanche Birdsong, the crime-fighting housewife from Arkansas—in a clearer light.

There was the faint sound of men chatting as James walked out the room and sat on an oversized couch next to a bowl with an array of fruit left for them by their hospitality matron. With his back turned to her and the view he asked, "Are you staying out there all night long?" Her fingers sounded like an ice cream stick in the spokes of a five speed. "Ava? You hear me. Are you going to stay out there all night?"

She'd mutter a question into the desert air—wait for its reply and resume typing.

"Ava?"

Again she spoke in her normal voice, but in a tone that held a pronounced singsong twang.

He knew she was wearing the headphones, but knew they were a buffer to avoid conversation. Often she'd wear them without the sound. Wearing them allowed her to stay in the world she'd created but James missed having her in the world he attempted to create for them.

Their eyes first met at the Zillionaire, a Memphis jazz club. James, who walked like a panther, was in the dimly lit establishment with several musicians in town to play with Boney James. He'd not been in a relationship since moving to the Volunteer State because he wanted to concentrate on his craft. Since he'd changed careers well past thirty, he could not afford a setback and felt if he were to be romantically involved his career would stall.

The air, the taste, the smell of the club was filled with rhythms. From the white-orange candles that twinkled like a child's dream to the smell of chicken and waffles, the room danced with harmony.

James, who'd frequented the establishment when celebrities were in town and he was assigned by the station to entertain them, sat at the WLCV table and ordered a round of drinks for the musicians. On occasion, a female would vie for his attention but few succeeded. Such occurrences were common since he had classic looks: tan skin, chiseled dimpled chin, hair pulled back to form a finger-length ponytail and just enough stubble to give him a dark middle-eastern appearance.

He often downplayed his looks by either wearing inexpensive clothing or thick bifocals. On this night he wore jeans, black boots, and a navy turtleneck. He also wore contacts and once he saw her, he could not look away.

She was statuesque and sat felinelike under a purple strobe. She sipped from a glass, which contained a red, orange, and yellow concoction—complete with umbrella—and James counted the number of men who walked up, dipped their head, or extended their hand before starting a conversation.

Eight had tried.

Eight were turned away.

James noticed a tension in her jaw as she closed her eyes and appeared to slide feet first into the music. Inside he felt if he could get her attention—if she would just look at him, he'd have a chance. But he never noticed her glance in his direction.

The crowd in the intimate club swelled from uncomfortable to aggravating but she was in the center of his sight as he sat at the VIP table alone. Ignoring an attractive female's request to dance, James decided to make his move after gentlemen ten and eleven were turned away. As soon as he stood, he adjusted the pleat in his pants and could feel someone take his seat at the VIP table but for some reason he didn't care. As he headed her way, he watched number twelve say a few words to her in anger. Even in the rhythm-filled room he could hear Twelve's voice shout, "Bitch, you stuck up anyway!" She continued to sip from her drink.

James paused for a moment. *How much time should I give her,* he thought. But then he straightened his back, raised his chin, and continued to maneuver himself through the crowd. *Females love confidence. Females love confidence.* As soon as he got within arm's reach of her—lucky thirteen extended his hand. She took it and they headed for the floor.

"Fuck me!" he said aloud. James looked back and noticed a woman sitting at his table, just inches from his Long Island Iced Tea. The rest of the band members were either on the prowl or had left for the evening. Feeling the momentary sting of "I wish I would have," James jingled the car keys in his pocket and headed for the room with the tattered M on the door. As soon as he opened it, he felt nauseous.

The sweat of thousands of patrons, gallons of piss, tons of vomit and shit hit him all at once. All three stalls were occupied and as he waited, he looked at himself in the mirror and debated. Should he wait for her to finish dancing and see just how lucky number thirteen was or should he just go home? After several moments a stall was free and James walked before the porcelain receptacle but refused to allow himself to look into it. He unzipped his slacks, pulled out his dick and thought about her. The floor was cum slippery and etched into the walls with abhorrence were the words, *I give good head, call 555-4818.* James zipped up his pants, returned to the mirror, and with the tip of his fingers yanked a brown recycled paper towel from the silver container and decided what he had to do. There was no way he would, could leave the club without talking to her.

As soon as the door opened, the voluptuous sound of Billie Holiday's "I Cried for You" drifted into the rest room. James looked over his shoulder and saw her leaning against the wall. His body was vexed.

With her arms crossed over her breasts she said, "You piss longer then any human being I've ever seen in my life." James turned to see if she was speaking to someone else. "You heard me," she shouted above the music. "I was going to leave, 'cause it looked like you were *never* going to speak to me. Then I looked at the table and you were gone."

"Yeah I-I was headed your way, I guess."

"I guess," she said as James walked to within a foot of her. He could feel the heat from her breath as she spoke. "But how can anything as tall as you get lost in the crowd?"

"I've had my eye on you." He leaned mere inches from her ear and lowered his voice to a soft purring roar. "I've had my eye on you alllll night long. Did you know that?"

"Damn." She softly sighed. "Please don't talk to me like that—at least not in a crowded place." She cleared her throat and said, "but, I saw you checking me out, Teddy P." She smiled and James felt the need to lean against the wall to maintain his balance. "I was actually going to come sit with you but then you were gone, so I danced with Dufus out there who kept stepping on my shoes and I saw you walking this way. I don't know what happened but it was something about the way you walked. The way you…it was the way you moved," she said, looking up to for the right phrase. "I just couldn't look away, so I left him on the floor. I guess he's out there kicking someone else's shins."

James held his tongue for a long moment and pondered the possibilities. There was no place to sit in the club. The bouncers were no longer granting admission, because it was a fire hazard and he didn't know this side of town so going for a walk was not an option. He could ask her to go for a ride and possibly take her to a quieter spot so they could talk or he could simply ask her to—"Excuse me?" he asked. "Can you say that again?"

She tilted her head, placed her fingers softly on his wrist and said, "You like making me repeat myself, don't you?"

"No. See the music is so loud and with so many—"

"I said come on and go with me. Come on over—to my place."

With the suddenness of a Coltrane riff, James and Ava Maria were in his champagne Range Rover headed to her midtown apartment. As they rode in the SUV there was a moment of deafening silence but then she grabbed his hand and before they could get out of the vehicle, his fingers were inside her body.

Within seven days, James and Ava Maria became one flesh. The small wedding was held at her parents' home and was attended by only a few of his family members and a few of her author friends.

It was after they said I do that they both found out how different they were. He never knew how she could be totally consumed by her writing to the point she took on the characteristics of the detective in her successful series of murder mysteries, Dr. Blanche Birdsong. Blanche was a housewife who gave up her practice to care for her family, and at times James did not know where B.B. ended and his wife began. Ava Maria did not know about James's paralyzing fear of heights. When he told her he felt sick just watching the movie *Cliffhanger,* she thought he was joking—until they went on a plane ride. Ava Maria watched him grip the hand rest until veins rose in his forearms and she was forced to ask the attendant for a bag, fearing he would lose the contents of his stomach.

After several months of marriage, both knew they'd plunged

into a lustful union yet neither wanted to walk away. They spoke to a marriage counselor, to their friends, and even their pastor, but something was missing. Something interfered with their ability to communicate and they knew that until they resolved the matter, their chances of surviving as a married couple were minimal. When Ava Maria accepted the offer from her publisher to take her character to the mysterious and romantic country, she agreed to do so in hopes that it would save their marriage.

6:15 A.M.

James awoke. He'd fallen asleep on the couch and could hear her fingers still tapping away. Slowly he stood, arched his back, and whispered, "This shit's over. I can't live like this."

The typing stopped.

"Dig, it's on you. I'm going to bed," he mumbled.

"Excuse me?" she replied and took off the headphones.

"I said, it's on you. I'm out."

"Why you find it so easy to walk away is beyond me."

Although she spoke in the Blanche persona, James resisted the urge to turn and look at her. "I can't live like this. I can't deal," he said and stopped in his tracks, "with not knowing who I'm gonna meet when I wake up in the morning or who I'm making love to at night. There was a time this character shit was cool but with everything I'm dealing with I need to know—"

"Well, sweetie, if it's too hot in the kitchen," she said in a high-pitched twang, "go in the bathroom."

James turned and looked at his wife and although it made him woozy, he stared at her on the balcony.

"This old girl has sold more than one million—hear me good now—more than one *million* books." A softer look came over Ava Maria's eyes. "I have fans in twenty-one countries all waiting to see what I'll do in this here foreign novel. If I'll ever find the diamond. If I'll finally find my mother."

"Ava, I support your creativity and all, but you've got to chill with this shit sometimes. I mean, when are *we* ever going to make love.

Every time you start with that crying shit, I know it's Blanche thinking about Ronald."

Ava Maria smiled as she stared at her laptop and tugged on her earlobe. She picked up a pencil, ran her fingers up and down its shaft, and looked at James. "Well, I've been through a lot, buster. A lot mo' than you'll ever know. Ronny cheated on me and I just can't walk away from him. Sometimes it's hard to tell him that. Sometimes the words get caught right here," she said, thumping her throat with the pencil eraser. "But it don't mean I don't care." Ava Maria's voice faded and she added, "but I'm a survivor and…and after I break up that drug cartel, everything's going to be fine and I can go back to the states."

James stared at his wife but only saw the silver-blond, creamy-skinned detective. "Well," he said and ran his spread fingers through the loose locks of hair that previously hung in his face. "You have to do what you have to do. I've got to deal with my career so it's on you, Ava. When you decide to deal with this situation, let me know. It's your move."

As he walked toward the bedroom, he heard his wife giggle in character, "You bein' mannish again? What did you just say to me, boy? "

James continued to walk.

"Seriously," Ava said, but this time James paused because she spoke in her normal voice. "What did you say?"

"I said, when you decide to deal with this situation, let me know."

"What else did you say to me?" James looked over his shoulder at his wife. With the moonlight in her hair, she'd never looked sexier. "Say it again?"

"Say what?" He focused on her eyes to block out the world below.

"What you just said. Say it again."

"I said, it's on you, I'm out. It's almost seven in the—"

"No, not that. You said 'it's your move.' "

"What are you talking about?"

Ava Maria's voice deepened and she sounded like a female quiet storm disc jockey, "Say, this is J Ride…and it's your move."

It struck James like electricity on raw nerves. He repeated the words to himself. He sat on the arm of the couch and felt them stir in his stomach and into his chest. Then he cleared his throat, did a quick warmup exercise, and said, "That was one of my favorite groups—Switch from 1978 and 'I Call Your Name.' You are listening to the irrefutable, undeniable, unbelievable earthquaking sounds of your night-time driver taking you to the stars and beyond and it's time to ride out. So without any further delay this is Mr. Teddy Pendergrass, and 'Close the Door.' " He looked at his wife. Her lips had parted. Of all the things that had changed in their relationship—the effect his voice had on her was not one of them. "And for all of you in radio land—" he lowered his already low voice by an octave—"this is J Ride and it's yoooouuur moooveee."

"Oh my God," she whispered in her natural tone, "that's the tagline. That's the one that you're going to use at the audition."

James smiled. He knew they had struck gold with the words. He could tell by the look in her eyes. No longer was she in character. She was fully engulfed by his voice. "It's your move." Ava leaned back in her chair. Although they'd had sex, he knew she wanted to make love to him on another level.

"Baby?"

"Yes," she whispered.

"Baby?" he said louder.

"Yes!"

"Baby, it's yoooouuur moooveee."

"Come—come," she said as her eyes rolled upward and then closed. "Come get me." James hesitated. He knew she had noticed that he had never wanted to as so much as stand on the balcony. Why would he— "James? Please come get me." Ava leaned back farther in the chair, spread her legs, and reminded him that she wore no panties on her shaved pussy. She pulled down the collar of his T-shirt and exposed her inch-long swollen nipples. "Come get me, James. I want to make love to you. Just you—" she opened her eyes and scanned his body from top to bottom—"and me."

Ain't no way I'm going on that balcony, James thought. Then he felt his dick fill with excitement. Ava Maria slowly rolled up the bottom of his T-shirt and slid it up her flat abs, over her breasts, and carelessly dropped it to the concrete tiles. "James, please come fuck me." The warm air blew through the curtains and cut through his body.

She sucked her bottom lip with her top and rolled her eyes downward. "I want to fuck you so bad—it hurts."

"Then come inside. We can go in the room. What if someone sees us out—"

"I'll come in the room, baby. I'll *cum* anywhere you want me to. But I want you to come...get...me."

Sexually frustrated, James put his hands on his hips and stared at her rotating mound. There was no way he could not go on the balcony. He walked to the sliding glass door and extended his hand. "Come on inside, girl." He could imagine the sweet aroma of her sex. "Let's make love."

"I want you to come get me."

"Baby you know as well as anyone," James wrapped his hand around his hard black satisfier, "that I don't do heights. Now come on inside and we can—"

"Baby I want you so bad." Her eyes were slits. Her back arched, and her fingers made slow, erotic circles around her navel. "But I want you to come get me." Ava Maria opened her eyes and whispered, "It's your move, baby."

James looked at the silver divider that separated security and fear and knew he had to make a step toward conquering a part of himself he hated most. He closed his eyes and took a single step across the divider. As soon as his foot touched the tile, he could feel his heart pound in his chest. His dick felt as heavy as a brick between his legs, but he had to do this.

"Baby, it's your move. Come get me." He took another step. He was totally outside of the hotel room. He wanted to look over the balcony but since he already felt dizzy, he kept his eyes focused on Ava Maria. "That's my baby. That's my baby," she said encouragingly.

He was two steps away but extended his fingers toward her. "Okay, I'm out. Now let's go inside."

"Come get me, baby." Her eyes closed again as she slid her fingertips over the folds of moist pink flesh. "It's all yours, baby. Come get it. Come fuck me."

James took another small step and noticed a strange bird fly past the balcony. *Oh shit, oh shit, oh shit,* he thought. He wanted to fall against the wall but knew if he felt its security he'd never take another step beyond the hotel room. He took one last step and stood inches from her.

She looked at his extended hand, spread her legs a little wider and pushed his hand aside. "Take me now."

"Into the room, right?"

She opened her legs as wide as she could, slid half her finger inside her pinkness and groaned. "It's your move, baby."

James dropped to his knees. He felt no fear or inhibitions. All he could feel was a desire—a need to be inside her body. A calming breeze whipped around the building and he could hear the brushing of the palms below. Gently he kissed the front of her bended knee, then the inside and allowed his tongue to slide back and forth on her thigh. "Baby, baby, baby…" she mumbled and deep-massaged the thick-roped muscles of his neck and shoulders. James inhaled the intoxifying musky scent between his wife's legs. He could feel her heat on his face and before he knew it, she writhed so he would be face to face with her love, grabbed two handfuls of his hair, and forced her pussy into his mouth.

Ava Maria let out a moan as he moved his face back and forth and swirled his tongue around her swollen pink bud. He could feel her hips jerk as her hand securely held the back of his neck. His tongue traveled between the pink, moist crevices of her body, and he could taste the dry-sweet menthol nectar that dripped from her. Ava Maria mumbled and then groaned again as she rocked her love in a circular motion against his invading tongue. James reached between his legs and stroked himself. He wanted to plunge it inside of her but resisted the urge until he felt her body move faster and faster against his face. "Oh shit, baby. Oh shit." She sighed. "Fuck!"

James knew she was about to cum early and hard. He wrapped both of his arms around her thighs, pushed them onto his shoulders, fastened her to his face, and dug his tongue as deep inside her pussy as he could. He felt the creamy residue of lotion on his face. Moving his face around and around he felt her legs stiffen. He felt her sink her fingernails into his shoulders. He felt her shiver and this time he heard no tears, only a hum that seemed to last forever.

James stood, and his cock automatically slid through the peephole of his silk pajamas, inches from her face. He wanted to feel her lips on him, but such thoughts succumbed to the desire to suck on her enlarged breasts. As James bent over and touched the tip of her nipples with his tongue, he started to suck them as if he needed to nourish his erotic desires. He'd forgotten about the heights, the audition and Blanche Birdsong, the crime sleuth. All he could think about was the taste of her body in his mouth as she slid her fingers through his hair with one hand, grabbed his dick with the other.

As he sucked her, she slowly ran her fingers up and down his meat. With James flicking his tongue over her nipples, Ava Maria moved her hand faster and faster, and every time she'd flick the head with her thumb, it sent a flame of pure fire into his legs and a drop of precum to the slit of his dick.

"James?"

"Yes, baby."

"James, fuck me. Fuck me like you love me. Fuck me out here under the—"

"No baby, let's go into the room. I want you on the bed, I want you on the floor, I want you in the shower. I want you in the kitchen pent up against the—"

"I want you under the stars." She opened her eyes. "I want to fuck you while the sun is rising." She then stood from the chair, pushed it aside and laid her completely nude body on the purple tiles. "Fuck me, baby. Don't make me beg you. Fuck me now." She droned and closed her eyes. "I want this to be our last memory of—" before she could finish the sentence, and without so much as a word, James tossed his pajamas to the floor and covered her body with his.

Their tongues circumnavigated each other's slow and sensuously and James grabbed his dick, rubbed it stiff it over her moist lips, and slid it inside of her pulsating body.

Her eyes opened and she stared at the burgundy sky.

Her mouth fell open and he could hear a low, nasty, guttural growl that turned into an outright scream as each inch disappeared into her pussy. When he'd worked himself halfway inside of her love, he felt her body shudder. It always amazed him that no matter how many times they made love, her body felt tight, wet, and virginal.

As James stroked himself in and out of his wife's pussy, he could feel her hands slide behind her head as if doing a sit-up and her body tighten with each push of his love. "You like this fat dick, don't you?" She opened her mouth but nothing came out. "You love my big black dick inside you. Tell me you love it!" James said and plunged himself to the root inside her body.

"I love it, baby. I love the way you fuck me." In the corner of her eye there was the first glimmer and unlike B.B's tears, this was a tear of passion. "I love the way—" she securely wrapped her arms around his head—"you *fuck* me." Ava Maria slid her tongue deep inside his mouth as he took control of her body.

Fuller, deeper, smoother.

"Baby, you feel so good. Your dick feels so…good." Ava laid her head on the concrete as James returned his kiss to her still-erect nipples and reached his large hands underneath her and squeezed her ass on each downstroke. "Damn baby, you feel *so* good!"

Fuller, deeper, smoother.

"You like it like that, baby? You like me digging in that tight pussy?" James could feel the head of his dick swell.

Fuller, deeper, smoother.

"Cum, baby. I want you to cum hard, baby." James knew she knew he was about to explode. "I want you to cum deep inside of me."

Fuller, deeper.

"Not yet, baby. I want to enjoy this pussy."

"Baby, I want you to drown me. Cum for me, baby." James looked at his wife and saw the pleading nature in her eyes to satisfy him. "Cum for me, baby. Cum hard."

Fuller.

James increased his pace and could feel the fire build. Then with one massive stroke he pulled back until the tip came to the rim of her pussy and before he knew it Ava Maria pushed him upward. She'd never done this before. She grabbed his dick and jerked it several quick times with her thumb massaging his head until he exploded his white sex all over her stomach.

"Yes—yes," she said, moaning. "That's what I wanted. I want you all over me." Ava Maria pulled her husband toward her and slowly their lubricated bodies slid together as one. "God, I've wanted to do that—for so long," she whispered in a breathy tone.

James was still settling to Earth from the moment he felt her teeth sink into the flesh of his chest. He loved it when she bit him right after the moment of climax because it sent him into another realm of ecstasy. As she bit him, he opened his mouth—still too excited to release a scream—and he felt her hand slide between their hips and into her pussy. She released the hold on his flesh, brought her lips back to his and sunk her tongue forcefully into his mouth. Then she brought her dry-sweet menthol fingers up to his face and under his nose. As they kissed, Ava Maria softly bit his tongue and slid her pinky into his mouth. The taste of her and the texture of their tongues sliding up and down her finger drove him wild. From nowhere he felt himself harden. Feeling him against her stomach, Ava said, "Let's go inside. Let's finish this on the bed. Let's finish this in the kitchen pent up against—"

James nudged her head back with his chin and bit her sensuously on the front of her neck. "I want you just like I got you. Under the sunrise."

"Baby, say it one more time."

From the tone of her voice, he knew what she wanted to hear. James opened his eyes slowly. Smiled at this woman who had the ability to amaze every inch of his body. With his thigh he pushed her legs apart and slid his dick between her still-wet lips. Then he said the words in a tone that would have made Barry White envious. "I enjoy being inside you and I enjoy doing you and doing you and doing you soooooo damn well. You move me."

"You groove me," she replied.

"And dare I say you soothe me, baby." He brought his lips to the edge of hers and slowly licked the inside. "This is your man fucking you like there is no tomorrow, and if you ever want to feel this again. If you ever, ever, ever want to return to heaven, just let me know. Because, my love, it is and will always be—yoooouuur moooooveee."

Watering Cherry's Garden
by
William Fredrick Cooper

*S*he captured my mind in a nanosecond, and then enslaved my body as one of her personal sex toys. The past week has been a study in surrealism; some Rod Serling meets Hugh Hefner moment in time; something Xaviera Hollander couldn't have brought to life for *Penthouse* had she tried.

Reminiscing on Cherry encounters—the chills we experienced when absolute physical satisfaction rendered us weak—a certain chocolate muscle between my legs pulses to life, threatening to bust the zipper of my gray trousers. My intense arousal blurs my vision, shortens my breath, and creates an erratic pounding in my chest. Perhaps comedian Bill Bellamy was right: memories of great sex can make you crash a car. *Damn, that shit was good.*

And to think, I have Yvette Melendez to thank for the satiation of my dormant lust. The genesis of this heat felt for Cherry was the result of a surprise visit to my lady's—check that, former lady's—Crown Heights apartment last Sunday. At the time, loving that Spanish/Mexican woman seemed so natural, just like walking, talking, and breathing. Little did I realize that the air inhaled that sunny April morning would be as stale as old bread.

Having pled with Yvette the night before to let me take her to the hospital because of her illness, I decided to surprise her with a teddy bear and card on my way to work. Mama Rivers had warned me years ago about unannounced visits, saying, "Vaughn, you always find out what type of woman is in your life by surprising them, seeing them without their makeup." I certainly got more than I bargained for when, upon scaling four flights of stairs, my six-foot, two- inch frame rushed into an open door, compliments of her Bajan ex. Bare-chested, with his little joystick dangling from paisley boxer shorts, he had the audacity to offer me a drink after inviting me in. His presence tore my ticker in two.

Then Yvette appeared from…*wherever.* Seeing her creamy, well-proportioned body draped in an orange football jersey with the bold white number 81 trimmed in blue, a jersey probably shed during…*whatever*—my football jersey—sent me reeling like a steel pipe had crashed against my bald skull. A migraine pierced my cranium and the tightness in my chest demanded immediate attention. Somehow, I remained calm through it all, but I will say this: that walk back to Utica Avenue and the Number 4 train, past the drugstore on Eastern Parkway where I'd purchased the card and stuffed animal was the   longest of my life.

Suffice it to say, my ambitious overtime shift that afternoon was an exercise in torture. Planted on a carousel of frustration, my head was spinning while my tattered heart was like a tennis ball being knocked back and forth on center court at Wimbledon by the rackets of betrayal and pain. My heaven on earth was now a living hell. But enough about Yvette; this is about Cherry.

I called my dawg Charles and told him about the sea of agony I was drowning in, and he in turn called another running partner, Ski, who contacted Crazy Hec who unbeknownst to me, suggested we go someplace to expel my demons over cheesecake. Little did I know the cake cut would be chocolate covered and Cherry in the middle.

Rollin' up on me in Hec's black Explorer at nightfall, my jean pockets were stuffed with money—"dolla, dolla, yo," Ski hollered—and a blindfold placed over my eyes. As Hec rolled up his tinted windows, the devious laughter from the trio gave me pause as the SUV sped away. *What an unconventional display of brotherhood,* I thought. Too late for inquiries regarding destination and knowing I would hear lies if I asked, silence and intrigue replaced my daylong misery.

A half hour later, our smoked-out vehicle stopped suddenly and car doors swung open. Pushing me out, Charles and Ski led me through an entrance where the thumping beat of my favorite groove rocked the room. Thinking I was at a dance club, my head bobbed instinctively while waiting for Michael Jackson's voice to accompany the deep base line the song provided. It never came. Only needing thirty seconds to realize the deejay was mixing the instrumental version of "You Rock My World," I needed another thirty seconds of shock recovery once the blindfold was removed.

To my amazement, we were at The Hideaway, a dim lit strip joint located in a seedy area of Brooklyn, down near Second Avenue. The fact that it was on a street you wouldn't want to be caught on alone at two in the morning was lost upon entry. Exotic, scantily clothed women of different races and builds filled the club's interior, serving the majority male patrons drinks while they viewed the more minimally clad dancers on a long, turquoise lit stage.

"Ass everywhere," Ski jovially announced.

Stationed at a back table, Charles told me they had been frequenting this place for some time, and because I was so enthralled with "that bitch Yvette," never mentioned it to me. Details from the remainder of the conversation are sketchy at best, for my attention was diverted to the voluptuous woman preparing to grace the stage.

Drooling like a dog in heat, I wanted her instantly. It seemed fitting Cherry would perform to "There She Goes," a Babyface cut. Strolling to the center of the dance platform, her five-foot, ten-inch, thirty-something caramel form glistened as if coated with baby oil. Seeing the combination of red glittery thong, bra, lipstick, fuck-me pumps, and natural thickness in some beautiful places hardened me immediately. I wasn't the only one she had at attention; male fans who were familiar with her either adjusted their seats closer, ran to the brim of the stage with dollars in hand, or craned their necks to get a better view.

Turning to face her growing audience, the younger dancers who left the stage upon her arrival, also took notice. Long on energy and enthusiasm yet short on experience and expertise, it was an education to them as well, once the music began. Wasting none of her movements, her sparkling brown eyes and wavy black hair complemented a warm smile that illuminated the whole nightclub. Not to mention that killer body—36-24-36—was an insult to Cherry. Possessing more than ample breasts that begged me to fondle them, her stomach rippled with exquisite musculature. With sinewy muscles in long, shapely legs that tightened and contracted with every sensuous body ripple, you could tell that her male admirers, obviously riveted by her aura and her presence, wanted to try out all kinds of pleasure techniques on this woman.

Cherry had everyone in the place under a spell, and the confidence she displayed while performing was so sexy. Rotating her large, firm backside to the crowd to reveal the cherry tattoo on her bottom would have been sufficient, as evidenced by the starving wolves eagerly placing dollar bills in her thong. But no, this temptress took it to another level by squatting in a catcher's position and making her cheeks bounce like a woman astride a stiff one. Embarrassed by my voyeurism, my bearded, chocolate skin was flush when she faced her audience once more. Sensing that she'd observed my reaction from afar, my intuition was realized when, upon lifting my face, our eyes met and held. Basking in her manifest power, Cherry almost made me cum in my pants when she winked those sexy browns at me and licked her lips with a long, lizardlike tongue at song's end. This image would bring me to self-gratification later.

Sure enough, two hours later, after my boys had dropped me at my Flatbush apartment, thoughts of Cherry became the lust within my fantasy. God, I longed to inhabit her liquid garden with a stiffened snake. Groaning carnally as I stroked my throbbing tool, instead of moving the tip of my index finger up and down the shaft, the meat of my hand was at the bottom of my thick, uncircumcised erection. It was so hard I envisioned her reflection in the tautly pulled skin of it. Reaching a desired rhythm, I increased the tempo only to slow it back down then speed it up again, as if simulating the pace Cherry would receive if inside of her. Too soon, that early Monday morning would end in satisfaction as I jerked myself to physical contentment.

"You must have finished docketing those cases since you're sitting here daydreaming."

My boss's voice rudely interrupted my musings of Cherry that Monday afternoon. Recalling the provocative swaying of her hips while gliding to the stage, her lively expressions of passion through movement during a splendidly choreographed performance and the exquisite lines of her sexy body, I had been unable to focus on my work all day. Falling behind in the numerous paralegal tasks that were awaiting my attention, all I'd been able to think about had been that cherry tattoo on her luscious derriere.

Eventually conceding that the day had been lost, I left my office at approximately seven- thirty that night. Arriving at my empty apartment with a take-out order of Chinese food, I turned on the television to ESPN as I ate in the living room. Soon, however, my thoughts returned to the seductive siren who'd imprisoned my mind and owned my libido. Automatically, my nature came to life in my drawers and since I was home, I unzipped my pants and released the swollen appendage. Reminiscing on the sensuous look Cherry had given me at the end of her set, my thoughts of her teetered on the precipice of obsession. Drifting deeper, my slacks were now ankle high as I envisioned us reversing traditional roles. Casting myself as the conservative virgin prince and her in the role of bold seductress, *mmm*, I didn't mind at all that she initiated the foray with a long, rapturous tongue massage. Relaxing her shoulders and neck with an oral object of my own, Cherry's eyes rolled to the back of her head as I laved her bosom, then her drenched channel with animalistic abandon. Feeling my hardness throb in her hand excited Cherry, for she gripped it, squeezed it, then stroked it, eventually drowning her hand in warm semen.

Tilting my world off its axis, that moment in fantasy sent cannons exploding in my head, and a different kind of discharge at my groin; for in the real world, a milky solution oozed from my manhood, down thick, tree trunk legs, and onto the black leather sofa. She had done it to me again.

Like Gator, the disheveled crack addict from *Jungle Fever,* I walked the office corridors of Randall, Morgan & Russell that Tuesday in a zombie like trance. In dire need of a Cherry fix, my fantasies sorely needed an infusion of new memories. I had to see her again.

Upon my arrival at The Hideaway later that night, I moved through the mixture of lap dancers and customers inconspicuously, knowing that a sighting by any of my boys would bring unwarranted ridicule and interrogation. *Phew,* none were there, but as fate would have it, the same back table where a certain cinnamon silhouette captured my interest from afar was vacant. The stage should have been unoccupied as well, for the white bag of bones rattling to Aaliyah's "Rock the Boat" was emptying the front seats.

"Fire poles are bigger than that bitch!" one patron screamed as the dancer slid down a pole on the left.

"I paid five dollars to get in this piece! Get that pogo stick out of here!" another screamed while walking away from the stage. When she was done, there were no dollars in her thong and nary a one on stage. Torn between humor at the moment and empathy, the latter won out; as she passed me en route to the changing room, I placed a five-dollar bill in her bikini and asked for a name.

"Sweetheart, which is your good ear?"

I pointed to the left one as she leaned closer.

"Precious," she whispered tenderly, then kissed my earlobe. "Thank you."

After enduring derisive taunts bordering on viciousness, the fact that she remained secure in herself, she deserved that Lincoln.

The sultry woman who emerged from the dressing room next deserved Ben Franklins, however. As Cherry glided to the stage amid refilling chairs, a brother gave her one, and was rewarded with a peck from full, ruby lips followed by a sexy, tongue flutter. Seeing that gesture made me wish she could lick the length of me with that long instrument, then clean up my gooey release with her mouth. Turning her back to the crowd, she bent over to pick up the green litter she enjoyed and provided those up close a glimpse of her well-groomed bush.

If every man in the room wasn't hard by now, what she did next was the coup-de-grace. Facing us once more, she wet her index finger with those luscious lips, adjusted her black thong to expose her kitty while squatting, then slid one finger, then two, in and out to the time of the song just beginning. Next, she parted her tunnel and rotated a finger on her clit while bouncing up and down on chiseled calves. Reaching for and receiving a black cowboy hat, you could tell Cherry was aroused as well; from way back you saw her quiver as she stood upright once more. Eyes slammed shut as she simulated female dominant positions to Ginuwine's "Pony," the thought of her feminine center stroking me, fucking me while sharing this rhythmic dance beneath her caused me to wipe sweat from my forehead. Visions of piercing this woman engulfed me, eliciting heavy breathing. Wanting her pelvis slapping furiously against mine, I watched her gyrations from afar, desperately hoping for eye contact once more.

My telepathy must have connected with hers at that instant. Winding her hips during body waves while scanning the room for someone to sing the chorus to, Cherry spotted my familiar face and smiled.

Every single portion of this beauty, from the circular motion of her waist to those luscious red lips and sultry stares, spoke to me, telling me she wouldn't fall off my stiff saddle if given the opportunity to ride. Feeling the temperature rise at my groin as she mouthed the lyrics my way, the climate below was so hot, trade winds couldn't cool it. Ascending quickly through me, I gallantly tried not to blush, but my efforts were futile. I felt embarrassed by the way Cherry kidnapped all my desires with the belly dancer quakes of her stomach. Craving her insatiably, the oar at my waist wanted to swim in her lake of lust.

Mercifully, her set ended without me messing up my black suit, and as she left the stage with enough money to pay three months rent, every tongue-wagging male eye in The Hideaway watched the stimulating, side-to-side tilt of her hips work the room, some throwing money at her when she neared their table. Thanking every admirer personally with a handshake or allowing a touch of her breasts or backside, that Cherry never approached my lonely table left me bewildered. Had this goddess been turned off by honest, innocent reactions?

The answer I sought came later. After Cherry's performance, the energy and excitement she injected into the strip joint dissipated, as her heart-stopping ability was akin to a comet sighting: sadly succinct, yet leaving behind brilliance in its wattage. The announcer realized this as well and quickly offered four-for-one lap dances, meaning, for twenty dollars a guy could get the beauty of his choice to grind on his groin for four songs. Watching as hot, horny fellas immediately grabbed ladies left and right, I wondered which lucky gentleman would get the honor of Cherry. Surveying the surroundings quickly, I didn't catch sight of her. Shrugging, I lowered my head to my Vodka and orange juice.

"Can I join you?"

I couldn't believe my eyes when I looked up from nursing my drink. Trying to conceal my surprise at the sight before me, I became mute as I smiled nervously. The woman was dressed in a black lace midriff that accentuated her lovely, dark brown nipples. Matching the top with short pants that sat low on her curvaceous hips, partially covering the thong she wore beneath them, the outfit clung to every contour of her fantastic shape. Obviously unaccustomed to being refused, she batted her long eyelashes and pulled up a chair before I could answer. Through brown and beautiful pupils, Cherry eyed me like a cobra about to strike at its prey.

"So, you're all by your lonesome tonight. Where's your crew?" Amazed that she had taken time to notice I was with my boys on my last visit, I had to be sure I was hearing correctly.

"What do you mean?"

"You were with some guys the other night. I've seen them in here before, but I've never seen you. You're new to this place. And two days later, here you are again. Sitting alone. Drinking alone." Acting like she had a master's degree in the art of seduction, her gaze never left my eyes as she pulled my drink out of my hands and took a sip. "Mmmm, a screwdriver," she announced, grinning impishly. "So, do you have a name?"

"Vaughn. Vaughn Rivers. And yours?"

"Cherry. That's all you need to know…for now." Pausing, she leaned toward me, invading my space and asked, "Tell me, are you fantasizing alone?"

Feeling the warmth of her body heat up mine through a simple grazing of the fingertips, I could smell her fragrance. It was Christian Dior's *J'adore*. I breathed in her essence while sitting up, moving back ever so slightly. Admittedly ambushed by her forwardness, my mind, normally reserved in times like this, had a devil on my left shoulder urging me to play the game, go along for the ride.

Deciding to do just that, I answered her. "Actually, I was fantasizing about you. I've always had a thing for cherries. Black cherries, bing cherries, wild cherries, maraschino cherries…even cherries that move like you."

Sensing the progress of our connection, her lips formed a sly, seductive smile. Seeing her reaction sent arrows of lustful thoughts through me, setting off fireworks throughout my body. The pieces of passion were now trying to make their way to her loins.

"I'll tell you what, Mr. Rivers. I'm never one to deny a man his pleasures. If you're really that crazy about cherries, I guarantee that I can give you the biggest, sweetest, most tasteful cherry you've ever had. What do you say about that?"

As her tongue hungrily traced pouty red lips, my body voluntarily answered her question for me through its erected state down below.

"What do you have in mind?"

Being the poor flounder that I was, those dreamy eyes of hers were the bait, and I'm not ashamed to say I was hooked. Licking those delicious petals of hers again as if in anticipation of a well-deserved treat, Cherry tilted her head to the side and gave me a smirk that let me know she was in control. "Come back Thursday night."

"What's happening Thursday night?"

Cherry sat up, pushing her full bust forward as her rebuttal came with a confident laugh. "You're invited to a private party. Just you and me, in the VIP room," she announced while pointing to the far left of the stage. Rising to leave, she added, "Be there at ten-thirty. And Vaughn, don't be late."

My anxious thoughts screamed, *nine-thirty. I'll be here by nine-thirty.* Totally overwhelmed, a couple of seconds passed before I realized she was leaving. Jumping up, I almost knocked over the table trying to stop her. "Cherry, wait!"

Looking back over her left shoulder, she turned around slowly and raked her eyes down my body, stopping at the obvious. I was too spellbound to be embarrassed—this woman could get my dick hard in a New York minute, and I really didn't care if she knew it. Her smile told me she did. "Was there something else…you want? You need?"

I reached over, grasped her hand, and pulled her back to me. Grabbing a twenty out of my wallet, I folded it in half and tucked it in the thong under her lace shorts. "This is for you."

Cherry gazed down at the bill and asked, "And what did I do to deserve this?"

"I appreciate your time. I know it's very valuable. Well, it is to me, anyway."

Though the allure left her face, it softened from the stripper mode, displaying a touch of warmth and a slight sheen of innocence. My body began to throb as she stroked my face, then kissed it softly. "You're right. My time is valuable, but Thursday's party is on me. Consider it my gift to you."

I stared after her in a daze as she walked away.

I was in a stupor later that night at home when dreams of Cherry manipulated my body once more. Envisioning myself introducing her to a whole new world of sexuality, the panoply of pleasures made regular intercourse seem pedestrian. My patient kisses had her head spinning like a carousel as the horizontal statue between my legs set off quivers and quakes of orgasmic turbulence. "Oh, shit, hit it good, Vaughn," Cherry uttered in a salacious tone upon my entry into her intimate cavern. "Please go faster," she ordered as my slow, sensuous strokes evolved into fast, furious thrusts. Shuddering, I released my sperm along the nexus of nerves of the walls of her vagina. The flight of this imagination crashed to earth when, upon awakening, I noticed a stream of my ejaculation had traveled to my stomach. Damn, Thursday couldn't come soon enough.

The Hideaway was packed that Thursday night, as evidenced by many Jeeps, Lexuses, and tinted-paned SUVs parked outside. Arriving just before ten, those last thirty minutes before my Cherry treat seemed like an hour as I watched a couple of dancers do their thing. A Latin cutie was ordered to "make that ass bounce" by somebody up front, and when she was unable to do so, the disgruntled patron removed the dollar he'd placed in her thong and gave it to a lap dancer passing by.

Shaking my head in amusement, I noticed the already dim lights in the establishment being lowered as Cherry graced the stage to Maxwell's "…Til The Cops Come Knockin'." Normally, the dancers would dance to fast music, but the deejay didn't seem to mind Cherry's sensuous waltz, especially since customers showered the platform with green before the selection even started good.

Appropriately attired in a midnight blue bikini set, I noted her indifference while sensuous beamers roved the crowd for a welcomed face. Mine. Relaxing when she saw me, Cherry smiled, fondled her breasts seductively, then unleashed a torrid dance routine that puffed the nature between my legs once more. The way she moved—her hips, her eyes, her thoughts, were in complete synchronicity with mine, despite the fact all were watching. Sticking that pretty ass of hers out as she placed her hands on the back mirror, the sea of patrons howled as I thought about locking her up in lust and passion for days. Needless to say, her scintillating, six-minute performance was the bomb. Twisting, exposing, enticing, teasing, seducing, and inspiring every man in the club to come out his pockets with cash, she walked off the stage and made her rounds to each man, yet keeping her eye on me in the back of the place. In the split second that I looked at my watch and saw it was ten-thirty, Cherry had made her way to me and whispered "Are you ready?"

Nervously, I nodded yes, and with that the woman of my fantasies grabbed my hand and led me past all kinds of dirty looks toward the VIP lounge. Approaching its entry, we were confronted by a bald, burly bouncer who placed a thick hand in my chest and demanded thirty dollars for the privacy.

"That's okay, Myron. This one's on me," Cherry intervened as I wondered, *how's a guy built like this gonna be named Myron?*

"You want me to come inside?" the big, bald wolf asked.

"No. I trust him," she responded while opening the door to a discreet paradise.

Walking by my tormentor, it took great restraint for me not to blurt out, "Ah ha."

The special room was mirrored and strobe lit red, with a long, blue sofa along the back mirror. To the left of the entry was a bar, where I treated myself to an Absolut and cranberry juice before sitting on the sectional.

Cherry had excused herself for two minutes and returned to my bulging eyes. Standing before me topless, her long, beautiful nipples protruded ever so sweetly. Her caramel body blending perfectly with the lighting, she motioned me to a metal chair she'd placed in the middle of the floor. Aggressively, she demanded my hands be placed behind my back. Feeling her tie them together left me wary and wanting simultaneously. The tingling at my groin intensifying, I yearned to release my erect friend from its cage.

After binding my feet together, she demonstratively bent close, her lips almost grazing mine as she said, "Vaughn, you can't touch me." No sooner than the command left her, Michael Jackson's "Butterflies" was a welcome intrusion to the moment. Dancing before me while mouthing magical melodies, the measured movements of her midsection were mystical as she backed away to exhibit this.

By mid-song, she moved from closer, suddenly, sensuously, pressing her full lips against mine. Next licking them tantalizingly with her teasing creature, this torture was pleasure and pain at its thinnest line. My erection was so hard at this point it could have drilled for oil in the center of Texas.

As the music changed to Janet Jackson's "Would You Mind," my seductress did the unimaginable. Straddling my stiffness, I was drawn into a sensuous tornado spinning round. Not wanting to get loose, I met her rhythm from above with my own grind. Moving together in such a way we failed to realize the time that passed us by; Cherry seemed heated by the connection.

She lost all focus on dancing as she pressed her luscious mounds against my face while astride my loins. Suffocating me with those succulent orbs, she ended up hugging me a lot, talking to me and telling me I was "dangerously sweet." Her eyes, her skin, her smell intoxicating me, she squeezed her breasts as if testing the freshness of cantaloupe at the supermarket. Placing her pointed nipples to my face, she demanded, "Kiss, but don't lick."

Obliging, pliant pecks from my lips touched them. My veneer now hopeless and helpless, Cherry's demands changed midstream. "Suck them."

Eagerly obeying her request, the sensuous groan that escaped her mouth was immediate. Losing control in the currents of lust flowing through this fantasy standing still, her body was jolted with electricity as I brought her pleasure by moving my mouth back and forth on each breast. Shivering and shaking against me, confusion matched her pleasure as her frame fought the loss of command.

I felt her thoughts. She wasn't supposed to be aroused by a customer; *this is strictly business,* her mind screamed. Having to choose between being obscenely entwined in passion and heat and maintaining her balance, the former didn't have a chance. Cherry doused the flames to the moment, reducing our VIP exposed foreplay to an aberration by removing her bosom from my brim and halting her hip grind.

"That's enough," she said stonily, rising slowly as if numb to the passionate freefall she'd experienced. Still feeling the aftershocks of her lap dance, my body stiffened, relaxed, then coated my Hanes boxers with spurts of warm satisfaction.

Cherry saw her power in those precious seconds and as my convulsions ceased, my eyes opened to her wicked grin.

"I hope you enjoyed your treat," she said, leaving me alone with my thoughts, my messy pants, and my legs and arms still bound to the metal chair, a prey to her game of seduction.

A minute later, the black metal door opened again and Myron entered the room with a disgusted mixture of envy and self-righteousness all over his face. Hell, there wasn't a man in the establishment who wouldn't have killed to have been alone in the room with Cherry, Myron included.

No words were exchanged as he untied my hands and feet, releasing me from my pleasurable bondage. Rising from the chair slowly, I stretched like a sated lover reenergized, awaiting more. Hoping the bouncer had no evidence that proved Cherry had definitely laid it on me, I quickly evaded his cutting stares and headed straight to the men's room. Needless to say, Cherry was nowhere to be seen when I left the strip club.

I had truly been drugged. Visions of Cherry overloaded my psyche, making it impossible for me to think of anything else. Recalling her heavenly scent, I could still feel the soft firmness of her breasts against my face. My mouth longed for the scrumptious taste of her skin. Her hypnotic beauty, mind-altering sensuality and sheer talent had me craving her like a drowning man needs air.

I sat at my desk at the job that Friday afternoon, having hardly accomplished anything, despite the fact a mountain of work awaited my undivided attention. Knowing that I could not leave the office until these tasks were completed, regardless of the hour of the day or night, I couldn't tear my thoughts away from her. I had to have this tantalizing temptress, if just for one night. She needed to know that despite my normally conservative nature, I could reciprocate the extreme pleasure she had given me.

I wanted an opportunity to give her a view of Vaughn the Voracious. *But how do I approach her?* I wondered. Cognizant that she regularly warded off advances from loyal fans wanting to fulfill their desires, I didn't want to be those dudes though. I had to show her that

I wasn't simply after a quick pussy fix. I wanted to worship her, even if for a brief moment in time. The need to revere a queen like her and her lovely body now emphatic, I was anatomically addicted to her; and if given the chance, my carnal passion would be put on full display.

Unable to concentrate on those inundating piles before me, I next found myself unconsciously, obsessively, writing her name repeatedly on the legal pad in front of me. Before long, the words, *Cherry, can I make you cum tonight?* appeared in front of me. Soon, my libido shouted its demands through pen.

Cherry, can I make you cum tonight?
Can I make you scale walls of ecstasy as I tickle and tease,
lick and please?
Can I start by pecking pliant petals while rubbing a purring kitten
aching to gush juices of satisfaction?
Can I lay you down, knead your ample cleavage with baby oil, then
rub my growing hardness between them?
Can I make you cum tonight? Cherry, can I make you cum tonight?
Can my mouth feel the cushion of your inner thighs?
Can I drink from your lusty treasure as you tremor with pleasure?
Can I make you cum tonight? Cherry, can I make you cum tonight?
Can I enter your wet tunnel and let you swallow me inch by inch?
Can I stroke you lovingly, in a fluid flow, tempo slow?
Can I increase the beat of my gyrations as you tighten your muscles
around my hunger, setting sensations aflame?
Can I bring you to a mental state of pleasure by thrusting deeper
into your soaked canyon?
Twitching helplessly as an orgasm leaves you, can I emit a soft groan
as I tense, then relax as my own eruption surfaces through spurts,
then subsides?
Please, Cherry let me make you cum tonight.

As I read this creation over and over throughout the day, the gambler in my body traveled to my mind. *She's gonna get this note.* Dreams of us grunting in simultaneous pleasure, the mere thought of ramming something hard and stiff inside of Cherry almost made an orgasm rise from the depths of my soul, at my desk. *She's gonna get this note,* I thought again. Visions of my growth moving in and out, then in circles against the cavern of her vagina caused a galvanized chill to wend through me. Longing to touch her mouth with mine as our sweat mingled in the dark, I saw Cherry squirming and screaming from the delicious, delectable torture I would inflict. The mind-blowing memory of her contact with me the night before still lingering in spirit, I wanted to drown my face in her womanhood. I knew I had to have her for one night. *Tomorrow night, she's gonna get this note.*

Returning to the erotic world of dimmed lights, plastic heels, skimpy lingerie, and reconstructed titties at eleven that Saturday night, I was a man on a mission. Instantly, my eyes searched the crowd of horny men and strutting lap dancers for Cherry, to no avail. As had been the case all week, the back table I had acquainted myself with was unoccupied. Seating myself in familiar territory, the dancers on stage were ignored as I stared at the white paper I pulled from my leather jacket. Reading the *Can I...* passage made my privates stiffen in anticipation. *She's gonna get this note,* I thought once more. My musing was interrupted by a familiar voice.

"Why hello, stranger." My private passion was standing before me. Looking more alluring than she had all week, Cherry was wearing a red, see-through peignoir with matching garter belts connected to her thong. I could see her hardened nipples as I climbed out of my chair.

"Hello, Cherry." Saying her name made my rod hot and hard, something she noticed immediately after a quick scan.

"From the looks of things, you either have a gun in your pocket or you're happy to see me. Which is it, Mr. Rivers?"

Her coated, red lips unnerved me for a sec, but I regained my composure and went for my wallet. Pulling out a twenty-dollar bill, I quickly folded it in the note. Leaning down slightly, I placed it at her hip and met her left ear with a whisper. "Read this note and you'll know the answer."

I had never been so bold in my life. Gazing into her pupils, I prayed my sensuous stare would tug at her passion. Like a wild boar in heat, the primitive sensations rampaging through me threatened to break out then and there, causing me to sit as quickly as I stood.

Her response was unrevealing. "I'll look at it, sweetie. I promise."

With that, Cherry quickly departed my presence to the changing room.

As my eyes turned to the stage, my thoughts remained on this goddess. I wanted to drink the dripping liquid between her thighs, suck those perky nipples, and capture her toes with my warm mouth. Envisioning the fusion of caramel and chocolate, skin and sweat, limbs and lust in the act of intercourse, the hard cable at my groin needed installation into her intimate cavity. But would these dreams be realized tonight?

My answer came instantly as Cherry reappeared in front of me. Dressed in a gray running suit with blue coat in hand, her heated stare pierced my soul. The look alone rattled me, but not as much as what came next from her pretty mouth.

"Yes Vaughn...you can. Let's go."

Leading the way outside, we passed Myron who inquired about Cherry's sudden departure.

"Early night, honey. I'll talk to you tomorrow," she replied as we exited. Feeling his resentment as I walked by, my eyes shifted to the dark blue Lincoln Continental parked in front of the club. Following Cherry to the vehicle, I immediately opened the door for her to enter. Once inside, with no hesitation, Cherry unleashed our hunger with her long, probing tongue. Initially startled by her urgency, my fears were quickly thawed by the burning fire before me.

Meeting her intensity head-on, the yearning passion in my soul took over as I joined the passionate tongue wrestle. As she straddled me immediately, my hands wandered slowly down the small of her back, finding her firm backside appetizing. Cradling her cheeks in my large hands and gripping them as if they were going to run away, a gentle squeal escaped the fantasy before my eyes.

"Shit, Vaughn...damn, baby. I should wrap your big ass up and take you home with me."

"Not tonight, Cherry," I rasped, barely able to get the words out. "We're going to my place."

After giving the driver directions, we resumed our mind-numbing foray. As the chauffeur adjusted his rearview mirror to get a better view of the action, Cherry decided to give him a show. Feeling her hands graze then grab my groin area repeatedly, she lowered her mouth to this region.

"I want to taste you, Mr. Rivers." Peeking up at me with a wicked smile, she unzipped my pants and roughly pushed them to my ankles. Doing the same to my silk boxers, she paused her assault on my erection to pay homage.

"Mmmm, Daddy got a lot down here. I can't wait to get him inside me." That would come later, I deduced; for now, she wanted a Blow Pop. Cherry cupped my testicles and loved the firmness of my sacs as they were drawn tight in passion. Removing her top, she surrounded my thickness with her ample cleavage. Damn, that shit felt good. Massaging the length of me with her breasts would have been sufficient, but she wasn't satisfied seeing my face war with ecstasy.

Cherry brushed a kiss against my swollen knob, and her oral lizard teased and pleased my member, licking it from stem to stern. Hearing my loud moan, Cherry returned to my face for a brief respite, stifling my noise with a kiss.

"You gotta cum once before we get home, Vaughn." As she resumed her hedonistic torture down south, my penis flexed in preparation for something warm and moist. Lining me up with her oral O, I felt her jaws stretch in hunger as she engulfed my stiff flesh, accommodating me easily. Taking a little more of me with each oral stroke, Cherry sent uncommon jolts of pleasure straight through to my bones. Oblivious to the front seat voyeur, she was so dirty, so wrong, and so nasty. And I loved it.

Bobbing up and down on my veined pole, slurping, sliding, and sucking me in a frantic, frenzied pitch, she was a skillful courtesan but my hands found the back of her head and aided the lustful lubrication her mouth provided. Responding to my assistance, Cherry sank her nails deep into my butt as she increased the pace of her pumping.

I began losing control of my body, as well as my senses. My fluid hips trembled and my body tensed as I groaned "Cherry...I'm gonna cum...".

"That's what I want, Daddy. Give me that juice, baby," she screamed between slurps. Hearing her call for my white honey made my body shudder as I deposited a warm, salty release in her mouth. Swallowing as much as she could, I could hear her hungry gulps as she suctioned almost every drop. Licking her lips with that active tongue, Cherry smiled deviously, then worked my sensitive tip with her brim.

Bringing her face to mine once more, I licked the overspill of my semen off her chin and kissed her approvingly. "Cherry, I can't wait to make you feel as good as you made me feel." No sooner than those words left me, the car stopped in front of my apartment. After quickly fixing our clothes, I went to hush Cherry's chauffeur with a ten spot.

"No tip necessary," he cracked, causing us to laugh. "Shit, I should be paying y'all." Cherry then winked at him.

"Thanks for the lift, Bernard. I'll see you tomorrow night."

We entered my apartment locked in a furious French kiss. After removing her coat, my object of every man's fantasy was pinned against a dim hallway wall. The diabolical desires raging inside took me over as I lifted her sweatshirt and attacked sensitive, swollen nipples with my mouth. Responding with a satisfied moan while quivering in the deliverance of her wont, the intense heat burning inside Cherry came to the surface, as her voice grew deeper in the throes of passion.

"Ooooh…yes, Vaughn. Mmmm…damn, baby. Take care of me, sugar."

Damn, the taste of her bosom turned me on, but I wanted more. She knew this as well, for after I removed her from her captive position, she guided me to my living room by the hardened object in my pants. Cherry's caramel complexion turned crimson as I gently aided her to the bearskin-carpeted floor and removed my clothing. Her sweatpants were damp with arousal as I ran my bald pate between her legs. Grinding slowly against my skull in an effort to match my freakiness, I felt her tremor as she issued a stern demand.

"Take them off, Vaughn!" Anxious to sample my caramel Cherry sundae, I eagerly obliged and to my amazement, saw her pierced and pantiless. Inhaling the scent of her femininity as my lips neared her entry, I decided to take my time with this dessert.

Cherry's gorgeous thighs trembled in anticipation as I kissed up and down those stems of delight leading to a liquid heaven. "Shivering is good, Cherry," I commented as I felt her shudder and shake, then release a confession as my fingers instinctively, intrusively invaded her garden.

"Damn, I've wanted you since Sunday. Please tame my kitty-cat with your tongue." That starving feeling below that craved her tingling slit would wait a little longer as I immersed my face within her slippery walls. Claiming every crevice while lasciviously licking her labia, juices flowed from this exotic goddess as a fluttering object between my lips cuddled her clitoris. Gripping my head for support, then releasing it to reach skyward for shit that wasn't there, Cherry exploded in ecstasy as I violated her vulva.

"Do that, Vaughn... Yes, Daddy, lick it...damn, baby, ooooh..." Hearing her moan intensified my tongue bath of her womanhood. Sensuous sensations numbed Cherry as I sucked her jewelry adorned, thumb-sized clit as though extracting a seed from her—only this one wouldn't be spit out. Soon, I would receive the warm liquid that gushed from her as she screamed primal sounds from pouted, red lips. Watching her tremble and thrash in gratification as I tasted the overflow of her nectar on my beard, the massive ache between my legs twitched and throbbed in anticipation of her pleasure chest.

"Come here, Vaughn. Let me kiss you," Cherry commanded between labored breaths. Meeting her face once more as we rolled into a reverse missionary position, our hips simulated the forbidden dance as our tongues tied themselves in knots again. Her bouncing, humping motion astride me had me begging to relieve the tightly wound coil of tension at my thighs. Her response to my passionate pleas was short and direct.

"Go get a condom." She didn't have to say it twice. Running to my bedroom, returning with a box of twenty-four and fitting myself in record time, the fantasy of going toe-to-toe in passion with Cherry was finally realized when she supplanted me deep in the moisture of her narrow, well-saturated canyon. Her strokes from above were deliberate and methodical at first. Staring deep into my eyes as if she were unfazed by my penetration, her coolness in the heat of the moment increased my arousal.

Making my nine inches disappear and reappear inside her with the genielike movements of her hips, I was getting turned inside out by an advanced aerobics instructor.

"You like that, Vaughn?" she purred while increasing the tempo. "I bet you never had it as good as this, have you? Have you, Daddy?" Cherry was correct in her assumption. I had never been dominated by a woman before. But I loved every minute of it. Squeezing the inner walls of her tunnel of lust around me, Cherry began showing cracks in her armor. Lowering her breasts to my mouth, she demanded that I bite her long, luscious nipples hard, then harder. Dutifully, I obeyed, and the core of her was awakened, sending her soaring, soaring and swirling into a vortex of ecstasy.

"Damn, Vaughn, you got me so hot," she moaned as we switched into the male-dominant position. Spreading her legs as wide as they could go, I held them hostage with my forearms as I drove into her crab-style so she wouldn't escape my measured, meaningful thrusts. Pounding her hot box urgently as our bodies bonded, her nails clawed into my back, drawing blood as our bodies slammed together, sending erotic moans ricocheting through the apartment.

"Vaughn, please go faster," Cherry wailed as her body experienced orgasm after orgasm. Shifting, groaning, panting, and moaning to the rhythm of my dance, a burst of ultimate pleasure seized her, creating an enjoyable commotion within. "Bite me, dammit!," she screamed as her body withstood tremors of delight. Hearing, then acting on this request, the kissing and licking on her nape evolved into sharp nibbles, propelling and prolonging her sexual apex. As I neared my own climax, the weirdest thing escaped my lips as my body felt the pressure of her pleasure.

"Oh, god, Cherry…thank you, baby. Thank you." Soon, I would shower the protective instrument I wore with warm juices. Cherry could feel my release as well, for we screamed simultaneously in harmony as she came with me. Totally satisfied, our exhausted, semi-lifeless frames collapsed in each other's arms.

As if joined at the hip, Cherry and I recovered and continued our game of naked Twister through the night and well into Sunday afternoon, contorted in every way imaginable throughout my apartment. Against the living room wall, in the dark hallway, on the carpeted floor again, the bathroom floor, kitchen sink, and the dining room table, everywhere—we just couldn't get enough of each other.

Cherry tried to leave frequently during the day, but the simplest touch would send us back to bed or wherever we decided to do it. Soon, the hours passed and, sadly, the object of my desire had to say good-bye.

Before allowing her to pass through my apartment door, I had to ask her, "Cherry, what's your real name?"

With a wistful smile, she whispered, "Faye," before softly pressing her lips·to mine. "Bye, Vaughn."

Initially, a sense of emptiness engulfed me as soon as she left. A silence in the air echoed that she was gone for good, having served her purpose in my life by fulfilling my fantasy. But I knew that wasn't entirely true, for the vision of seeing her perform one last time would be the ultimate way of closure.

It was ten o'clock when I returned to The Hideaway that night. I had no intention of staying; I had only gone to once again give Cherry my thanks. She had turned my world upside down, and with no illusions of sharing anything more than we had, I wanted to her to know how much I appreciated the indescribable joy she had brought into my life. What had begun as an attempt by my boys to brighten the melancholy caused by a broken heart had turned into a fantasy come to life.

I ordered a screwdriver and took the same table I had occupied on every excursion to this den of salacity. As the place filled to capacity, my eyes scanned the surroundings hoping to get a glimpse of her before the show started. I felt a twinge of disappointment when my efforts were futile, but I found solace in the fact that she would see me during another sensuous routine and engage me with a between-the-lines smile.

Impatiently waiting for Cherry to appear onstage, I was restless and bored by these women who suddenly all appeared to be trying too hard. Try as they might, no one had enticed me the way that Cherry had and definitely would again, tonight. So I waited patiently, knowing they were saving the best for last.

Quickly downing a second drink as the show neared its end, my disappointment turned to distress as I noticed that big, bald bouncer, Myron, near the entrance. In search of an explanation, I rose from my seat and started toward him.

"What happened to Cherry tonight?" I blurted out.

"What?" he barked.

"Is Cherry dancing tonight?"

"Who's Cherry?"

"What do you mean, 'who's Cherry?' " I asked, certain that my face revealed my puzzlement.

"Did I stutter?" Myron meanly asked.

"You know her! She took me back into the VIP room just a few days ago, and you stood guard at the door," I emphatically reminded him.

"Nigga, I ain't never stood guard at no door, and I ain't never seen your ugly mug before today. Now why don't you sit your ass down or get the fuck out!" Myron ordered.

"Whadda you mean, you've never seen me before? I've been in here damn near every night this past week. And Cherry's been dancing here every night I've been here. I've come back each time just to see her!" I informed him, hearing my own desperation in my tone.

Another bouncer joined us then, and asked, "What's going on, Tommy?"

"Who in the hell is Tommy?" I screamed.

"I'm Tommy," Myron brusquely answered. "And you're leaving. Now!"

"But Cherry…" I started as the two brawny ballbusters grabbed my arms and pointed me toward the exit.

"I've already told you, ain't nobody named Cherry dance here. Now get the fuck out!"

Within seconds I was looking at the closed door of The Hideaway from the vantage point of the deserted street. My mind was trying to wrap itself around what had just happened. *How could there be no Cherry? I was just with her this afternoon.*

Needless to say, I was clueless. I felt like my head was spinning. Then there was this annoying ringing in my ears.

Next thing I knew I was at home, in my bed, the covers twisted annoyingly around my legs. My alarm clock was piercing the silence of my apartment and driving me insane. When I reached over to turn it off, I felt the wetness on my sheets, and a dripping emission in my shorts. *Oh shit, was this whole thing just a dream?*

Blue-Collar Lover
by
Sandra A. Ottey

*B*lue-collared testosterone emanated the thick air as Gina Blackwood browsed the tool department at Home Depot. Fingering a lady's drill, she slyly swerved her head left to check out the fine black men as they busied themselves examining and choosing their tools to go perform their physical labor. Watching their chiseled physiques pass by in muscle shirts and shorts Gina crossed her legs and pressed her thighs together, trying to suppress the hyperactive sexual appetite that enveloped her. That didn't help. It merely sped up her adrenalin and wet her panties.

But she had never dated a blue-collared man, she mused. In fact, she had never even thought about dating anyone besides those lying attorneys, illiterate professors, and ailing physicians. With her upper-middle-class upbringing: a maid, Ivy League schooling, and now her prestigious position on New York's powerful Wall Street, her ego had always soared.

But I shouldn't be blamed for having dated only white-collared men. Quite frankly, I have lived only what I have been taught. "In order to live a happy, successful life you need to marry a highly educated man who will be able to let you live at or above the standard of living to which you are accustomed," Gina's mother would drill into her young, blossoming brain. *But it's not all about money. Many blue-collared workers make a lot more money than the so-called white-collared ones! Besides, I make more than enough money to take care of myself! And another thing, who said that blue-collared men are uneducated?*

And when her dad was out of earshot her mom would add in a sly whisper, "Just make sure that the man you choose can give you a good you-know-what, in bed." *Okay, Mama, I agree with that one. But shouldn't men who perform physical labor be able to satisfy their women in bed, since those men get their exercise by simply doing their jobs? On the other hand, an office man who simply sits at his desk all day can quickly develop a beer belly even without the beer!*

Then Gina's highfalutin' mama would chuckle and add, "Gina, darling, you have to mix with the best of the best, the cream of the crop." *But who decides which caliber of men is the cream of the crop?* Gina wondered now as she stopped to check out a small hammer. *Hammer. Hammer.* She imagined the pounding of a hammer against wood and wished she was being fucked just as hard, right here and right now. She chose a slender hammer with a wooden handle, just feminine enough for her to handle. She placed it beside the drill, in her orange-colored shopping cart that matched the store's interior and the employees' aprons. Further down the aisle she picked up a screwdriver. So now she had the three basic tools a home owner should own: hammer, drill, and screwdriver. *Hmmm. Screwdriver. Screw. Why do the names of these tools sound so sexually suggestive and add to my sexual drive? Hammer...drill...screwdriver.* She answered her own question: *It's PMS time. Oh God, I hate periods. The monthly red curse is only a few days away, and my libido is at its peak. Besides, no one has shared my bed in the last seven months.*

She started to head for the cashier when she saw her next-door neighbor Phyllis Johnson pushing an empty trolley in her direction. As a West Indian, when Gina had moved into her Long Island neighborhood two months ago, she was happy to learn that her new neighbor was Guyanese. At least they had certain customs in common, she had thought. "Hello, Miss Blackwood," Phyllis said.

"Hi, Phyllis. What's up?"

Looking into Gina's shopping cart Phyllis smiled, nodded approvingly and said, "I see you're stocking up on some must-haves. That's very good."

She smiled. "Well, I'm purchasing them, but that doesn't mean that I know how to use them, though."

They shared a laugh.

"Well, girl, welcome to the neighborhood."

"Again."

"But please do not join the group of single women on the block who have to shovel their own snow during the winter months. They need to get themselves some men. Remember those terrible snowstorms we had last year?"

It was the middle of July but Gina shivered just thinking of the wallop of snow that nature had continuously dumped on New York. Mountains of snow that turned into ice, then sleet that turned the streets into skating rinks.

Phyllis said, "Well, you should see those single home owners out there shoveling like men while I just lay in bed while my Jimmy did all the cleaning up for me. And don't forget you have a big corner lot. Now, that's a lot of cleaning up. Girl, I don't want to scare you, but as a single woman it's not easy to own a home and live alone. You are a foreigner like me so I have to share the knowledge with you. You need someone you can call on when any one of the tons of things can go wrong in the house. I'm tellin' you. A house is not a home. If you buy a house you're gonna need a man. Call him whatever you want—handy man, lover man, maintenance man, plumber man, some kinda man.

"I'm not going to get a man simply because I don't know how to shovel snow or use a drill. I can afford a snow blower."

"I've only known you for a short time but let me tell you straight up, Gina. You're too choosy."

"But that's the way I was brought up."

"Well, it's time you stop blaming your parents for the way you choose your men. My mother also told me the same thing your mother did: 'Never settle for less than what you deserve.' But what *do* I deserve? A kind, gentle, loving, honest, caring man who will love, trust, and care for me and support me in all my endeavors. Well, my man is a plumber, and he can fix my sink anytime."

Gina chuckled. "I know exactly what you mean. My mother has this mentality that a man has to dress up like a mannequin in a tailored suit every day; and this is the albatross that's keeping me from finding my joy. Real men also go to work in sweatshirt or a simple T-shirt, jeans and sneakers, or boots. They don't only manage our portfolios, represent us in court, or write prescriptions when we're sick; they also repair our plumbing and electrical work, fix our boilers and air conditioners, renovate our bathrooms and clear our cesspools."

"You know it. Not to mention the fact that some of these blue-collared men make a hell of a lot more money than these so-called white-collared idiots. By the way, what about that sexy guy that installed your central air?"

She smiled and crossed her legs. "Who? Dante?"

"Gosh, Gina, he is cute. And I know you like him."

"I do."

"An' what a pieca body him have. Damn, my Jimmy doesn't look half as good, but anyway Jimmy the snow, fixes little things around the house, but most of all we love each other and I'm no longer lonely."

"Good for you. I haven't been touched for so long that my you-know-what has become an anatomical landmark. But I've never slept with anyone except…you know…"

Phyllis said, "Listen, when winter comes, you don't want any-one slipping or sliding, purposely or accidentally, in front of your door-steps and then turning around to sue you simply because you didn't take care of business. Stop being so choosy. And you're now what…thirty-three?

"Thirty-two!" Gina snapped. "Don't push it. I'm scared of old age."

"You're going to be even more scared if you end up alone. A man's occupation doesn't make the man."

"You've said it and I know it, Phyllis."

Phyllis said, "Well, let me go sniff on some cedar wood and then go pick out some plants at the nursery.

Gina lowered her voice. "Sniff on what?"

"The scent of cedarwood turns me on. Jimmy always wonders why I always feel overly sexy after a trip to Home Depot. You should try it, Gina."

"Girl, if I get turned on anymore tonight I'll explode."

The parking lot was scanty as Gina packed her bags on the backseat of her red Camry. She sat behind the wheel and felt a faint thrust at the back of her car. *No, someone did not hit my car!* With her mouth angrily ajar she swung her head around to look behind her. A burgundy GMC Savanna was parked behind her. The thrust was mild and she didn't think there was any damage to her vehicle. *But why*

touch my car? There's more than enough space to park.

She quickly opened the car door and jumped out just in time to see Dante walking toward her, a big grin on his handsome dark face, his teeth sparkling into the night. "Oh, Dante, it's you."

"Only me. And don't worry, no harm done. Just bumper to bumper. I just did that because I know how you feel about your baby," he said, smiling and raising his brows at her car.

"Now you know if you mess with my car you're going to have to fix it and fix it good."

"You know I can fix everything and anything. And I fix it good too."

And he was right, she thought. Dante was a perfectionist. This sexy man could break a whole house down and put it back together again, only better. He wore a white T-shirt paired with matching shorts. A faint hint of his seductive cologne floated in the tepid air. "So what are you doing here?"

"I should be asking you that question. Home Depot is like my second home. I'm always here."

She heard her vehicle arm itself. A soft wind whistled in her ear. She pointed to his burgundy van that featured two small windows with blinds on each side. "Oh, this is a lovely van. How many vehicles do you own? I've never seen you with this one before."

"Yes, you have. You just weren't paying attention. "Would you like to check it out?"

"Sure."

He opened the front passenger door. She started to help herself into the van, but Dante's strong hands swept her off the ground. Surprised but enchanted, she hung on to him and sniffed his cologne. He put her on the front passenger seat, slammed the door, and walked around to the driver's door.

She grinned at him in the driver's seat. "I know you're strong, Dante so you don't have to show off. I've seen you lift my 25,000btu air conditioner as if it weighed ten pounds." She turned to look in the back of the air-conditioned van and noticed that a pair of navy blue drapes separated the two front seats from the back of the van. "So what do you have around there? Tools and stuff?"

"Something like that. Why don't you go find out?"

"It's your van, you lead the way."

He led her to the back of the van that featured a small hoisted television and upholstered seating. Dante pressed a button on his remote control, and Marc Anthony's sweet, soothing voice filled the vehicle. Then the seat they sat on quickly converted into a sofa.

Her adrenaline gushed as he took her right hand and gently kissed the tips of her fingers with his soft, full lips. She trembled as he planted tender kisses on the inside of her arm all the way up her shoulders and neck.

Dante hungrily covered her mouth with his and kissed her fiercely, and she met him with the same fiery desire. He probed his tongue in her mouth and hungrily sucked on her tongue. He cupped her breast and tweaked the erect nipple that hardened and was ready for his mouth. She quickly peeled off her tube top and shivered as his hot mouth devoured her nipples, one at a time, nibbling, sucking, and milking away her loneliness. She moaned in excitement as he masterly brought the two nipples together and teethed them both. The tantalizing mixture of Marc Anthony's crooning, Dante's sexy cologne, and the excitement of making love in a vehicle in Home Depot's parking lot set her on a high, and she gasped in anticipation of what was yet to come.

On her back, she unzipped her shorts and quickly wiggled out of them. Dante used his teeth to peel her panties down to her ankles. She kicked off the flimsy apparel and then her sandals.

Dante quickly shrugged off his shirt and shook off his shorts and then unleashed his tool from the captivity of his briefs. He knelt in front of her and pulled her by the thighs closer to the edge of the sofa and to his waiting tongue. He spread her lips apart, traced a finger over her clitoris, stuck the finger inside her, and gently scooped it around like a spoon and discovered the crevices and corners she never knew she had. The skillful finger inside her elicited a satisfied heave from her mouth.

"You like that, baby?" he asked her.

"Ooo, I love it."

He stuck that same finger into his mouth and sucked her juices from it. He buried his head between her trembling thighs and used his teeth to comb the scanty public hair. *Now, that's new,* she thought. He captured her clitoris between his teeth and nibbled on it ever so gently. She stifled a scream as she exploded. Like a starving man he kept his head buried in the quivering moistness between her legs, made small circles with his tongue and then licked ferociously like a cat lapping milk.

A gasp escaped her throat as she sizzled from his experienced masterful tongue and teeth tricks, alternately sucking and nibbling her public area and placed moist kisses on the inside of her thighs. For getting where she was she started to scream, but he quickly clamped a hand over her mouth. He released the hand and stuck her finger in her mouth. Sucking on the finger she imagined it was his penis and moaned in earnest ecstasy while he feasted hungrily on her love organ.

But she had to have her feast too. He ejected his face from her vagina and stood up. She quickly sat up and rubbed her face in his crotch. He smelled so good she guessed that he had included down there as one of his pulse points and had dotted some cologne there too. She started at the shaft near his testicles and wagged her tongue all the way up to the tip where she found he, too, had excreted some liquid. She clamped her mouth snugly over his beautiful tool and pumped him in and out of her mouth. She liked what he did to her with his teeth so she gently scraped his penis with her teeth.

He made a seething sound and smiled. "Oh, baby, that's sooo good."

She gave him some more teeth on the sides, and then used her tongue to paint him up and down from under the shaft to its smooth head. *Aaah, the pleasure of the flesh.*

On her back she spread her legs apart and his beautiful being fit right in, groin to groin, heart to heart, soul to soul. Sweeping her exploring hands down his rippling loins and chiseled buttocks she faked a protest, "Oh, I can't believe we're doing this." His soft, hot lips quickly circled hers and gently sucked on them, one at a time, just as he had sucked on her other two lips below. He entered her in sections, slowly, almost teasingly, and then ejected from her. "Please, please, give it to me...please...now," she begged.

"Don't you worry, baby. I'm going to give it to you, baby. I'm going to fuck you like you've never been fucked before." Her pressed his penis against her clitoris and then traced it around the circumference of her vulva area.

"Do it to me now."

She circled her legs around his neck. On his knees, he raised her buttocks, bringing her vagina closer to meet his pending thrust. He drilled into her with full force. She inhaled sharply and smiled as she again exploded.

She looked up into the ceiling, expecting to see a tool pan or some other blue-collared worker's possessions and gasped as she saw herself in heat in the mirror.

He lowered her left leg and thrust into a part of her that she never knew existed. She wanted to scream so badly. She grabbed a piece of clothing, which turned out to be his undershirt, from the floor, and screamed into the cologne-tainted garment to suppress her screams of ecstasy. Next she lowered the right leg and kept the left one around his waist, and experienced the same discovery.

Gina lowered and then closed her legs while Dante continued to drill into her. With such friction she thought she felt the beat of his blood in the veins of his penis. He went up on his hands and toes in a push-up position, pushed down and pounded into her faster and harder. Forty strokes later he uttered some unintelligible words. His entire body trembled with pleasurable satisfaction. He inhaled sharply and them exhaled slowly. His body relaxed.

Swept away by this man's experienced, masterly lovemaking she again slowly spread her legs, allowing his dripping body to settle between them. He hugged and kissed her and brushed her wet hair from her face. After a moment of silence he said confidently, "I knew it would happen. I just wasn't sure when or where."

Tracing his toned biceps with her finger she concurred, "We were gravely attracted to each other right from the start. It just had to happen."

She liked the way he cuddled her after sex. It showed that he really cared about her. Her sex sabbatical had been ended by a man other than a white-collared worker. Mama was wrong, she thought. Blue-collared men were just as loving, caring and sensitive as any other man. Her hang-ups were over.

Moonlight spilled through the blinds as she stretched and took a quick peek outside.

They looked at each other and laughed softly.

"It's pretty empty out there," she said.

"Empty is good."

"I'd better make my escape before the lot crowds up again."

"And I'd better get dressed and go purchase the materials I came here to buy in the first place."

She hurriedly got dressed and shot from the van and drove home with a broad grin on her face. *Blue rules!*

Jonesing
by
Linda Dominique Grosvenor

*C*iara Holland stood in the mirror and brushed her thick head of hair back into a ponytail and clipped silver bobby pins at her temples. She smoothed out her eyebrows and glared at her reflection and said it out loud finally: "I love him." Ciara loved her man, Dennis. She loved every caramelized, tongue-tantalizing inch of him. He was blessed with a business savvy that too few men had mastered in this town where the average job was in automotives and would bleed you until you retired with a mediocre pension and a gold-plated tie clip. Dennis Caldwell towered a little under the mark at five-eleven but had the softest hands this side of Lake Michigan. Ciara smiled. His hands did wonderful things to her. Things that made her quiver just thinking about him late at night when there was no one around to fulfill her insatiable longing. Descendant of African kings for certain, Dennis's demeanor crowned him with a persona that made every woman take notice. Ciara didn't mind other women looking but it was hands off from day one.

Sex. They hadn't gone that far yet but looking at his lips sure took her there mentally. She shook her head at the way she convinced him that fondling alone wasn't breaking the rules of celibacy. She said she was saving herself for marriage. It was then and only then that Ciara would let any man ravish her. She was saving herself for Dennis, supposedly. She didn't dare trust him yet with the true reason that she wouldn't sleep with him. She was afraid of how he'd take it. She was honestly afraid of things that her mother had told her about various shades and ethnicities. She was afraid that she'd have dark-skinned babies just like her mama said. Her mother warned her repeatedly, so she promised herself that she would wait. Too many times men proposed marriage just to get the sex and then they would start an argument about anything, leaving the woman feeling used, ugly, and worthless as they walked out of the door to her life with a ring they would later return to the jewelers. Dennis wasn't like that, she was certain of it, but she agreed to wait for him anyway. Hopefully she'd get past her issue of shade. Her love for Dennis was stronger than that— or so she hoped.

She had been with other men. She wasn't a virgin, but at this point in her life she wasn't trying to get her feelings and her mind all tangled in a heated desire that she knew could never been quenched once she got started, so sex could wait. Women had more willpower than men and she knew that one day soon she would have him. They had abstained however excruciating, even though it didn't seem like much of a virtue anymore. But then again sex was overrated, unless you were in love, and that she was, madly and deeply.

Her mother's underlying issue with skin color, which she had perpetuated to her child was what Ciara prayed wouldn't do her relationship with Dennis in. Her mother was relentless and wanted to rule her life even though she had just turned thirty. Light skin versus dark skin, an old issue that her mother wouldn't let die along with other old wive's tales. "He'll give you dark seeds," her mother said. She dismissed her mother's words whenever she said it but the determination in her mother's eyes wasn't letting it go. A tiny part of her worried whether all the things that her mother said were true. Wanting every portion of her life to line up, Ciara struggled with the thought of wanting to give in to Dennis and worrying about how her mother's words would curse her and come back to haunt her life with dark seeds if she did.

Her mother often told her that dating was one thing but that contemplating forever with someone like Dennis was something totally different. Ciara couldn't see the difference, no matter how hard she looked. Her heart knew what was right. Did that mean defy her mother and have her saying I told you so until the day she died? When Dennis proposed to her the month before she broke his heart, shattered it in a million microscopic pieces. She looked at the ring in the box, stared right into his eyes, and told him that she'd have to think about it.

Now he was gone and hadn't called in more than four weeks. Parts of her wished it wasn't more than but she knew there was no way to mend a pain as deep as the one she had created in Dennis.

She remembered the day he proposed like it was an hour ago. Dennis had met her in front of her job. The summer sun was high and he was sitting in his late-model car with the engine running waiting for her to come out of the building. Ciara pressed through the door with a hoard of workers making their mass exodus at 5:00 P.M. directly behind her. Ciara looked up and glanced his way as if she could feel him there drawing her to him. She whispered good-bye and waved to her two coworkers, promising they'd do lunch the next day. They eyed Dennis, too, and then headed off in the opposite direction. Ciara had on Dennis's favorite red dress, which accentuated her full breasts and svelte body. The hem of the dress grazed slightly above her knees. He waved her over, and she headed in his direction her long legs strutting and her purse resting delicately on her shoulder.

Everyone who met Dennis loved him. His charismatic manner of speech lured them to him like an old friend. Ciara was no exception. He had a hearty laugh and hands that were expressive and large enough to make you think it was a common theme in his anatomy. She initially had no idea what he had planned for the evening. Dinner probably, she thought, but she wasn't hungry so it didn't matter. Whenever she got a feel for wanting to be touched she lost all of her other senses. She couldn't hear anything and she'd lose her appetite. All for the pleasure of being touched. He drove to their favorite place by the water near the lake and watched the other cars file in waiting for the sun to disappear completely beyond the horizon and for the darkness to engulf them and offer them all discreet moments in the backseat of their cars.

He turned off the engine. Their eyes met without hesitation. It took him little or no time to fall into the mood and respond to her. Dennis's lips sucked at hers hungrily. He unbuttoned her dress and pulled it open, groping her flesh impatiently. Her plump breasts pressed out beyond her black lace bra and his lips were instinctively drawn to them and the thick nipples that rose in the chilly air. Ciara remembered looking down at his lips and what they were doing to her. He ignored her eyes and focused on going as far as she would let him. With her breasts cupped in his hands and his warm lips on her body Ciara wanted all of Dennis. His hips thrusted toward her in the throes of passion like a movie on the Spice channel. Parts of her wanted to wait, other parts wanted her to shut up and enjoy the moment because she remembered how good it could be if both partners willing to please each other beyond the limit. Good girls had sex. Virtuous women did too. Naughty girls had fabulous sex—sometimes with husbands, sometimes with boyfriends that would one day become husbands. She wanted to let Dennis. He talked about putting his mouth on places that would make her forget how to speak, places that would make her shudder and leave earth momentarily. With the same lips that said he loved her he wanted to taste her and dine on the goodness of her sweet flavor. She had made up her mind to let him that night. She wanted him to, badly. Her mind was relishing his hot breath breathing down there, returning her to a succession of warm orgasmic waves that she missed so much.

Dennis's hands were at it again now. His hands disappeared under her red dress. She raised her hips and he slipped her panties down with little difficulty. She sighed, moaned, and squirmed in the seat, assisting him with anything that would quicken her pleasure. Her eyes were closed, anticipating a soon coming pleasure. It had been such a long time. She desperately needed to feel that wonderful pleasure again. Dennis spread her legs and caressed her between her thighs. She was wet with a hunger for him. Her sticky honeycomb moistness was all over his fingers as he foraged his way through her tight snatch of curly brown hair, a spot she was saving for him. He made her feel like a woman. He kissed her everywhere. With almost no effort she was ripe with excitement. She closed her eyes again and touched his manhood. She wrapped her fingers around it, gripped it, and moved up and down awkwardly as it throbbed in her hand. His index finger fished for her opening and delighted itself in teasing the swelling of her womanhood. Dennis was starting a fire that would burn in her until someone quenched it. She spread her thighs wider for him, giving him access to all of her honey, which he would skillfully lick from her pot.

Like a flash, her mother's words took up residence in her mind again and echoed. Dark seeds. She saw the words in her head as clear as if they were printed on paper. She closed her legs and gathered her senses, pushed Dennis away, and reached for her panties, which were sitting in a ball under her dashboard, as she pulled at her clothing to cover herself. She told him that she couldn't. Not now. Not yet. In her mind she wondered if she ever could, and if not, why she was leading him on. He urged her to listen to him. He told her that she *had* to please him tonight. He said that she *had* to make this real for him.

"I have to?" She frowned.

Dennis shoved his hand in his pocket and retrieved the cute red velvet case and pushed it down between her breasts.

"Yes. You have to, woman. I love you." He grinned. "Ciara, will you marry me?"

The expression on her face said it all. She was shocked. Her body trembled and panic set in.

"Ummm…" Ciara's next words were unexpected. She hadn't planned on hurting him but each syllable was like an obscenity to his heart. "I have to think about it."

She couldn't accept a proposal without her mother's approval, and as dark as Dennis was, no matter how much money he currently made or how much of that impressive Caldwell business savvy he had, she knew her mother would never give her consent. He absorbed the sting of her words.

"Think about it?" He scowled. "What's the real reason, Ciara?" He rubbed his chin. "I know you love me. I know that I make enough money to take care of you. Is there someone else? Who is he? What's his name?" His demeanor turned cold and his erection subsided.

"You're too dark, Dennis. My mother won't allow it." She couldn't believe that she was actually saying it.

"What are you saying, Ciara? Are you listening to yourself?"

"She doesn't want dark grandchildren," Ciara said.

"You and your mother have lost it!" he said, then started up the car and dropped her off in front of her home without uttering another word. That's where she'd been ever since. At home for weeks, not able to eat or drink or think about anything else but Dennis Caldwell.

Since she was seven Ciara pretended to be the perfect bride wobbling around in her mother's high heels and a sheet draped across her head like a veil dragging behind her practicing to be the graceful soon-to-be Mrs. Somebody walking down the aisle holding anything she could bunch together and call a bouquet. "I do." The words sounded so dutiful, like a purple heart awarded for bravery. In her bourgeoning twenties she watched as friends paired up and set off to plant seeds of their own and stake claims to a life that was waiting for them behind fences that weren't always picket or painted white. Shortly thereafter some were getting divorced, cheating, or dating men who belonged to other women just to have a name, number, and sometimes a memory on their caller ID. Some of her friends just lined up any available men they could find and dated them like a turn at bat, having sex like it was going out of style. Getting men to marry them then refusing them pleasures and playing head games. A bunch of mixed-up women. She vehemently denied being one.

All those years Ciara had waited and screened potential men for commitment phobia and now here she was still alone, all because she believed the myth that if he was dark, her kids would be dark and they wouldn't have as good a life or as good features and hair as they would if she married someone more her complexion. *Don't dark kids play well with others?* Why was the beauty that was supposed to encompass a race limited now to hue. Sometimes she thought it silly and other times noble to think that far ahead for her children and their children's sake. Her mother didn't think it was sensible to abandon all of her fine lineage for a roll in the hay with a dark man. She wondered if he didn't like his color either and only dated her because she was lighter and he was jonesing for a little milk in his chocolate or was she the only one contemplating these issues? She wished she had thought this all through before she had fallen in love with him. How unfair of her it would be to abandon her emotions now too.

Dennis loved Ciara. She knew it. He turned down a job as VP in a Los Angeles company making double what he made in Detroit because he couldn't bare having a long-distance relationship with her. He didn't dare limit their love to holidays, three-day weekends, and airport layovers. He needed to see her, hear her, touch her, speak to her, and ultimately taste her. He told her so. Foreplay was the furthest they had gone. Just once she wanted to be able to defy her own mind and her mother's too. She wanted Dennis back. She needed him back. His strong presence and his gentle way of doing things. When Ciara finally stopped crying and called her mother and told her about Dennis's proposal that night in the car all her mother said was, "maybe it's for the best." Now here she was jonesing for her dark chocolate lover, wondering how much he missed her and after all these weeks and still no phone call, if he ever cared.

    Ciara paced her apartment. She looked out of the window at the schoolkids filing onto the block, oblivious to the weather. It was lunchtime. Her heart absolutely could not take it anymore. Dennis. She had it bad. All she could think of were his hands, his lips, and his fingers. She closed her eyes, revisiting the times they spent together and took a deep breath. She couldn't bear the thought of it being over. This distance between them was putting a hurting on her. Boredom and anxiety both had chosen this particular day to pay her a visit. She had spent the morning linking paperclips together and planting peppermint-flavored kisses on Dennis's picture in a frame. It was raining heavily outside, cats and dogs, and she never thought that she would actually go out in it since she hated the rain and hated getting her hair wet even more, but hours at a time every day sitting at home trying to figure out how many days he would let pass before he called her and asked to come over and talk was driving her mad.

    His love—or the lack thereof—had her doing lots of things that she didn't normally do on the regular. She didn't dare call Dennis at his office because he was always too busy trying to work his way up the corporate ladder to have a leisurely chat with her. It would also look like she was giving in if she called first. So instead of calling Ciara dragged herself to the shower, freshened up, put on some clean clothes, and snatched up an umbrella and strolled over to the downtown district, making her way through the maze of people who were trying to get to and from somewhere with less than an hour to spare. She walked quickly between the people and crossed the street. She was standing only feet from his building rethinking what his response to her being there might be.

    For some reason Ciara stopped dead in her tracks. Dumbstruck, she froze, her head lifted and her brown eyes focused slowly before knowing what it was that she was looking at. There he was at least twelve feet ahead of her, tall and slender. Dennis. Her man and some skinny dark-skinned woman with a red umbrella who was twirling it and splashing water everywhere. The woman had on a red rain jacket belted tightly around her waist and red heels that must have been at least three inches high. Dennis must have had a way of making all of his woman wear red. Ciara scrutinized them closely. She couldn't believe that he would do this to her.

A ferocious anger slowly worked its way to her face and matched the frown now smeared across her forehead. Ciara wanted to run and hide, just like the love he claimed to have for her must be doing deep down inside of him. His love was nowhere to be found that day. Standing next to a blue mailbox with a colorful umbrella, there Ciara was peeping at him as if she was the one who had a secret worth hiding. She watched how Dennis and the woman smiled at each other and looked into each other's eyes like they had been lovers for years.

Within moments and totally oblivious to Ciara's presence the woman was slowly and methodically putting her tongue in Dennis's mouth, kissing his lips sweetly, leaving him wiping the corner of his mouth, satisfied and content to go back to his office and accomplish some things with the rest of the day. The mere thought that she had to stand in the rain and witness such infidelity when she had been oh so monogamous from the beginning to the end worked Ciara's last nerve. But Ciara bit the bullet and watched as this woman followed Dennis in the building and back to his office.

Ciara's thoughts were raging but her women's intuition told her to be calm. Just breathe and give him a moment before she went up there barging into his office acting crazy and uncouth. She stood on the corner a moment longer and counted to fifty then went inside of the building too. She shook off her umbrella on the clear plastic runner and looked down at her shoes, which were now soaking wet and knew that it was all his fault. Despite the umbrella the rain still wet her clothes and gave her a chill too. Her hair was frizzed up but she didn't care. She slowly filed her way into the elevator and pressed the button to go up to his office.

When Ciara made her way to the reception area she tried to put a smile on her face. "Is Dennis in?" she asked the secretary who widened her eyes and covered her mouth as she chewed a mouthful of sandwich, unable to respond.

The woman glanced at Ciara's frizzy hair, and down at her

nipples that were pressing through her rain-soaked blouse, then looked away. Ciara got impatient.

Ciara couldn't wait for an introduction. She knew that the two of them were in there doing only God knew what. She walked up into Dennis's office and didn't knock, just turned the knob, flung the door open and stood there looking at him as he sat with his head down shuffling through papers that were still more important than she was standing there right in front of him shivering with her umbrella dripping all over his burgundy office carpet.

"Where is she?" she yelled.

"What do you want, Ciara?" His jaws clenched.

Before common sense could warn her of the repercussions of her actions she barged over and began tossing everything off his desk— reports went flying, paper weights toppled over, and his precious desk plate landed in a potted plant and lunch or what looked like corned beef on rye with Swiss cheese ended up face down on the floor, inedible. She took a second to look at the cup of coffee sitting there just begging for the same treatment she had given everything else on his desk. He eyed her and Ciara thought, *what the hell*, and pushed the lukewarm cup of coffee off the desk too.

"What's wrong with you?" He stood and glared at her. The cufflinks that she had bought him last Christmas caught her eye.

"You are what's wrong!" She pulled him by his jacket and then pushed him down into his chair with all the force she could muster as he looked up at her baffled.

The woman emerged from his office bathroom with freshly applied lipstick and eyed Ciara.

"Am I intruding on something?" Ciara spat before the woman could get a word out.

Dennis cleared his throat. "We were just—"

"Going," the woman said. "I was just going. I'll call you, Dennis." She waved.

Dennis nodded.

"Stay awhile. Don't rush off on my account," Ciara said.

"Listen, Ciara, is it?" Ciara waited for her to continue. "I don't do drama, so you can stand here ranting and doing it all by yourself." The woman secured her purse at her side and walked out of Dennis's office.

"Who is she, Dennis?" Ciara spat.

"What do you care?" He shrugged. "I'm too dark, remember?"

"That's not what I said. And that's not what I meant."

"Well, you can gloss it up any way you like, it's what it all boils down to." He continued to arrange the papers and files that she had thrown to the floor.

"You're changing the subject. I saw you with that woman. Kissing. Standing outside of this building for the whole world to see." She put her hand on her hip.

"Don't make this about me. Too dark, too light. I can't honestly believe that you are as intelligent as you are and you buy into all of that. Now that woman," he said, pointing, "she didn't have an issue being with me or showing me affection for the whole world to see, regardless of shade."

"Birds of a feather…" she said sarcastically.

"What does that mean?" Dennis demanded.

"Look at how dark she is. Of course she doesn't mind being seen with you."

Dennis looked at Ciara disbelievingly.

"I can't fathom how on God's green earth I ever wanted you to be the mother of my children. Of anybody's children. Especially if this is the kind of thing you'd teach them. That good hair/light skin thing is for people who don't have anything else that they can be proud of."

"Dennis, it's just—"

"Over," he said. "It's over. Please leave, Ciara. I really don't want to look at you right now and I don't want to have to call security."

Flowers. Lilacs. Dinner, an apology, and a skimpy outfit too. She promised that she'd give him a long, drawn-out heartfelt apology. The kind he deserved. She loved him and she owed him that. She'd be his if he wanted her still. And she promised that she'd give him anything he wanted. Even kids who deserved a mother without a hang-up about color. As a child everyone told her that she was pretty. Her mother had lived through it. The teasing, the ridicule, the comments, and her unruly hair. She married light so that Ciara wouldn't have to suffer through that. Ciara shook her head. She was suffering through the loss of a love. She had a man who loved her, now he was gone; color hadn't done anything for her except run him away.

After seven messages he had relented. When he rang her door-bell she answered the door.

"I just brought over a few of your things. I honestly don't think we have anything to talk about."

"Dinner, please. That's all I want."

Dennis eyed her suspiciously before agreeing.

Ciara served dinner in the dining room and they ate in silence. Tender barbecue beef ribs, stuffed potato salad and garlic sautéed snow peas that they washed down with a hearty red wine. Ciara eyed Dennis as he ate everything on his plate.

"Thank you," he said. "It was delicious."

Ciara cleared the table and took the bottle of wine to the living room. She sat facing him on the sofa and he wouldn't look at her but she'd say what she had to anyway.

"Dennis. I'm sorry. I was wrong. So wrong."

"Ciara, how come you didn't tell me before now that this is how you felt? Or how you think?"

"Dennis, I don't really. My mother just goes through these long, drawn-out scenarios about what the children will or won't have based on their complexion."

"Well I don't believe it." He shook his head. "We have what we strive for in life."

"I know that."

"So, why do you let her tell you these things and ruin us?"

"I don't know, Dennis. She's my mother."

"I understand that, but if she's poisoning you, you don't just sit there and let it happen just because she's your mother."

"She's not poisoning me, Dennis."

"Yes she is, your mind. She's poisoning your mind."

"I'm sorry that's the way you see it."

"Let me ask you this, Ciara, is this whole color thing the real reason we haven't slept together after all of this time?"

Ciara couldn't look Dennis in the eyes.

"We're being honest here, right?" he asked.

"Yes."

"I need to know then," he said.

"Yes…" She nodded. "It's the reason. My mother said that if we—"

"Snap out of it, Ciara. Please?"

Ciara's eyes were drawn to his.

"I love you. That's all that matters. Nothing else. Not people, their opinions, or their personal views on what they think our kids will endure."

"I love you, too, Dennis." She caressed his face and brushed the frown from his forehead with her fingers.

"Prove it, Ciara."

"Prove what?" she asked.

"You love me. I need you to prove it to me."

"Prove it how?"

"Let me make love to you."

"Dennis, I—"

"You can, Ciara. Say you can. I've got to know if you love me that much."

"I do."

"Show me," he said.

Ciara leaned forward and Dennis wrapped his arms around her. He kissed her and told her that she was special. The most special woman that he had ever met. "That other woman means nothing to me. Absolutely nothing."

"Then why were you kissing her?"

"She was kissing me." He grinned.

Ciara was missing him too much to argue. She let it slide.

"I want to make it up to you," she said. "I never meant to hurt you either. That wasn't my intention."

Dennis turned her face away from him and kissed the side of her face, her earlobe. He slowly unzipped the back of her dress and slipped the cap sleeves from her shoulders. She had managed to quiet her mother's words, finally. She wouldn't let them ruin her evening, their wonderful evening that they were about to have together.

His lips tickled her neck, back, shoulders. His warm hands went between her legs instinctively. His fingers found her split first, and he grinned. She had shaved it for him. He liked her bald and she knew that. She tried not to tremble from his touch. That night was it. She knew she would let him indulge in her as he lowered himself to the carpeting and pulled her legs gently apart. They skipped all of the formalities and cordial exchange; she put it in his mouth. She didn't squirm. She relaxed and welcomed the heat of his breath, the thickness of his tongue and the sucking of his lips as they tugged gently on her femininity. Her legs dangled over his shoulders as he indulged face first in her juices and devoured her.

"More…" Ciara cooed.

She had waited so long for Dennis that she wanted him to spare nothing. Ravish her. She wanted to be ravished. He moved her dress out of the way and he released his pent-up passion from his pants. "Touch it," he said.

Ciara wanted to feel him, deep inside, but not in her hands. He was enlarged, throbbing, and about to burst with excitement, wanting desperately to be hugging her walls and making her call heaven.

"You want it? Say you want it." His fingers teased her mercilessly until she was ripe enough to be plucked.

"Please, hurry, Dennis. Don't make me wait," she gasped.

"In a minute," he teased. "Tell me how bad you want it." He tossed the sofa pillows on the floor.

"Oh, goodness, I want it really bad, Dennis," she said. "Please, put it in now." She clawed at him.

He was about to oblige her. Their naked bodies tangled in passion, her light flesh against his dark skin. He pushed the coffee table out of the way and positioned her on the Chinese carpet and kissed her down her back. He nudged her legs apart, used his fingers to open her up wide, and slid his thickness into her tight little offering, making her love every inch. Shade didn't matter as they both relished the feeling of being one.

The rocking rhythm assisted in making the moment a feverish bliss. They were both lost in the lust of the moment, eyes closed, him holding her shoulders and digging into her deeper and deeper as her breasts jiggled and she moaned his name. She thrust her hips against him voraciously, wanting more, wanting faster, wanting every drop he had in reserve.

They didn't even hear the key in the door or feel the prying eyes of someone standing there watching them get down and dirty.

Dennis was making Ciara his. Branding her. He was tapping on that G-spot and it made her knees weak.

"Is it good to you?" he asked.

"Yes…" She breathed rapidly.

Dennis turned her on her back and lifted one of her legs in the air and sucked her toes. He looked down and watched as all of him got lost inside of her. Ciara moaned and trembled delightfully. Her orgasm had found her.

A dozen more deep, lengthy strokes and Dennis let out a deep moan and shuddered as he filled her with an entire load of his thick, dark seed.

Ciara basked in the afterglow and ran her fingers through his hair as he rested on her chest, exhausted. She frowned recognizing the voice the second she heard it.

"Ciara?"

"Mama!" She scrambled for her clothes. "What are you doing here? How did you get in?" She wiped the sweat from her hairline.

"I have a key, remember? And I'm here to make sure you're okay but I see Dennis here has got that covered."

Dennis stepped into his pants and maintained his cool.

"I'm leaving," her mother announced. "We'll talk later."

"Mama, there's nothing to talk about. I love Dennis. I'm marrying him."

"Don't let sex cloud your brain, Ciara."

"Why are you meddling? Go home and let her live her life," Dennis demanded, fastening the buttons on his shirt.

"This is none of your concern." Her mother shot the words at him.

"She's my fiancée, so it certainly is." He looked at Ciara as he reached in his pant pocket. "Will you—" he handed Ciara the velvet box—"make me a proud man?"

Tears filled Ciara's eyes, even as she looked at her mother she knew that she had the power to make her own decisions.

"Yes, Dennis. I will."

Her mother turned and marched out of the apartment. Dennis pried open the red velvet case and pulled out the ring and slid it onto her finger.

As the tears slid down Ciara's cheeks, Dennis lifted her and carried her to the bedroom. In there they would talk, cuddle, and make plans for a future together.

Sunday morning brought Ciara breakfast in bed. Dennis was a good cook to boot. Ciara looked down at the tray and picked over Belgian waffles, fresh fruit, and juicy sausage links. She sipped the orange juice and smiled at Dennis, sitting next to her on the bed.

"I'm sorry about yesterday, Dennis. My mother, she—"

"Don't apologize."

"I have to, that was an intimate moment and—"

"You love me. Mothers have a sixth sense. She knows that you love me. Eventually we would have consummated that love." He touched her face softly. "Now your mama knows exactly how much," he teased.

She swatted at him.

"So what do you want to do today?" he asked.

She shrugged.

"I know a little place that sells love stamps and prints custom-made wedding invitations and engagement announcements." He winked.

"Yes." She nodded frantically. "We can do that." She removed her tray from her lap and squeezed him tightly in her arms.

"I love you, Dennis."

"Forever?" he asked, holding her just as tight.

"Forever." She looked down at the ring on her hand and noticed how it sparkled as if it was supposed to be there on her finger, making her day, her night, and her future. Her mother would have to accept her decision.

"I can't eat now." She grinned.

"Well, let's get going." He cleared away her tray.

They spent the better part of an hour in the shower lathering up each other's body and satisfying each other against the tiled shower walls before they tore themselves away and finally got dressed.

Arm in arm they headed out to find that place that Dennis was talking about where they could pick out the perfect invites and get busy planning the celebration of their engagement. They hadn't set a date. It was too soon for that, but she did know that when they did tie the knot that she would be Ciara Holland-Caldwell. They agreed on that because with her mother finally off her back she needed her individuality badly, and no matter how much she loved Dennis or how good he felt to her, she was still her own woman.

Please Come Again
by
Eric E. Pete

*R*ise and shine," he says in that accent of his. It's the kind that puts me on edge yet gets my juices flowing. He pulls the sheet off my face, sending the warm light of day flashing into my eyes, causing them to blink rapidly as they adjust. He simply laughs.

"Don't want to sleep the whole day away now, do we?"

"Good morning to you, too, Sam," I answer with a false lilt to my voice as I try to imitate his cadence. I fail. I don't sound even half as sexy.

I hear the waves crashing onto the rocks below. It's just as I remember. Even the smell of sea salt in the air tells me this is not a dream. I smile deeply.

"I've missed you, Melanie."

"It's only been a week," I say. I'm blushing slightly. Sam has a different look on his face this time.

He licks his luscious lips and moves his braids aside. "It's been one week too long."

I look out of the open windows and stare out into the Atlantic. "This was a good choice. It's so beautiful."

"As are you. Where would you like to go next week?"

"*Next week?* That's pretty presumptuous of you." I say this while being barely clothed. As I walk around the room, Sam's following me, slowly tracing my path across the creaky wooden floor. My bare ass is exposed to him.

"Melanie," he calls out in his deep, seductive tone. "I know you. I probably know you better than anyone out there."

Another wave crashes and I breathe deeply. One of my breasts pops out from under the white cotton fabric, which barely conceals it. Perspiration's beginning to form on it. I move to cover it again, but see Sam watching—he wants me. He always wants me. I lower my hand and leave it out.

His face contorts, giving life to the scar across the side of his face. I hate perfect men. It's funny because for his imperfect features, Sam is perfect in every other way. He's attentive, listens to me, and surprises me when he provides me with insight about myself. If I didn't love fucking him so much, he'd make for a good therapist.

Sam looks at me and then back down to my exposed breast. He squints and a cool, stiff wind blows in as if by command. The drapes flail about wildly as the gust whips in through the open windows and swirls around me. I'm startled as it blows between my legs and up into my shirt. The knot that was tied in it is no more for it has fallen completely open. The wind is still tugging at my shirt as if trying to rip it off my body.

I am completely exposed to his gaze and he smiles approvingly. He still hasn't moved from his perch in the window next to me, but motions for me to look down. My large brown nipples have sprung awake. Blood flowing into them has them swollen and eager. Below Sam's massive caramel chest and tight stomach, I can see blood is flowing to parts in his torn, faded jeans. My thighs begin tensing as they remember the delight inflicted between them by his thick, black cock every time we have a rendezvous like this.

"Are you thirsty?" he asks.

"Uh-huh," I respond. I'm thirsty alright, thirsty for the lovin' he gives like no other. No one makes me cum like Sam.

Sam hops down from his window seat and walks over to the side of the bed, all the while never taking his eyes off me. I watch his defined back muscles as he bends over. It looks like he could hold the world upon that beautiful back of his. I imagine it in action with him plunging in and out of me and feel the warm honey beginning to percolate inside my pussy. An open bottle of red wine appears in his hand with two delicate crystal goblets. He pours himself a glass first, wafting it under his nose before taking a small taste. A drop lingers on his lip.

I bring my hands up and rest them on each breast. I smile and he smiles back. He slows his walk toward me just enough to savor the view. I close my eyes and gently grasp each chocolate hill. Imagining Sam's hands instead of my own, I begin soft yet firm. Then I fondle each of them in circular motions, moving outward toward my nipples, which are yearning to be touched and tasted. The wind blowing outside picks up. I can sense Sam. He's nearby, but just out of reach. He's still watching…and wanting me. I know his cock is as hard as marble right about now.

I let out a moan and begin moving my hips like so. I'm really getting into it now as I dance and sway to unheard music in front of the open window. No one can see me besides Sam and the exotic birds flying overhead in the clouds. I giggle as I raise one breast up to my mouth and lap my tongue across the top of my sensitive, bulbous nipple. My other hand goes searching and finds its way down to my waiting clit. As two of my fingertips trace across the sweet spot, goose bumps pop up all over my body. My fingers continue on their journey and wind up inside me where I bury them deep inside my wet treasure.

As I feel Sam upon me, I open my eyes and look at him. He's poured me a glass of wine as well.

"Still thirsty?"

"Yes. But I don't need the glass."

Before I can take a breath, he's upon me, pinning me against the wall. I rest my hands on the windowsill and arch back. I feel his lips running over my neck and sucking on my ear. I let out a kittenlike purr to show my approval. As he holds me steady, he raises the glass precariously over my head. I tilt my head back and let him pour.

The crimson wine rains down into my mouth and splashes down the front of my exposed, trembling body. My shirt is stained and probably ruined, but I don't care. As I swallow and gasp, Sam is right there licking and kissing all over me. I am a puppet in his powerful arms as he moves me around to better drink the wine off my neck, then off my breasts, followed by my stomach, then between my legs where the last few drops have sought refuge. With him down on his knees, I choose to hold him there. The wine is gone, but it's time for Sam to taste the *real* intoxicating drink that awaits him.

I orgasm more times than I can count, sending my nectar spilling out as if released from floodgates. It streams down my thighs but Sam catches most of it before continuing to generate more with the dance of his tongue against my clit.

"Do you love me?" I ask while coming down briefly from my last eruption.

"I live to serve you," he answers. "And I love you because you let me."

Tears stream down my face as I brace myself against the wall because my legs are failing me. Emotions are sweeping over me, but I control them rather than letting them control me.

Without warning, Sam effortlessly picks me up, which is no small feat. I'm not the smallest of women, but I am carried with as much effort as the lifting of a pencil off a desk.

I feel on Sam's muscles and kiss his large, full lips with my own. His braids are between my fingers as I push his mouth against mine and suck his sweet tongue.

"Is it hard?" I ask, already knowing. With Sam, it's *always* hard.

He simply smiles with a mischievous twinkle in his eye.

I expect a thud as I fall onto the bed, but it's like landing on a bed of feathers. I smile eagerly, almost high, ready to accept what Sam has to give. I discard my wine-stained top then enjoy the view as Sam begins to unzip his jeans. I crave the cock that rolls out before me. I slowly crawl across the bed as if possessed by unseen demons. Sam has dropped his pants to his ankles and stands before me at the foot of the bed.

He spreads his massive arms and grasps the bedposts. It's as if he is at the altar paying tribute to me, his nubian queen. His rod is a sacrifice I gladly take into my mouth. For the first time today, I see weakness in Sam as his legs buckle slightly. I feast on the head of his swollen penis and hum with delight, which causes him to tremble yet again. He holds steadfastly to the bedposts as I swallow more and more with each stroke of my head into him. I could go on and on sucking him, but I have other parts of my body longing for a taste. Besides, I know our time is limited this day.

"Melanie," he coos with satisfaction as I move off him, leaving a beaded trail of moisture between my mouth and the head of his dick that I catch and swallow before it falls off.

I back farther onto the bed, sliding my body lazily across the sheets. He begins to follow like a hungry lion. I then turn over to expose my plump ass to him. I want him to see and admire all my curves.

"You know how I want it," I say as I rise up onto my hands and knees. I'm still moving away from him, but he overtakes me. I grunt when I feel his cock part my moist pussy lips. A woman can try to be all prim and proper and tell you she has another favorite position, but nothing beats doggie style.

Sam's firm hands grip me tight around the sides of my hips and hold me steady. I spread my legs farther and move my ass higher. My face is down into the bed itself and I am ready to take every inch inside me.

"You like that?" he asks teasingly.

"Harder. Fuck me harder."

Sam spreads my ass cheeks as he delivers just what I needed up in me. Skin on skin smacks for what seems like an eternity. Talk about hurting so good. I bite the sheets to keep from screaming, but lose all sanity when I feel him reach around the front of me and stimulate my clit further as he hammers home. My juices gush all over his dick, covering it with a thick cream. Like I said before…no one makes me cum like Sam.

When I think I can't take it anymore, I fall onto my stomach. He doesn't stop though as he rides me down into the bed, his pelvis grinding all up into my ass. The change of position and of his stroke brings with it a whole new set of sensations, and I let out a yelp of delight as I discover I still have farther to go to reach my limit. He is going to take me there.

"Oh yes!"

Sam rides me farther, reaching underneath me to take firm grasp of both breasts. I feel his fingertips tweaking and toying with my overly sensitive nipples and his hot breath on my neck as a passion mark is beginning to form there.

We are covered in sweat now and during the scant seconds I'm able to focus, I see that it has turned from day to night. The sun's still out though. A storm has begun to blow in and the black clouds are filling the sky.

We continue fucking even as the wind picks up and the rain begins to fall outside. Sam suddenly stops and turns me over.

"I want to see you," he says as a loud thunderclap startles me and causes my ears to ring.

"Don't stop. Please don't stop." Lightning now flashes through the room in one window and out the other.

I part my legs and let him slide between them as he comes to rest on top of me. Our fingers interlace as he holds my hands down on the bed. I feel him sucking on my breasts and I begin ascending to heaven again.

The storm outside has come in.

"I love you, Melanie."

Drops driven by the wind land on my face and I taste the ones that land on my lips. At first they're sporadic—driven in only when there is a large gust. The rain starts coming down harder with each boom of thunder and crackle of lightning, but we don't care.

"Mmmm. Love me, Sam. It feels so good, baby."

The rain on our bodies now replaces our sweat. As the storm grows in intensity, so does our lovemaking. I spread my legs out farther and run my toenails across the sheets, which are now falling off the mattress.

When I've gone beyond heaven, I urge Sam on.

"Cum in me, baby. Yeah, that's it. Give it to me. Mama wants to feel you."

I feel his intensity rise as he builds toward his climax and it turns me on even more.

"Mel…"

"That's it, baby. Don't disappoint me. I want it allllll."

"Oh gawd."

"Yesss."

"Oh gawd."

"Yesss!"

"Oh gawd!"

"Mmmm. Give it to me," I purr.

He spasms for a second before his back arches, then spasms again. I let out a gasp and feel the hot rush of his cum as he explodes and slams into me. Normally, I wouldn't let a man go off in me, but Sam's not just any man. He's different, you see. As we lay there locked in an embrace, the storm outside begins to subside and move on. The sun has begun to reassert itself. The floor of the room is still damp with small puddles of water here and there on the wooden floor.

Rather than rolling over and going to sleep, Sam plants gentle kisses on my cheek. I smile and enjoy the tender moment in his arms. I know it's about to end until our next rendezvous.

"Care to join me in the shower?" he asks.

"No. I think I'll just lay here and reflect."

"It was good for you, right?"

"When is it ever not good?"

"Very well then," he says, chuckling. Man, how I love his accent.

Sam finds the strength to somehow rise. I stare at his braids and into his dark brown eyes.

"What?"

"I want another kiss before you get in the shower," I say.

"I think I can oblige."

He leans over and gives me a soft, sensual kiss. He pulls slightly on my bottom lip before letting it go.

As he begins to walk off, I call out in a low tone, "Sam?"

"Yes?"

"Paris, next week?"

He thinks to himself, then answers, "Paris it is."

I blow a kiss to him, then he's off to the shower. I sigh. I really want to join him, but it's not in today's plans.

I find one semidry sheet on the floor and pull it up into the bed with me. I breathe deeply, then take one final look around the bare room. The wine bottle and the goblets are overturned on the floor by the window. A smile of joy fixes on my face as I close my eyes and pull the sheet over my face.

Darkness. Again.

Out of the darkness, I see a tiny red light. It's flashing, but barely visible. I focus on it, and it gets larger and brighter.

Eventually, I'm enveloped in the red light, which has stopped flashing. The waves I heard crashing on the rocks are gone like a faded memory.

A series of chimes echo around me now and I listen to their cue. With my right hand I reach out and pull. And bright lights flood in.

I'm a little disoriented at first as I step out through the hatch I just opened. I carefully remove the goggles I'm wearing and unzip the yellow bodysuit I'm fitted with. I pause for a second, then proceed cautiously down the steps.

I stop to run a gloved hand across the smooth, metallic skin of the sphere I had just been inside. A feeling of melancholy sweeps over me.

"Good-bye, Sam," I say with a hint of regret and sadness in my voice.

I let out a sigh then stroll off to the dressing room to change clothes. On the sphere, just below where I had run my hands are the words engraved "Sexually Automated Maintenance" or S.A.M. for short.

When I emerge from changing into my executive wardrobe, I approach the front desk of the facility with gym bag in hand. The same gentleman is manning the counter.

"Was everything to your liking today, Madame President Palmer?"

"It always is, Herschel." I stick my hand under the blue light of the scanner and watch the beam of light move across the barcode on the back of my hand. My account has now been deducted.

"Same time next week?"

"Yes, but make it *two* appointments. One of them for Paris. I'll call when I decide about the other."

"Of course, Madame President. And as we always say to our satisfied customers…Please come again."

"Don't worry…*I will*."

Possessive Passion
by
Jacquie Bamberg Moore

*S*adé was spinning in the CD changer as Jada bit into the soft suede cushion that covered the arm of the sofa. She directed all of her concentration to the sweet lyrics being crooned by the sultry songstress and away from the dull ache that was beginning to form in her lower abdomen.

Her boyfriend, Trevor, had had her bent over doggie style, for the last ten minutes, banging her with a driving force that made his breathing jagged and his words choppy as he asked her questions that all warranted the same answer: "Yes, big daddy."

Despite the fact that Trevor's large hands were locked around her waist, her body rhythmically jarred with every forceful stroke causing her knees to dig deeper into the sofa and her already very sensitive nipples to rub against the plush material.

What is he trying to do? Push my uterus up into my throat? she thought as she reached back and placed her hand firmly on his thigh. "You're hurting me," she said a little sexier than she intended.

Trevor grabbed her wrist and bent his body over hers, planting her hand back on the sofa. He whispered in her ear, "Do you want me to stop?"

She could feel his heart thumping against her back. She shook her head, "Don't stop. Just go easy." She turned to face him and opened her mouth to receive his tongue.

Trevor slowly put space between them as he let his kisses move from her lips to her shoulders, then gently down her back and over her ample buttocks.

Jada jumped and a small noise escaped her throat when his

tongue came in contact with her anus. She oohed and aahed and moaned and groaned as Trevor went to work licking, biting, and sucking on everything that was usually shielded by her silky panties.

"Don't move," he ordered sexily before slapping her lightly on her ass and walking toward the back of her apartment.

Jada obeyed, holding her pose as Sadé told her the story of the "Sweetest Taboo." She looked up when she heard Trevor return to the living room. She took in the fullness of his toned naked body as he lessened the distance between them—warm eyes, sweet smile, broad chest, tight abs, and a ten-inch, bobbing penis in her face. She stuck out her tongue, lightly touching the head.

Trevor gently stroked his shaft before grabbing the back of her head and guiding himself into her mouth. She locked her jaws in a sucking position and tried to keep up with his pace. Trevor eased out of her mouth and positioned himself behind her.

Jada was ready for him this time. She pushed her ass up as far as she could and waited for him to fill her with delight. He began fingering her wetness, making her moan with pleasure. "Give it to me," she begged.

"You want it?"

"Yes, big daddy."

Jada squeezed her eyes shut tightly and held her breath as Trevor slowly entered her ass with his large penis. It hurt like hell. She tried to bear it because she wanted to please him, but she couldn't take the pain. She jerked away and turned to face him.

"I can't take it—"

"Yes, you can." His words were soft. "I'll put more lube on." He picked up the tube from the coffee table and applied a healthy amount to the top of his dick. "Turn over."

Jada hesitantly returned to her position. *So that's what he went to get,* she thought. When she felt Trevor's hand clamp down on her waist to steady her, she sucked in her breath and began massaging her clit to help ease the pain.

"Tight," he grunted between clenched teeth as he guided himself in and out of her with easy strokes at first, and then deeper, faster ones until there was no movement at all except for their labored breathing.

Trevor backed out of Jada and sat next to her on the sofa. This is how it has always ended—no cuddling, no soft-spoken words or breathless kisses—just silence. She stood and headed for the bathroom, then turned back and glanced at him, as he lay spent from their lovemaking. His limp penis was on his thigh, the condom halfway down the now-soft flesh.

In the bathroom, Jada stepped into a hot shower and let it massage her sore spots. She was lathering up when Trevor joined her.

"Hey," he said as he stepped into the tub and right in front of the flow of water.

She stepped back and made room for him. "Hey, yourself." She smiled big, like a woman in love.

He returned the smile and took her washcloth from her. "Let me get your back."

She turned around and he ran the soapy cloth across and down her back and finally around to her breasts. He cupped them gently with his soapy hands and stroked her nipples.

She twisted so that she could look up into his warm eyes. Jada wanted to tell him that she loved him, but she dared not try that again. The first—and only—time she uttered those three words, Trevor stormed out of her apartment and didn't speak to her for weeks. He told her that love further complicated their already complicated relationship. So she never said it again—*aloud*. But it was in her heart and it was loud and clear in her actions and the good deeds she loved doing for him. It was especially apparent in their intense lovemaking.

By the time Trevor was dressed and ready to leave, her mood had become somber. For her, this was the hardest part. Seeing him leave always made her feel desolate and desperate.

He was standing at her front door with his hands tucked inside his jacket pockets. She was sitting across the room on the arm of the sofa. She pulled her robe closer around her and asked, "When am I going to see you again?"

"I'm not sure. I'll call you."

That was the rehearsed answer she got every time. That's why she hated herself even more for asking.

Trevor turned the locks and reached for the doorknob. Her heart leaped in her chest. She wasn't ready for him to leave. She had to say something quickly to get him to stay awhile longer. She stammered and came up with, "Before you go, I just want to know if we're going to see each other next weekend?" She stood and went over to him.

"That sounds good." He opened the door a little. "I'll call you," he repeated.

"Okay." Her eyes were on his sneakers when he kissed the top of her head and left.

She sighed deeply before locking her door and going to her bedroom. She clicked on the TV and checked her answering machine. She always turned her phone off when Trevor was over.

She had two messages. She hit the play button and listened. The first caller hung up, and the second caller was her best friend, Kim. "Hey, Jada, I'm trying to catch up with you. I thought you might want to see a movie tonight or something. Trevor is out with his boys doing that male-bonding thing and I'm kind of bored. Call me when you get in. Bye."

Jada closed her eyes and sat on the edge of her bed as guilt crept up on her and covered her from head to toe.

Why did she ever let this *thing* happen with Trevor? She didn't even know how it got to this point, and how was she supposed to keep it from going any farther?

She was torn. Part of her wanted to end things with Trevor because he had been dating her best friend for the past two and a half years. But the other part of her had fallen so deeply in love with him that she couldn't imagine being without him.

She was hooked from the first time they'd made love four months ago on her living room floor. She'd never forget it. It was the day she had moved into her apartment and Kim was supposed to spend the morning helping her clean and get settled before the moving company arrived with her furniture and boxes.

Kim called her very early that morning and said that she had gotten her period and was on the verge of dying from menstrual cramps. She told Jada that she felt bad and promised to send Trevor over to help with whatever he could.

Jada got to her new one-bedroom apartment at seven in the morning with mop and bucket in tow. Trevor strolled in around noon and the moving company, which was scheduled to deliver her belongings at two o'clock, didn't show at all.

By the time six o'clock had rolled around, she was sitting in an empty apartment—except for the things she'd brought over in her car—angry, frustrated, and hungry. She started complaining and Trevor whipped out his cell phone and ordered a large pie with toppings and a two-liter soda from Domino's.

They had been chitchatting all day, but they were halfway through the pizza before any real conversation started. Jada began, "Have you spoken to Kim?"

Trevor nodded, with his plastic cup still up to his mouth.

"Is she feeling any better?"

He took his time swallowing before answering, "She's feeling a little better. I spoke to her earlier when you went outside to look for the moving van."

"Oh. You really should be there with her. But I'd be lying if I told you I didn't appreciate the company."

"No problem. Don't mention it." He smiled.

Maybe it was something in his words, perhaps something in the way he smiled at her. Whatever it was, the light on their innocent meeting had shifted. The pizza in her mouth became dry and tasteless, but her pussy was alive and wet.

Jada drained her cup and started to stand. Trevor put his hand on her forearm and his touch made her stop in her tracks. She looked down into his face and there she found the unmistakable mask of desire that every woman longs to see on her lover's face.

She sat back down. "Trevor, I—"

He put his finger to her lips to silence her. He was looking so deeply into her eyes, she thought he might be able read her mind. Then their lips met. The first touch was soft and brushlike. She pulled away slightly, but he would have no resistance. He leaned into her body, cupped the back of her neck, and kissed her firmly. His tongue danced in her mouth, then flicked at her chin and earlobe before he finally found her neck and collarbone.

Even in the heated moment, Jada knew it was wrong—as good as it felt—still, it was wrong. She fought her way out of his kiss and scooted across the hardwood floor away from him. She could barely catch her breath as her common sense wrestled with her body for control. She stared at him. He stared back.

"Jada—"

"Leave."

"Jada—"

"Get out, Trevor," she said weakly.

He didn't move immediately. He just stared at her in silence.

She was afraid to look at him because he might see that she was struggling to maintain control. She only looked up when the front door opened and closed. Even then, she didn't move.

Her mind immediately became jumbled with thoughts. She had to get to a pay phone and call Kim and tell her what a lying, two-timing dog Trevor was. But what if Trevor twisted the story and said she'd made the first move? Kim would never believe that. Had she made the first move? Did she say or do something that may have been misleading? Not that she could recall. Maybe she should just keep quiet. Kim would never have to know and from now on, she'd just keep her distance from Trevor. No. Kim was her best friend and she had to know about this.

Jada stood and stretched before resting her hands on her hips in disbelief and took the whole scenario in. Fine-ass Trevor had just made a move on her. *He probably wanted to do it all along,* she thought as she bent to collect the trash.

She checked the pocket of her jeans for her new key and ample change for the pay phone, and then headed out of the door where she bumped into Trevor standing in the hallway.

Jada nearly jumped a foot into the air and the pizza box made a loud echoing sound as it hit the floor. "Trevor, what are you doing?"

"I couldn't leave." His voice was soft and mellow.

She wasn't expecting that kind of response and immediately began to weaken. She mustered up as much attitude as she could before speaking. "Well, you might want to try because I'm going to call Kim right now and let her know what just went down."

He stepped into her space, causing her to back up into the wall. "Why would you want to do that?"

She couldn't answer. Her mind was a complete blank. It could have been the rock-hard dick that was pressed against her waist that held her logic and her words captive.

Before she knew it, Trevor had her back inside the apartment and butt-naked on the cold hardwood floor, sucking his big dick and begging for more as he fucked her long, hard, and continuously.

She never made that phone call.

Jada rang Kim's doorbell and waited. She was ready for their shopping spree at Green Acres Mall on Long Island. She had on her comfortable shopping shoes, her cute shopping clothes, and had all of her credit cards ready to be swiped. She was going to hit Sam Goody first to get Luther Vandross's latest CD, then she wanted to get a gift for her mother's birthday at the end of the month. She was deep in thought when Kim finally snatched the door open in a furry.

"Well, good morning to you too." Jada was speaking to Kim's back as she stormed toward the kitchen.

Jada closed the front door and followed her lead to the laundry room where Kim was separating clothes on the floor.

Kim reached into the pile of dark clothes, picked up a navy blue ribbed turtleneck and shoved it at her.

"What?" Jada took a step back.

"Smell it!" Kim ordered sharply.

Hesitantly, Jada leaned into the sweater and inhaled. The scent was familiar. The scent was hers. She struggled to meet Kim's eyes. "So?"

She dropped the sweater, picked up a T-shirt and held it out to Jada, and again she sniffed. Same smell.

"You recognize the fragrance?" Kim was almost yelling.

Beads of perspiration began forming on Jada's brow and her heartbeat had quickened tremendously. She wanted to speak, but her mouth had suddenly become extremely dry.

Finally Kim answered her own question. "It's Happy by Clinique. I don't wear that shit!" She threw the T-shirt back onto the pile and turned and leaned on the washing machine with her face buried in her hands.

Jada was suddenly afraid. Everyone knew that Happy by Clinique was her favorite and she wore it all the time. She was busted! *Oh, God, why did Kim have to find out like this?* she thought. Her mind began racing with excuses and apologies, but just as she was about to give up her story, Kim's hands moved from her face to her hips and she slowly faced Jada.

"Jada, let me tell you something," her voice was surprisingly level. "I suspected this. A few weeks ago, Trevor pulled a disappearing act and when I questioned him, he gave me some shady excuse that didn't make any sense. Then, I really put the pieces together the other night when I called you and left that message about us going to the movies."

Jada was literally shaking. She didn't know if she should stay or run, admit to the indiscretion or lie about it. She cleared her throat and tried to moisten her lips with her parched tongue. She found the folding table and leaned against it for support.

"See—" Kim cocked her head to the side— "right after I called you, I got a call from one of the guys Trevor was supposedly hanging out with. That's when I knew, without a shadow of a doubt that Trevor was up to no good. But why, Jada? What have I done to deserve this kind of treatment?"

Jada didn't know what to say, so she just decided that she'd try to explain her actions and tell Kim that she never meant for things to go this far. "Kim, I, don't know what to say." She croaked and wiped her wet face.

Kim stopped ranting and stared at her for a minute before her own tears started falling. "Why, Jada?"

Jada silently shook her head. She could find no words to explain her betrayal.

Kim inhaled deeply and wiped her face with the back of her sleeve. "Jada, you're my best friend in the whole world." She sniffed. "That's why I know when I find out who this tramp is, you're going to help me break her fucking neck!"

Jada was stunned motionless. Her mouth dropped open and she managed a strained, "Huh?"

"I know what you're thinking: I should be trying to kill Trevor's ass. And I am. I'm going to make him sorry he ever thought about disrespecting me."

Still rebounding from shock, Jada was uncertain of her next move. She wanted to make an excuse to leave, but couldn't think of anything good enough. She certainly didn't feel like going shopping.

In fact she didn't feel like doing anything except crawling in a hole and dying.

"I'm sorry I upset you, Jada. You share my pain and hurt. You're a true friend." She smiled and gave Jada's arm a gentle squeeze before leaving the laundry room.

Yeah, right, Jada thought and followed Kim back into the kitchen. They both sat at the table where Kim poured them tall glasses of her delicious lemonade.

"I know I spoiled your shopping mood," Kim said.

"Don't worry about it. We can shop anytime. Are you going to be okay?"

"Of course I am." She smiled devilishly.

Jada became nervous again. If Kim began digging too much, she was sure to discover that it was Jada on the other end of her pain. "What are you going to do?" She didn't try to hide her concern.

"I'm not sure yet. I need time to think." She took a long drink from her glass before meeting Jada's eyes. Her words were soft when she spoke. "I loved him. I thought he was going to be 'the one.' " She made quotations marks with her fingers while fresh tears eased down her face. She stood and went over to the window.

Jada's guilt was getting the best of her. She had an overwhelming urge to confess, to take on all the blame so that she could ease her best friend's broken heart, but how could she when she too was so very deep in love with Trevor? She was also hurting. For the past few months she had lived with the pain of not being able to have him all to herself. But if Kim no longer wanted him, that left endless possibilities for her relationship with Trevor to grow.

Jada went over to Kim and rested her hand on her shoulder. "I know you love him, but you don't need the aggravation. In fact what you need is someone who's going to love and respect you in return."

"You're right," Kim softly agreed.

"And if Trevor doesn't want to treat you right, then there are thousands of men out there who will."

Kim turned around to face her friend. "Everything you're saying is true, but it doesn't make it hurt any less. Trevor is cheating on me. He's hiding things from me, lying to me, and he felt he couldn't be honest with me. If he wasn't happy being with me, he could have told me. That's what bothers me the most." She shook her head woefully. "I thought that everything was great between us and I was totally un-aware that our relationship was in trouble."

"This is not your fault, Kim. You couldn't have known."

"Why couldn't I have known? I live in the same house with him and sleep in the same bed. We've spent almost three years together. Why couldn't I have known?"

"It's not your fault that Trevor is good at being a liar and a cheat. Remember, you haven't done anything wrong."

"True. That's why when he gets home tonight I'm going to let him have it. If he wants to be with this other woman so bad, then she can have him. I won't hold him back from doing anything he wants to do. Jada, you're absolutely right, there are thousands—no, millions— of men out there who would love to have a fine, sweet thing like me."

"Yeah, let her have his ass. I can always move on and find somebody better." Kim went to the table and picked her glass of lemon-onade. "A toast to new beginnings." She held up her glass.

Reluctantly, Jada went to the table, retrieved her glass and tapped it against Jada's. "New beginnings," she repeated softly.

Jada drank her lemonade and pretended not to see the hurt look in Kim's eyes. After all, Kim and Trevor's breakup was the best thing for everyone involved.

For the remainder of the afternoon, Jada listened to Kim vent, cry, and then vent some more about how undeserving she was of this kind of treatment. Jada was lost in her own guilty thoughts when Kim stomped passed her, "… And I'm not washing his clothes. Let his whore wash his funky drawers!"

Kim stomped up the stairs and Jada followed. She stood in the doorway of Kim's bedroom and watched her as she went about throwing clothes into her suitcase. She stopped in the middle of the floor and scratched her head before turning to Jada. "I need to stay at your place for a few days. I hope you don't mind."

Jada gave her a reassuring smile before going over and hugging her tightly. "Kim, you're doing the right thing by getting out of this relationship." She stepped back and eyed Kim closely. She looked so sad, Jada's determination almost wavered. She quickly looked away and busied herself with Kim's suitcase. "We're going to have a great time staying together. It'll be like living at the dorm again." Her words were full of forced cheer.

"I need to get some files for work next week," Kim said quietly before leaving the room.

Jada covered her eyes with her hands to help keep her tears inside. She had no idea that this was going to be so emotionally draining. She took several deep breaths in an effort to compose herself and went into the bathroom to collect toiletries she thought Kim might need. She was trying to decide if she should pack a pedicure set when she unmistakably heard Trevor's truck pulling into the driveway. She went back out into the hall and Kim was standing at the top of the stairs with her suitcase.

"He's home," She said softly.

"Kim, listen, don't give him the satisfaction of seeing you upset. Let's just leave peacefully."

"The hell I will!" She snatched up her suitcase and went down the stairs.

The last thing Jada wanted was to be around when this confrontation took place. She waited a moment and listened.

"Hey, what's up with the suitcase?" Trevor asked casually.

There was a brief pause, then Kim's wails echoed through the house and sent Jada into a panic. When she got to the bottom of the stairs, Kim's petite five-foot, two-inch frame was all over Trevor, landing a series of blows on his face and chest. "I hate you! I hate you! Why, Trevor? Why?" Kim screamed again and again.

Trevor tried to shield himself from the surprise attack and finally managed to grab her wrists and shake Kim out of her rage.

They stood, breathing heavily and staring each other down. Kim was the first to break. She crumpled to the floor in a fit of uncontrollable sobs and Jada ran to her side to comfort her. She stole a peek at Trevor as he slowly backed away from them and sat on the arm of the sofa until Kim rode out the wave of emotion.

When she was able to pull herself together, Kim raised up from the floor and spoke in a shaky voice, "I want you out of my house by Friday."

Trevor looked directly into Jada's eyes and asked, "What is this about, Kim?"

"You know what this is about." Kim said and picked up her suitcase.

If looks could kill, Jada would have been assassinated right on the spot. She knew what he was thinking: that she had betrayed him. She wanted to run into his arms and tell him that she'd never do that. Their secret was safely locked away within the confines of her heart. She wanted to let him know that this was just a twist of fate and that she hadn't planned it.

Trevor turned to Kim and grabbed her arm when she started for the door. "We need to talk about this."

She yanked free. "Go to hell!" she barked as she went out the door.

The first three days Kim stayed at her house, Jada spent most of her time, playing two roles: hostess and home wrecker—neither of which she was very good at. She took extra care with Kim's feeling and tried not to seem too pushy when making suggestions about how to handle Trevor. And when Trevor called, she always did Kim the favor of running interference by taking the call and gently asking Trevor not to call again.

At the same time, Jada was keeping in constant contact with Trevor, in a vain effort to convince him of her loyalty to him and to their secret. She filled her conversation with lies about how Kim was totally through with him and ready to move on. She also told him that she asked Kim to give him another chance but she was unwilling to listen to reason.

Wednesday evening after work, Jada and Kim met at Two Steps Down restaurant for dinner and a chance to loosen up all the tension they'd both been under.

The waitress delivered their food and Jada immediately started in on her smothered chicken and macaroni and cheese. She was venting about her day and enjoying the atmosphere when she finally looked up and noticed that Kim had barely touched what was on her plate.

She put her fork down. "What is it?"

"Huh?" Startled, Kim focused on Jada.

"What's on your mind?"

"How long have we known each other?"

Jada shrugged. "Ten years. Freshman year at Indiana State."

Kim smiled, "Remember how excited we were when we discovered that we were both from Brooklyn? That was something."

Jada nodded and took a sip of iced tea to wash away the lump that was forming in her throat.

"And ever since then, you have been taking care of me." Kim shook her head sadly and Jada reached across the table and gave her hand a gentle squeeze.

"You took care of me when we were pledging our sorority, you always kept me encouraged when I didn't do well in my classes, and I can never thank you enough for holding me together when my mom suddenly died after we graduated."

Weighed down by guilt, Jada could barely lift her eyes to meet Kim's, so she focused on her shoulders instead. "You've done a great job at supporting me too. You really came through for me when my parents got divorced. That was a difficult time in my life."

"I've never told you this, but I've always admired your tough exterior, your tenacity and ability to get through a crisis with minimal bumps and bruises. Sometimes I wish I were more like you—"

Jada held her hand up, "Kim, you're fine just as you are. Now, we came here tonight to have a good time and enjoy ourselves. Let's change the subject."

"Jada, I'm not enjoying myself. I need more time before I can just jump back into the swing of things."

Jada flagged their waitress and asked to have Kim's meal wrapped to go. The emotional roller coaster she was riding was beginning to get to her.

When they got to Jada's apartment, Trevor had left a sugary message declaring his love for Kim and begging her to call him.

"The nerve of that bastard!" Jada accidentally said aloud.

"I think he sounds sweet and sincere," Kim said softly.

Jada shot her a look. "I think he sounds guilty and full of shit. If he continues to call, I'm going to have his number blocked." She was hurt and angry that he could leave such a message knowing that she'd hear it.

No sooner than the words left her mouth, the phone rang, causing them both to jump. Kim was closer to the phone and picked it up.

"Hello?"

"Yes, Trevor. We just got in."

Jada dashed to her bedroom and picked up the extension. "Trevor, I have asked you several times not to call here."

"Kim, I miss you and I want you to come home."

"I will as soon as you're gone," she said with false bravado.

"You don't mean that." He kept his voice smooth.

"Look, Trevor, I know you're seeing someone else. I don't want you to have to lower yourself and sneak around like a dog in heat. So, I'm going to bow out gracefully. Now you and your girlfriend can be together without having to look over your shoulder all the time."

Jada held her breath and listened as Kim delivered the breakup speech that would land Trevor and her together.

"You're right. I'm not going to lie to you. I was seeing someone else, but it's not what you think."

"How do you know what I think?" she asked angrily.

Jada's heart soared to her throat and she immediately became so overwhelmed with trepidation, she had to sit on the side of her bed. She wanted to interject, but her voice was lost.

"Look at how you're behaving. Why can't we sit down and talk like rational adults?"

"Who is she?" Kim demanded to know.

"W-w-who cares?" Jada stammered. "What matters is that she means more to him than you do." Her breathing was jagged.

"Is it important?" Trevor asked.

"Obviously it is. You jeopardized our relationship to be with her. She sounds pretty important."

"Well, she's not."

Jada almost lost her mind. She couldn't believe what she was hearing. In a fit of rage, she slammed down the receiver, rushed into the living room, and almost broke Kim's arm trying to wrestle the phone from her and threw it across the room.

Kim jumped up, "What the hell is wrong with you?" she shouted. "I almost got him to tell me who this tramp is!"

"Kim, don't lose focus! You want to be respected for standing strong in the face of adversity. Well this is your chance to get started."

"I want to know who she is!" Kim was almost in tears.

"Then what? After you find out who she is? What is it going to change?"

"Nothing."

"Right. It's not going to change one thing about that fact that he was sneaking around to be with her and how much he hurt you."

Defeated, Kim sat back down and closed her eyes. Jada turned away from the sad sight and massaged her forehead. "I need some air," Jada finally said.

Kim let out a long sigh. "I'm going to take a shower and go to bed."

Jada waited until she heard the water running in the bathroom, then called Trevor's cell.

"We need to talk," she said when he answered.

"About what?" He snapped.

"Meet me at the spot in thirty minutes." Jada cleared the lined, dialed 411, then hung up and left.

When she pulled into the parking lot of The Motor Inn on the North Conduit, Trevor's truck was already there. As she approached the driver's side, he stepped out and she immediately noticed how tired he looked.

"We're in Room 119," he said without meeting her eyes.

Jada led the way and as soon as the door closed behind them, she broke down and cried. She ran into the bathroom and waited for Trevor to come in after her, but when he didn't, Jada eventually forced herself to go to him.

He was sitting at the small table with his head in his hands. He must have sensed her standing over him. He lifted his head and looked at her through teary eyes.

She went to him and wrapped her arms around his neck and held on for dear life as they openly wept together.

Jada pulled back and looked into his sad eyes. She used her thumbs to wipe the tears from his cheeks. He looked so vulnerable and yet so incredibly desirable. She could no longer resist the urge to kiss him and brought her lips down softly on his eyelids, then his nose, and finally his mouth.

His desire matched hers and he returned the kiss with just as much fervor and passion. He lifted her and planted her on her feet in the middle of the bed. She towered over him and stroked his head with her hands as he stroked her navel with his tongue.

He expertly unhooked, unbuttoned, and unzipped everything

until there was no barrier between them.

She didn't realize that she was still crying until Trevor eased her onto her back and tears slid into her ears.

Trevor took his time, gently probing her openings with his tongue, just as she liked it.

Jada massaged her nipples and moved her hips in rhythm with Trevor, until the thrill became too much for her. She moaned and pulled away from him, but he followed, still holding on to her sensitive clit. She began bucking like a wild woman, but Trevor had her legs locked in an open position with his strong arms.

"No! No! I can't take it! Trevor!" She tried to wiggle out of his grip, but he would not let up until she reached a second climax. Only then did he release the hold on her and kiss her inner thighs. He took a deep breath and blew a steady stream of cool air on her wetness, which caused her to shiver with delight.

She was still trying to regulate her breathing when Trevor crawled up her body until his hard dick met her slippery opening and found its way in.

Jada gasped for air and dug her fingernails into his firm ass. "Trevor." His name left her lips in a whisper. He felt so good to her, she could hardly stand the intense pleasure.

Jada maneuvered her body from underneath his and put her lips around the head of his dick and began sucking vigorously.

Trevor took a handful of hair and held it away from her face, so that he could see her lips move up and down his thick shaft. With his free hand, he rubbed her perky nipples.

Ready for more action, Jada stood and Trevor assisted her in mounting him. She moaned loudly as their bodies met and shifted her weight back and forth until the friction caused her to see double. She began to lose her rhythm, so Trevor took control and moved inside of her until she begged him to stop.

"Turn me over," she demanded breathlessly.

He stood, picking her up as well. They shared a heated kiss before she got on her feet and turned her back to him. "I want you to put it in my ass." She bent over and gripped the cheap, stained bed-spread.

Trevor's hard-on had increased. He spread her cheeks and slid his tongue into the tight opening before attempting to enter.

"Oh, God!" Jada screamed.

"Want me to stop?"

The pain had rendered her speechless.

"It's halfway in. I'll leave it like this." Trevor leaned over and used his fingers to help her relax.

The sensation made her moan and after a while, she began to push back against Trevor. She actually enjoyed the painful stretch of her body as it accommodated him. She moved in rhythm with him until he jerked away from her and she felt the hot streams on her back.

Trevor was breathless, and his forehead and chest were covered in perspiration. He turned away from her and headed for the bathroom.

Jada followed silently, too lost in her own emotion to be offended by his dismissive attitude.

By the time Jada and Trevor were showered and dressed, it was after eleven o'clock. They were standing awkwardly by the front door when Jada finally spoke. "I just want to let you know that I didn't tell Kim anything."

He stared at her blankly and waited for her to continue.

"When I got to the house last weekend, she was ranting about suspicions she had."

"And what did you do to encourage those suspicions?" he asked calmly.

Jada's eyes went to the floor.

"I thought so."

She began wringing her hands. "What are we going to do now?"

"*We're* not going to do anything. *I'm* going to try and talk to Kim."

She would have preferred to get hit by a truck than to receive Trevor's words.

She tried to remain composed. She stammered, "B-b-but, I thought you—"

"Jada, listen to me, I'm going to work things out with Kim."

"Trevor, I'm in love with you and I—"

"I told you in the beginning about that."

Injured, Jada spat, "Kim said she doesn't want to be with you. Why are you trying to be with someone who doesn't want you?"

"Ask yourself that question." He moved around her, opened

the door, and left without looking back.

Feeling hurt and used, Jada ran after him screaming, "You wanted me an hour ago, dirty bastard!"

Trevor's tires left tracks and a crumpled Jada on the parking lot pavement.

The following afternoon, Jada had moved beyond the previous hellish night with Trevor. She expected him to say whatever sounded best at the time, but his touch, his kiss revealed his unspoken feelings. Besides, all of his efforts to get back with Kim were in vain. Kim's mind had been made up to close this chapter of her life.

Jada snatched up her ringing phone and masked her annoyance with a pleasant voice. "Post office. Jada speaking."

"Hi."

"Hey, Kim. Are you feeling a little better? You didn't look so good when you left the house this morning."

"I know." She sighed. "I was just calling to let you know that I'll be a little late tonight. I need to go to the house and get some things."

"Oh, Kim, you don't have to go all the way out to Queens. You're welcome to wear anything in my closet you'd like."
"Thanks, Jada, but it's not clothes that I need. I have to get some files for work."

Jada sensed Kim wasn't being totally honest and pressed. "Do you want me to come with you?"

"Nah, I got it. I need some time alone to think."

"Are you going to be alone?"

Kim took a deep breath. "Jada when I got to work this morning Trevor was here with this big bouquet of flowers and he started rattling on about how sorry he was."

Jada sat up in her chair.

"My coworkers, foster parents, and children were all around us. I didn't know what to do, so I took him in the back to my office and I heard him out."

Jada huffed loudly into the phone.

"Don't start with the lecture."

"No lecture. I've already told you what I think you should do."

"I appreciate your input because I know you care about me, but Trevor and I talked and he's truly sorry. I believe him and I'm considering giving him another chance."

"What was there to talk about?" Jada snapped.

"We talked about a few things. For starters, that tramp is history. Trevor said she was just an easy piece of ass and she didn't mean anything to him. In fact, she's already been cut off."

Jada sucked her teeth. "He has to say that. He wouldn't dare tell you he was in love with her. And he was probably fucking her last night for all you know."

"In love with her? Are you insane?" Kim let out a dry chuckle. "Everybody knows the other woman never gets any love."

"What else did he say?" Jada wanted to know.

"Nothing much. We're going to talk more later," Kim said not going into details.

"Why are you holding out on the information? I bet you did more than talk."

"So what if we did do more than talk?" Kim said angrily. "I told you I'm thinking about forgiving him. He's entitled to a second chance."

"Do what you want, Kim, but trust me when I tell you he's going to see her again. It's not over like Trevor said."

"Jada," she said softly, "I'm in my office. We're going to have to finish this conversation another time."

"Whatever, Kim." Jada hung up without a good-bye.

When Jada got home that night, she called Kim's house and left a couple of messages on her answering machine, letting her know that she was worried and reminding her to stay strong. Jada waited up for her until after midnight, than reluctantly went to bed.

The next morning when she got to work, the first thing she did was dial Trevor's job number and left a curt message instructing him to call her back immediately. Then she waited.

The morning dragged by without a word from him. By the time she returned from lunch, she was completely unnerved. She called his office a second time and was told that he'd taken the day off. She hung up and called Kim's job and was told the same thing. Now, she was irate. All kinds of scenarios began playing in her mind. Trevor and Kim were somewhere together living it up when he was supposed to be with her. How dare he! Her heart had been in constant pain since speaking to Kim the day before and hearing her talk about Trevor.

After trying both of their cells phones, which were off, Jada retreated to the ladies' room for a good cry. She was at the sink fixing her face when her coworker Barbara walked in.

"Hey, Jada, are you alright, girl?"

She shook her head and the tears started again.

Barbara hugged her tightly. "Do you want to talk about it?"

Jada pulled away and went back to cleaning up her face.

"There's not much to talk about. My best friend is sleeping with my man." She whimpered as she lied. Was it a lie? Trevor was *her* man. She had just as much right to him as Kim did.

Barbara shook her head sadly. "Jada, listen to me when I tell you to let her have him. If they would sleep together, neither of them could possibly care about you. Find a new friend and a new man, you'll be better off."

Back at her desk, Jada couldn't concentrate. She continuously called Trevor's cell phone and left one angry message after another. When she got tired of doing that, she told her supervisor that she was ill and left for the weekend.

Jada had no idea what she was going to do, but nonetheless, she was in her car and on her way to Queens. She had already figured the two of them had been making love all day and the thought made her heart ache.

Jada slowly drove passed the house and just as she suspected, both cars were in the driveway. She circled the block a couple of times to build up enough courage to get out of her car and ring the bell. When she finally did, there was no answer. She stood there ringing for more than twenty minutes before she gave up and headed home.

As soon as she walked into her apartment, she started dialing every number she had for Kim and Trevor and listened to their recorded voices. She had stopped leaving messages since what she needed to say would be better received face to face.

Jada paced the floor all night until her body gave out from

exhaustion. By the time she nodded off, the sun was rising and when she finally woke up, it was after two in the afternoon. The first thing she did was check her answering machine. Nothing. She managed to shower and get dressed before she started dialing again. It wasn't long before Jada was in her car and heading back to Queens.

She instantly knew that the loving couple wasn't home. Their cars hadn't been moved. She parked a few houses down and waited for the sun to dip behind the trees and as darkness began to fall, Jada left her car with her Club in hand, marched up to the back of Trevor's truck and with one mighty blow, glass shattered all around her.

Half scared and half thrilled, Jada ran back to her car and sped off, leaving behind the wails of Trevor's alarm system.

A little mischievousness must have been just what she needed because by the time she returned to her apartment, Jada was more relaxed. She put the kettle on, made herself a large cup of tea, sat down at her computer, and surfed the Internet until she was ready to retire.

She made a second cup of tea, ran a hot bath, and enjoyed them both along with an Earth, Wind & Fire CD.

The following afternoon, Jada was in her kitchen preparing a small pan of lasagna when she received her first frantic call.

"I know you fucked up my truck!" Trevor barked.

"You don't know shit," Jada responded and slammed the phone down as satisfaction crept up on her. She sprinkled more Mozzarella on top of her dinner and slid the pan in the oven.

She was in the middle of ironing clothes for the upcoming work week when the second call came.

The static on the line let her know that Trevor was calling on his cell phone. "Jada, what's wrong with you?"

"I don't know what you're talking about," she said innocently.

"First you try to sabotage my relationship with Kim and now my truck!"

"I didn't do anything to your truck and as for Kim, that was your handiwork."

"Jada, Kim told me you were advising her to break up with me. For what? So that you and I can be together?" He laughed sarcastically.

She wasn't going to let her hurt be known. She took a deep

breath and fought her tears. "I can't tell Kim to do anything. She has a mind of her own. And if you weren't so careless, we wouldn't even be having this conversation right now."

Trevor was in the middle of responding when their connection was lost. Jada hung up the phone and waited for a third call, but it never came.

Monday mornings were the hardest for Jada and this Monday was no different—in fact, it was worse. Because she left early on Friday, her workload was backed up and piled high on her desk. To add more drama to her life, the lie she told Barbara had spread like a wildfire through her office. The stares and whispers wouldn't have bothered her so much, if the rumor she'd started were true. Now she was the center of gossip in her office.

Jada had been at her desk all morning, shifting papers from one side to the other without actually accomplishing anything. She was lost in her thoughts when Barbara came over and asked if she was all right.

Jada started giving her a few bland answers when her phone rang, saving her from the conversation.

"Good morning. Post office," she answered wearily.

"Hey, Jada, I got your messages. All of them," Kim said smartly.

Jada rolled her eyes. "This is your idea of being strong?"

"You know what? I'm tired of you!" Kim huffed. "You're really getting on my nerves trying to convince me that I'm weak and stupid just because I chose to forgive Trevor."

"Why do I have to convince you of the obvious?" Jada shot back.

"Why are you trippin' so hard over this? Why can't you just be supportive of my decision?"

Jada could hear the emotion in Kim's voice and a tinge of guilt silenced her. But she couldn't back down now, if she could get Kim to break up with Trevor, it would only be a matter of time before he'd come running to her for comfort.

"Lately, you have been nothing but rude and insulting—"

"You're right, I'm sorry." Jada interrupted. "It's just that I'm concerned about you. Like this weekend you disappeared without a word. I was worried. Where were you?"

"I'm not sure if I should tell you. I don't feel like arguing with you."

The hair on the back of Jada's neck stood at attention. She inhaled deeply and prayed that her toned stayed level. "Kim, you can tell me anything."

"Not when it involves Trevor."

"You and Trevor went away this weekend?"

For the next thirty minutes, Jada was silent as Kim gave her the details about Trevor's proposal and how he whisked her away to the Cayman Islands for a beautiful private sunset wedding on a white sandy beach.

Jada bit her tongue until she tasted blood when Kim gushed about making love to *her* man for hours on end until it was time for them to return home.

By the time Kim was finished with her story, Jada felt sick to her stomach.

"Jada, are you still there?"

"Uh, I'm here." Her voice was barely audible.

"Are you okay?"

"Yeah, I'm just a little overwhelmed by your weekend," Jada admitted.

"I know it's a lot to take in at once. I'm Trevor's wife!" Kim squealed and the grip around Jada's heart tightened.

She cleared her throat in an effort to fight off tears. "Speaking of Trevor, how is he doing?" Jada waited to hear about Trevor's reaction to finding his truck vandalized.

"Oh, Trevor's just great. We're both very excited. In fact, we talked about having a few people over to the house this weekend to announce our nuptials. I know you don't particularly like Trevor any-more, so I won't pressure you to come if you don't want to."

"Are you kidding me? I wouldn't miss it for the world." Her tone dripped with sarcasm, which Kim ignored.

"Well, I guess I'll see you Saturday at eight o'clock. I know you're at work, so I won't keep you on the phone another minute."

"Okay, later."

"Uh, Jada, one more thing. I hope you can get over whatever it is you feel for Trevor by Saturday. This is going to be a celebration and I really want it to go smoothly."

"No problem."

"Great. Bye."

Not really sure of how she did it, Jada somehow managed to make it through the rest of the day without completely falling apart.

The next morning, she called in sick for the remainder of the week, shut off her phone, and locked herself in her apartment. Thinking about Trevor and Kim day and night was truly making her ill, but she hadn't figured out if it was mental or physical.

Jada was consumed with thoughts of the newlyweds making love, having babies, and living happily ever after while she watched from the sidelines knowing in her heart that it should be her making beautiful memories with Trevor instead.

She wrestled with her conscious about the rights and wrongs of the situation and tried to determine if she loved or hated Trevor, if she truly cared for Kim as her best friend, and how she even felt about herself. Decent people didn't do the things she'd done over the past few months, but all of her logic and rationale went to hell when she thought about the way Trevor made her feel—his large hands on the small of her back and the way he nibbled her ears and neck, the skill he showed as he suckled her perky nipples and anxious clit, the long phone calls late at night and the deep kisses that lingered on her lips hours after he was gone. He was the best thing that ever happened to her and nobody could ever know—or could they?

Confession. She thought about it a hundred times, but at this point would it do any good? It may cause her to lose her best friend. It may also lead to the breakup she so badly wanted.

Jada massaged her temples in an effort to ease her headache. The mental battle had her physically beaten. She wasn't eating or resting properly and her matted hair went well with her dark, swollen eyes.

She had been locked away for days and no one had even come to check on her. Kim was probably too busy party planning and most likely, Trevor was somewhere baby-sitting his truck.

The week had easily slipped away and it was already Saturday morning. The night before, Jada had taken a big swig of Nyquil to help her sleep. It got the job done, but now she was nursing a small hangover.

She dragged herself to the kitchen and fired up the kettle for a cup of tea. She couldn't resist the urge to sneak a peek at her answering machine and came face to face with the big red zero. She almost started to cry, but stopped herself.

"Pull yourself together, girl," she reprimanded herself before preparing her tea. She took the mug, went into the living room and put a Mary J. Blige CD in the changer and sang along with the singer to an old jam.

She took a quick shower, pulled on a sweat suit, and headed toward the beauty salon so her friend Lionel could hook her hair up for Kim's soiree later.

When she got to the salon, Lionel was just pulling up the gate and two other ladies were already standing outside waiting.

"You won't believe the kind of night I had," Lionel said as he opened the door for them. He disappeared somewhere in the back of the salon and in an instant the shop was illuminated and buzzing. The lights came on, along with the television and a few other electrical things.

Lionel reappeared, still talking—to no one in particular. "I left here in a hurry last night trying to meet this guy who was paying for me to go to a star-studded affair and I was just one minute late and he was beefing. So you know what I did, right?" He paused dramatically. "I danced all night long with this fine chocolate-colored hunk and left him there looking angry and foolish." He snapped his fingers. "I ain't got time for that kind of shit. I was looking good too. Wait 'til I show you the pictures."

Lionel took a peek at himself in the mirror before turning to one lady. "What are you having done, honey?"

Jada waited almost an hour before Lionel motioned for her to sit in his chair. He ran his fingers through her scalp. "You're ready for a touch-up, Jada. And I can tell you haven't been conditioning. Your hair looks damaged."

This was her first human contact in days and she felt like throwing her arms around Lionel's big shoulders and asking him to hold her, but instead Jada sighed heavily. "I've been under a lot of stress lately."

Lionel swung the chair around and eyed her carefully. "You don't look like yourself. What's wrong? You can tell Lionel all about it."

And she did. By the time Lionel put her under the dryer, he—and the other women in the salon—knew the whole story.

The woman seated under the dryer next to her lifted the heated hood and rolled her eyes in Jada's direction before sauntering over to Lionel's chair. Once she was seated, she said, "I know you said you love this man and everything, but you're wrong."

"Yep," quipped the lady seated at the dye bowl.

"She's wrong?" That was Sandy, Lionel's shampoo girl/shop-keeper who had come in shortly after them. "What about his trifling ass? He's wrong!"

"Yeah, he's wrong too," the lady in Lionel's chair agreed as Lionel brushed out her roller set.

He stopped in mid-stroke and pointed the brush at Jada. "I always say, all's fair in love and war."

The woman craned her neck to look up at Lionel. "I would have agreed with you when they were just dating, but now that they're married, you need to leave that woman's husband alone."

"Married, single, gay, straight, black, or white. None of it matters. It's all about the sex," the woman at the dye bowl jumped in. "You don't have to leave him alone. Stop giving him sex, and he'll leave *you* alone."

"It was more than sex with Trevor and me," Jada said defensively.

"It couldn't have been too much more. He married somebody else," the woman in Lionel's chair said.

Sandy stopped sweeping up hair from around Lionel's work-station. "It may be only about sex for him, but not for Jada. I've been on both sides of this situation and I can tell you, whoever winds up winning the man still turns out to be the loser because what has she won? Long nights of wondering where her man is when he's supposed to be out with his boys? Who needs that shit?" She sucked her teeth and continued sweeping.

Jada had never thought of it that way. She was coming out of this situation the true winner because she had the freedom to move on and meet a man who'd treat her well.

When Jada left Lionel's salon, she had a new do and a new attitude. One conversation in Lionel's salon had given her a whole new lease on life.

She felt so good about herself that she made a quick trip to the mall and bought a new outfit before returning home. As soon as she walked in the door, she hit the power on her CD changer and blasted the Mary J. Blige track she was listening to earlier.

She got out of her clothes, re-wrapped her hair and tied it down with her headscarf before starting her shower. She made sure that the water was warmer than she usually liked it and switched the showerhead to the massage setting.

In the shower, Jada wasted no time squeezing shower gel over her breasts and used her thumb and forefinger to make her nipples stand firm. The more she rubbed, the hotter her pussy became. She released the showerhead from its holder and directed the steady stream of water on her full clit. She let out a long, deep moan.

Usually when she masturbated in the shower, it only took a few minutes for her to climax but this time, whenever she thought she might cum, Jada shifted her aim of the showerhead until the feeling passed, then she'd continue, making the sensation last.

After her shower, Jada ran an iron over her new jeans and V-neck knit top and got dressed. She let her hair down, put in her large silver hoop earrings, spritzed herself with Happy by Clinique and was out the door.

Jada could hear the music before she even turned onto Kim's block. It was only eight-thirty, yet she couldn't find a parking spot on the entire block. It was late May, and even though the sun was beginning to set, the eighty-degree heat made it feel as though summer was already in full swing. She finally found a spot one block over from Kim's and took her time walking to the house. She was in no real hurry to help the newlyweds celebrate, even after her therapy session in Lionel's salon.

Kim's front and back doors were both open and from the porch, Jada could see straight through to the backyard where people were standing around holding plates of food and drinks. She opened the screen door and went directly to the kitchen.

"Hey, Jada." Kim's aunt came over and hugged her. "I was wondering if you were going to make it. Kim told me you were feeling under the weather this week."

"Hi, Aunt Carol. I'm feeling better now."

"Good. You remember Kim's cousin Felicia and her husband, Troy?"

"Hi, nice to see you again." Jada shook their hands.

"Let's go out back where everyone is. I'm sure Kim will be happy to see you. She was concerned that you wouldn't make it." Aunt Carol led the way to the backyard.

Jada was doing all right up until she saw the large banner that read: "Congratulations, Trevor and Kim." She immediately felt a stab of jealousy in her gut. She froze when she saw the couple of the hour posing by a large wedding cake and smiling brightly for the photographer.

Kim was dressed in a beautiful soft pink, ankle-length dress that flowed in the occasional breeze. Trevor was looking as handsome as ever in a pair of beige linen slacks and matching shirt. They were both tanned and looked like they should be standing on top of the wedding cake, not in front of it.

Jada was just about to turn and run back through the house and out the front door, when Trevor caught her eye. Instead of acknowledging her, he turned and whispered in Kim's ear. She looked over and gave Jada a big, toothy smile.

She was brought out of her stupor, when Kim's cousin Kevin came over and put a drink in her hand. "Hey, long time, no see, Jada. You look like you could use this." He indicated the cup.

She took a sip and forced a smile. "It was all so sudden. I guess it just hasn't sunk in yet."

"Yeah, I feel the same way. I hope Trev can still hang out with us from time to time," he joked, but Jada was in no joking mood. She drained her cup in one long gulp and patted her mouth with the napkin.

"Damn, girl, that's not Kool-Aid, you know."

"I know." Jada was embarrassed. She quickly surveyed the room before asking Kevin to get her another drink. "This time make it a double," she said as he walked away.

"Hey, Jada." Aunt Carol was quickly approaching her with a guy. "I don't think you've met my nephew Patrick. He just graduated from the University of South Carolina and is visiting with us for the summer." She turned to Patrick. "Pat, this is Kim's best friend, Jada." Jada smiled warmly and managed to hold a brief conversation until Kevin came over with her drink.

"Take it easy with that," he scolded playfully. "It's more gin than juice."

"Thanks for the warning." She took a sip and discovered that he was right. It was strong—just how she needed it to be. "Excuse me, gentlemen." Jada left the two men standing in the yard and she disappeared into the secluded compounds of the kitchen so that she could down her drink in private.

She went over to the sink and filled her cup with water to douse the fire in her abdomen. She was starting to feel the immediate effects of drinking strong alcohol too quickly.

"I thought I saw you come in here."

Jada spun around at the sound of Kim's voice and held on to the side of the sink to balance herself.

"I was wondering if you were going to speak to me."

"I was going to make my way over," Jada mumbled.

Kim opened the freezer and pulled out two big bags of ice. "Are you enjoying yourself?"

"Yeah." Jada could barely raise her eyes to meet Kim's.

The silence between them made the hum of the refrigerator sound like a freight train. Jada needed a seat. Her head was beginning to spin.

Trevor entered the kitchen and looked from one woman to the other before settling his attention on his wife. "Is everything okay in here?"

Kim nodded.

"Let me get this." He took the bags of ice from her and kissed her forehead. "Don't stay in here too long. We're ready for the toasts."

"I'll be out in a minute," Kim said softly.

Trevor left without uttering a word to Jada. She reminded herself that she was the true winner in this situation, but that didn't stop her eyes from filling.

She turned back to the sink and took deep breaths until the

urge to cry passed, but when it did, anger quickly took its place. *I hate him!* the voice in her head screamed.

Jada turned to Kim who was watching her intently. She squinted in an effort to read the expression on Kim's face. It was blank.

Kim's mouth finally curled up into a tight smile and she released a long breath. "Are you coming out?"

Jada followed silently.

The sun was completely gone and the lights had been turned on in the yard. Aunt Carol met them at the back door. "Your husband is waiting for you, dear." She draped her arm around Jada's shoulder, "You can come sit at my table."

The music stopped and Trevor's older brother was standing in the middle of the yard with a microphone in his hand. He started off with a couple of jokes about how much he'd miss Trevor on the basketball court now that he was married and then went on to wish the couple well. Jada almost choked on her drink when he said he couldn't wait for the babies to start coming.

When he was done, everyone raised their glasses and saluted the newlyweds.

Aunt Carol spoke up and announced that as Kim's best friend it was only right that Jada also toast the newlyweds. Out of the corner of her eye, she saw Trevor stand in objection, but Kim grabbed his arm and quietly convinced him to be seated.

Jada was shaking so badly on her way to the microphone that she almost knocked it over. She had to clear her throat more than once in order to find her voice. "I wasn't prepared to have words, but having known Kim for so long, there are a million and one things I could say about her. She has always been a very caring and loving person and having seen her and Trevor together over the past two and a half years, I've witnessed those characteristics grow and intensify."

She cleared her throat and glanced in Kim's direction. She had that vague look on her face again. Trevor's face held unmistakable anger. "So instead of congratulating her, I want to tell Kim how sorry I feel for her because she's been blinded by a selfish man who has no respect for her and has been cheating on her for the past several months." Trevor was up on his feet again and this time Kim was by his side. There was murmuring among the guests and someone even cursed her in the distance, but she had come this far and wasn't about to stop now. "I'm sure everyone here wants the best for Kim, but Trevor's not it. He's a lying, cheating, sneaky, conniving dog."

In an instant, Kim had crossed the yard and was standing in front of her. She snatched the microphone from her hand and held it at her side, but the frequency still picked up their voices, broadcasting their hushed angry tones.

"How dare you!" Kim whispered between clinched teeth.

Jada shook her head sadly. "I truly feel sorry for you."

"Not half as sorry as I feel for you," Kim snapped. "Trevor's not the only one who's a liar and a sneak. Jada, on the way to the Cayman Islands, Trevor told me that the two of you have been fucking for months. I know the whole story. I forgave him and then I married him. And despite how betrayed I felt, I loved you enough to forgive you too. All I wanted was for you to be honest with me. But you just couldn't take the high road. Instead you did everything you could to convince me that being with Trevor was the biggest mistake of my life. After this performance here tonight, I know what my biggest mistake was."

There was nothing Jada could say. She thought she was doing the right thing, but the disappointed stares made her wish she had kept her mouth shut.

Trevor and Aunt Carol were standing together with his parents in one corner of the yard, looking at her as if she were a demon. She made eye contact with Kim and was met with the same vague stare that she now recognized as hurt. It tore at her heart, but she held her head up high and moved around Kim and toward the door.

She was on the street and heading to her car when someone called her name. She kept walking and soon Kevin was in stride with her.

"Jada, wait." He grabbed her arm to keep her from moving.

She gave him a look that told him that she didn't feel like being bothered.

"I know that must have been really hard for you, but I couldn't let you leave without giving you my phone number. If you ever need someone to talk to, I hope you'll consider giving me a call."

She took the slip of paper, stuffed it in the front pocket of her jeans and continued walking. When she approached her car, she immediately wished this living nightmare would end. All of her car windows had been knocked out. Her knees weakened, she dropped to the ground, and let out an animal-like scream that pierced the darkness around her.

Jacques in the Box
by
Léone D'Mitrienne Williams

y affair began just last weekend. I was in New Orleans on business for the annual jazz festival. My company was one of the sponsors for the concerts, and I was there as a representative. This had to be the best part of my job. As a promotional director I was provided with a suite and VIP tickets to all of the events. My husband, Dominic "Nick" Dupuis, hated when I went away to events like this...especially since that weekend was our two-year wedding anniversary and Nick didn't have to work. He travels frequently as a talent scout for a major record label, but took the time off for our anniversary.

Nick and I met two and a half years ago at the same jazz festival that I was attending. His concern was not only that we wouldn't be spending our anniversary together but also that I was going to be at the same place that we first met. I had suggested that he come with me, but he said that I would be working most of the time and that he hated all the schmoozing that goes on at these events, especially since he had to do the same shit with his job. He told me that we could celebrate our anniversary when I returned.

It was a sweltering Friday night when Nick placed me under his spell. I was working as the promotional director's flunky at the time. I was at the jazz festival to help set up and break down venues and fetch coffee whenever my boss needed it. I was allowed to have free time, usually after eleven in the evening. By that time all I could think about was getting into bed, but it was Saturday night and I would be heading back home the next morning, so I decided to put on my sexy clothes and hang out.

As I headed back to the hotel from the convention center, I took note of all the good-looking people and stragglers hanging out on the street. My hotel was located in the French Quarter, which was about two miles away. I wanted to take advantage of the time I had left, so I caught a cab. The ride took about twenty minutes because of the heavy traffic and the crowds. The streets were bumping and I was about to join in.

I couldn't wait to get to my suite. I immediately stripped myself of the somewhat sweaty clothes I had worn all day and threw them on the floor. As I headed for the shower, I stopped in front of the mirror. I looked at my body and thought about how long it had been since I last made love—or fucked for that matter. It was too long. This body needed some tender loving. My body needed it from the nape of my neck, over the tips of my nipples down to my stomach, and straight between my thighs—especially between my thighs.

The shower was hot and the water was coming through the showerhead with full force. *Oh,* I thought, *this feels so good.* After allowing the warm water to relax and refresh my body, I was ready to party the night away. I left the steamy bathroom, put on my robe, and went outside to stand over the balcony to get a taste of what the night had in store for me.

The hotel was situated in the heart of the French Quarter on Bourbon Street. I was in one of those old hotels that represent what New Orleans is all about. The ones that you see on the *When School Girls Go Wild* video commercials, so I had a perfect view of the area. The building was more than one hundred years old with the steel balcony and soft pastel-like pink paint. On the inside, the room was a light ivory with a king-size canopy, draped with an oversized down comforter, and a light gold silk screen that covered the entire bed. The white oak armoire and matching rocking chair complimented the room's theme. The cherry-stained oakwood floors had an area rug that covered the space under the bed. It would have been very romantic, had it not been for the fact that I was completely alone.

I could see from the crowd outside that that night was going to be a blast. The people were getting their party on. There were droves of women with daiquiri cups in hand and brothers sipping their malt liquor out of brown paper bags. I could see the young local kids on the street corners tap dancing for money using bottle caps on the bottom of their shoes. The streets were alive and breathing in the bayou called New Orleans.

It took me less than thirty minutes to get dressed and get my groove on. I decided to put on this cute little dark jean mini—and I do mean *mini*—skirt. I had a fitted black rayon top to wear with it that showed just a hint of my stomach. To tie it all together I wore my sexy strap sandals that wrap around my ankle. Oh, and let's not forget the toe ring. Makeup wasn't a big deal for me because I don't really need it. I was blessed to get my mother's flawless light caramel complexion. All I needed was some mascara and lipgloss to accentuate my already rosy lips.

I walked slowly down the corridor to the stairwell where I received confirmation from the bellman that I was looking pretty nice. It was something about the way he tripped up the stairs, nearly breaking his neck while checking out my legs and then turning around to sneak a peek of my ass. I was glad he didn't really hurt himself and thanked him for the compliment. As a twenty-five-year-old African-American woman, I had to admit that I had it going on. I was in great shape physically and mentally. I made sure that I worked out at least four times a week and read at least one book a month.

I was the youngest and only black person in my position at my firm and made some very good money. Before me the position was only given to young white boys whose daddies probably got them the job to begin with. I won't deny that my shapely hips and succulent lips were partially responsible for my decent salary. The old fart who hired me, Mr. La Bauve, couldn't take his eyes off me during the entire interview. I played him very well and even got a free lunch out of it. I was reminded time and time again that my salary was "just between us." We continued to have this "nice" relationship in which I tolerated his flirtatious winks and comments. I found out that Mr. La Bauve had a thing for black women. He even divorced his wife of thirty years for one. It turns out that he was sleeping with the nanny and impregnated her. Once the child was born, he professed his love for the nanny and divorced his wife. Mrs. La Bauve was well taken care of and was even given their mansion, but chose not to take it. Instead she took a hefty settlement and moved to Virginia with her sister. As a southern woman, she was too embarrassed and humiliated to remain in the same town. In cooperating with him and his sometimes-wicked comments, I was promoted in no time from entry-level file girl to being able to travel to all of the different forums our company held across the country. Three years later, Mr. La Bauve promoted me to promotional sales coordinator. He did this just before he retired, knowing that his replacement would never let me grow above being an assistant manager. He personally thanked me for brightening up his days and said he was happy to be able to be home with his beautiful wife. Not bad for a young black girl without a degree.

As I left the inn, I could feel the heat of the city. The people were colorful and the streets were packed. My first stop was the dai- quiri place on the corner. It took what seemed like forever to get to the bar. The patrons had created their own dance floor, which made it hard to pass. The bartender had a warm smile with beautiful white teeth. He spotted me immediately and guessed that I was a Hurricane girl. I actually wanted a 190 octane, but the Hurricane would do for now. I paid him and took my drink to the streets. I couldn't believe how hot it was outside. There was a slight breeze, but the humidity made the air moist. The coolness from the drink refreshed my body and began to relax me as I set out on my hunt for fun.

In no time I had a nice buzz. I stopped at a club once I finished my drink and began to dance by myself. I found it amazing how a little alcohol could simply relax me so I could just enjoy myself. The music was pumping from the speakers and my body was working with it. My hips gently moved in a figure-eight motion while I raised my hands in the air, swaying them from side to side. I must have been sending out some type of smoke signal because the next thing I knew there were two hands behind me helping my hips get their swerve on. I was so involved in the music that I didn't bother to turn around. I just looked down and saw a set of brotha's hands holding on to me. From the looks of his hands he was tall and packing…if you know what I mean! Oh yes, a woman can tell a lot from some hands.

The beat seemed to grow as did the body behind me. The stranger with the hands had moved closer behind me when he realized that I was not going to shoo him away. I could feel the thrust of his hips moving closer to my body. I felt my behind moving in motion with him. I became intoxicated, feeling his manliness grow against my ass. How could I be feeling this good? I didn't even know this muthafucka! But damn he felt good...and big. Suddenly the music slowed and his arms wrapped around my waist. With no hesitation I moved toward his chest and leaned my head back. He was tall all right. I could feel that my head was resting on his chest. I knew I would have to turn around soon, but I would wait until the song was over—just one more song. As I continued to feel the music, his hands began to feel me. They began to wander around my waist and back down to the sides of my hips. They moved up and down and found their way around my waist again, then they moved down...down...down, barely touching the top of my private spot. Had he gone any farther he would have touched my...you know.

His hands slowly rose up my sides and right underneath my breasts. Although he was not cupping them, I could feel his fingers gently caressing the bottom of them. I became flushed and nervous that someone I didn't know was taking his time to seduce me in this crowded place. I had to know who this was, what he looked like because I surely knew his touch. In a matter of seconds the man with the wandering hands read my mind and went from behind me to directly in front of me, and still I did not see his face. I stood there with my face at his chest, still pondering the thought of when I should look up to see who this mysterious dancer was. Once again he read my mind and took his hand and placed it underneath my chin to take a look. As his gentle yet strong fingers raised my face, I looked up and saw an amazingly handsome face.

"Bon jour," he said through beautifully shaped full lips. His almond-shaped brown eyes also said *bon jour* as they gazed into mine. *Bon jour* was all I remembered as he took my hand and pulled me close to him as another slow jam played and he stroked my back. With the smell of his freshly showered body and feel of his tall athletic frame, *bon jour* was all he needed to say to take me to his bed.

The pounding sound of a new Jay-Z song snapped me out of my trance. I looked up at him, smiled, and nodded for us to get out of there. I was never so bold before, but I was about to have him and needed to make use of my newly found confidence. He followed without hesitation, and as we were leaving he whispered in my ear, *"Bon jour, bon jour, bon jour."* This beautiful Creole man had all the right ingredients to fill me with some good Cajun loving, and in the blink of the eye, we were in my room.

He went to the radio and turned to the classical radio station. He set me on the bed and removed my sandals. He slowly lifted my right foot and gently took my toes one by one into his mouth. His tongue circled each and every one of them with such gentleness. I cold feel a warm tingling move slowly up my thighs. Once he finished, he set my foot back on the ground and introduced himself. "Dominic Dupuis is happy to have made your acquaintance."

"Francesca Xavier is charmed," I replied.

Nick and I had a long-distance romance for six months before he asked for my hand in marriage. Some would say that our relationship had no time to develop, but I believe that fate brought us together and we weren't going to alter it. Our short weekend trips back and forth from Atlanta to New Orleans were always filled with passion and sometimes got a little nasty when we where apart for too long. Nick decided purchasing a house in Atlanta was more cost efficient and moved there to be with me. Now that Nick is in Atlanta, he believes that toe sucking among other things aren't quite as necessary—at least not on a regular basis. The man I met with the beautiful hands had to be in the mood to give me those pleasures. I still love him so very much, but I wish I could get my Nick back.

Thursday

The story of Jacques is quite ironic. I ran across Jacques in one of those erotic shops the night I arrived in New Orleans. My company had arranged a dinner meeting that night and let everyone leave early to get some rest for the next day's activities. A couple of the other promotional representatives were heading to Pat O'Brien's for drinks, but I would see enough of them during the week and politely declined. I wanted to add some spice to Nick's and my love life, so I walked throughout the French Quarter and ran into an erotic toy store. I wasn't looking for anything in particular and hoped something would jump out at me. As I looked around I noticed how all the patrons looked just as normal as me. I always had an image of people with tattoos and body piercings being the only types that shopped for sex toys. The shop was filled with videos, games, books, and toys—lots of toys! I was too embarrassed to ask about the different gadgets, so I decided to get one of the sex games they had for sale. I used my cellular and called my sister Liza in Atlanta who knows all there is to know about sex. As a thirty-one-year-old independent woman she has had more erotic encounters with men than anyone else I know. I remember her telling me about a ménage a trois she had in college and that she was going to be meeting up with one of the guys again soon, but I never did get the information from her on what happened after their date. Her latest conquest was some comedian.

"This is Liza. Talk to me."

"Hey, big sister. How they hanging?" I said with a laugh. We always joke about her being the one with the balls in a relationship.

"Oh, girl, I am so glad that you called. I want you to bring me back some pictures of all the fine men out there and be sure to give them my number too."

"Liza, do you always have dick on the brain?"

"No," she replied. "I sometimes think about having it inside of me." We both burst out laughing. The patrons in the store were staring, so I walked outside to finish my call. One thing about Liza is that she has such a dirty mouth, but that's what I love about her. She is so honest with her sexuality.

"Okay, all jokes aside. I need some help. I'm at one of those erotica shops and I'm looking for something to spice up my marriage. Do you have any suggestions?"

"Hmm," she thought aloud. "I know one thing that you can do for your man…naw, you're not ready for that. I'll tell you about that in two years when you turn thirty." Liza giggled.

"What the fuck is that supposed to mean?" Anyway, I'm not going to beg you, so just tell me what to get."

"Francesca, darling, I think you should get those love coupons. I know how much in love you are with your man, and he would really appreciate that. You could put one in his bag when he goes on his business trips, that way he will have something to look forward to when he comes back home."

"That sounds pretty good—"

As I tried to complete my sentence, Liza interrupted to tell me that somebody named Noah was on the other line and that she would have to call me back later. I'm sure it was another one of Liza's conquest that I will hear about when I get back to Atlanta.

I placed my phone in my purse and walked back into the store. As I scanned the shelves, I was surprised with a beautiful vision. Jacques Noir was thick and chocolate and ready to please. *Ummmm*. The thought of Jacques inside of me made me wet on the spot. I couldn't believe that I was thinking of another inside of me, but Nick wasn't pleasing me and I was yearning for some sexual release. Besides, maybe Nick, Jacques, and I could spice up our currently dry sex life.

Without completely thinking out the repercussions of my relationship with Nick I left the store with Jacques, only thinking of my own personal needs. We stopped at the package store to get a bottle of wine before we headed back to the inn—the same inn where Nick and I first made love. I ran a bath and had a glass of wine before Jacques and I began our interlude. I lay naked on the bed with the comforter pulled back. There was no need for foreplay. The anticipation of Jacques entering me was satisfying enough just before entry. My slight nervousness was replaced by nirvana as Jacques entered the warmth between my legs. It began between the lips, pulsating on my clit, and easing slowly inside of me just a little at a time. Jacques went deeper and deeper until I couldn't control my breathing. My heart was racing and my body was on fire. I began to feel surges of electricity run down my chest and inside my private spot, and the feeling from all this stimulation slowly eased down between my ass. I took a moment to catch my breath and gain my composure. For the last few minutes I had forgotten where I was. My entire being was transported to another place, a place where I knew I would go again before I began to work in the morning. I considered getting rid of Jacques, but it was late so I let Jacques stay. *Just wait until the morning,* I thought.

Friday

My appointments didn't start the next morning until eleven, so I had set my alarm for 8:30 to give me enough time to play since Jacques was still there, shower, and have some breakfast. I woke up just before the alarm went off and got an early start with Jacques. The thickness of this marvelous chocolate bar had me yearning for the extraordinary orgasm I had the night before. The sensation I felt exceeded anything I'd ever felt before. I had to bite my lip to keep from screaming out in sheer pleasure. I was thoroughly aroused and pleased at the way my body was able to answer to that amount of intensity. Jacques was good...real good, but I knew I would not be able to continue this when I got home to Nick.

After showering and dressing, Jacques and I parted ways. I headed downstairs for breakfast. I couldn't believe how hungry I was. My breakfast consisted of a three-egg, cheese, and veggie omelet; turkey sausage; home fried potatoes; and two slices of wheat toast. I had forgotten how hungry a good orgasm could make me. I had to walk off all that food, so I headed to the convention center by foot.

The sky was clear and the air was warm. I could tell from the humidity that it was going to be another searing day in New Orleans—and maybe another hot night. I made it to the convention center in no time. My assistant, Carol, waved to me from our booth as she was setting up for this evening's concert. Carol reminded me of myself at that age, twenty-two and ambitious. Even though Carol worked for me, I wanted her to learn the business and grow with the company, not fetch my coffee, do my banking, and pick up my dry cleaning, which some of my counterparts thought was part of the job description. I walked toward her and asked how things were going.

"Not as good as they seem to be going with you," she replied.

"What do you mean?" I asked. Carol gave me a devilish smile. One thing I liked about Carol when she first came aboard was her honesty. She always made sure she let you know what was on her mind, and I could appreciate that. I was just wondering what insightful observation she was going to make now. She told me how I was smiling as I walked in, and that I looked like I had a secret. This young lady had great vision and very good perception. I was in a good mood all right. Who wouldn't be? I had the ultimate orgasm this morning and some delicious breakfast to follow. My day had started out perfectly.

The day continued to go pretty smoothly. My clients who consisted of concert event coordinators came and went. A few of the artists scheduled to perform over the weekend also stopped by for promotional pictures and autograph signings. Lunch finally came, and I took Carol and one of my female clients out to this nice little tucked-away restaurant called Napoleon's. The inside of Napoleon's was furnished with dark wood and reminded me of an Irish pub. The real reason I liked the restaurant was the outside seating, which was actually closed in by an apartment in the back. It was a backyard stone garden in northern Italy with iron chairs and tables for seating. The food was also rather delightful. The tuna-filled avocado salad and the Bruschetta were my favorites. They were unlike any I have had before. The French bread was covered with a light layer of fresh Mozzarella cheese, topped by plum tomatoes, and drizzled with olive oil.

It was almost as good as Jacques. Mmmm, Jacques. We ordered our lunch and because I was in such a delightful mood, I ordered a bottle of wine to accompany our meal. What a lovely day, I thought. We ate our meal and drank the wine while we spoke of our loves and our drama just as women do. There were two empty bottles of wine on the table by the time lunch was over and a nice buzz to go with it. These conventions were the only time I really got a little untamed.

On the way back to hotel, after a long day's work, my mind went back to thinking about Jacques. I figured I could sneak in a little somethin' somethin' with Jacques. I told Carol to close up the booth and that I would see her later that night at the concert and afterward we could go club hopping to all of the after parties I had invites for. Carol raced back to our display to get out of there to get ready for the evening. I called Nick to tell him about my day—leaving out my time with Jacques of course. I missed being with Nick, but at the same time I couldn't wait to have Jacques inside of me again. The thought was so heavy in my mind that I began to talk dirty to Nick. I shared all of my mischievous thoughts with him and what I was going to do to him when I got home. He used to like when I did this, and it had been a while since we had done it on the phone. I decided to get extremely descriptive with Nick. I could tell that he had missed our talks, too, because deeper into the conversation his breathing became harder and he spoke less and less.

"Nick?"

"Yes, baby," he answered with his sexy, deep voice.

"Will you help me with something?"

"Anything you want, baby." His breathing slowed as he anticipated my next move.

"I need you to unzip your pants and take out my big chocolate candy, and after you take it out I want you to close your eyes."

"Okay," he replied, not denying me my simple pleasure.

"Now, Nick, I have to tell you that I'm extremely wet right now. I'm going to have to have to spread my legs and sit on top of you."

The continued silence let me know that Nick was stroking himself. I went on to tell him how good it felt to have him between my thighs and deep inside of me.

"Nick, o*h honey!* I wish you were here to hit my spot."

I told him how I would squeeze his thickness as I felt him growing inside of me. Now all I heard on the phone line was heavy breathing and moaning.

"Yes baby, yes!" I whispered as he began to reach his peak. Before I knew it I was imagining Jacques between my thighs, stroking my insides. How could I be doing that with Nick on the phone? He wouldn't know…he couldn't know. Nick was too busy being pleased by my sexual thoughts, as was I. He let out a low howl as he came. In the meantime, thoughts of Jacques pleased me. Nick called my name a couple of times as I basked in the rapture of my own ecstasy. Although he had already received his pleasure, the thought of me enjoying myself, too, was quite a turn-on for him. I could hear his distant voice urging me to cum. He asked me how wet I was. He asked if it was soft and warm. Nick said he wanted to be with me so that he could slowly rub his hands over my body to hold me tight. I was mesmerized by the whole experience. I continued to revel in excitement with the sound of Nick's voice and thoughts of Jacques as I began to climax.

Silence took over as we lay there feeling worlds apart. I thought about how much pleasure I received from Nick...and Jacques. I wondered what Nick would do if he found out about Jacques. Would he mind Jacques joining us? Who was I kidding? I couldn't possibly let Nick know about my night with Jacques. It would ruin everything that we had built in our relationship. I was once told that fucking had nothing to do with love, but somehow I believed that Nick wouldn't understand that concept. Nick has been very good to me aside from the recent setback in our sex life. Maybe I simply needed to adjust my priorities in life.

"Nick?"

"Yes, baby?"

"Do you love me?"

"Does a bee love honey?"

"I love you too, Nick."

"I love it when you call me Nick. You haven't in so long. I miss that."

"I know, baby. It has been a long time. Maybe we should have calls like this more often. We both travel so much. Lately I've felt so distant from you because you're too tired to even touch me. I really miss that."

An uncomfortable silence passed through the phone line again as Nick sighed. *Please say something Nick,* I thought.

"Sweetness," Nick began, "there is nothing on this earth that I wouldn't do for you. I realize that lately I haven't been giving you the lovin' you deserve, but there's a reason for that. I've been working real hard to make sure that I'll be able to take care of us. I don't want you to ever have to worry about a thing. I cherish you. You are my beginning and my end. I couldn't imagine not having you in my life."

"Nick, honey...."

"Shhhhh. Please let me finish."

What more could he say?

"I think you should know that from the time I saw you on the dance floor I was in love with you. You had this aura of beautiful light surrounding you as you swung your hips. I had to know what you were feeling. I had to feel you. And when you didn't flinch or move away from me I knew that you and I were destined to be together. I was reassured when you began to back up to me and began to rub that nice ass on me. I still remember it like it was yesterday. I think about it every night when we're not together. I'm in you every night. The moment I close my eyes you appear. I made love to you that night like I've never done before. You made me feel things that dreams are made of. I wanted to tell you that I loved you then, but I didn't want to scare you away. I need you, baby! I'll do whatever it takes to keep you in my life. I promise. *Je t'aim.*"

A sigh of relief came through the phone line. Damn, I loved this man. Nick had been working extremely hard and I had a beautiful wedding ring to prove it. My heart just couldn't help but want him more than ever. I would simply have to suppress my sexual urges and realize that I had one hell of a man who could satisfy me in more ways than one.

"Oh, Nick, you are my everything," I exclaimed almost in tears. How could I be so deceitful to this wonderful man? I had no idea how deep Nick's feelings were from the beginning. I always believed that a man's main concern was sex, and began to accept that. But Nick, oh Nick...what a godsend!

I realized that I had to dismiss Jacques as a temporary setback. Just like drugs, Jacques felt real good but could end up costing me everything if I didn't let go. With that, Jacques was dismissed. Nick and I reconfirmed our love for each other over and over for almost an hour, neither of us wanting to hang up. When we finally did it was nearly 10:00 P.M., and I knew Carol would be at my door any moment.

I took a quick shower and no sooner did I dry off before there was a knock on the door. I opened it without asking who it was because I knew how prompt Carol was. She was dressed to the nines. Carol reminded me so much of myself of the younger, single-and-ready-to-mingle me. I wanted Carol to have a wonderful time as I had had in the past, so I let her know that everything was taken care of for the evening and all she needed was her identification. Carol was ecstatic and ready to hit the streets. We giggled and discussed how much fun we would have as I dressed. I have to admit that being in love and experiencing an orgasm before you go out really helps with one's confidence. I felt bad about the whole Jacques thing, but at the same time I felt so sexy knowing that I had a man who cherished me at home. My ego was soaring high and the night was just beginning to take flight.

Carol and I walked out of the hotel and all eyes were on us. It was like walking down the runway in Paris. The only thing missing was the flashing cameras. We made our way to the front of the hotel when the concierge signaled me that our limo was ready. We entered the limo, which had been arranged by one of the artists we sponsored as a thank-you. We ignored the scowling looks and tight lips of our white counterparts, as I'm sure they probably thought we were either prostitutes or kept women. All I knew was that I was in love and I was going to have fun. Carol and I toasted with champagne as we made our way to the first party. We drank two glasses of champagne before we arrived, and that alone made me a little tipsy. Although my body was ready to party the night away, my mind began to stray between my love for Nick and my lust for Jacques. I don't understand why alcohol makes me so sexually motivated—not that there is anything wrong with that. I personally feel that sex is a beautiful and organic way of expression. What's better than sex? Hmmm. I'll have to think about that.

Our first stop was an extremely exclusive party for the artists performing at the concerts throughout the weekend. Security was tight and no was allowed to enter without a V.I.P. pass and proper identification. I was overwhelmed by all the effort taken to make the ballroom look so magnificent. There was nothing left undone. You could see food and beverages one end to the other. There was even a 1950s style cigar lady passing out Cubans. I knew they were Cubans because I decided to take one for myself. I had to laugh out loud as I took one from the woman as the Bill Clinton "cigar story" went through my head.

The attending artists came lingering around sipping on everything from the pricey Perifino water to Kettle One vodka martinis. One of the artists, whose name I will not mention to protect his privacy and his wife, was making passes at just about every nice-looking woman in the room. I have to say there was plenty to take in. Some of the women—oh excuse me, I mean hoochies—were so obvious with their skimpy clothing. It was as if they had just left their brothel. I thought about all the action I could get if I were single, but I knew deep down that because I had my Nick to love me forever, being single wasn't going to happen. Oh, man, how I wished he was there with me. Well, thanks to modern technology, he was.

"*Bon jour,* may I speak with Monsieur Dupuis?"

"*Oui, oui!*" Nick said with excitement in his sexy voice. "To what do I owe this pleasure of your beautiful voice again today?" he asked.

"Well, I'm here at this V.I.P. party with Carol, who's missing in action and I felt like something was missing here. Then it hit me. It was you. Happy anniversary, Nick!" A brief silence passed and all you could hear was the music and talking in the ballroom. I wondered for a moment if maybe the cellular signal had been lost.

"Francesca, my love, you never cease to amaze me. You are out there with all the happening people and I know you're driving somebody wild out there with your sexy self. I bet you're standing in the corner somewhere sipping on some champagne and doing your usual people watching. I know you've got some man salivating over you right now as he watches you talk on the phone. Do you really love me that much, Frankie?" Nick's voice cracked slightly.

I imagined him lying in the bed wearing just his shirt and boxers with a book in his hand. He was always reading something. When I left he, was reading a book called *Encounters* about this woman and her different sexcapades, so he was probably thinking about the damage I could do in New Orleans—that is if I didn't love him.

"Nick, I want to show you how much I love you."

"How are you going to do that, baby?"

"I'm walking to the bathroom right now."

"Why? What's going on with you? Is my baby a little buzzed right now?"

"Be patient, Nick. I'm in the bathroom now and I'm walking into the stall. You should see this bathroom, sweetie. The floor is a yellow marble with silver veins and the walls are dark mustard and there are small cushiony velvet chairs all around. The walls are lined with mirrors everywhere. And guess what? There are only five stalls, but there is one of those chairs inside. And guess what else, baby?"

"What, Francesca? You know you got me trippin' on you right now. Are you sure you're okay?"

"Hon, I'm okay. I just wanted to tell you that I'm not wearing any panties."

"Is that right?" Nick's voice mellowed once I told him that. He knew if I called to tell him that I wasn't wearing panties that it was going to be on! I locked the stall door behind me and hung my purse on the hook before I sat in the chair.

"Nick, are you still there?" I whispered because I didn't want anyone else to know what was going.

"Yeah, baby, you got my attention." Little did I know that on the other end of the phone Nick's manhood had been at full attention and he took the initiative to keep it growing.

"Baby, I have one of my legs hanging over one of the arms of the chair waiting for you. What should I do next?" Nick loved it when I surrendered to him and he took full control.

"Francesca, baby, you know what I want." I took my hands-free earpiece out my purse and hooked it up to the phone. I knew I would be using my hands for much more important things.

My hand slowly maneuvered up the inside of my thighs where I could feel the heat pulsating in anticipation of my finger's exploration. Nick had my hips twisting and turning. My body lifted from the chair as he dictated my every move. He had me thoroughly hot and wet and completely under his spell. I could hear him struggling to give me commands to please myself while his own elation was happening at home. The beat of my heart grew stronger with every word that Nick managed to get through the phone. He spoke my name—no, he sang my name—over and over.

"Francesca...Francesca...Francescaaaaaa." The sound of his voice was like a classical opera concerto. At the last call of my name, my body became a whirlpool as the fluids rushed from my chest down to the open space between my legs. Once I regained my composure, I could hear Nick moaning from the stimulation he was giving me—and himself for that matter.

"Nick? Nick? Do you feel how much I love you?" Still breathing heavily, I waited for his reply.

"Oh yeah. I felt you and heard you too, loud and clear. I guess that means you love me."

We both laughed out loud and Nick told me to get myself cleaned up and get back to the party. He didn't want any of my scent to be sniffed by any of the dogs wandering around acting like men in disguise. I felt a little disloyal as I straightened myself up before I went back to the party. I wanted to get back to the room and have Jacques inside of me once again, because my Nick was too far away right now. I would only have Jacques one more night and be done.

Saturday

The day would be leisurely until 6:00 P.M. Two of my associates and I would be taking our clients to dinner at Emeril's restaurant and then accompanying them to the main concert event. I knew that that would be very taxing on me so I had scheduled a therapeutic body massage and facial after my workout first thing in the morning. The pilates body-sculpting class I took really kicked my butt, so I was looking forward to the relaxing touch of strong hands caressing my sore body. I took a shower and was instructed to remove my towel and lie on the massage table and use the sheet provided to cover my lower half. The air was filled with the scent of apple-mango burning oil in the small burnt-orange room, along with the sounds of YoYo Ma playing in the not-so-distant background. I closed my eyes and began to drift away once the massage began. Luke, the young beau who was massaging me was very sexy, was a mixture of Andy Garcia and a young Harry Belafonte. Most Creole men looked that way. In light of my recent activities with Jacques, I was hoping that Luke's touch would not prompt me to want more than just a massage. Luke's fingers worked magic as he rubbed the scented oil from the nape of my neck to the small of my back. Once he felt his job was done on my upper half, his hands lifted the sheet of my left leg and began working his miracle there. He began by giving individual attention to each of my toes, and then running his fingers through them. The same attention was given to the right foot. Both of his hands provided my upper thighs with the extra attention they desired. As Luke's hands approached the lower part of my ass, I let out a light moan.

"You like that?" Luke said to my surprise in a deep but low whisper.

"Uh huh," I replied.

"Yeah, I was hoping you would. You've got quite a beautiful body. I feel like my hands were made to give you pleasure."

Please on, baby. Please on!

I chose not to speak because my mouth has been known to get me into trouble. I fell asleep and heard Luke calling my name as he caressed my hair to wake me up. Luke's touch was so tender I almost thought I was at home in bed with Nick. I thanked Luke for relaxing me and gave him a nice tip as I left the spa and fitness club. As I walked down the street looking for food I decided to check my messages. I missed the most important call of the day. Nick called to wish me a happy anniversary, since it was officially the first day of our lives together—forever. I hung up immediately to call home and there was no answer, so I, too, wished my sweetheart a happy anniversary. I stopped at the Royal Sonesta Hotel for a light breakfast and called

Carol afterward to see if she wanted to go shopping with me. Carol sounded like she had company, so I told her that it was okay. I wondered if she was with my business partner, Trevor Banks. He was always checking her out.

Nick was on my mind as I strolled the River Walk. I also thought about Jacques. I hoped that Nick never found out, but by the same token part of me hoped my temporary freakiness would rub off on him so that we could rekindle our wonderful lovemaking. I went directly to the Body Shop and had the salesgirl assist me in putting a basket of men's body oils, lotions, and bath soaps together. I planned on treating Nick to a day of relaxation for our anniversary. This would include a hot bath, followed by an all-over body massage and some good loving. I didn't know what Nick had in store for me, but I knew he loved my massages and I wanted him to feel good when I returned home.

I went back to the hotel to shower and prepare myself for dinner and the concert. I phoned Nick and still there was no answer. Jacques showed up, so I decided one last time wouldn't hurt before I went home the following morning. After an intense orgasm, I showered and tried not to miss Nick so much. Once dressed, my business partner Trevor called to let me know that he would meet me downstairs in fifteen minutes. The form-fitting backless black halter dress I chose to wear for the evening was a gift from Nick. He bought it for my birthday along with a pair of one-carat diamond earrings and matching necklace. I wore the entire ensemble to remind me of Nick for the evening since he was not with me.

Trevor was at the bottom of the stairs waiting for me as I carefully made my way down, hoping not to trip on my dress. He advised me that the clients would be meeting us at the restaurant, as it was one block from their hotel. Trevor arranged for a limo to pick us up and wait for us as we dined, then take us to our next engagement. My mind drifted to another place as we dined on our five-course meal. All I could think about was Nick and how I missed his touch. Before I knew it we were at the concert and in the V.I.P. area where the bar was open and the dance floor was alive and kicking. I couldn't even remember getting there. I knew I had to snap out of my daze and thought a Belvedere martini was just the trick. As I sipped my martini and had small talk with my clients, I gazed upon the dance floor and decided to loosen up by going out there and shaking my thing. I instructed my clients that it was time to boogie and they followed me to the dance floor. We formed a circle and began grooving to the music.

My client Estelle Graves whom I took to lunch the other day and her husband, Mark, moved pretty well for white folks. They did the bump and had the bounce down pat. I was definitely impressed. I knew there was something I liked about her. The music slowed and the couples began to move closer together. I slowly moved back, but still continued to move to the music. *Oh, Nick, why aren't you here with me?* I closed my eyes momentarily and tried to visualize Nick caressing my body. Damn, he felt good touching me. I was so caught up in my daydream, that I could actually feel Nick's hands caressing my hips as they swayed from side to side. His hands moved from my hips down my ass and back up my sides. I tilted my head and took a deep breath and felt his lips kiss my neck. The softness of his lips and the warmth of his breath were so real that it caused me to open my eyes. When I did, I looked down at the hands I felt. They were real and I had not been dreaming.

"*Bon jour,*" I heard a voice whisper from behind.

I am awake, aren't I?

I knew those hands. I knew that kiss. I knew that voice. I let out a sigh and slowly turned around to find that my beautiful and loving Nick had come for me. I smiled in delight as Nick lifted my chin to plant his warm kisses on my lips. I had never felt such happiness in my life—except for the night Nick and I first met.

"Hi," was all I could say as I stood there in astonishment. A single tear fell from my eye. As it rolled down my face, Nick kissed it away. We gazed into each other's eyes for what seemed like eternity. I realized then that Nick was my only love forever. Like the story of Sampson and Delilah, Sampson's hair was his strength as Nick was mine, and nothing would change that, not even Jacques, my big black dildo.

Twist

by
Tracy Grant

*I*t was happy hour, but Harvey Barron wasn't too thrilled as he strolled into Mercury, his buddy Chuck's new favorite hotspot in Chicago. As he scanned the crowd, Harvey could see why Chuck liked the place—it was filled with sweet-looking young women. The music was good too. Were it not for Chuck, Harvey wouldn't know such trendy places existed.

"Harv. Harv, over here!" Chuck was calling him from a small table. He had a drink in one hand and in the other, a voluptuous, caramel-colored sister in a dark blue pantsuit.

"Janet, this is my good friend Harvey Barron. Harvey, meet Janet."

"Nice to meet you, Jan."

"You too. Chuck, I'm going home."

"Okay, I'll call you." Both the men watched as Janet sauntered off, her hips moving east and west. Harvey laughed as he sat down.

"You like them thick ones, don't you?"

"Oh, and you don't? You can't front on me, Harv, I've known you too long."

"Right. Chuck, we both have to leave tomorrow, so what are we doing here?"

"Hanging out, like everyone else! You want a drink?"

"No, thanks."

"Doing the workout thing again, huh?"

"Just for a while." Harvey had to smile; his friend knew him well.

"I knew it, Harv. Whenever the NSBE conference rolls around, you get all anal, like you have to prepare out the ass. It doesn't make sense. That's why I insisted you come out."

"Yeah, but why the night before we leave? Tonight was my last chance to get some work done! And we're in here clubbing like we're still in school."

"So you have to be in school to have fun? That's crazy. See, that's what's wrong with you right there."

"Ain't nothing wrong with me."

"I know. Network engineer with nice contracts, one of the top consultants in town, always the first to get your certifications. Successful, a home owner, nice Lexus outside. But dude, if you can't appreciate some of the mamas in here, what's it mean? Did you see the ass on Janet? She's got friends, you know."

"Thanks, man, but that's all right. I appreciate what you're trying to do. This just wasn't the best night."

"Harv, the conference is in San Diego. The National Society of Black Engineers, all in San Diego. It's about eighty-six degrees! You must admit it'll be nice to get out of Chi-town."

"You've got me there."

"Uh-huh." Chuck waved a waitress over and ordered another drink.

"Harv, there is something else I thought you should know."

"What's that?"

"Devin's going to be there."

"Devin? For what?"

"She's giving some kind of presentation."

"Devin works in human resources. What could she possibly—"

"That was then, brother. Have you talked to her lately?"

Harvey couldn't contain his surprise. "You know I haven't."

"Well how long has it been?"

Harvey mumbled his answer.

"What?"

"More than a year."

"Damn, Harv. And you wonder why I bring you to Mercury."

"I thought about her, Chuck, but there just wasn't anything to say."

"You haven't been with anyone since Devin, have you?"

"So what?"

Chuck held up his hands. "Easy, easy. I just wanted you to know she'll be there. But I also want you to have a good time while we're out there. You'll get a lot out of the conference, but life isn't all work. Let's play some golf, man, meet some of these chicks!"

"I hear you, man," Harvey told him, "I hear you." Harvey stood to leave, to the dismay of his friend.

"Where are you going?"

"Home to pack. I'll see you at the hotel."

That night at his house, Harvey did his last bit of packing as the news sunk in. Devin knew he would be at the conference, as he was every year. Yet she wasn't going to tell him she was coming. Typical, he thought. If Chuck hadn't found out that she would be there, he would have been completely caught off guard. As he closed the Gucci suitcases she had bought him, the memories came back. When he looked at the plush, tasteful décor of his bedroom, he recalled the arguments. Harvey thought of himself as traditional, but Devin had called him a chauvinist; it was one of the main reasons why they hadn't worked out. She was too independent for him and Harvey knew just what he wanted. When Devin proved unwilling to adjust to Harvey's needs, he had been man enough to let her go. He was genuinely happy for her success, which he thought had been in human resources.

Harvey decided to shower that night to leave himself extra time in the morning. Afterward he went into his basement, which he had converted into a small gym. He turned on the TV, found a movie he liked, and launched into a workout on his Nautilus system. He did set after set, building his already muscular arms and chest. But the workout didn't help, Devin was firmly planted in his mind. In addition to the drama, there were of course, good times, not the least of which involved the kind of lovemaking he hadn't known before or since. Before Devin, Harvey had usually been with sexually conservative women whose bodies more than made up for their lack of imagination in bed. Devin James had given him the best of both worlds. Her lovemaking went from basic to experimental, depending on her mood. He loved her flexibility, the way she could twist herself in different directions during the act. And her body, Harvey thought, shaking his head. It was nothing short of artistic. When Harvey closed his eyes, he imagined her smell and felt the smoothness of her blouses, her skirts, her dark stockings. Harvey opened his eyes and returned to reality; the delights of Devin were history, regardless of whether he was going to see her. Still, he'd have a hard time getting to sleep that night.

Harvey woke up the next morning with renewed focus. He gathered his materials for the conference and checked in with his clients over the phone. He arrived at Midway Airport two hours early; Midway was less congested than O'Hare. While waiting on his flight, Harvey looked over the conference schedule and decided which workshops might be best. He also did some work on his laptop, mapping out possible system solutions for his clients's computer networks. Much of this was done in the name of keeping Devin off his mind, but Harvey didn't care—he was happy to use the time productively.

Four hours and a nap later, Harvey set his watch to Pacific Time. While leaving the plane he checked his mobile phone, but only Chuck had called.

Harvey emerged at ground transportation area and took a deep breath. It was a balmy eighty-two degrees and the sun was out. *Chuck was right,* Harvey thought. *This'll be nice.*

"Harvey Barron." It had been months since he had heard that voice, but Harvey knew it anywhere.

"Devin James. Hi."

"You headed to the convention?"

You know I am! Harvey thought. "Yes."

"Care to share a taxi?"

"Sure."

Moments passed as the two of them sat in the back of the taxi.

"Nice suit," Devin complimented him.

"Yours too. I like the pants."

"Ha ha," she said with sarcasm. "I see you haven't changed."

"I'm sorry. I'm just surprised to see you. I didn't know what I'd say when I ran into you."

"How about 'nice to see you'. 'How have you been?' That would have been nice."

There was another pause between them as the taxi drove on.

"You're right," Harvey admitted. "I hope you'll give me another chance."

"Sure."

The taxi pulled into the La Jolla Hyatt, where the conference would convene. Harvey offered to pay the driver, but Devin insisted she pay instead. Once they reached the lobby, Harvey was at a loss for words.

"We'll catch up later in the week, Harvey. Right now I need to prepare for the conference."

"Right. I'll see you later."

The opening night reception was held in one of the hotel ballrooms. Harvey came in about an hour after it started and the room was packed with presenters and attendees. Harvey recognized old colleagues as well as students, who were more excited and bright-eyed than the more seasoned engineers. Corporate attire was the norm, and as usual, everyone was all business, discussing job opportunities and the upcoming workshops. Harvey spotted Chuck in the crowd and waved; Chuck's face lit up with excitement as he made his way over.

"What's up, player! When did you get here?"

"A few hours ago. You play golf today?"

"Fa sho. Still got the nine handicap."

"That should be enough to take care of these clowns."

"Yep. Hey, Devin's here."

"I know. I shared a cab with her."

"Yeah? How did that go?"

"Not great, but we were civil."

"That's good. Whoops, speak of the devil."

Chuck pointed to the crowd and there was Devin, chatting it up with a couple of male attendees. Chuck laughed.

"Those brothers don't fool me, talking all that bullshit. They don't care nothing about what she's doing here. They're just trying to kick it to her."

Harvey fought back a smile.

"You know I'm right, dude."

If you only knew, Harvey thought.

The workshops began at 10:00 A.M. Harvey was pleasantly surprised by the globalization panel, a session where he actually learned something. He found the sessions on effective networking and mentors a bit too basic for him, though they were good for younger attendees. A couple of hours later he stood outside one of the conference rooms. He checked his phone messages and answered a client's question. After his call, Harvey saw Chuck speaking with someone about the session they'd just attended. Harvey approached and he saw that the guy with Chuck was very engaged in the discussion.

"...so I was just happy that they covered all areas of product development," the guy told Chuck. "I go to these conferences and they always go into marketing, but they never deal with engineering properly."

"That's true," Chuck agreed.

"All you computer guys are taking over."

"Yeah, whatever. I was in aeronautics before I touched a computer. I started from scratch—Unix, C+, C++, Oracle, all that. You still on your MCSE."

"But I was just saying—"

"Just be careful who you're talking to," Chuck warned him. "You might need a job one day."

The young man looked somber. Chuck offered his hand. "Hey, it's all good. No hard feelings."

"Thanks." Chuck sent the man on his way as Harvey watched.

"Still putting the young boys in their place."

"That boy don't know. I didn't even come here for all that."

"How was your session?"

"Pretty good. I'm going to Telecom next."

"Me too. How about some lunch?"

"Sounds good."

Just then, Devin approached. Harvey played it cool, but inside he was anxious.

"Hi, Chuck."

"Devin James, hello!" Devin watched Harvey as she embraced Chuck.

"Long time no see, miss lady."

"Long time indeed. You gentlemen have plans for lunch?"

"Maybe you'd like to join us," Harvey offered.

"You know what? I've got to catch this guy from Dell," Chuck said. "You two go on ahead." Before Harvey or Devin could react, Chuck was gone.

Devin and Harvey found a beachfront restaurant in La Jolla, near the hotel. It gave them both a chance to see some of the gorgeous La Jolla area. After their food arrived, Harvey felt like he was in a staring contest.

"Aren't you going to say anything?" he asked.

"I'm engaged, Harvey."

"Wow. That's saying something. When's the wedding?"

"September."

"Seven months from now. Congratulations."

"Thank you. Do you mean it?"

"Of course. You're happy, aren't you?"

"Yes. I was a little nervous about telling you."

"Nervous? Not you."

"Very funny. I can be nervous sometimes."

"Could have fooled me. Who's the lucky guy?"

"His name is Michael."

"I see." Harvey considered what he'd just heard. He was silent as the news sank in.

"Don't look so surprised, Harvey."

"It wasn't what I expected, that's all."

"What *did* you expect?"

"Nothing. I didn't expect to see you here, now this. Why are you even telling me?"

"Would you rather I didn't?"

Harvey was stumped. The conversation was too unpredict-able.

"This is why I was nervous," Devin admitted. "I knew you might act funny."

"How is this funny?"

"Harvey, you walked away, not me."

"And you stayed out of touch."

"Of course. Me and rejection don't get along."

"Oh. So now you're looking for closure, is that it?"

"Maybe," she admitted before sipping her wine. "I always felt I could talk to you when I needed to. Don't ask me why," she asserted, rolling her eyes. Harvey couldn't help but smile. He hated showing even that much emotion, but she had truly comforted him with the comment.

They walked back to the Hyatt, sightseeing along the way; it was another hot day.

"You used to talk, Harvey."

Harvey looked down at her. He didn't want to ruin the moment with a misplaced comment.

"What does Michael do?"

"He's a schoolteacher."

"Ahh, a teacher. In public school?"

"Yes."

"So you'll be the breadwinner."

"That's irrelevant."

"Sure it is. Would you be engaged if he made more than a nickel?"

"Don't be an asshole, Harvey. I know it's a strain."

"I'm just saying—"

"You have nothing to say about Michael, trust me." They found themselves in front of the hotel.

"The next session started already. I'm late."

"Devin, wait."

"Thanks for lunch." Harvey watched her storm off. Frozen with regret, he could only think of how he'd ruined lunch by being a smart-ass. He'd forgotten that beneath the proud, self-reliant exterior, Devin was a sensitive woman. He'd also forgotten that he had touched her heart as much as she had touched his.

Harvey sat through the remaining sessions that day, but he was too distracted to get anything out of the workshops. He never dealt with losing Devin, but since she'd been there, he had to now. Dammit, he thought. Maybe if he'd faced facts, admitted he'd made a mistake, he would have handled seeing her better. Instead, to use Chuck's words, he had played himself.

The NSBE conference held its annual Funk Jazz Café that night in the hotel restaurant, which was crowded as usual. Instead of the usual suits and jackets, everyone looked less formal, including the women. Harvey found Chuck at the bar.

"Hey, player."

"Hey, Harv! I was looking for you."

"Here I am. What are you drinking?"

"Hennessy."

"Me too. Bartender, two Hennessys."

Chuck looked at his friend wide-eyed. "What happened to the workout?"

"I'm taking a break."

"All right. What happened with Devin?"

"Nothing."

"Harv, this is—"

"She's engaged."

"Oh." Harvey didn't bother to hide his dismay. "Brother, it could be worse. She's a good sister and fine as hell, but that's over."

"Yeah, well seeing her didn't help."

Chuck was silent, but his eyebrows were raised. Harvey knew what he was thinking—*I told you so,*—but he didn't want to say it.

"You're right," Harvey admitted. "I had my chance."

Hours later, Harvey could barely stand and Chuck had to help him back to his room. Harvey woke up at 8:30 the next morning, fully clothed with his shoes still on. He looked a mess in the mirror. When he took a shower, he was met with a fierce headache, yet he was relieved somehow. *At least it's done,* he thought. Though the rest of the conference would be a wash, now he might have a meaningful exchange with another woman.

At the hotel's buffet breakfast, Harvey checked his messages while wolfing down scrambled eggs and orange juice. One client needed him immediately, but he finished eating before calling him back from the lobby. It was there he saw Devin again, just passing by, in her usual business suit, this one olive. That day she wore a skirt and his favorite dark stockings with black lines along the back of her legs. Now he couldn't concentrate, but he had to walk his client through his system problem. He did so over the phone, but not without fighting off a fierce erection. After the hourlong call, Harvey kept imagining her backside and the erection was still there. Ridiculous, he thought. He could have cut glass with it.

"Don't look so troubled," he heard someone say. He looked down and recognized her heels.

"Client call," he replied, putting his hands in his lap.

"Look, I finished my presentation, so I probably won't see you."

"You leaving? Cause I'm done too."

"Harvey, it was good to see you."

"You don't have a few hours? We could check out the aquarium."

She considered the offer.

"I know you've got things to do. I just didn't like the way our lunch ended."

"I thought about the aquarium."

"You can tell me more about Michael."

Devin cracked a smile, indicating her consent. Harvey could have jumped for joy.

They took in the Birch Aquarium's exhibits, which included sharks, sea horses, and all kinds of exotic fish. Harvey peppered Devin with questions about Michael, but she was evasive. They found themselves at a pier outside the aquarium overlooking the beach.

"Why don't you want to tell me about him?" Harvey asked. "I might learn something."

"Michael has nothing to do with what went wrong."

"You've got me there, but I have to ask."

"You both have your qualities," she told him. "Not that that's any of your business." She walked to the edge of the pier. His eyes were on her backside, which was as plump as ever. Harvey came up behind her and pinned her to the gate with his body.

"Devin, I am sorry—for everything." She held on to the rail and he placed his hands over hers. Before long, he felt the bulge in his pants against her skirt. She squeezed the gate. He put his face near her neck and breathed in her scent. She began to rub her behind against his erection. His hands made their way into the front of her blouse while he gently nibbled on her neck. He could hear himself panting.

"Make sure no one's around," she told him. But all of San Diego could have been there. It was sensory paradise, her muscles tensing, her perfume, the silky feel of her pantyhose under her skirt. He lifted the skirt and ran his hands along her behind, which was still wrapped in a taut pair of panties. He was big enough to hide what he was doing behind her, so he lowered her panties just enough to make room for himself.

"Use a condom," she instructed. Harvey was delighted, but nervous all at once, like he had been as a teenager. He dropped his wallet on the pier while fumbling for a condom. Devin grunted once he was inside and her feet were a few inches off the ground; she was pinned. Harvey was frantic, keeping his nose around her neck and shoulders, moving in and out with little control. Her nipples were extra long, just as he remembered.

"Easy," she told him. Her feet were now moving up and down with him. She took her right arm, grabbed the back of his neck and somehow twisted herself around until she was almost facing him for a long kiss. Harvey knew she could get hurt against the rail, but he couldn't help himself. As tight as she was pinned, he felt Devin backing herself into him, moving quickly then stopping. Seconds later he shuddered and almost fell. Devin arched her back and braced herself as she'd always done; Harvey let out a loud grunt as he exploded inside of her. He kept kissing and licking, but Devin gently pulled herself away and fixed her clothes while looking around for bystanders. Harvey knew she was satisfied, but he was overcome with sadness. She looked sympathetic.

"You never had trouble in this area," she declared. Harvey looked down at the pier. "I agree, Harvey, it's a shame," she told him. "*Now* you come on strong. *Now* you're passionate. Go figure."

"I was wrong," he blurted.

"Yes," she agreed. "But it doesn't make you a bad person."

"I can change," he insisted.

"No need. Take care," she said before giving him a peck on the cheek. Harvey looked as if the world were ending.

"I'll send you an invitation. Promise." Before he could react, she was walking down the pier, headed back to the aquarium. Harvey could only watch her as she left. Suddenly, nothing else mattered, not even the client calling on his mobile phone.

He could never replace Devin, but he did grow because of her. At least he hoped so.

Holdin' It Down
by
Courtney Parker

*P*ortia Banks entered her two-bedroom downtown Los Angeles apartment, shaking off the tear-sized raindrops from her leather coat. Of all the nights for Mother Nature to be kind to southern California by blessing the usually sunshiny state with rain, she had to be gracious on the day of Portia's standing Thursday hair appointment. And with Los Angeles being the "pressed hair" capital of the world, Portia knew her hair was practically ruined for the rest of the week.

Tossing her keys on the nearby end table, Portia bent to pick up her mail. As she lifted the letters from the base of the door one by one, she couldn't help but notice the sage-green envelope with the ivy trim, a gift she gave to her boyfriend Jamal last month for their anniversary. Although the stationery was a bit girly, Portia wanted to make sure that the letters Jamal was writing her from jail would not arouse the attention of her curious neighbors unless the postman paid close attention to the return address. As far as she was concerned, Jamal was in the military on a tour of duty in Germany, although, Portia knew Ms. Jenkins, her nosey-ass neighbor across the hall assumed differently. Gloria Jenkins knew better than to ask Portia inappropriate questions about her personal life especially since Portia's father corporate mogul and attorney Porter Gates had saved their building by purchasing it and maintaining the rent-control policy that had been incorporated years ago by the former owner.

Portia's life had always been a bit on the rebellious side. First it was her attempts to drop out of her prestigious prep school to pursue her dream of modeling. It was evident by her 4.0 grade point average that school was definitely where she belonged. Then there was her continuous acts of defiance with her chosen male suitors. Never were they the prodigies of her father's very influential friends, instead they were always the roughest of the rough boys usually from cities like Compton, South Central, or Watts. Portia liked them hard—Ebonics talking, chronic smoking, and khakis sagging. She liked everything about the act of surviving in the ghetto, even though it was a long stretch from her parents' seven-bedroom Brentwood home in the hills. Whenever her mother and father would encourage Portia to go right, she insisted on going left. And as their only child by circumstance rather than choice, they learned to accept her for who she was rather than what they wanted her to be.

Portia looked around her designer décored mini palace (a gift from her father upon agreement to go to college as a political science major) and smiled. Even though she liked her men rough and rugged, she insisted on only the best. Jacques Monrovia, L.A.'s top interior designer, decorated her plush pad with unique pieces of Italian brush-suede furniture, with only the riches of deep mahoganys, olives, and plums. Her rugs were personally handpicked by Jacques on his trip to Persia, all of course at her father's expense.

Portia placed the group of letters on the table next to her keys, keeping the one from Jamal in hand as she headed to the phone to check her messages. She grabbed the cordless phone while slipping out of her new three-and-a-half-inch Napa leather taupe heels and walked toward her couch. After carefully punching in the code to voice mail—so as not to mess up her freshly manicured nails—Portia laid on the couch, as thoughts of Jamal flooded her soul. She placed Jamal's letter on her copper-colored coffee table, grabbed a cigarette from her pack of Virginia Slims Lights, lit the stick, and allowed the butt of the cigarette to kiss her doll-like thin lips.

First message: "Hi, honey. It's Dad. I wanted to thank you for going over the McKinley briefs for me. With Aaron in Michigan closing the Freedmen deal, I didn't want those documents to go ignored. By the way, I know you have some exams coming up but as soon as you get some free time, your mother and I would love to have you over for dinner. Outside of work, we barely get to see you. Sweetheart, call your mother, you're all she has, you know. We love you very much, princess. Bye."

Message erased. Second message: "You have a collect call from the Los Angeles County Jail. To accept this call, please press five…"

Message erased. Third message: Portia slowly exhaled a small circle of smoke, tapped the extension of ash unto the corner of an ashtray, then smiled. The mere thought of Jamal made her weak in the knees. *Damn, I miss that,* she thought, brushing her auburn-colored bangs away from her eyes.

"Hey, Portia, it's Chris. Listen about last night…maybe things did get a bit out of hand with you trying to be faithful to Jamal and all. But I just couldn't resist you any longer. I have no regrets…and I hope you don't either. Damn, you do it for me. Please call."

Message saved.

Portia took a long drag then released a cloud of nicotine. *Chris is definitely going to be a problem,* she thought. Even though she'd written Jamal about her new relationship, with the guarantee that it was nothing, the last two months of this so-called platonic friendship had taken a drastic turn in a very unfamiliar direction.

Portia hung up the phone, place the half-finished cigarette into her Waterford crystal ashtray, and picked up the letter again. The thought of her most recent letter to Jamal brought a huge grin, as well as uncontrollable blush. The last few letters had been extremely explicit yet the latest included a variety of pictures of Portia in an array of nude, sensual poses. Kevin Salvage, ex-photographer for *Playbunns* magazine, had agreed to shoot Portia at her request. Five hours and twenty-five hundred dollars later, she and Kevin had created not only pictures of sheer enjoyment, but also Portia's first experience with masturbation—both of which she would later experience again and again.

She remembered making love to the very pen she used to write Jamal's letters. The feeling of the warm marble finger-width pen in and out of her pussy heated her all over again. Taking slow, deep breaths, Portia unbuttoned her chocolate tailored slacks and pulled them off, exposing her crotchless nude pantyhose. With a hasty hand movement Portia managed to unfasten all five buttons of her taupe silk blouse. As she stroked the traces of her satin Wonder Bra with her left hand, she fanned herself with Jamal's letters using the other. She closed her eyes remembering the words of her letter. As the words softly replayed in her mind, she imagined the expression on her Alan Iverson look-alike man making love to every sentence on the page:

I'm loving myself thinking about you right now, using my hands to do all the things yours can't. Tasting all of me, the way I know you would if your tongue could kiss the lips of my throbbing center. Sucking on my nipple hard then soft, then hard again, until the redness of my skin aches with desires. J, my body's exploding as I imagine you inside me. You being the man that you are, I'm feeling you tangled inside me like a fly caught in a spider web, wild...desperate to escape but trapped inside my love. Your thickness pounds in and out, softly banging the walls of my pussy like an African drum. The rhythm is in sync, echoing with that of my heart. Ohh, baby...I feel you...I feel you...growing harder with me getting wetter and wetter. I know you like it juicy, so I've made it nice and juicy for you. I'm using the juice of my love to write this letter. If you smell the pages, they carry my scent. The sweat, the sweetness, it's all for you. I want you to cum all over this letter. Look at my pictures, see my ass, touch my pussy, lick my breasts, cum all over me...do it for me, baby. Do it now, as you read this. Take me...just like that...I need you...I miss you... Fuck me, J...fuck me with your mind.

Portia opened her eyes, not realizing that she'd slipped into the past. She wondered if Jamal did all the things she'd told him to do in her letter. She hoped that he had as much fulfillment reading it as she had writing it.

Anxiously, she opened his and read:

Hey, love,

Just got the pictures you sent me. A nigga can't believe how phat that ass has gotten since the last time I saw you. Twenty-two months and counting to be exact with only two months to go. Portia, I know I told you to wait for me, and deep down I want to believe that you have, but when I see your face in these pictures, see your ass bent over like that, I wonder who's been swimming in my love. Fuck it. Shit like this will drive you crazy in here so I'll be the nigga that I am and suck it up. 'Cause, I know the last time I was in it, I put my name on that pussy, and it belongs to me. You really fucked a nigga up though with that last letter. You had a nigga nuttin' on the drop of dime. Damn, I miss you, too, boo! It's been a minute now, seems like forever though. I don't like you going out and making new friends. This Chris sounds like trouble. I mean, from the way it seems, shit, you been spending a lot of time with that nigga. You say it's nothing, so a nigga's got trust you, just know this, boo. No matter who's gotten or gets in those skins while I'm locked up in this mutherfucka, that ass belongs to me. I'm gonna get out of here and serve you up right even if I have to fuck a mutherfucka up for feelin' you. A nigga can't think right now. My dick's aching and my head's all fucked up looking at these pictures. Tonight, I'll make love to you the way you asked me to, hell, the only way I know how to in here...with my mind. Holdin' it down.

J.

Portia smiled as she pulled the letter close to heart. Twenty-two months behind them with two months to go. Those were the words that rang in her head. Portia was lucky that Jamal only had to serve two years for the drugs he was trafficking, especially since he got caught with a kilo of cocaine. With Portia's help and strong support, the two of them convinced the D.A. they didn't know what they were transporting, and as a favor to a friend who had recently been shot, they were dropping off the package in Texas. Portia with her good-girl image and wealthy father's money was assigned someone within her father's firm to get her completely off the hook and Jamal received twenty-four months in the county jail. Because of the extreme nature of his crime and the firm warning from her father, Portia wasn't able to visit Jamal under any circumstances while he served his sentence. So they communicated once a week via phone and every other day by mail.

With one final exhale Portia rose and sauntered in the direction of the bathroom. With only two months left to go, she was sure she could manage her feelings for Chris long enough for them not to matter. Jamal would be out soon, and she knew he wasn't going for the thought of sharing his woman with another—or would he?

With the proper convincing, he may be down with the possibility of a threesome. Hell, for all she knew he may have experimented while in jail himself, so he might actually be comfortable with the idea of sharing, at least one time. She and Chris had crossed the line the other night, which was to be expected after three Long Island Iced Teas, and a shot apiece of tequila.

Chris was a second-year attorney at Portia's father's firm. Tall, dark, and absolutely divine. A favorite of her father's, Chris possessed all the qualities Portia's father wanted for her and was someone he wouldn't mind hanging out with his only daughter. In his efforts to form a bond between the two, he often arranged for Portia to assist in Chris's cases as an understudy, since Portia had only one year left in college. At first Portia resisted because there was an uncomfortable vibe between she and Chris from the beginning, one she verbalized to her father.

"You could learn something from Chris," her father protested. "I think you're overreacting, in an attempt to not meet and mingle with someone decent. I will not have you throw your life away on that thug in jail. Chris can help you, maybe even introduce you to new things, ideas, and people."

Never in her wildest dreams did Portia feel her father was going to be right. Chris had exposed her to new things, ideas, and people. Together they had explored new territories, and much to Portia's surprise she accepted the change with cautious but open arms. Within two months Chris had taught Portia more about herself than Jamal or her parents had in the past seven years of her life. Chris knew how to make Portia feel like a woman. Not just any woman but a strong, self-serving, confident, self-loving woman. From the way Chris complimented her to the way they touched each other, Chris made Portia feel complete. The night before, even in all its splendor, Chris opened up a whole new feeling of intimacy in Portia. Even through just touching and kissing, Portia's body fell into total incomprehensible passion and submission. And although her mind begged her to stop, her soul screamed out for more. Chris had unleashed an inner being that had been trapped inside Portia's body for her entire twenty-three years and now that the awakening had begun, there was no way she would put it into hibernation again.

Portia turned on the shower and removed the remains of the clothing from her body, then got in. The warm water trickled against her chocolate smooth skin, calming her fiercely stirred emotions. Just as she began to unwind with the water gently massaging her body she was interrupted by the doorbell.

"Who in the hell!" she exclaimed as she pulled back the shower curtain, awaiting a second ring.

Once she heard it, she reached for her terry-cloth robe and slid her misted body into it. The drips of water from her body traced her steps as she made her way to the door.

"Who is it?" Portia snapped.

"Portia, it's me...Chris. Can I please come in? I really need to see you."

Oh shit, Portia thought, as she peeked through the peephole. Not knowing exactly how to react, Portia turned the lock and slowly opened the door.

"Chris, what are doing here? Is everything alright?"

Chris leaned in close, forcing the door open. "Can I come in?"

"Um...yeah...come on in." Portia cracked the door a tad bit farther, allowing Chris enough room to slide past her. Without hesitation, Portia repeated her question. "Chris, is everything alright?"

"No, Portia. Everything isn't all right. I'm all fucked up now. I keep wondering and thinking about us...and last night... and I just need to know." Chris moved in close, but Portia politely stepped back. Chris sighed. "I need to know if it meant anything to you. But I can tell now by your reaction, last night meant nothing."

Portia stood still, wanting to embrace and comfort Chris, but wasn't exactly sure how she felt about responding. By comforting, she didn't want to lead Chris on, yet by not doing anything, she risked Chris feeling rejected, which truly wasn't her intention.

"Last night was amazing," Portia stated while cautiously keeping her distance. "I just don't know what to do though. I love Jamal. I still crave his touch...I love him."

"I don't want you to choose. But I do want to be with you again." Chris moved in close again. Only this time Portia didn't resist. Within moments the two of them were kissing and touching with the same intensity and passion as the night before, both moaning with desire...both lunging toward the other.

Chris slid off Portia's robe, then followed her into the bathroom. Portia stepped back into the running water, leaving the shower curtain open—an invitation for Chris to join her—and within minutes the two of them stood naked with massages of the lukewarm water and each other's fingers caressing their bodies. Chris kneeled down and licked the lips of Portia's pussy with long, slow strokes eager to go farther than they had the night before. Smiles crossed both of their faces as Chris mastered the act of providing oral love.

"Let me do you," Portia whispered, pulling Chris up then kneeling herself down.

Taking turns they continued providing each other with sensual pleasure and fervor. For minutes they groaned and moaned in delight, so much that neither of them noticed Jamal standing in the doorway, full of rage—and lustful desire.

As fate would have it, a shipment of illegal Mexican aliens had been caught trying to smuggle themselves and more than two thousand pounds of marijuana across the border in an eighteen wheeler, so Jamal was granted an early leave due to overcrowding.

With what seemed like an eternity, Jamal stood in the doorway, with an array of mixed emotions and fears, and in awe watched the woman he loved, make love to another.

"Oh my god!" Chris said, covering her firm mango-sized breasts with her hands.

Unable to speak, Portia's eyes froze on Jamal's full muscular frame. Finally after a brief moment of awkward silence, she whispered… "Jamal."

Portia stood paralyzed as Jamal just looked at her, breathing heavily, dick hard, and tears streaming down his cold, pain-stricken face. She knew that never in his wildest thoughts, could he have imagined his girlfriend being with another woman.

"J," Portia tried to speak as she watched him slowly remove his shirt, then kick off his shoes, and drop his pants. Now wearing only his boxers, Portia wondered what he was thinking as he darted a cold glance at Chris, motioning her to move in close to Portia. Trembling, Chris stepped toward Portia without saying a word.

Almost methodically Portia imagined what she would do if she was Jamal, yet clouded with confusion and fear she stood silent witnessing his actions.

Jamal removed his boxers to expose his fully erect penis. As he looked at the two naked bodies before him, it was obvious that his lust was overtaking his anger. Gradually, he moved the shower curtain back and got in. Still in silence he reached for Chris, bending her over so that her butt was aligned to his hard penis. He shoved himself inside of her, and fucked her in the ass while looking at Portia with the same cold, pain-filled eyes. Chris moaned with agony and delight as Jamal thrusted in and out of her ass. After repeated strokes, twenty-four months of cum began to gush from his penis as he pulled out. Gently pushing her to the side, Chris balled up in a fetal position in the corner of the shower, while Jamal closed in on his woman.

Portia threw her arms around Jamal's neck, praying that he still loved her.

"I love you, J," she whispered in his ear, her heart pounding, her voice faint.

"I love you too, boo," he answered. "I love you too."

Love at First Sight
by
Tracy V. Green

*H*ey baby, what's up? Whatcha doin'? I'm comin' to get you!"

Chris always seemed to ask questions, not really wanting the answers. Chris could be so stank at times but I loved him. He was sensitive when we were alone, friendly toward others, and zealous all the time. Chris was the love of my life. I had met him my freshman year in college. He was a sophomore and very popular. I used to see him and his posse in the cafeteria. My girls Mia, Rochelle, Asa, and I used to watch them and make up stories from what we heard or wanted to hear.

"That dark skin guy is a cutie. He looks so mean. I never see him smile. He must be from Brooklyn," I said, never taking my eyes off him as he passed our table in the cafeteria.

My Spanish friend Mia said, "He's a dog. I heard he be with crazy girls. He tried to talk to me the other day. You know he's in my African Studies class."

To this day Chris denies ever trying to talk to Mia. He said she used to sweat him and ask him stupid questions just to start a conversation. Rochelle, my buddy and roommate, said, "Lauren, he's definitely your type. He hangs around my calculus class on Thursdays to pick up his homeboy Kevin. Here he comes," Mia said in a loud whisper. He walked by and his eyes met mine. I smiled shyly and he kept on walking, peeping me from the corner of his eye.

"He looks a little crazy to me, girl. I don't think you want to mess with that. I can see you now, crying because he beat the shit out of you," Asa said, shaking her head, her mouth turned in disapproval. She was always negative. Never wanted to see anyone happy unless she was happy.

I remember seeing Chris on the yard at school with this light-skinned skinny ugly girl riding on his back. He was actually giving her a piggyback ride. Mia saw them first. "Looka here, looka here. Lauren, see what I told you. He's a German shepherd. Girls hang all over him. And you know them dark-skinned brothers always got to get them a light, bright, near white bitch."

Asa was nodding in agreement and stuffing her fat face with a hot dog. With her mouth full, she spit out, "I heard he's fucking her. Lauren, girl, I tell you, you don't want him. Shoot! You don't need a man to be happy. Shit, as long as there's cable, my girls, and horseback riding class I'm straight." We all laughed because we knew that Asa would cut many of her classes, but never the horseback riding one.

I agreed with them aloud but I still found Chris sexy and had to have him. I knew I was hot. At five foot seven inches, size eight, light-brown honey skin with slanted eyes, chin-length bob haircut (I used to be called China), I had lots of guys knocking at my door. Chris should be easy to get, I hoped. He was tall, six foot two, dark brown smooth skin, puppy dog eyes with long eyelashes, large nose, and sexy full lips. His body was strong and slim since he played basketball almost every day. He was bowlegged and had the cutest behind I'd ever seen. He wore a fade and his haircut always looked fresh. He never smiled but I knew he was witty because he could be found in the poolroom on campus in the afternoon (in between his classes) cracking jokes. He used to play for money and would always win enough to pay for dinner for two.

Thank God for Rochelle. She ran back to our room and said she told Kevin that I thought his friend was cute and that Friday at the Halloween party they were going to introduce us. I was in a complete frenzy. I hated her. I didn't know whether I wanted to kiss her, slap her, or punch her. "No! Why'd you do that? Did Kevin say he liked me? Why Rochelle, why? I'm not going, forget it. He might have a girlfriend already. What about that light-skinned girl?"

Rochelle laughed at me for a long time and I mushed her in the head for complicating my already confused life. She finally answered all of my questions. "I did it because you like him. And plus every time we see him, he always makes eye contact with you, not the rest of us. Kevin did say Chris had mentioned you to him before, but Kevin pretended he couldn't remember what Chris said. You're going to the party. And fuck that light-skinned girl, Kevin said that Chris ain't fuckin' with her, she's just on his shit."

After that first meeting at the Halloween party, Chris and I were inseparable. I remember the first time we made love, it was heaven. I stayed in his room. He had a single suite and it was on the top floor. It was like staying in a treehouse because of the view of the trees that surrounded the campus. Bobby Brown's "Tenderoni" was playing on the stereo. Chris held my hand softly and pulled me toward him. He put his other hand around my waist and leaned in and whispered in my ear, "You smell so good. Can I have a taste?" I began to giggle and my coochie began to flow like Niagara Falls. He grabbed me tighter and we began to sway to the music. I could feel his penis against me and my entire body began to pulsate. He planted small soft kisses on my neck and whispered, "I thought about you all day." He reached for my chin in order for us to be face to face. He kissed me on the lips soft then firm with his hot tongue rolling around with mine. His strong hands began to massage my back, undo my bra, and pull off my shirt. We kissed like we never kissed before, like the world was going to end if were not one. He grabbed my breast with his left hand while the other hand firmly held my waist. His kisses trickled down my neck to my breast and he licked the nipple then looked at me and licked again. He put the entire breast in his mouth and lured me over to the bed where I ended up on top of him. He smelled so good and I began to kiss his neck then suck his nipples. His hands were on my behind and he was rocking me over his dick. My hands ran down his muscular body to find a large throbbing penis waiting to please my every desire. He took my hand and placed it around his dick and guided me to move up and down.

By then I heard Prince's "Adore" blaring in the background. I massaged Chris's throbbing dick and he continued to suck my breast and squeeze my ass. Chris whispered, "Can I make love to you to-night?" I was so wet and scared that all I could do was nod. He rolled over on top of me and we kissed again. Our tongues flickered frantically back and forth. He reached inside my panties to feel the moisture between my legs. The nappy dugout was more than ready. He used his fingers to play with my clitoris. His kisses and licks moved toward my belly, my inner thigh, and then my clit. My body began to tremble. Chris continued to lick and suck me while he inserted his fingers in and out of my vagina. I exploded in delight as I had my first orgasm with this wonderful, beautiful man. He smiled and then gave me his signature sly grin. He entered me with force and we began to rock to the rhythm of the music. Feeling him inside me heightened my orgasm and I came again. When I thought I couldn't take it anymore, he put my legs over his shoulders and continued to move in a rhythmic groove. His body seemed to be magnified—his back and all his muscles were immense and glistening. At the same time his skin was so soft next to mine. His thrusts became harder and our moans louder. I began to squeal because I was having my third orgasm and Chris yelled "bring it home, baby" and then he came. We laid in each other's arms and he softly kissed me on the lips and cheek.

I could hear Asa yelling at the window, "We know she's up there. She's coming with us to the party." After that night, on many occasions, my girlfriends would have to come to Chris's dorm room to get me to hang out. Asa would look at Rochelle and she would say "Damn she's turned out."

Rochelle would reply, "It's called good dick! Besides, he's whipped too. I don't see him hanging out with his boys much anymore either."

Years Later

I can even recall some of our dates after college. They were amazing. "Hey, baby, what's up? What are you doing'? I'm coming to get you!" Chris's low but happy tone on the phone made me giddy. It was Saturday night, be-with-your-girl night since the guys hung out together on Thursdays and Fridays. This dating ritual was reasonable to me at first because I got to hang with my girls those nights. Later it became a problem. Chris and all things with a penis seemed to really believe that what women liked to do was not important and could only be happening on a Saturday night.

I couldn't wait. "Where are we going?" I asked.

Chris replied with a you-know-better-than-to-ask any-questions-when-I'm-trying-to-surprise-you tone. "You'll know when we get there."

"Come on. Give me a hint."

"Would you rather know now and just not go?"

"No."

"Well, be dressed in an hour—and I mean an hour. Don't have me waiting fifty hours like you always do. All right!"

"You want me to look good, don't you? I'll only be twenty hours this time. All right!"

"Yeah, yeah, one hour. See ya."

When Chris rang the buzzer I still wasn't ready. I knew I was going to hear it, but he knows me. "Tell him I'm on my way down," I told my sister, Camille, who everyone said looked liked me but was a smaller version with longer hair.

"You're never ready," Camille said.

"So, he wants me to look good, right?"

"But you still look busted. You need at least a week to get ready."

Don't you just love sisters? I should have been the only child, but Mother had to be hot and horny and have three more sarcastic brats. Fortunately, I love them and wouldn't trade them for anything in the world. We all get along great. The buzzer rang again after ten minutes.

Camille yelled again, "She's coming down."

Chris yelled back, "If she's not down here in five minutes..." Camille let go of the intercom button.

I ran out of the door, down the stairs and was looking into the face of a black man with a bald head and no patience. Damn, he was sexy.

"I've got to admit, you do look good. But it shouldn't take more than an hour."

"Sorry, but Alisa called with some urgent news."

"What happened now, she couldn't pull up her panty hose? Or is there a sale at Macy's that you girls can't miss? Nah, I know what happened. Her man woke up and realized she's an ugly bitch!"

"Ha! Your mama."

"Damn, Lauren, I was only kidding."

We drove to this little restaurant in Manhattan called Jezebel's. It was the best southern food I ever tasted. She knocked Sylvia's out the box. Later we went to the movies and afterward we drove out to Jones Beach on Long Island. We sat on a sand dune away from the lampposts. Chris lifted my skirt and squeezed my firm ass. He began to spank me playfully and kissed me on my neck. I removed my panties for easy access and straddled him with my long honey-brown legs. He loved when I was on top. My kisses always started at his bald head then traveled to his full lips. He held me so close I could feel his heart beating against my chest. I don't know if it was the sound of the ocean or the moonlight but beach sex made me wild. Chris knew my body— my hot spots, my weak spots, and my sweet spots—better than anyone.

"Your pussy is so sweet," Chris said while I was grinding him in slow motion.

"I want you to fuck me," I replied in a low, sexy voice.

I rode his big, beautiful dick until we both began to howl at the moon. I was completely whipped. This man's smile could make me wet. His touch made my heart beat faster. His warm lips made me shudder with excitement. I always felt safe and loved in his arms.

The Wedding

The sun is shining. Yes! I prayed the whole week. *Please Lord, I'm a child of God and I would love to have a beautiful sunny day for my outdoor wedding.*

I'm so psyched. I awake around 9:00 A.M. The alarm goes off playing some rap remix by Biggie Smalls and Puff Daddy. My girl-friends Gina, Dana, and Renee roll over in their beds and stuff pillows over their heads. Gina and Dana are up from Maryland and the Washington, D.C., area. Renee lives in Brooklyn, but she stayed over to help me dress, drive my brothers to the wedding, and most impor-tant to help me stay calm. I'm a little hyper and need someone to hold me down sometimes.

I decide to shower at my studio apartment then go over to my mother's house to get dressed with the rest of the family. I couldn't believe the day was finally here.

"A marriage! Just like anything else in life—you work hard, you sweat, you plan, and you work hard again for the big climax. It's always over in a matter of minutes but it's the memories that keep you smiling," I said to my girlfriends while getting ready.

"What are you talking about?" Renee asked. She laughed, looked at Dana and Gina as if to say "this girl is crazy." "You've only been planning for four months. You haven't worked that hard and I sure don't see any sweat."

"You know what I mean, girl. We went to college for four years busting our butts but it only took Dr. Richardson two minutes to call our names and hand over the fake diploma," I said.

"Yeah, I know what you mean," Dana said. "I've been working for two years at my firm trying to get my well-deserved recognition and raise. My freaking boss casually states in a weekly meeting that I have been doing a great job. He spit it out in less than a minute in front of four staff members and later told me about my shitty three percent raise. What happened to my plaque, my fifteen percent raise, and my grand announcement in front of all the staff, especially in front of the partners? I was robbed."

We all start to laugh. Renee yelled for me to hurry up and get showered. "Lauren, you are going to get married today, right?"

"You better," Gina said. "I spent too much on your gift. So get to steppin'. Dana and I will see you at the restaurant."

Chris and I dated for eight years. His greatest asset: He's always there for me and his body is gorgeous. He has the softest, silkiest dark brown skin. His aspiration: To become a lawyer. His crutch: He's sloppy.

My greatest asset: I am compassionate and I have the sexiest toes—suckable ones. My aspiration: To be a sitcom writer. My crutch: I'm a sucker for baldheaded dark brown skin men who want to be lawyers. It was our wedding day. I couldn't be happier.

At the suite I laid on the king-size bed and closed my eyes and prayed. *Lord, I can't believe I'm married. I really love him and I hope we will continue to be happy together.*

"This is a phat suite," Chris said as he came from the bathroom holding a bottle of champagne. I looked at him and he knew what I was feeling. I started to speak but he cut me off.

"Shush! No more talking tonight," Chris said as he put his fingers over my lips.

"But I just…" I replied. But he quieted me again and stationed himself in front of me on the bed. He brought me to my feet and held my face with both his hands and kissed me long on the lips. He turned me around and lifted my wedding dress to find that I was wearing a white lace thong and thigh-high white stockings. He bent me over, kneeled down and kissed my right butt cheek then my left one. I could feel his tongue lick the inside of each cheek. I tried to turn around but he held me tight. His hands reached for my thong and I could feel his fingers inside my wetness. I tried to turn again and he spanked me. His tongue began to trace the length of the thong, sending chills up my spine. This man was a freak. He moved my thong and placed his tongue in my ass. Chris's firm grip would not allow me to turn, so I decided not to fight it anymore. It felt so good. Next, I felt his finger enter slowly into my ass. At the same time, he was massaging my clitoris.

My anxiety kept me motionless. Chris did not say a word. He began to undress me. Our naked bodies pressed together, my back to his front. His body felt like silk next to me and his dick on my behind was the best feeling. His kisses down my back were erotic to say the least. He explored my body with his hands and mouth, touching, licking, and kissing all of me. I was so hot. I was begging him with my body to take me. He laid me on the bed face down and parted my legs. He entered me from behind slowly while kissing me on the lips. It took a few attempts and a lot of squirming but his dick filled me up and we began to move together. The heat that came over my body was extraordinary. Our moans became sweet music as we climaxed together.

"I love you and always have since that first day I saw you in the cafeteria," Chris whispered in my ear.

"Shush," I replied with a smile.

Happy Anniversary?

"Hey, Lauren, can you get some time off around the end of this month?" Chris questioned on the other line.

"Why?"

"Well, I want us to take that second honeymoon that I promised you. You pick the place. Anywhere you want to go."

"What about buying the house?" I questioned curiously.

"We can hold off on that right now. I want you to be happy. I even talked with management and there's a one-bedroom available. We can move in next month."

"What about the wedding in Jamaica?"

"I'm still going. My ticket is nonrefundable. You can go if you want. I mean I would like you to go with me."

"I'll have to think about it. We've had a rough year. I don't think any of this is a good idea."

"I'm going to pick you up from work this evening. We can talk more about it tonight. All right?"

"Okay."

"I love you." I was silent and I could hear him breathing on the other end. "I'm waiting," he said.

"I love you too," I said.

Chris picked me up for dinner and we headed to the Boathouse in Central Park. We had been talking over the phone for most of the month. He came over to our studio apartment a couple of times to talk. Twice we had sex and nothing was resolved so I refused to meet him at the apartment. It is our one-year anniversary. He picked me up from work looking so sexy with his freshly shaved head. If Michael Jordan only knew how his look had transformed black men into gods. Chris looked like a huge chocolate bar and I just melted. That's why I gave in so easy those times at the apartment.

He was wearing some gray slacks with an off-white v-neck sweater and a T-shirt underneath. The sweater fit him so that you could see his broad shoulders, back, muscular chest and arms. I was looking cute myself in a black pantsuit with a fitted purple silk button-up shirt underneath it. Of course I unbuttoned enough for him to see my cleavage and black lace bra.

He pulled out the chair for me. We sat on a deck over the water and the scenery was beautiful. There was a pond or something and all around us was greenery—the trees and plants were relaxing. In the corner a jazz band was playing and the setting was quite romantic. It brought me back to our wedding. He ordered a bottle of white Zinfandel and a shrimp appetizer for us. I was impressed because I loved both choices.

"You look hot," he said after staring at me for about five minutes.

"You look good yourself," I replied, enjoying the music and looking at his lips.

"Okay. I'm sorry. I see your point and I'm just rebelling. Eric said that you wouldn't let me go to Jamaica so I bought the ticket anyway. I contradicted my own rules but you can't get so mad all the time. I really thought it would be nice to go back to Jamaica again."

I gave him a look as if to say "no you didn't go there." He noticed and changed his tune real quick.

"I know that we were supposed to do a real honeymoon and I just thought we could combine both activities. I know we've already been to Jamaica but we loved it so much I didn't think it would hurt to go back." He hesitated, probably amazed because I didn't cut him off once. I decided to let him talk this whole dinner. It seemed I was the one always talking, yelling, and complaining. Well if this marriage was to work…he had to open up more.

A waiter brought the wine for Chris to taste and poured our drinks. Another waiter brought the shrimp appetizer along with some bread and Chris smiled at me. He began again. "Lauren, you are not the easiest person to live with. You always want your way. And I know I want my way. We definitely need more space and I agree with you—and two TVs couldn't hurt either." I couldn't believe that he was quoting me. Maybe all my ranting and raving wasn't in vain. I still sat silent. It was hard but I drank the wine, ate the shrimp, which was the bomb, and listened.

Chris saw my plan and used the opportunity to get everything out. "I don't like to clean. I never had to and I don't want to start now. I'm sloppy and that's who I am. You have to just get over it and leave it alone. Lauren, you talk a lot. You are always yapping on the phone with your girlfriends and you are too neat. Everything doesn't have to be in its place all the time."

I arched my eyebrows like I was about to say something. Instead, I simply nodded in acknowledgment of what he was saying. The bread was soft and warm and the sun was setting. We began looking at the menus and I finally broke the silence. "What are you going to order? Both the salmon and crusted tuna look good to me," I said.

"Let's get both," Chris said. He put in the order with the waiter and looked out at the pond. I could tell that he didn't know what else to say without starting an argument. He was trying to choose his words wisely. He was so used to me cutting him off. He hadn't gotten this far in a long time.

"I want to come home for good. I know we've had a rough first year but once we move I know it will be better. More space. I'll try to compromise. I know I'm not good with that but sometimes I won't and you can't throw knives or forks at me. We must both control our tempers and not provoke each other. Do you agree?" Chris asked with his infamous puppy dog gaze.

Finally, I could speak. He asked me a question and I wanted to lay down the law and tell him that he's the selfish one and I always compromise. I would never buy a ticket because my friend teased me into it. I would talk to him about it first. I don't say one thing and do another. I put him first not my friends. I don't run home to my mommy when I have a test or need a break (except once and I came back home that night). Although my brain went on a tangent, my mouthed cooed "I agree."

We decided to go to Curacao. It's one of the ABC (Aruba, Bonaire, and Curacao) islands, north of Caracas, Venezuela. We signed the lease for the one bedroom and moved in over the weekend. We planned to stay there until we could save up enough for a house. The place was a mess but we agreed to fix it together when we got back from our second honeymoon.

"Lauren," Chris yelled from the living room, "make sure you pack my deodorant and stuff because I don't have enough room in my bag for it."

"Okay."

He came into the bedroom where I was packing neatly and he pushed the suitcase on the floor. He grabbed me by the waist and turned me onto the bed. I giggled, saying stop it. He started unbuttoning my blouse and kissing me all over. I laughed hysterically.

"We have a whole week in Curacao to do this, you know."

"Yeah, but I need you now…. What if the plane crashes before we land?" he said before he planted another kiss on my sweet spot.

"Don't say that. You don't want to jinx our trip, do you?"

He pulled off his shirt to show me his chest and I pinched his nipples. He rubbed his hands through my hair and moaned. We kissed and his tongue was hot and flickered quickly against mine. The moisture began to flow. The dampness between my thighs forced me to unbutton his jeans and pull his dick through the hole in his boxers. He smiled and whispered "kiss it." I kissed it, sucked it, and made love to it until he was in a frenzy and was about to release. I got off and said, "We've got to stop and finish packing."

Chris looked at me like I was insane and threw me down on the bed and forcibly inserted himself in me to finish what we started. I shouted in delight as I reached orgasm and he groaned loudly—"Oh yeah, that's what I'm talking about"—as he reached his climax. It was wonderful. We rocked together. In all the excitement we didn't realize that he didn't pull out as he usually did.

Early the next morning we boarded the plane for our honeymoon. I was excited about the night before and couldn't wait for our weeklong fuck fest. Just us talking, swimming, reading, relaxing, and being together. It was our best anniversary ever.

I rated that month a ten-plus. I hoped the second year was all tens. I was looking forward to being his wife again.

Idiot
by
Michael Presley

he visions in my head are getting worse. She is lying next to me and I can't even touch her. I swear I hate her. It hasn't even been two weeks since we met. Please excuse me if I ramble a bit here because I'm going through some pain right now. You know the one you can feel but can't touch. I'm sure you do. I think anyone over the age of five has felt that kind of pain before. I feel used. I have not left this apartment in two weeks. A trip to the supermarket created this problem for me. I met Loretta in the refrigerator section. We both put our hands on the same half-gallon container of Tropicana orange juice. In two weeks I had fallen as hard as one of those big trees in the forest.

Now my soul mate is lying here looking all innocent, fast asleep, not a care in the world. I feel like putting my hands around her throat and squeezing the life out of her. But I am not a violent man; it doesn't pay to be violent. My father told me that ten years ago. He said, "Son, if ever you decide to become violent, remember the immediate gain is not worth the life of pain." I listened to him too. My father was a very smart man. He didn't graduate from Harvard or any of those Ivy League schools, no he got his education from good old City College at a time when a college education was almost free. Back then there weren't that many minority students attending the CUNY colleges. Now my father says the education at the CUNY colleges is not worth the paper it's written on. I agree with him too. That's why I got my computer science degree from Polytechnic Institute of Technology. I had an Asian woman, too, but that was before I met my love.

Yesterday my love said that she was leaving me, going back home. You ever ask yourself if a woman is supposed to be your soul mate then how come she would hurt you? Don't look at me. If knew the answer I wouldn't be asking you the question, would I? I should have known better, after all, look at where I met her. My father told me about places to meet a good woman. He said the best place to meet a good woman was in church after she came from confession. A woman should never spend more than ten minutes in confession. If she did, either she did too many bad things or she was having an affair with the priest.

Oops, she's waking up now.

"Hi, honey. You had a good nap?" I said.

"I sure did. What time is it?"

You know why she is asking the time, right? Come on. Everyone who's guilty always asks the time. She hasn't left the apartment and I know she's guilty. It is like the person is announcing to the world that she needs to know where she is. I'm sure when Monica Lewinsky and the president was smoking the cigar, one of them asked the time.

"It's eight o'clock?" I said.

"Why didn't you wake me? Did you have dinner?"

"Yeah, you know me. I put some leftovers in the microwave, and I was happy."

That's the next thing they like, to make sure that your stomach is full. A man on an empty stomach is a raging idiot. Scientists say it has to do with our central nervous system. Do you think that I should ask her or keep playing it cool? I think I should just ask her and get it over with. But what if it's true, then what? I'm sure she told her girlfriends. Women always go and tell their girlfriends. They must have code words they use when I'm around. You know, something like the oven is open or the iron is hot, shit like that. If I ever find out that they are laughing at me I'm going to hurt somebody. I'm not a violent man but I already told you that so I won't go through it again.

"I love you so much," she said, rising to kiss me on the lips.

I hate when she says that because it confuses the hell out of me.

Her mouth tastes like cotton candy. I don't know how she does it but her mouth has these different sweet tastes and it doesn't matter what time of the day it is. I think that's the main reason I fell so fast. I have never met a woman whose mouth changes flavors. Is there a product on the market that gives a woman a sweet-tasting mouth? I would like to know. Every morning she wakes up with a sweet-tasting mouth. Maybe she wakes up in the middle of the night and goes and sucks on candy or something. Today she tastes like strawberries, yesterday it was peaches. As she kisses me I'm wrapping my hands around her waist to pull her sweet, soft, gentle self to me. She doesn't resist, as if I expected her to. Her body feels so good, it's hard to describe but let me try anyway: What was the best thing you felt in your life? Think about it. But make that thing edible and think of it again. As I kiss her face I could feel myself getting excited. Damn, she does it to me every time whenever I'm in her arms, I fall apart. This evening she's wearing a short blue silk nightgown; her body smells like fresh fruit. It is a lingering scent that slowly creeps into you—well not you, me. Her arms are over my neck now and I turn to kiss her right hand then her left. I'm kissing because it is the sane thing to do. I would really like to eat her arms. I want to bite into that sweetness but then you and the world are going to think I'm crazy, but I'm not.

Now she has started to kiss me, not with her lips but with her tongue. Of course her lips are touching me but her tongue is what is driving me crazy. Her tongue is warm and a little bit sharp. I don't mean sharp in the sense that it would cut you, I mean long and thin as opposed to short and round at the end. I'm shaking my head as if I was Diana Ross trying to get my weave right. It feels real good. She is kissing all the way up my neck. I lay back on the bed because it is the only thing that will make me understand where I am. I feel like I'm floating. I'm getting really lightheaded. She has totally taken over the lovemaking now. She continues to work her tongue down from my neck onto my nipples. She takes the first one and licks around it over and over. Then suddenly she bites it and my whole body lifts off the bed.

I told you her tongue was sharp and I meant it but her teeth are sharp as a steak knife. I don't want you to mistake it for a butter knife. Most butter knives require a lot of strength to cut and that's not the case with her teeth. I quickly look at my nipple to see if it is still there and yes, the little black raisin is still place. As quickly as she bit it her tongue runs over it bringing pain and pleasure together to provide an unnerving sensation. She continues to play with my nipples while her hand traces down my body to my erect penis. She moves her hand up and down the shaft as she runs her tongue down the middle of my chest all the way to the nappy curls above my penis. Well you know what

I'm thinking as my lower body tries to connect with her face. But she doesn't let me. Instead she kisses around my balls and back up to my nipples. As her tongue goes back up my body, her pubic hairs graze upon my stomach making me even more excited. I told you before that I felt like eating her, well this time it is even worse. She stops kissing me and starts to use her pubic hairs as an airbrush on my chest. My whole body is on fire. I reach back and grab her forcefully by her buttocks, holding on for dear life. She reaches out and grabs me by the throat. I'm holding on to her ass for dear life as she squeezes on my throat. I know I'm about to cum.

"I'm cum—" before I could complete the phrase, her fingernails dig into my neck.

"No," she says.

My body reacts more to the pain than the pleasure and the orgasmic feeling dissipates. I let go of her ass and as I do that she brings her vagina right up to my lips. That is my only weakness. A thing that is indescribable. My tongue reaches out. Adam was a fool, Sampson was stupid and I am an idiot. Her pussy smells like apricot. As soon as my tongue touches her pussy lips the convulsions start as her body shakes uncontrollably.

"Now," she says, "I want you in me right now."

There is a loud knock on my door.

"Don't answer it, it's him," she says. "Just fuck me. Don't answer the door."

I look at her pussy dripping with cum and the knocking on my door becomes louder.

I feel like shouting that I'm not at home. Of course I know that would let the person at my door know that I am home but it would also let him know that I don't want to be disturbed. The knocking is getting louder. I'm looking at the door and she is just staring at me, daring me to make a decision. I already know what is behind door number one. Should I leave it and go to door number two?

I get off the bed and turn around. She is looking at me. The knock is getting louder and someone is saying something. I can't hear because I have her ankles in my hand. I spread her legs apart. I come forward and slowly inch myself into her warmth. Blood runs through my body as her vagina embraces me. It is again an indescribable feeling. It is the purest of natural pleasures. When a man enters the sweetness of a woman, his body is transformed. It is a feeling that really cannot be measured by anything scientific because it is constantly changing. The tip of the penis going in feels different than when the complete penis, for a lack of a better word, is submerged. As I withdraw halfway to go back in, the weakness in my legs has made my body start to shake. I have learned how to control that shaking—what I do is go in all the way and make my thrusts short and quick. I'm pumping as she brings her body to me with every thrust.

"I know she's in there," the voice shouts.

Well of course I do, too, because I'm fucking her. You're wondering who's at the door, right? Well I could make it easy and just tell you.

"Are you ready?" she asks.

"Yes," I say.

She pushes me away then slides down in front of me. She takes my penis in her mouth and starts to suck on it as if it was a Slurpee on a 100-plus day in Vegas. The noise she is making would have woken up the mummies in the tombs in Egypt. I take deep breaths as I try my best not to explode in her mouth. I still had a job to do. I grab her by her hair and pull her away from my dick. At the same time she clamps down on it. As I pull her away, she left four long marks on my penis. I am angry. I push her down on the bed, so that her head is down and her butt is sticking up. I drive my penis in her as I pull her head back. I do that for at least fifteen strokes, each going deeper and deeper. She is wailing. I don't know if it's from pleasure or pain. To be honest with you at this point I don't care. I climb up on the bed, making sure my penis remains in her. I crouch on top of her so that my penis goes straight down into her pulling at her vagina.

"Fuck me hard," she says as I continue to drive into her. "Write your name inside this pussy."

I don't know if I forgot to tell you this but talking dirty to me while having sex will keep my dick hard all night.

I drive into her harder and harder, using my legs to pump with all my strength. It is at the fortieth stroke that I feel that same thing from earlier. It started in my toes and raced through my body. I pulled my penis out of her and cum spurts, traveling all the way from her butt to her hair.

"I guess you won't need a perm today," I say as I collapse onto the bed.

"Aren't you going to get the door?" she asks as she lies down beside me.

"Should I?" I ask.

"Just because I told you who it is doesn't mean that you should be rude," she says. "And when you're coming back, bring me my dildos because you came too fast. If you keep this up I'll have to go back to my husband."

"What do you expect? It's been two weeks since we've been in this apartment fucking. I can't go two-hour marathons ten times a day," I say and walk out of the bedroom.

"Then I don't need your sorry ass," she shouts to the closed door.

I walk past the small kitchen, which I never use, on my way to the front door. I pull the chain off the door then I unlock the deadbolt. I open the door naked as the day I was born.

"Where is she?" a tall, athletic-looking black man asks as soon as I open the door.

"Your wife?" I ask.

"Yes, my wife? Who do you think?" He puts his nose out and sniffs me like a dog. "I see you been kissing her too."

"Among other things," I say and leave the door open for him to come in. I go to the refrigerator and take out a Budweiser. "You want one?"

"No, motherfucker. What do you think this is?"

"A friendly visit," I say and take two dildos out of the freezer. I look at them and I realize I am losing her.

"I see you can't satisfy her either," he says, looking at the frozen glittering dildos, a small film of ice covering them.

"At least I lasted two weeks. She said you were finish in four days," I said, a little angry because he was telling the truth.

"I'm sure you thought you were doing something."

"I'm doing better than you," I say and go into the bedroom with the two frozen dildos. I throw the dildos on the bed and walk back into the living room.

"Button, Loretta told me that you were coming. I didn't expect you so soon though. What happened? The clues weren't good enough,"

I say as I take a seat opposite Button who had found comfort on my black leather couch.

"The address and phone number she left on the answering machine weren't clear enough," he says sarcastically.

"She told you she wanted a divorce but you said no," I say, placing my hands on the arms of the recliner. "Now you understand why."

"She also said that you had a bigger dick than me but that's not true," he says, looking at me.

"Well now is not the time to judge," I say, looking at my flaccid penis.

"So what would it take to get you out of my wife's life?" he asks. "Money? Drugs? Another woman?"

"None of the above. You tell me how much it would cost for me to end that sham of a marriage," I say.

The moaning from the bedroom has gotten louder.

"Judging from the noise coming from the bedroom, I don't think you will last much longer either," he says, a stupid smile coming across his face. "She's all yours."

He was right. I didn't satisfy Loretta.

"That's right. I'm the man in control of this pussy from now on," I reply, not knowing what else to say.

"I think you're fooling yourself. You don't know who you're dealing with," he says and stands. "You are not the first and you won't be the last. Loretta will come back to me or move on when she's finished with you."

Loretta walks out of the bedroom and points at Button.

"I want a divorce," she says, holding a big black dildo.

I watch him and start to smile. I have won.

"And you, put this dildo back in the refrigerator and come back in the room and fuck me," she says, throwing the dildo toward me. I catch it and get up.

"The lady has spoken," I say and go to open the front door.

Button walks out a dejected man. I go into the room to handle my business.

Six months later

I climb the stairs two steps at a time. I hold the piece of paper in my hand tightly as if my life is scribbled on it. When I reach the front door I start to pound on it with all my strength. There was no answer. I continue to pound on it until my knuckles start to blister. I pound some more until I am tired then lean on the door an angry, despondent man. Twenty minutes pass before the door opens. The bulky black man looks me up and down before he says, "Your wife said you were coming."

My Specialty
by
Tracy Price-Thompson

*L*ook!" Kirah said, pointing into the crowd of moving bodies. "Get him. The tall dude coming toward us in the baseball cap and the Bermuda shirt. He's a live one, Spark. Gurl, go get him!"

I sucked my teeth and groaned. Not another funky old goat. Tuesday was retiree day on base. They turned out in droves to take advantage of the low prices at the commissary and post exchange, and after skinning and grinning in their faces all day I'd had enough pats from blue-haired little old ladies and leers from gray-balled horny old men to last me a lifetime.

We'd been at it for six hours. Walking up and down the length of the Army and Air Force Exchange mall, clipboards and pens in hand, stopping military shoppers and begging them to complete a Morale, Welfare, and Recreation survey. Extra-duty punishment was a bitch. This Army shit was a trip. All kinds of stupid rules and regulations you had to follow. Well, my first sergeant didn't have to worry about my ass showing up late for duty anymore. As much as the head hoochie-mama liked to party by night and sleep by day, I'd learned my lesson. I was gonna save up my money and buy me a car. Get my own ride, so if I wanted to fuck out all night and creep in before dawn I didn't have to depend on a soul to get me home by o-dark-thirty when the military day began. Yeah, I know I signed up for this hup-two-three-fo' drama, but damn if a city girl like me is used to all these early mornings and manual labor. Up at the crack of dawn buffing floors, polishing brass, cutting grass, and pulling weeds. Hell, that was men's work, wasn't it?

A man, I was not.

I was built for pleasure, not for toil.

Okay, I admit it. I'm a hoochie. A fly-ass hoochie. Hooching is my specialty; and it was hard enough trying to keep my perm from going raggedy under those Army black wool berets, but mess up my nails too? Sheeiit. I was glad today's detail of collecting surveys and tomorrow's chow detail for the battalion change of command exercise would put me back in my hip-huggers and thongs and free me from the bondage of wearing this hot-ass camouflage pickle suit twelve hours a day, fourteen days in a row.

My feet were squealing in my new jump boots as I ran my thumb over the dwindling stack of papers on my clipboard. We'd started out with close to two hundred surveys, and now there were just five more clowns to con. Five more asinine surveys to complete and I'd be free.

"Gone." I felt Kirah nudging me in my back. "Smile and go get with the brother."

"I ain't asking him!" I shook my head stubbornly and held my clipboard behind my back. "I got those last two old guys. Broke-down dead dicks smelling like Fix-a-Dent and Buckley's Back Cream. It's your turn, Kirah. Besides, look at him range-walking with those long-ass legs. Ducking and dodging. He's probably trying to get into the PX, purchase his Vaseline and girlie magazines, and get the hell back home to his blow-up doll."

"Bullshit." Kirah snatched me by the sleeve of my battle-dress uniform and pulled me toward the tall, ebony-skinned man who was beating feet in our direction. "He'll do it. A niggah always has time when a fine sistah needs it. Just show your teeth and get up in his face. Push your titties out now. Damn! Unball your lips! You wanna scare the brother away?"

Despite my misgivings, I complied and positioned myself so that I was directly in his path. I stood waiting; legs slightly spread, clipboard in one hand, the other perched easily on my sultry hip. He tried to veer around me, but I sidestepped left, then followed his lead and danced right.

"Good afternoon, sir," I craned my neck and looked up into a face that struck me as both nerdish and oddly attractive.

He gave me a startled look as I did like Kirah'd said and arched my back so that my ass shot straight out and the twin melons of my breasts jiggled beneath the fabric of my uniform. Got-to-mighty-no! I blinked hard. Nerdy, yes, but he was also a Frankie Beverly—looking somebody. His moustache and sideburns were neatly trimmed and flecked with tiny bits of gray. The glasses he wore didn't do a thing to hide the sensual length of his eyelashes, and although there were character lines in his face that hinted at wisdom and experience, all it took was a tiny whiff of his cologne to assure me that he was quite a few years away from taking the Ben Gay Walk for the Elderly.

"Umm, I...umm," I reached up and smoothed my hair, my carefully memorized speech saying *adios* and flying from my brain as I stared into his eyes. They were so dark, so intense, I was sure the fire belting from their centers would crack his lenses and send them shattering all over me. But instead, he locked his gaze on mine and I felt us *connect*. Merge. Those eyes seemed to bore so deeply into mine that for a moment Kirah, the milling shoppers, the taco man, the one-hour photo girl—everyone—fell off my radar screen, and the only thing in my reality were our breaths and the sensuous pounding of my heart.

His voice was like liquid velvet when he spoke. Low, thick, and blacker than the ace of spades. "Can I help you?"

"U-Umm," I stammered and swallowed hard. It took everything I had not to turn that clipboard around and fan at the heat that was suddenly rising from my cleavage and swirling about my crotch. I almost laughed out loud. Damn if I wasn't standing there catching vapors from a strange man. And an older one at that. I mean, yeah, he was tall like I liked them, a real slim goody. And yes, his skin looked like the outside of a perfectly toasted marshmallow, but damn! Dude was wearing a loose-fitting button-down shirt that had no doubt come from a duty-free gift shop at some tropical airport, and that little apple-jack number on his head had seen better days. Besides, I was sure he belonged to the hard-bottomed-shoe–wearing generation. One of those proper men who wouldn't be caught dead in a pair of Timbs, and whose idea of a decent pair of sneakers was a generic cross between New Balance and Pro Keds.

"Yes?" His eyes released me and darted toward the PX entrance where a white-haired old lady stood checking IDs.

Curiosity. Impatience too.

"Yes, umm. My name is Private First Class Sparkle Henderson and I'm conducting a blind survey for the Fort Benning Morale,

Welfare, and Recreation offices." He canted his head a quarter turn. "Do you have a few minutes you can spare?" I asked, my voice syrupy sweet, my lowing back throbbing as I fought to keep that artificial C in my spine.

He smiled and I almost lost it. It's a shame what some men can do with a tube of Colgate. Thirty-two of the most beautiful little white Chiclets I'd ever seen. "Sure do," he answered, following my swaying ass over to a table near the taco stand. "I can give you whatever it is you need."

I glanced over my shoulder and saw Kirah eyeballing us and pumping her fist over her head. *You go, girl, my ass,* I thought and rolled my eyes.

I sat down and crossed my legs as he towered above me. It was hard to meet those embers glowing in his sexy gaze, so I pretended to ignore him as I scrawled X's near the boxes I needed him to fill out on the form. Our fingers touched as I passed him my pen, and I felt my scandalous pussy twitch of its own volition.

"Oh!" I jumped up and squeezed my thighs together as he sat down on the bench opposite me. He looked at me and grinned again. "Something wrong, Private Henderson? You okay?"

I swallowed hard and grinned right back. "I'm fine."

His gaze raked me from head to toe and he nodded slowly. Appreciatively. "I can see that."

Black as I was, I blushed all the way down to my damn toenails as my nipples tried to poke two holes through the pockets on my uniform jacket.

"So." I snuck and wiped a film of moisture from the back of my neck then rubbed my damp hand across my ass. I wanted to know more about him, but didn't want to make it seem like I was jumping all up in his business. "Are you active duty?" What I really wanted to ask was, are you old enough to be retired?

"Yes." He nodded and went down the form checking off boxes. "I'm active duty."

"Hmm. What branch are you in? What's your job, your MOS?"

He looked up at me and locked me in a gaze that made my juices leak. "Killer."

I laughed out loud. "Killer?" I'd taken him to be the admin or medical type. You know, paper pusher, bean counter, pill dispenser.

"Yeah, Killer. I kill things for a living."

I just couldn't call it. For the first time in a long while I found myself without a snazzy comeback. He finished up with the form and handed it back to me without another word. He left my pen lying on the table. Left me with an unexplainable rush of disappointment. The least he could have done was handed it back to me, touched my fingers, and scorched me with his heat again, but instead he was walking away. Striding with a purpose. As I stared at his retreating back and admired his long-legged fluid swagger, he turned and touched me once more with those magnetic eyes, then moved his tongue like a windshield wiper and mouthed five short words that nearly made me swoon.

My response was a dumb nod as I stood transfixed, rooted in my spot. All thoughts of my aching feet, the surveys, and my extra duty were lost in the pit of desire I was sinking into.

"Goddamn!" Kirah slunk up beside me. "Close your mouth, girl. Why you lookin' at dude like he's a slab of prime rib when you got that fine-ass Pierre waiting for you back at the room?"

"Shut up, Kirah," I snapped. "I ain't looking at him like nothing." I snatched my pen from the table and pushed it and the clipboard into her flat chest. Suddenly I was mad—at myself, at Kirah, at that sexy-ass Killer with garden-snake tongue. "You can get the rest of these filled out. It was your fault we got extra duty in the first place. Believing that lying-ass Leon was gonna get us a ride back to base in time for formation. Shoulda known his ass was shady when he showed up to pick you up riding that truck-ass bicycle."

"Girl, them bikes used to be the shit back in the day."

"Kirah," I said nastily, my misdirected emotions bouncing off my girlfriend. "Grow the fuck up. If you wanna be a real hoochie, quit playing with those little boys and go find yourself a grown man."

I turned on my heels and strode toward the outer doors, heading for the bus stop where the post transportation van would deliver me back to my barracks room and into the arms of my latest squeeze, Pierre. A few bricks short of a load, no doubt Pierre had ridden one of those little short school buses as a kid and when he got horny he stuttered something fierce, but in the state I was in, none of that shit mattered. My stuff was throbbing and I was gonna ride that donkey dick until one of us passed out and fell into a coma.

I felt Kirah's eyes shooting daggers into my back. Heard her call, "go beat it up yourself, Sparkle," as I left her holding the clipboard and tried to switch nonchalantly away. I didn't give a good goddamn about Kirah. Couldn't have cared less. Because all I could concentrate on was those five little words ole boy had mouthed at me. And the growing puddle of heat sliding down between my legs.

It was Wednesday morning and I was happier than a pig in shit. The last day of our two-week long punishment. For two whole weeks the first sergeant had kicked our asses from east hell to west, kept us scrubbing toilets and pulling kitchen duty, and if I could make it through this day I swore all out that I'd be a better soldier. But that damned Kirah? I glanced over at her empty bed. Please, Mister First Sergeant, kick her ass some more. Sister hadn't learned a damn thing. Still catting out all night like the ball-breaking scallywag she was.

The sun streamed in from our lone window and cut a rectangle across the olive drab green blanket on my bed and I stretched lazily, my nipples erect, one dark breast bulging out the side of my sleeveless T-shirt. I was alone, Pierre having vanished before I arrived home the evening before. I suspected he was probably out swinging his bat in another nappy dugout, but what the fuck. Easy come, easy go. Instead of spending the night getting my bucket tipped, I'd taken a shower, ironed my uniform for the next day, then spent two whole hours dipping my finger alternately in Kiwi polish and a watered-down alcohol mixture and spit-shining my new Corcoran boots.

Kirah and I weren't due in the orderly room until 08:30 hours, so I lay back and closed my eyes, enjoying the serenity of a morning without waking up to Kirah's snores, or worse, the high-pitched panting of her lovemaking as she got it on with the latest man she'd chosen to capture her prize. Most times it wasn't her uninhibited sounds of sex that distracted me, but rather the heady smells that wafted across the room and tantalized my senses. I'd duck beneath the covers and put the pillow over my head, but no dice. My coochie would gush, clit popping, nipples straining, until I either jumped up and fled the room, or gave in and moved my own fingers to the beat of the bucking asses in the bed across the room. I'd rub myself like crazy, then bite my lips and cum with a silent roar as the dick-stoked scent of hot pussy washed over me.

Immediately, Killer flashed through my mind. Dude was a bit slim for my liking, but he looked hard. Wiry. Muscular. And you know what they say about them no-assed, long-legged brothers. Dick for days. And his eyes. I'd damn near cum on myself just looking into them. Felt like he was sucking me down into a swirling pool of hot quicksand. The fact that he was an older man was also a turn-on. Meant he was mature, not into playing head games. Had experience and dick control. And didn't they just love sweet young pussy?

Just the thought of his smile had me squeezing my legs together, and before I knew it, my fingers were inside my panties, dipping into my wetness and rubbing my clit. I moaned and flexed my hips, rotating gently as I imagined my hand belonged to him. He explored my tender folds, reaching deeply into my well and gathering my juices as he rubbed softly around my outer lips. Then he spread his index and middle fingers apart and placed them on either side of my clit and squeezed and massaged until I exploded, my pussy blinking like a broken traffic light as I moaned and writhed, then fell back against my pillows and drifted back into slumber.

The pounding at my door sent me bolting to my feet. Clad only in my panties and T-shirt, and with the aroma of my own sex still hugging the air, I rushed to the door, glancing at the clock in dismay.

"Dammit, private!" The voice of the first sergeant scraped at me through the thick wood. Open this goddamn door! You were due out on the field site an hour ago!"

I flipped the lock and snatched the door open without thinking. "I'm sor—"

"Sorry my ass! You'd better come on line, soldier. Your shit is raggedy and the Army is downsizing—"

He stopped spewing as his jaw dropped and his eyes bulged in his handsome, coffee-colored face. I followed his gaze and looked down at myself. Slinky panties cutting a bright ivory swatch between the darkness of my taunt stomach and shapely thighs. Wifebeater shirt riding high and exposing the dimple of my navel. Juicy titties, raisin-sized nipples erect and heaving above my pounding heart.

I jumped behind the door and poked my head out as the first sergeant licked his lips, his anger dissipating into the air as his lust took charge.

"I'm sorry, first sergeant," I said in my most seductive tone. I thought Kirah, I mean Private Walters, was going to wake me up on time—"

"Forget it, Henderson," he said, cutting me off with a wave. "Private Walters is already on site. Doing your job and hers as well. Get dressed and get downstairs. I'm letting you know," his voice was harsh but Lord knows I know what I read in his eyes, "I'm writing your ass up. Recommending that Colonel Washington, our new battalion commander, take some disciplinary action that's sure to get your attention."

I closed the door and swore. How could I have fucked up so royally on my last day of extra duty? It was that damned orgasm. None of that ladylike get your rocks off and let's cuddle and talk shit for me. I took my nut like a man, rolled over, and tuned straight the fuck out. To hell with a cigarette and some light conversation. Sleep was the only thing that could rejuvenate me. And Kirah. How could a skank who stayed glued to the bed manage to hang out all night and still get to work before me?

Thankful that I'd prepared my uniform and boots the night before, I rushed into the shower and dressed quickly. Twenty minutes after the first sergeant had bammed on my door, I was downstairs climbing onto the back of a deuce-and-a half truck laden with marmite containers of cold salads and other side dishes it was my duty to serve up at the change-of-command luncheon.

Out in the field, I waved away biting flies and mosquitoes as I helped a detail of basic trainees on KP duty set up the serving line. There were massive charcoal grills smoldering, tons of hot dogs and hamburgers, and a boiling vat of corn on the cob so large I could have pushed Kirah's ass in it for not coming home to wake me up.

I kept rolling my eyes at her even though I knew it wasn't her fault that I'd overslept, but still, the thought of her getting off extra duty and the new punishment I was sure to face at the hands of the new BC was enough to make me totally irrational. Not to mention the fact that my earlier self-stimulation had been like dipping a teaspoon into the ocean. Although it was a pleasant distraction (after all, I know how to please me), it was far from all that I needed and desired.

We spent the next two hours dishing out chow and watching the officers and senior enlisted soldiers guzzle beer and wine coolers. More than two hundred soldiers were present, and most members of the battalion were dressed in battle-dress clothing, with the exception of those soldiers participating in the color guard and other change-of-command activities. There were a series of testosterone-laden war games scheduled for the afternoon, because you know how hard it is for a bunch of jock-heads to get together without needing to have a pissing contest to prove who was the better man. They'd step all over one another trying to make points with the incoming battalion commander, whoever the hell he was. I paid no attention to such matters. As long as the Army hit me in the pockets on the first and the fifteenth, I didn't give a rat's ass who was in charge.

I'd just scrubbed my hands with a bar of rough Army soap and was holding them under a spigot at the end of a water buffalo tank when I felt a tap on my shoulder.

"Private Henderson."

I swung around, hands dripping. "Yes, first sergeant?"

"The mission is about to begin. You and Private Walters have been assigned to the Alpha team OPFOR, which will be aggressing Bravo Team and probing their perimeter during the exercise. Suit up in your MILES equipment and combat gear, and meet your team leader on the hardball road in fifteen mikes. And move like you have a purpose in life."

What the fuck? I thought incredulously. Sure, I'd played all the bang-bang, shoot 'em up, cowboys and Indians games back during basic combat training, but hell, I'd never expected to have to muddy my knees or scrape up my shins like that again. And in MILES equipment, no less. That shit was heavy and awkward to wear, and if you took a "hit" from a weapon, your sensors went off beeping and making all kinds of noise until you found a squad leader with a key to turn you off. The good part about it was, once hit, you were out of the war and were corralled back to the rear with the other mock prisoners and casualties, thus freeing you from splashing into creeks, bounding across fields, and rolling into underbrush as you fled the enemy who was trying his damndest to take your hill.

Alpha Team was broken down into two twenty-five-man squads, and after waiting thirty minutes until Bravo Team had reconned the dense foliage, established communications, and taken up their defensive positions, we huddled over an arial map and received our marching orders.

Since I was only a private and not too long out of training, most of what they said went straight over my head. I hadn't paid much attention to this type of shit in basic, relying instead, on that pussy-hurting specialty I was putting on my drill sergeant to ride me into graduation, so what made them think I was about to pay any attention today?

Lanes of fire were assigned, orders were given, and I took off into the woods at a full charge right along with everybody else. I knew exactly what I had to do. I followed along in the woods, crawling with green bodies for roughly half a mile. I didn't even have to pretend to fall behind the rest of the team. As one of the few females, it was all I could do to move fast enough to keep them in my sight.

I trudged along, slipping and sliding, falling down on one knee and dropping my weapon until I was panting with exhaustion. As soon as I heard the first dummy rounds being fired, I caught a surge of energy and hauled ass in the direction of the fire fight. It took me about fifteen minutes, but I managed to immerse myself right in the middle of an intense gun battle right on the perimeter of Bravo Team's phase line.

"Get down! Take cover!" I heard them yelling, but I'd be damned if I had any pride. Fuck if I wasn't going to get hit. A few seconds later, the telltale buzzing of an active hit rang out through the air, and the red buttons dotting my equipment began blinking and lighting me up like a Christmas tree.

"Goddamnit, Henderson!" The first sergeant did a combat roll and low-crawled toward the spot where I stood beaming. I was damned proud of myself. First flippin' casualty of the war! Time to head back to the rear. Yippee!

I stood hiding my grin as he extracted an oddly shaped key from his ammo pouch and turned it in the lock near my top left shoulder. "Sorry, Top," I said, mustering up as much earnestness as I could. "I guess I gotta head to the rear. Don't worry, I'll find my way back."

"Like hell." The first sergeant stared at me with a wry expression. "We've set up a holding area for prisoners of war and casualties. Where's your map?"

Whatchoo talkin', Top? Holding area? My eyes were as big as saucers as I pulled my map from my cargo pocket and handed it to him.

"Here." He scratched two letters and eight numbers along the margin of my map. "These are the grid coordinates to the holding area. Shoot yourself an azimuth, do a pace count, and stay there until End-Ex is called."

My mouth was opened so wide Top could have wiped his feet on my tongue. Damn! Not only didn't I get to go back to the rear and possibly to the barracks, I had to find my own way through the woods in the opposite direction of everyone else.

It took me a full fifteen minutes to plot the points on my map, draw a line for distance, and measure the angle with my protractor. After using my compass to shoot my best approximation of an azimuth, I emptied the water out of my heavy canteens and took off marching through the woods, the silky-smooth voice of my drill sergeant echoing phantomly in my ear. Instead of hearing his lilting Hispanic accent ringing, "Damn, baby girl, your honey pot tastes so good," or "Give it up to *papi, mamasita,* c'mon, throw that fat black pussy over here," I heard his voice commanding, "Keep your compass out front and your map oriented north. Turn your body, not your map."

Twenty minutes and several insect bites later, I stumbled out of the woods and into a small clearing, my boot strings trailing behind me in the dirt. Although I'd lost my compass, ripped my map, and had broken off two of my Lee Press-On nails, I'd made it. Ahead were two yellow signs marked "Holding Area" that bracketed a shady, boot-raked area that held a five-gallon water drum and several wooden benches.

I fumbled to free my empty canteen and flung myself toward the container of water, sweat rolling into my eyes. After filling my canteen to the rim, I turned it up to my mouth and swallowed greedily, gulping and slurping like I was auditioning for a deep-dick-sucking contest. I was wiping at the puddle dribbling from my chin when I finally noticed that I wasn't alone.

"Shit!" I hollered. "How long have you been sitting there? You scared me!"

I took a step closer and froze, unable to believe my lying-ass eyes. So I wasn't the first casualty of war after all. If I had to be second to somebody, thank God it was him! He sat sprawled on a bench, deactivated MILES equipment on the ground before him, his hands at his sides, his back resting against the bark of an old oak tree. His feet were planted about two feet apart, his right leg swinging back and forth lazily. It was him. Lawdhamercyjeezus! It was him!

"Finally," he said, "some company."

"Umm, oh shit. I mean, umm, yes, sir."

His laugh was easy and deep. It rose from his belly and softened his eyes. "I'm a man of my word, Private Henderson," he said. A steaming mist rose from my body that had absolutely nothing to do with the strenuous journey I'd just taken. "You do remember what I promised you when we saw each other last, don't you?"

"Killer." I breathed and almost melted. There was something about this man that made me broil. Straight turned me the fuck on. Call it charisma, sex appeal, animal magnetism, call it down-home Weeziana mojo if you wanted, whatever it was it had my pussy dripping instantly.

He rose from the bench and sauntered toward me, that sexy long-legged walk of his barely concealing the power in his undulating body. I glanced at his collar and nearly shit. Damn if he wasn't a killer. An infantry man. A full-bird colonel. Colonel Washington, my incoming battalion commander.

He watched me reading his uniform and grinned. Stupidly, I dropped my canteen and saluted, forgetting to come to the position of attention first. He stepped up to me and returned my salute, and when his arm fell, somehow it landed naturally around my waist. He pulled me into him and ground himself against me as I whimpered and parted my lips to receive his kiss.

Now it's no secret that I like to fuck. Been fucking since I was fourteen and once I started I was like a dick junkie. Fucking became my specialty. Just couldn't get enough of it. I mean, let's just call a hoochie a hoochie. I'm a sistah with a big appetite. That's one of the reasons I joined the Army. Men. Black men. In all sizes, shapes, and colors. But in all my life I'd never jumped a man's bones as fast as I plastered myself to Killer. His hands were everywhere—on my breasts, between my legs, in my hair. And his tongue. Lord have mercy. He had that thing so far down my throat I could only imagine what other areas it could reach with relative ease.

Buttons flew and belts were snatched off in our haste to shake off those uniforms. Coming out of my boots was no problem since they were already untied, and when I pulled off my military T-shirt and pushed my battle-dress pants down over my hips showing him my spicy red panty and bra set, his eyes crinkled in the corners as a huge smile of appreciation split his face wide open.

"Now, soldier." He panted, unbuttoning his trousers. He was naked from the waist up and I marveled at the sight of his taunt, muscular body. Sunlight glistened off the bits of gray speckling the dark forest of his chest, and while I realized there was probably a significant age gap between us, I wasn't hardly mad at him. It was obvious that Killer took good care of himself. Judging by his lean, but chiseled physique, he was in top condition, and while he might have had the wisdom and experiences of a man more than twice my age, he had the body of a thirty-year-old stud. "You're out of uniform. Those are not regulation panties, so I'm going to have to give you a few orders."

"Yes, sir," I said, reaching greedily into his pants to free the log I longed to feel burning between my thighs.

Killer barked the orders and I obeyed his commands. We lay down on the blanket of our uniforms. My breasts were like hot torpedoes. Brother could suck him some titties! He nibbled and slurped and suckled until that nerve that ran from my nipples to my clit became engorged and electrified and tore a scream from me that sent my back arching and my orgasm flooding my pussy and dripping between my legs in a slick puddle.

Killer moved down and licked at the fireballs leaping around my navel, then plunged his head lower and fulfilled the promise of those five words he'd spoken after completing my survey. He worked his tongue like an all-you-can-eat patron at a smorgasbord. It was everywhere all at once—teasing my clit, parting my lips, delving deeply into my pussy, and toying with my asshole all at the same time.

I felt feverish, and I clamped his pretty head between my thighs as my second orgasm tore through me like a freight train, my screams sending birds fleeing from their perches and rooting armadillo scurrying for cover. I needed a chance to rest, to catch my breath, but Killer wasn't having it. Moving up on his knees, he held his dick in both hands and guided it toward my trembling lips. Now, if I couldn't do anything else, I knew how to suck me a mean dick, and I went to work on Killer like his was the last dick I'd ever suck. I nibbled along its base, applied pressure to that main vein, swirled drops of pre-cum around his beautiful mushroom-shaped head, and then deep-throated that mutherfucker like I intended to swallow it whole.

I felt his nut rising, felt his balls contracting, and suddenly he pulled himself from my mouth and stared into my eyes. He reached for his pants and pulled a condom from his wallet.

"You want this?"

"Yes, " I begged hoarsely, my fingers already wandering down between my own legs as he rolled the thin film of rubber down over his thick dick.

"You sure?"

I lay back and spread my legs in answer, motioning at the exact spot I wanted him to hit.

He plunged into me and I screamed for the third time.

"Oh, Killer! Goddamn, baby! You're *killing* me!"

He moved like a piston, plunging in, withdrawing halfway, then diving back inside of me, filling the center of my universe with all ten inches of his thick, glorious black dick. Beneath him, I worked my ass like there was no tomorrow, worshipping that dick upon my altar, bowing down to its magnificent power, blossoming like a flower under his long, powerful strokes.

I came twice more before I felt his back stiffen and arch. He thrust his tongue down my throat and grabbed two handfuls of my ass as he impaled me on his throbbing sword. I almost blacked out when I felt his hot fluid scorch the back of my pussy where it sat bubbling inside his condom. We lay together for several long minutes, laughing, kissing, getting to know each other, and admitting that this was something we wanted to do together on a regular basis. Killer sure knew how to make a sistah feel good. He stroked my body and my ego, and made me feel beautiful.

I marveled at the fact that despite our age difference, Killer had given me a dick whipping unlike any I'd ever had before. I visualized myself sexing him in all kinds of ways. Saw myself cooking a brother dinner and shit. Fixing breakfast for him wearing nothing except one of his shirts. After only one session under his touch, I was whipped. Straight sprung. Killer had laid that thang on me from every angle, filling my every need, attending to my every sexual desire, and before I could check myself, I found my mouth wide open telling him so.

His response scared me, for somehow I knew it revealed our destiny. "It's fate, baby. From the moment I saw you, I knew I had to have you," he confessed. "I've been divorced for more than a year, and there hasn't been a woman who crossed my path who had the ability to turn my head—until you."

I smiled in satisfaction and snuggled closer to him, breathing in a scent I knew I could be happy with for a really long time. Uh-uh. I did my best to steel my mind from the thought. I couldn't even entertain the idea of settling down with one man. With one dick. I mean damn, what kinda hoochie would I be then? Never heard of a one-dick hoochie, have you? Well, me neither. But then again, I'm known for setting trends, trying new shit. Developing fads. Bending roads. Carving paths. That's my specialty.

The Naked Truth
about the
Contributors

Rochelle Alers is the author of more than twenty-five nationally acclaimed romance titles including; *Rosie's Curl and Weave, Welcome to Leo's,* and the popular Hideaway series. Rochelle is one of the genre's best-selling writers. She has been nominated for a Romantic Times Career Achievement Award, and has won a Gold Pen Award, six Emma Awards and is the first recipient of the prestigious Vivian Stephens Career Achievement Award for Excellence in Romance Novel Writing. She has consistently made bestseller lists; No. 7 Vows Ingram top 50, No. 1 Essence and Blackboard for *Rosie's Curl and Weave* and *Della's House of Style.* Many of her titles have gone into multiple printings, and have been selected for the DoubleDay, Black Expressions and Literary Guild Book Clubs. Her name and titles have appeared in articles in *Publishers Weekly, Heart and Soul, Upscale, Today's Black Woman* and *The Writer.*

William Fredrick Cooper is an "ordinary guy" born in Staten Island, New York; raised in Brooklyn; and presently residing in The Bronx. A litigation clerk at Proskauer Rose LLP, one of New York City's largest law firms, he is the proud father of a lovely daughter, Maranda. Due to Fredrick's unflagging sensitivity, warmth, and generosity, as well as proudly being an admitted romantic, he has been aptly and affectionately labeled "Mr. Romance." A true sports aficionado and dance enthusiast (he loves hip-hop, salsa, and meringue, and does a dead-on impersonation of Michael Jackson), the sensitive characteristics Fredrick owns were put on full display in his self-published debut novel, *Six Days In January.*

Currently, Fredrick is working on *Damaged Goods*, his mid-to-late 2003 follow-up to *Six Days in January* as well as a yet-to-be titled compilation of erotic musings, samples of which can be found on the nebpublishing.com Web site he calls home.

Phill Duck resides in Central New Jersey with his wife and daughter. He is the author of *Sugar Ain't Sweet* and a short story, "Flimsy and Raggedy," to be released in summer 2003 in the anthology, *Proverbs for the People*.

Lolita Files is the bestselling author of four novels: *Scenes from a Sistah* (Warner Books, 1997); its follow-up, *Getting to the Good Part* (Warner Books, 1999); *Blind Ambitions* (Simon & Schuster, 2000), and *Child of God* (Simon & Schuster, 2001). Her novels have appeared on a number of bestsellers lists, including Blackboard, Barnes & Nobles, and Ingram's Top 50. Lolita—a native of South Florida, sometimes New Yorker, and current resident of Los Angeles, California—has developed a reputation as a writer with a sharp wit and skill for dialogue, both of which have made her a favorite with national reviewers and fans.

Lolita is currently at work on her fifth novel, *Tastes Like Chicken,* a follow-up to her most popular characters, Misty and Reesy, from the novels *Scenes from a Sistah* and *Getting to the Good Part*.

Nancey Flowers is the author of the novels *A Fool's Paradise* and *Shattered Vessels* and the forthcoming 2003 novel, *The Other Woman*. Nancey attended Morgan State University in Baltimore, Maryland, where she received her bachelor's degree in mass communications with a minor in journalism. She is presently working on several anthologies and a non-fiction series entitled *I Have Dreams*. Nancey is presently the program director for the Harlem Book Fair and is slated to be the host of a new national XM Radio program, Black Scrolls.

Tracy Grant is the author of *Hellified,* a freelance journalist, and an adjunct English professor. He is a frequent contributor to *Today's Black Woman, Black Men, Black Issues Book Review* and *Mosaic* literary magazine. Tracy is currently working on his next novel. He lives in New York City.

Marlon Green, the author of *Making Love in the Rain,* is a die-hard romantic who is winning the hearts of readers worldwide with his keen insight and understanding of women, men, and relationships partnered with great writing. His next book, *I Just Wanna Love You,* is a scorcher and will be available on shelves this fall. Marlon currently resides in Prince George's County, Maryland.

Tracy Green is a resident of Brooklyn, New York. She is a graduate of Morgan State University and earned a master's in public administration from John Jay College of Criminal Justice. Tracy is a financial consultant working on her first great novel *Sleeping on the Edge.*

Linda Dominique Grosvenor was born and raised in New York by parents of Caribbean descent. She is the author of several novels *Fever*, *Like Boogie On Tuesday,* and *Sometimes I Cry* and a collection of poems enitled "Love Lingers." She currently resides in North Carolina with her husband, John. She welcomes readers to visit her Web site at: lindadominiquegrosvenor.com

Joylynn M. Jossel is a resident and native of Columbus, Ohio. She is a graduate of Columbus State Community College's Associates Degree program and Capital University's bachelor degree program. Joylynn is a multigenre writer who, in addition to her erotic contribution, has written titles such as *Please Tell Me if the Grass Is Greener* and *World On My Shoulders.* She plans to publish the five children's stories she has written as well as two volumes of poetry and is currently working on a novel entitled *Harlem's Blues.* She enjoys writing songs and is collecting data and doing research for an urban *Sex in the City* column titled "He Said, She Said," which will attract a major magazine to print.

Timmothy B. McCann is a Florida native who started "writing" short stories at the age of eight. As he grew older, he attained numerous accolades in sports, which provided him with the opportunity to play football on thecollegiate level.

After graduating from college Timmothy established Timmothy McCann and Associates, a financial planning firm. The agency achieved national recognition within its industry, but Timmothy sold the business to pursue his true passion, which has always been writing, and a gift that began as a child grew into his first novel, *Until*. He is a national best-selling author with three other titles *Always, Forever,* and *Emotions* currently in print. Timmothy is also a motivational speaker, teaches a course entitled "The Art of Commercial Fiction" on the collegiate level and is a proud single father of two children, Anna and Timmothy II (Jake).

Jacquie Bamberg Moore is the author of the acclaimed novel *All I Need*. Jacquie's love for the written word began at a very early age. Her earliest memory of receiving praise for her writing was in the fourth grade. She wrote a short story entitled, "My Thanksgiving Vacation," a vivid tale about a family chasing a frightened turkey through their home. That was the first of many writings for which she would receive recognition. Jacquie Bamberg Moore is currently a resident of Brooklyn, New York, where she lives with her husband, Dave, and their daughter, Irene.

Courtney Parker is a novelist on the move, looking to make both of her novels number one bestsellers. Courtney has been writing since before she could read, scribbling poems on pieces of paper as early as five. Although her novels are not yet published, Courtney has written several essays, short stories, debates, oratories, prose, and poetry pieces; winning both National and Catholic Speech Competitions of America. She has written several columns for both newspapers and magazine publications, including the *Los Angeles Sentinel.*
Single and living in Los Angeles, Courtney is a full time writer.

Eric E. Pete was born in Seattle, Washington, and raised there as well as Lake Charles, Louisiana. He is a graduate of McNeese State University and currently resides with his family in the New Orleans area. He is a member of Delta Sigma Pi Professional Business fraternity, the Black Writers Alliance, and the Young Council of Greater New Orleans. His released novels include *Real For Me* and *Someone's in the Kitchen*. He has toured extensively across the United States and has been a featured author at such events as the Essence Music

Festival and the African American Book Club Summit at Sea. Eric is currently working on his next novel.

If you have any comments or wish to reach Eric, he can be contacted at heyeric@att.net. Eric's Web site can be visited at: www.ericpete.com.

Michael Presley is the author of Black Funk II No Regrets, No Apologies and Black Funk. Born in Grenada, West Indies, Michael migrated to the United States (Brooklyn, New York) in 1978. Upon graduation from George W. Wingate High School., he obtained a bachelor's degree in English literature from Stony Brook University. He has written various short stories, specializing in fiction. He continues to live in Brooklyn where he is working on his next novel, *Tears on a Sunday Afternoon.*

Sandra A. Ottey is the author of *Jamerican Connection*, the story of Rose Thorn, a high school dropout trapped in an abusive marriage and her struggle to get back on track to realize the deferred dreams and career ambitions she had put on hold for too long. Sandra is presently working on her second novel and a sequel to *Jamerican Connection.*

Tracy Price-Thompson is the author of the national bestselling novel *Black Coffee* (Random House, 2002) A Brooklyn, New York, native and retired army engineer officer, Tracy was recently awarded a Zora Neale Hurston/Richard Wright Award for literary excellence. She recently co-edited *Proverbs For The People*, (Kensington, 2003). Her next novel *Chocolate Sangria* will be released in January 2003.

Léone D'Mitrienne Williams is a native of Los Angeles, California. She resided in Atlanta for nine years and worked at Warner Bros. Syndication before returning to her hometown in the spring of 2002. Léone is an artist at heart and sketches many beautiful pieces and has always been passionate about writing. She is presently working on her first novel *Encounters* scheduled to be released in 2003.

Recommended Reading

Addicted —ZANE
A Fool's Paradise—Nancey Flowers (aka Nancy Flowers Wilson)
After Hours—Tracy Grant (Contributor)
All I Need—Jacquie Bamberg Moore
Always—Timmothy B. McCann
Black Funk—Michael Presley
Black Funk II: No Regrets, No Apologies—Michael Presley
Black Coffee—Tracy Price-Thompson
Black Silk—Lolita Files (Contributor)
Blind Ambitions—Lolita Files
Child of God—Lolita Files
Chocolate Sangria—Tracy Price-Thompson (2003)
Della's House of Style—Rochelle Alers (Contributor)
Fever—Linda Dominique Grosvenor
Forever—Timmothy B. McCann
Encounters—Léone D'Mitrienne Williams (2003)
Getting to the Good Part—Lolita Files
Hellified—Tracy Grant
Hideaway series—Rochelle Alers
I Just Wanna Love You—Marlon Green
Jamerican Connection—Sandra A. Ottey
Like Boogie On Tuesday—Linda Dominique Grosvenor
Making Love in the Rain—Marlon Green
Please Tell Me if the Grass Is Greener—Joylynn M. Jossel
Proverbs for the People—Tracy Price-Thompson (Coeditor, 2003)
Real For Me—Eric E. Pete
Rosie's Curl and Weave—Rochelle Alers (Contributor)
Shame On It All—ZANE
Scenes from a Sistah—Lolita Files
Shattered Vessels—Nancey Flowers
Six Days in January—William Fredrick Cooper
Sleeping on the Edge—Tracy V. Green (2003)
Sometimes I Cry—Linda Dominique Grosvenor
Sugar Ain't Sweet—Phill Duck

Tastes Like Chicken—Lolita Files (2003)
Tears on a Sunday Afternoon—Michael Presley (2003)
The Heat Seekers—ZANE
The Other Woman—Nancey Flowers (2003)
The Sex Chronicles: Shattering The Myth—ZANE
Until—Timmothy B. McCann
Welcome To Leo's—Rochelle Alers (Contributor)
World On My Shoulders—Joylynn M. Jossel